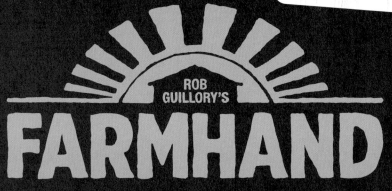

ROB GUILLORY'S
FARMHAND

VOLUME 2
THORNE IN THE FLESH

Created, Written and Drawn by
ROB GUILLORY

Colors by
TAYLOR WELLS

Letters by
KODY CHAMBERLAIN

Graphic Design by
BURTON DURAND

IMAGE COMICS, INC. • Robert Kirkman: Chief Operating Officer • Erik Larsen: Chief Financial Officer • Todd McFarlane: President • Marc Silvestri: Chief Executive Officer • Jim Valentino: Vice President • Eric Stephenson: Publisher / Chief Creative Officer • Jeff Boison: Director of Publishing Planning & Book Trade Sales • Chris Ross: Director of Digital Sales • Jeff Stang: Director of Direct Market Sales • Kat Salazar: Director of PR & Marketing • Drew Gill: Art Director • Heather Doornink: Production Director • Nicole Lapalme: Controller • IMAGECOMICS.COM

• Deanna Phelps: Production Artist for FARMHAND •

FARMHAND, VOL. 2. First printing. September 2019. Published by Image Comics, Inc. Office of publication: 2701 NW Vaughn St., Suite 780, Portland, OR 97210. Copyright © 2019 Rob Guillory. All rights reserved. Contains material originally published in single magazine form as FARMHAND #6-10. "Farmhand," its logos, and the likenesses of all characters herein are trademarks of Rob Guillory, unless otherwise noted. "Image" and the Image Comics logos are registered trademarks of Image Comics, Inc. No part of this publication may be reproduced or transmitted, in any form or by any means (except for short excerpts for journalistic or review purposes), without the express written permission of Rob Guillory, or Image Comics, Inc. All names, characters, events, and locales in this publication are entirely fictional. Any resemblance to actual persons (living or dead), events, or places, without satirical intent, is coincidental. Printed in the USA. For information regarding the CPSIA on this printed material call: 203-595-3636. For international rights, contact: foreignlicensing@imagecomics.com. ISBN: 978-1-5343-1332-3.

DEDICATION

For those in the hereafter.

Special thanks to Kody Chamberlain,
Ben Richardson and LaToya Morgan
for their endless support.

And thanks to April for tolerating me
while I struggled with this story.

CHAPTER 6

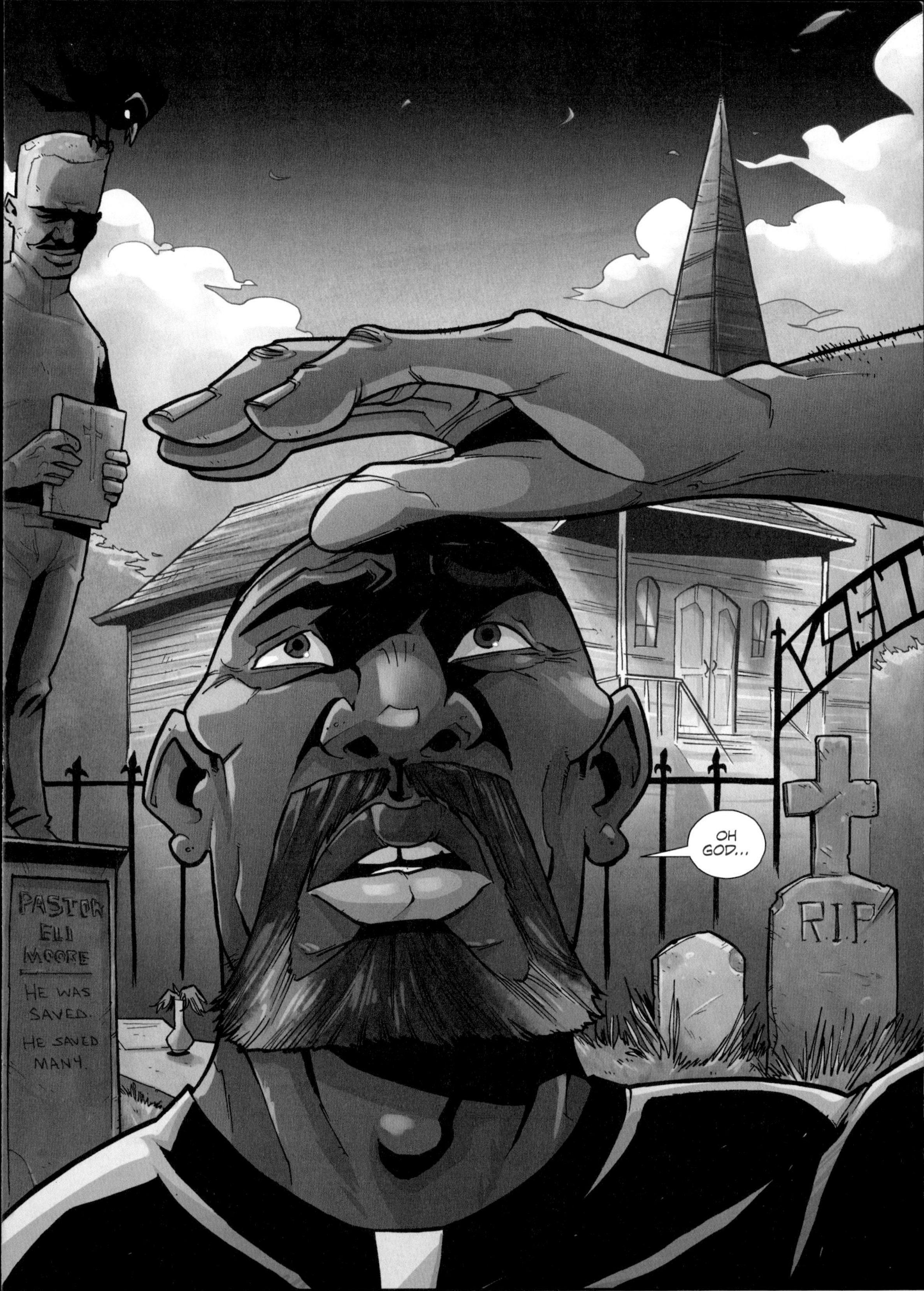
PASTOR ELI MOORE
HE WAS SAVED.
HE SAVED MANY.
OH GOD...
R.I.P.

CHAPTER 6: ReCreation.

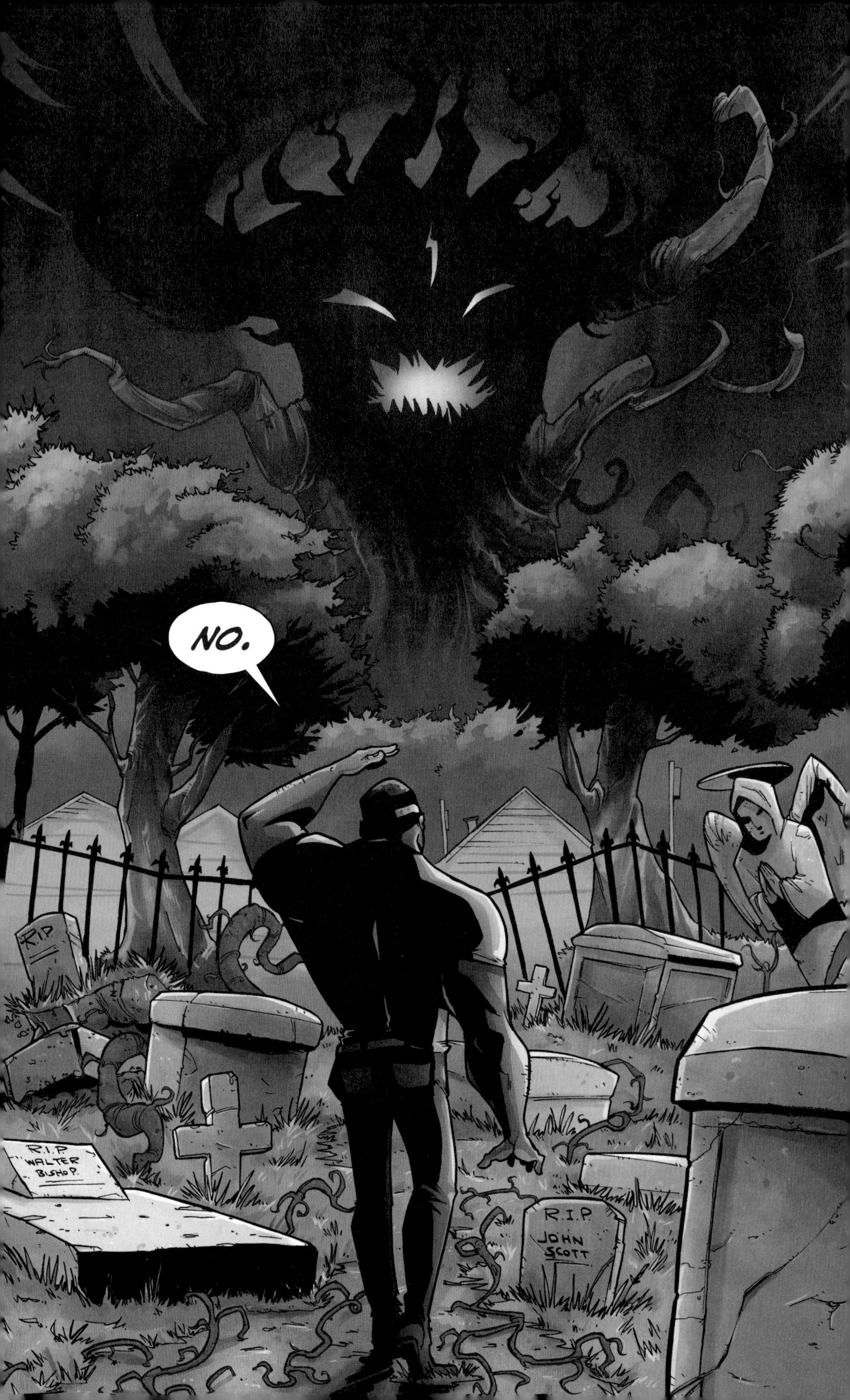
NO.
R.I.P.
R.I.P
WALTER
BISHOP
R.I.P.
JOHN
SCOTT

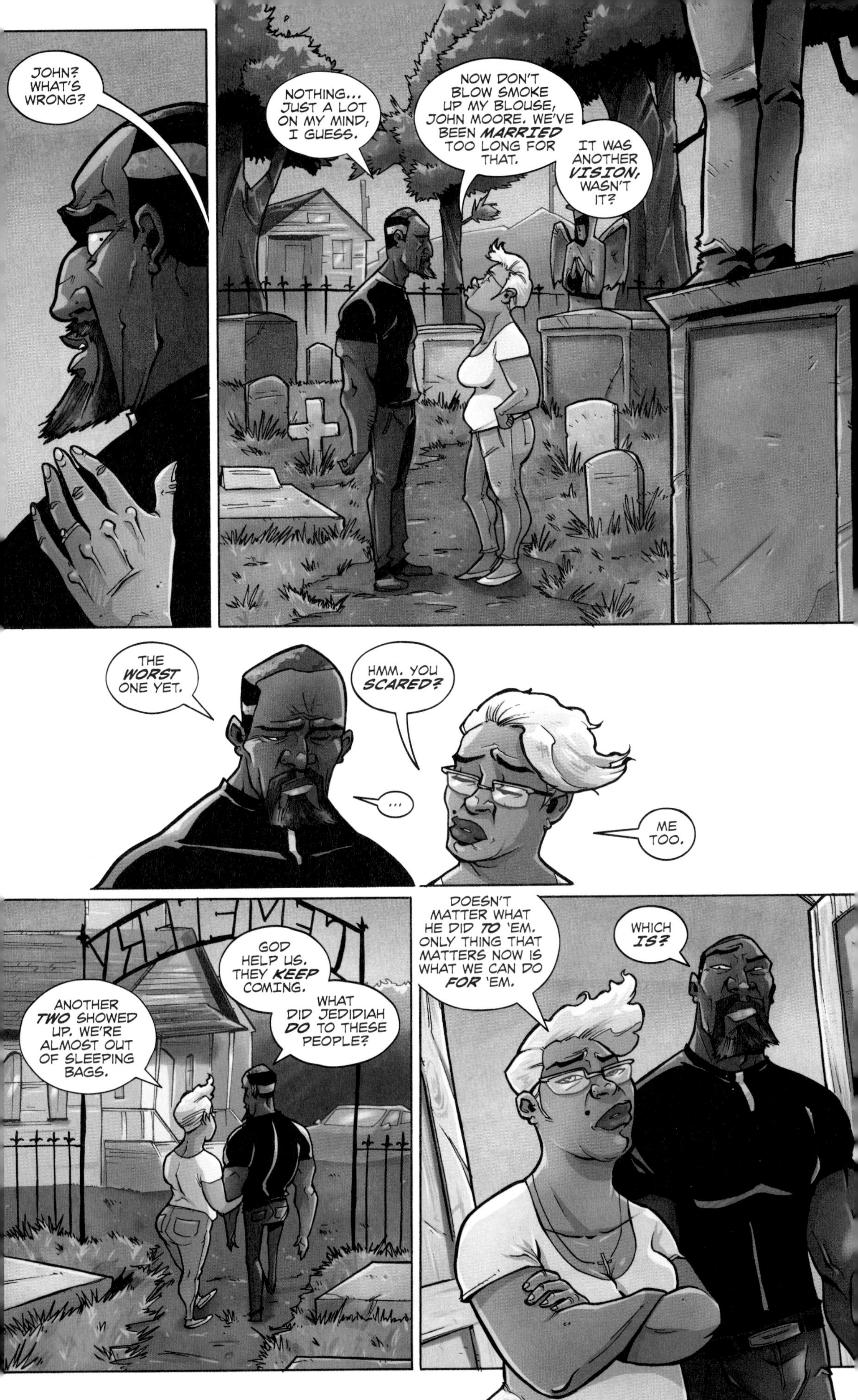
JOHN? WHAT'S WRONG?
NOTHING... JUST A LOT ON MY MIND, I GUESS.
NOW DON'T BLOW SMOKE UP MY BLOUSE, JOHN MOORE. WE'VE BEEN MARRIED TOO LONG FOR THAT.
IT WAS ANOTHER VISION, WASN'T IT?
THE WORST ONE YET.
HMM. YOU SCARED?
...
ME TOO.
ANOTHER TWO SHOWED UP. WE'RE ALMOST OUT OF SLEEPING BAGS.
GOD HELP US. THEY KEEP COMING.
WHAT DID JEDIDIAH DO TO THESE PEOPLE?
DOESN'T MATTER WHAT HE DID TO 'EM. ONLY THING THAT MATTERS NOW IS WHAT WE CAN DO FOR 'EM.
WHICH IS?

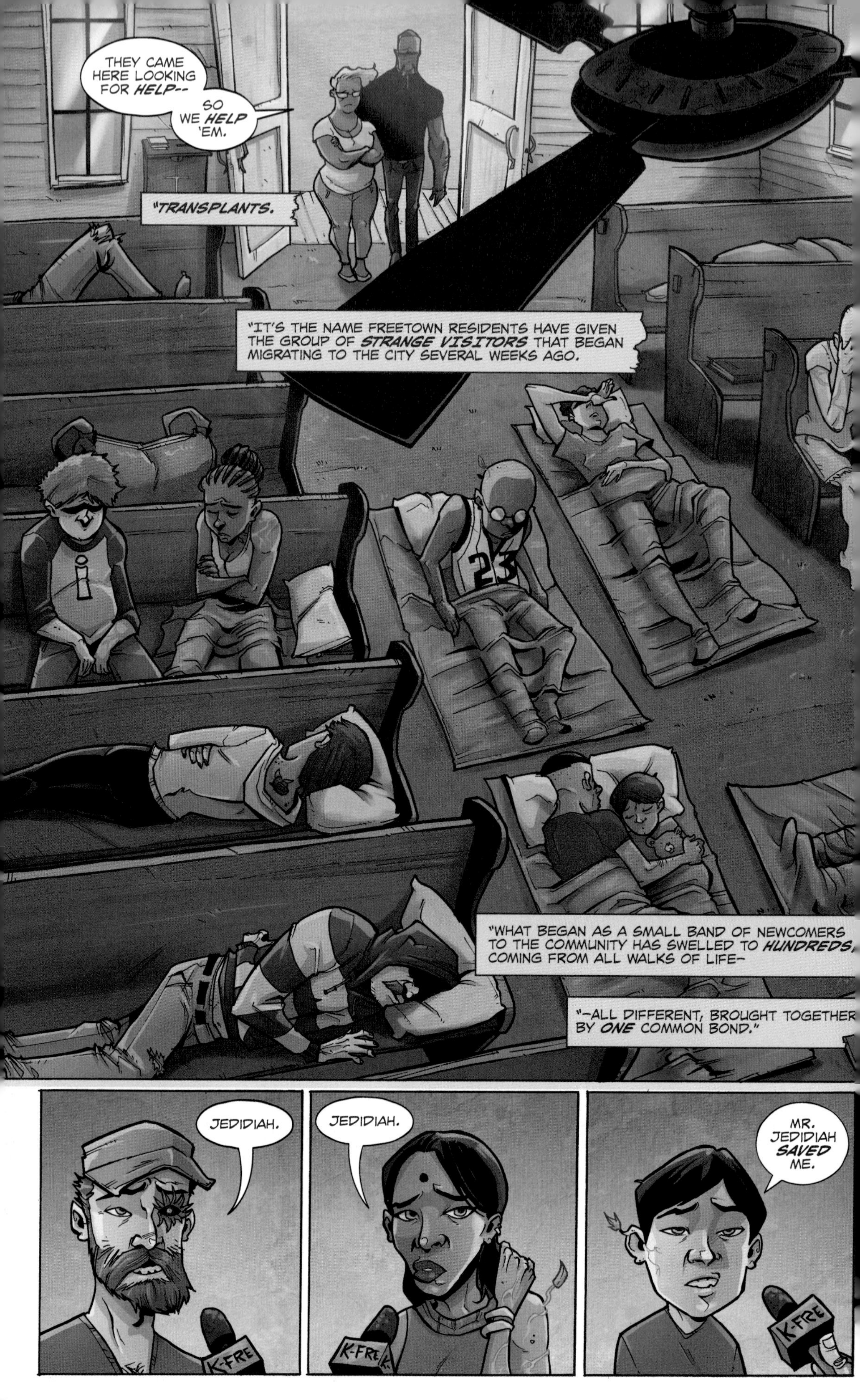
THEY CAME HERE LOOKING FOR *HELP*--
SO WE *HELP* 'EM.
"*TRANSPLANTS.*
"IT'S THE NAME FREETOWN RESIDENTS HAVE GIVEN THE GROUP OF *STRANGE VISITORS* THAT BEGAN MIGRATING TO THE CITY SEVERAL WEEKS AGO.
"WHAT BEGAN AS A SMALL BAND OF NEWCOMERS TO THE COMMUNITY HAS SWELLED TO *HUNDREDS*, COMING FROM ALL WALKS OF LIFE-
"-ALL DIFFERENT, BROUGHT TOGETHER BY *ONE* COMMON BOND."
JEDIDIAH.
K-FRE
JEDIDIAH.
K-FRE
MR. JEDIDIAH *SAVED* ME.
K-FRE

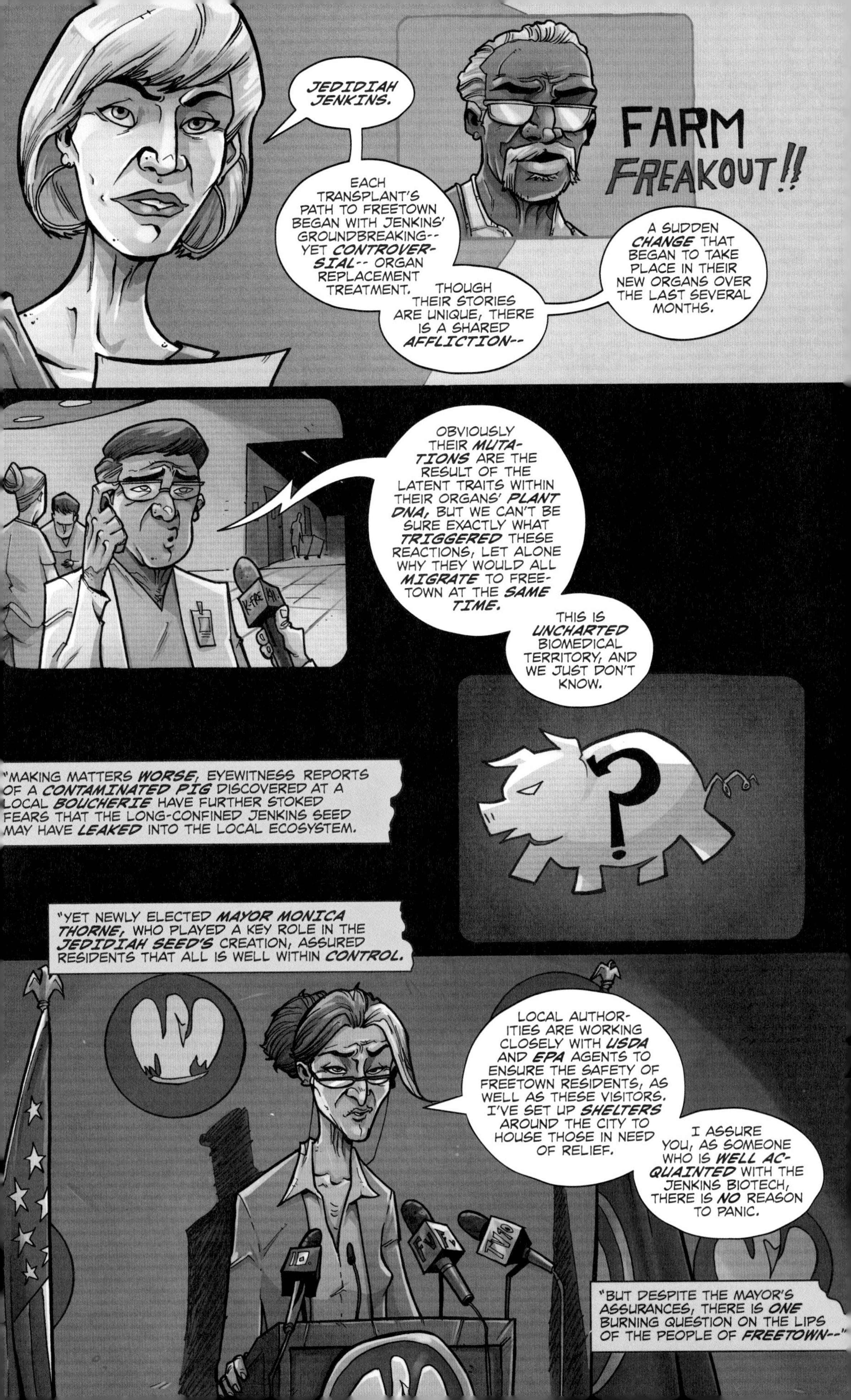
JEDIDIAH JENKINS.
FARM FREAKOUT!!
EACH TRANSPLANT'S PATH TO FREETOWN BEGAN WITH JENKINS' GROUNDBREAKING-- YET CONTROVERSIAL-- ORGAN REPLACEMENT TREATMENT.
THOUGH THEIR STORIES ARE UNIQUE, THERE IS A SHARED AFFLICTION--
A SUDDEN CHANGE THAT BEGAN TO TAKE PLACE IN THEIR NEW ORGANS OVER THE LAST SEVERAL MONTHS.
OBVIOUSLY THEIR MUTATIONS ARE THE RESULT OF THE LATENT TRAITS WITHIN THEIR ORGANS' PLANT DNA, BUT WE CAN'T BE SURE EXACTLY WHAT TRIGGERED THESE REACTIONS, LET ALONE WHY THEY WOULD ALL MIGRATE TO FREETOWN AT THE SAME TIME.
THIS IS UNCHARTED BIOMEDICAL TERRITORY, AND WE JUST DON'T KNOW.
"MAKING MATTERS WORSE, EYEWITNESS REPORTS OF A CONTAMINATED PIG DISCOVERED AT A LOCAL BOUCHERIE HAVE FURTHER STOKED FEARS THAT THE LONG-CONFINED JENKINS SEED MAY HAVE LEAKED INTO THE LOCAL ECOSYSTEM.
"YET NEWLY ELECTED MAYOR MONICA THORNE, WHO PLAYED A KEY ROLE IN THE JEDIDIAH SEED'S CREATION, ASSURED RESIDENTS THAT ALL IS WELL WITHIN CONTROL.
LOCAL AUTHORITIES ARE WORKING CLOSELY WITH USDA AND EPA AGENTS TO ENSURE THE SAFETY OF FREETOWN RESIDENTS, AS WELL AS THESE VISITORS. I'VE SET UP SHELTERS AROUND THE CITY TO HOUSE THOSE IN NEED OF RELIEF.
I ASSURE YOU, AS SOMEONE WHO IS WELL ACQUAINTED WITH THE JENKINS BIOTECH, THERE IS NO REASON TO PANIC.
"BUT DESPITE THE MAYOR'S ASSURANCES, THERE IS ONE BURNING QUESTION ON THE LIPS OF THE PEOPLE OF FREETOWN--"

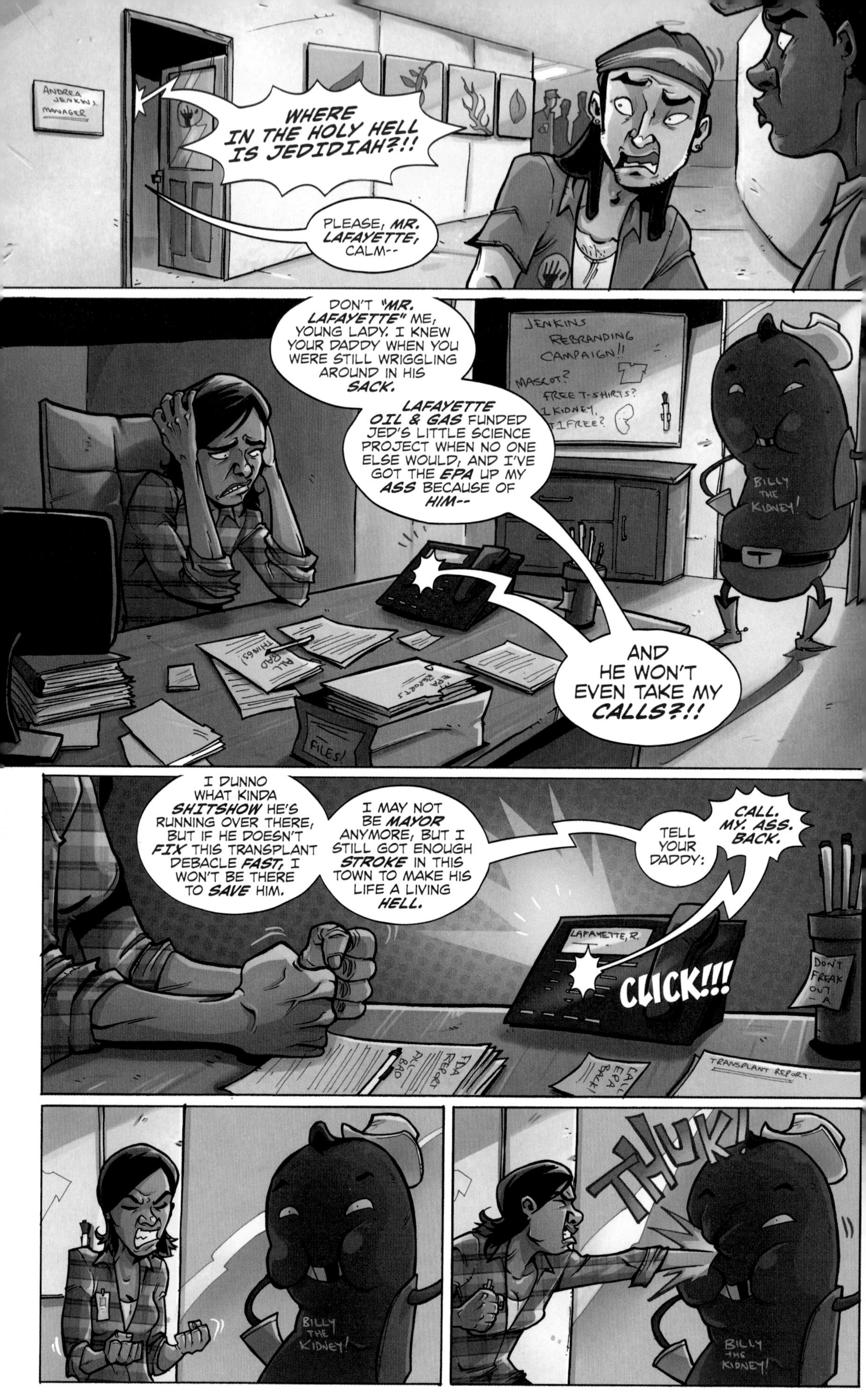

ANDREA JENKINS, MANAGER
WHERE IN THE HOLY HELL IS JEDIDIAH?!!
PLEASE, MR. LAFAYETTE, CALM--
DON'T "MR. LAFAYETTE" ME, YOUNG LADY. I KNEW YOUR DADDY WHEN YOU WERE STILL WRIGGLING AROUND IN HIS SACK.
LAFAYETTE OIL & GAS FUNDED JED'S LITTLE SCIENCE PROJECT WHEN NO ONE ELSE WOULD, AND I'VE GOT THE EPA UP MY ASS BECAUSE OF HIM--
AND HE WON'T EVEN TAKE MY CALLS?!!
JENKINS REBRANDING CAMPAIGN!!
MASCOT?
FREE T-SHIRTS?
1 KIDNEY, 1 FREE?
BILLY THE KIDNEY!
ALL BAD THINGS!
FILES!
I DUNNO WHAT KINDA SHITSHOW HE'S RUNNING OVER THERE, BUT IF HE DOESN'T FIX THIS TRANSPLANT DEBACLE FAST, I WON'T BE THERE TO SAVE HIM.
I MAY NOT BE MAYOR ANYMORE, BUT I STILL GOT ENOUGH STROKE IN THIS TOWN TO MAKE HIS LIFE A LIVING HELL.
TELL YOUR DADDY:
CALL. MY. ASS. BACK.
LAFAYETTE, R.
CLICK!!!
DON'T FREAK OUT. —A
FDA REPORT
ALL BAD
CALL EPA BACK!
TRANSPLANT REPORT.
BILLY THE KIDNEY!
THUK!
BILLY THE KIDNEY!

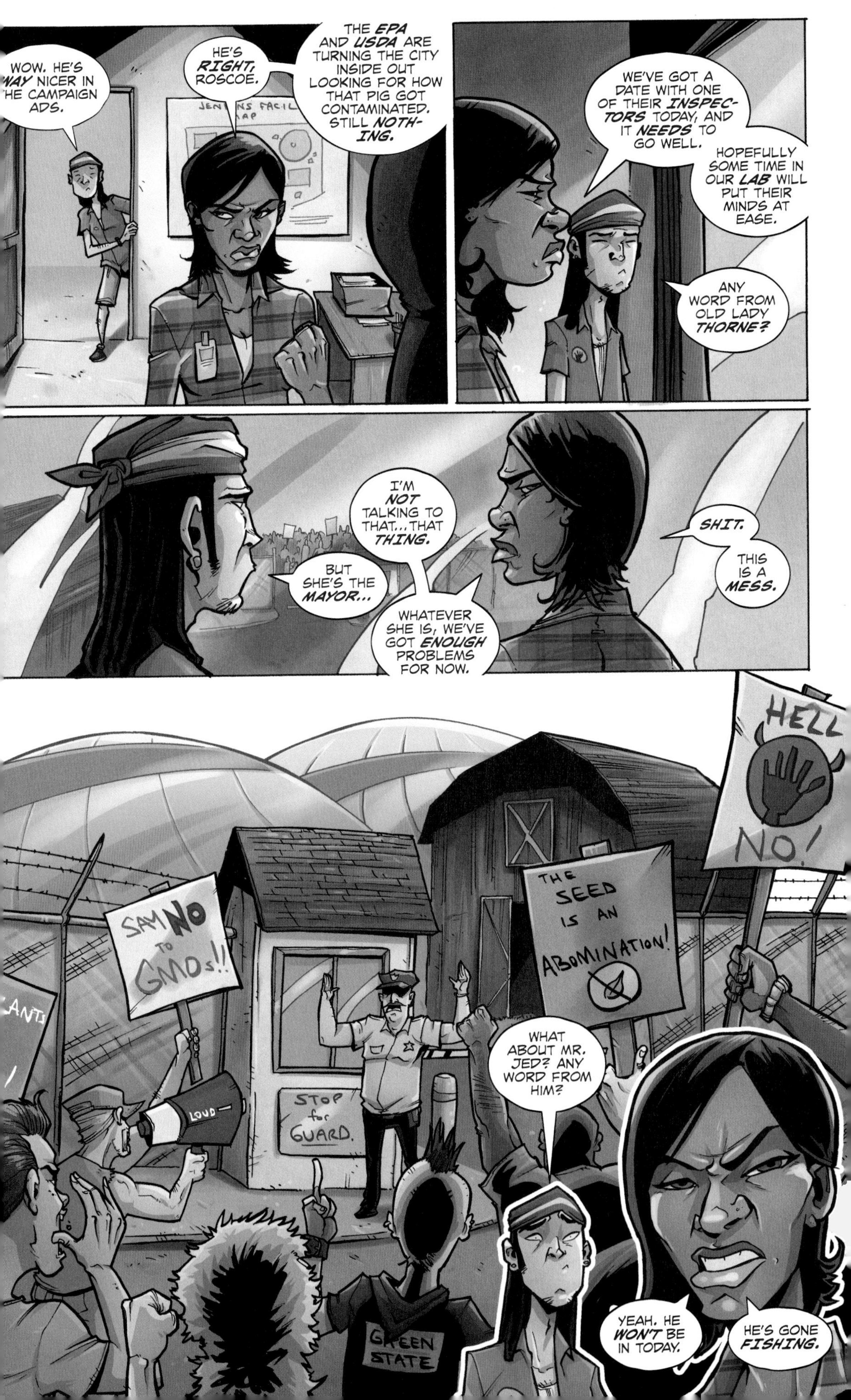
WOW. HE'S WAY NICER IN THE CAMPAIGN ADS.
HE'S RIGHT, ROSCOE.
THE EPA AND USDA ARE TURNING THE CITY INSIDE OUT LOOKING FOR HOW THAT PIG GOT CONTAMINATED. STILL NOTHING.
WE'VE GOT A DATE WITH ONE OF THEIR INSPECTORS TODAY, AND IT NEEDS TO GO WELL.
HOPEFULLY SOME TIME IN OUR LAB WILL PUT THEIR MINDS AT EASE.
ANY WORD FROM OLD LADY THORNE?
BUT SHE'S THE MAYOR...
I'M NOT TALKING TO THAT... THAT THING.
WHATEVER SHE IS, WE'VE GOT ENOUGH PROBLEMS FOR NOW.
SHIT.
THIS IS A MESS.
HELL NO!
SAY NO TO GMOs!!
THE SEED IS AN ABOMINATION!
STOP for GUARD.
LOUD
GREEN STATE
WHAT ABOUT MR. JED? ANY WORD FROM HIM?
YEAH. HE WON'T BE IN TODAY.
HE'S GONE FISHING.

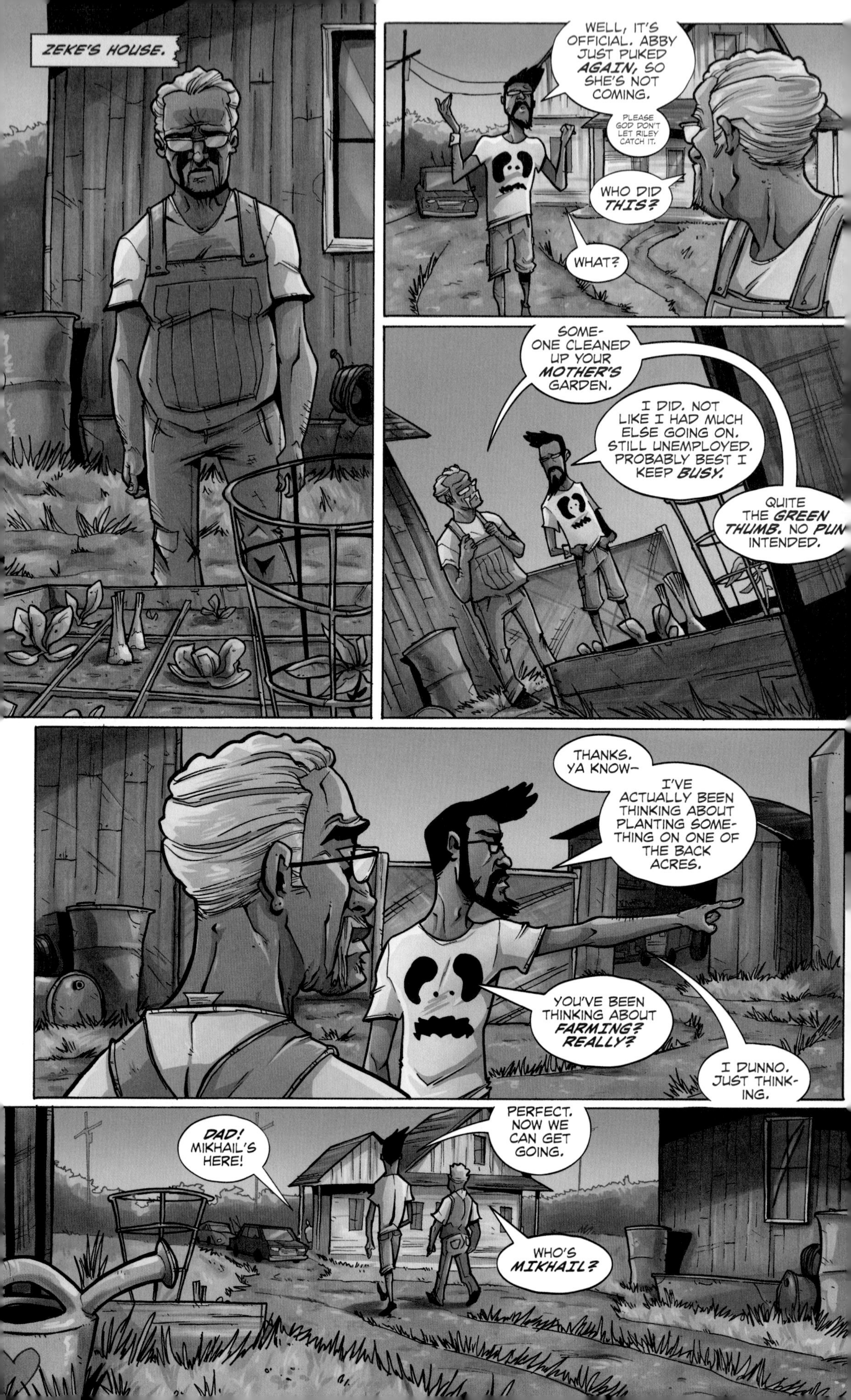
ZEKE'S HOUSE.
WELL, IT'S OFFICIAL. ABBY JUST PUKED AGAIN, SO SHE'S NOT COMING.
PLEASE GOD DON'T LET RILEY CATCH IT.
WHO DID THIS?
WHAT?
SOME-ONE CLEANED UP YOUR MOTHER'S GARDEN.
I DID. NOT LIKE I HAD MUCH ELSE GOING ON. STILL UNEMPLOYED. PROBABLY BEST I KEEP BUSY.
QUITE THE GREEN THUMB. NO PUN INTENDED.
THANKS. YA KNOW–
I'VE ACTUALLY BEEN THINKING ABOUT PLANTING SOME-THING ON ONE OF THE BACK ACRES.
YOU'VE BEEN THINKING ABOUT FARMING? REALLY?
I DUNNO. JUST THINK-ING.
DAD! MIKHAIL'S HERE!
PERFECT. NOW WE CAN GET GOING.
WHO'S MIKHAIL?

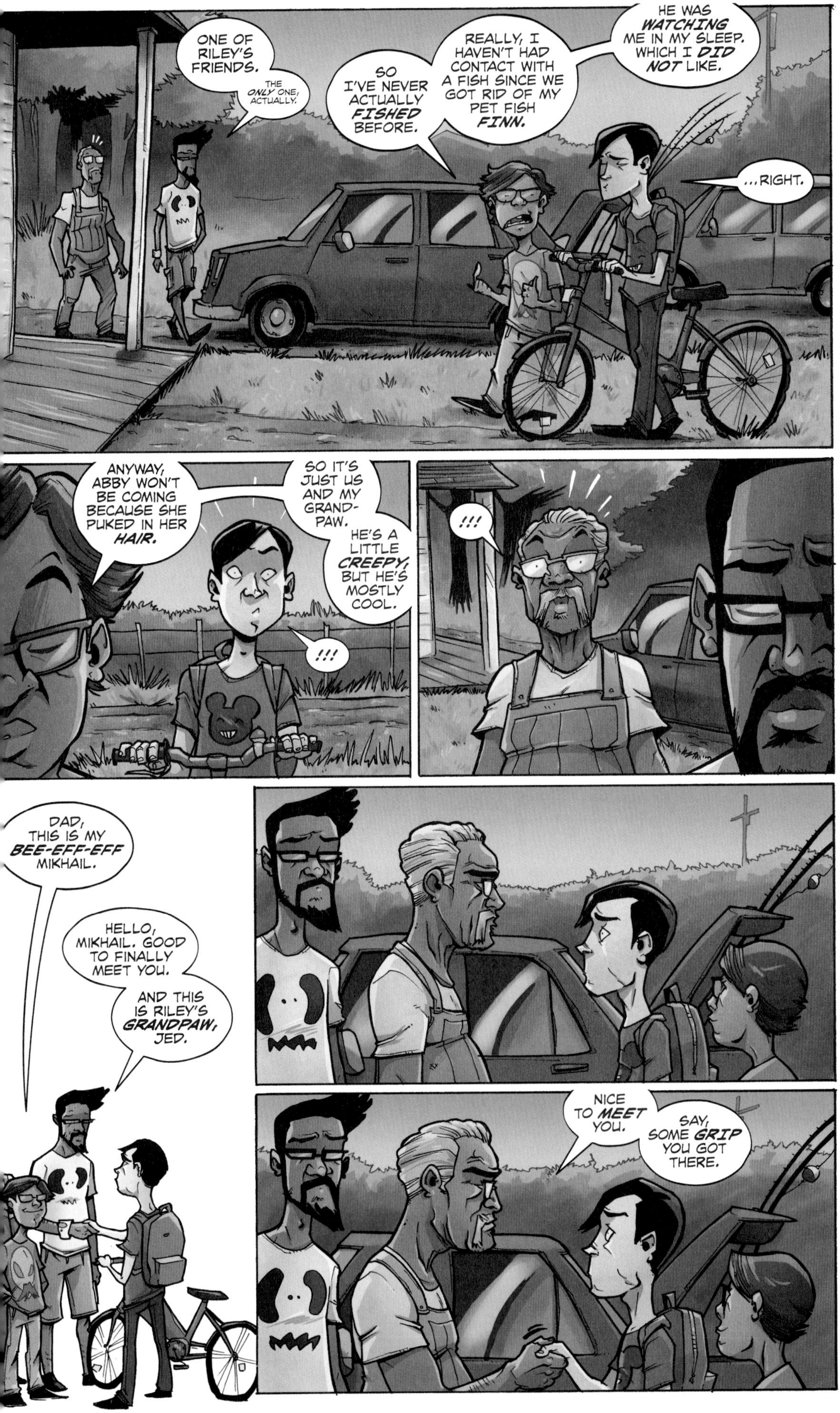
ONE OF RILEY'S FRIENDS.
THE ONLY ONE, ACTUALLY.
SO I'VE NEVER ACTUALLY FISHED BEFORE.
REALLY, I HAVEN'T HAD CONTACT WITH A FISH SINCE WE GOT RID OF MY PET FISH FINN.
HE WAS WATCHING ME IN MY SLEEP. WHICH I DID NOT LIKE.
...RIGHT.
ANYWAY, ABBY WON'T BE COMING BECAUSE SHE PUKED IN HER HAIR.
SO IT'S JUST US AND MY GRAND-PAW.
HE'S A LITTLE CREEPY, BUT HE'S MOSTLY COOL.
!!!
!!!
DAD, THIS IS MY BEE-EFF-EFF MIKHAIL.
HELLO, MIKHAIL. GOOD TO FINALLY MEET YOU.
AND THIS IS RILEY'S GRANDPAW, JED.
NICE TO MEET YOU.
SAY, SOME GRIP YOU GOT THERE.

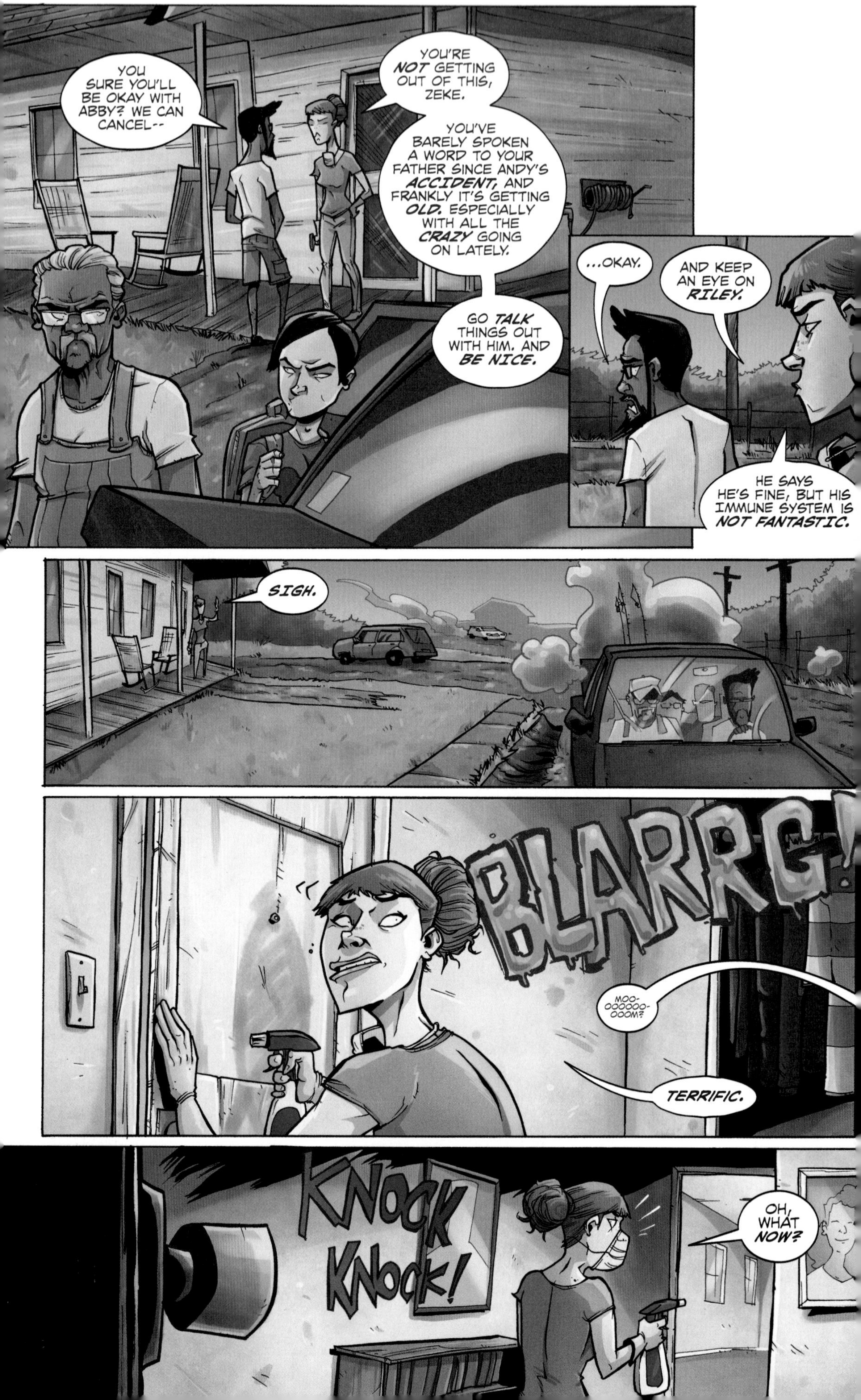
YOU SURE YOU'LL BE OKAY WITH ABBY? WE CAN CANCEL--
YOU'RE NOT GETTING OUT OF THIS, ZEKE.
YOU'VE BARELY SPOKEN A WORD TO YOUR FATHER SINCE ANDY'S ACCIDENT, AND FRANKLY IT'S GETTING OLD. ESPECIALLY WITH ALL THE CRAZY GOING ON LATELY.
GO TALK THINGS OUT WITH HIM. AND BE NICE.
...OKAY.
AND KEEP AN EYE ON RILEY.
HE SAYS HE'S FINE, BUT HIS IMMUNE SYSTEM IS NOT FANTASTIC.
SIGH.
BLARRG!
MOO-OOOOOO-OOOM?
TERRIFIC.
KNOCK KNOCK!
OH, WHAT NOW?

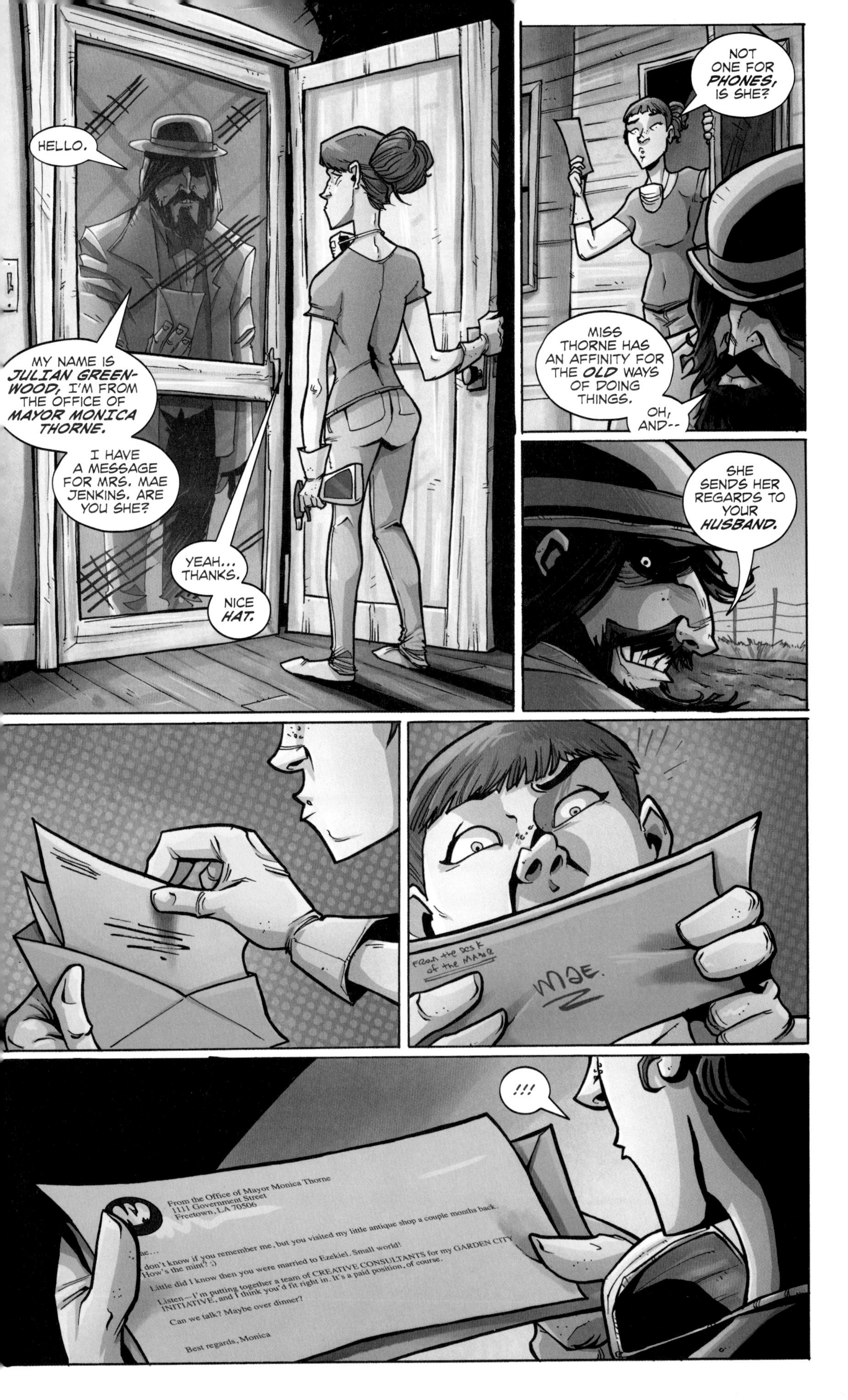
HELLO.
MY NAME IS JULIAN GREENWOOD, I'M FROM THE OFFICE OF MAYOR MONICA THORNE.
I HAVE A MESSAGE FOR MRS. MAE JENKINS. ARE YOU SHE?
YEAH... THANKS.
NICE HAT.
NOT ONE FOR PHONES, IS SHE?
MISS THORNE HAS AN AFFINITY FOR THE OLD WAYS OF DOING THINGS.
OH, AND--
SHE SENDS HER REGARDS TO YOUR HUSBAND.
From the desk of the Mayor
Mae.
!!!
From the Office of Mayor Monica Thorne
1111 Government Street
Freetown, LA 70506
ae...
don't know if you remember me, but you visited my little antique shop a couple months back.
How's the mint? ;)
Little did I know then you were married to Ezekiel. Small world!
Listen—I'm putting together a team of CREATIVE CONSULTANTS for my GARDEN CITY INITIATIVE, and I think you'd fit right in. It's a paid position, of course.
Can we talk? Maybe over dinner?
Best regards, Monica

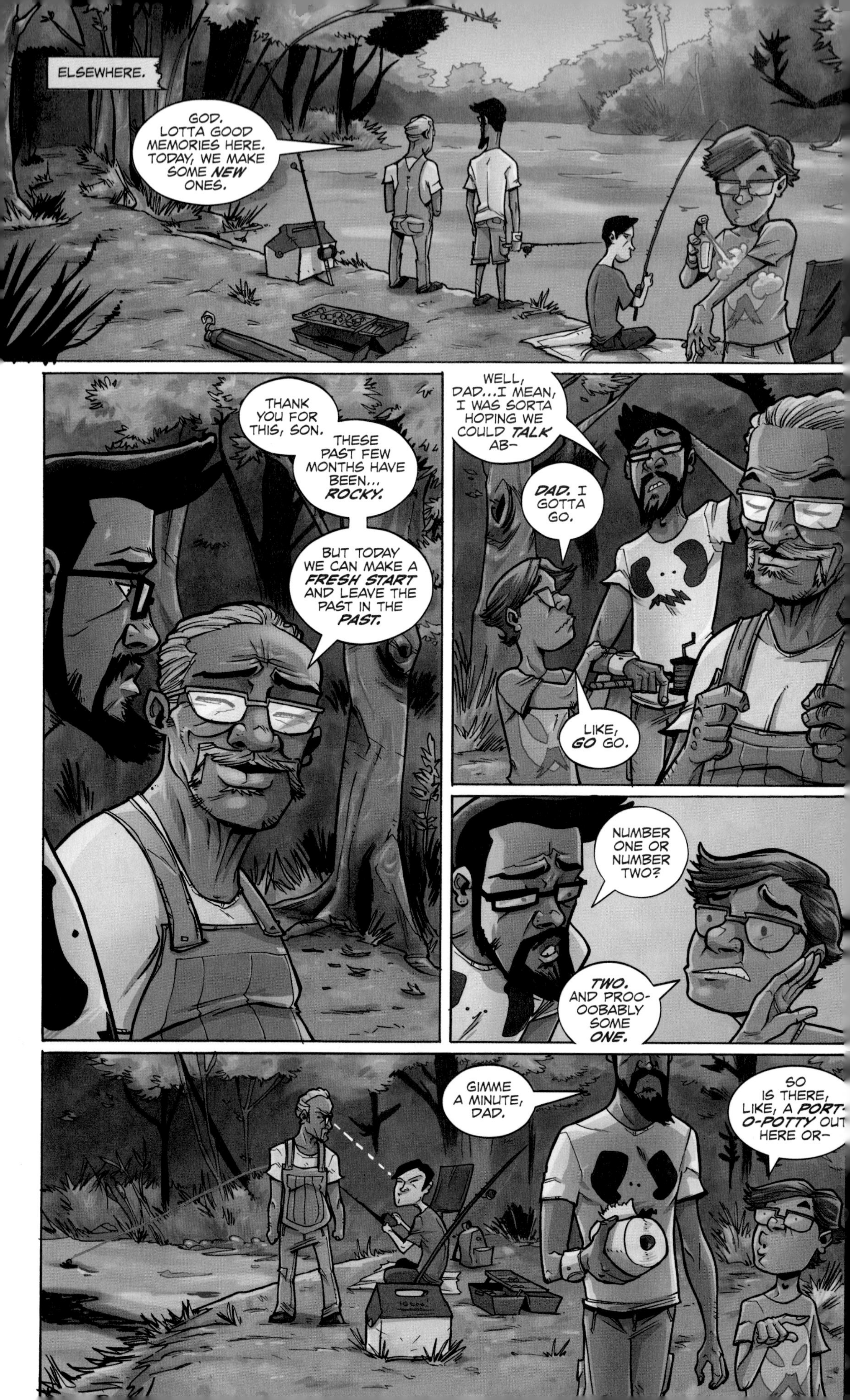
ELSEWHERE.
GOD. LOTTA GOOD MEMORIES HERE. TODAY, WE MAKE SOME NEW ONES.
THANK YOU FOR THIS, SON.
THESE PAST FEW MONTHS HAVE BEEN... ROCKY.
BUT TODAY WE CAN MAKE A FRESH START AND LEAVE THE PAST IN THE PAST.
WELL, DAD...I MEAN, I WAS SORTA HOPING WE COULD TALK AB–
DAD. I GOTTA GO.
LIKE, GO GO.
NUMBER ONE OR NUMBER TWO?
TWO. AND PROOOOBABLY SOME ONE.
GIMME A MINUTE, DAD.
SO IS THERE, LIKE, A PORT-O-POTTY OUT HERE OR–

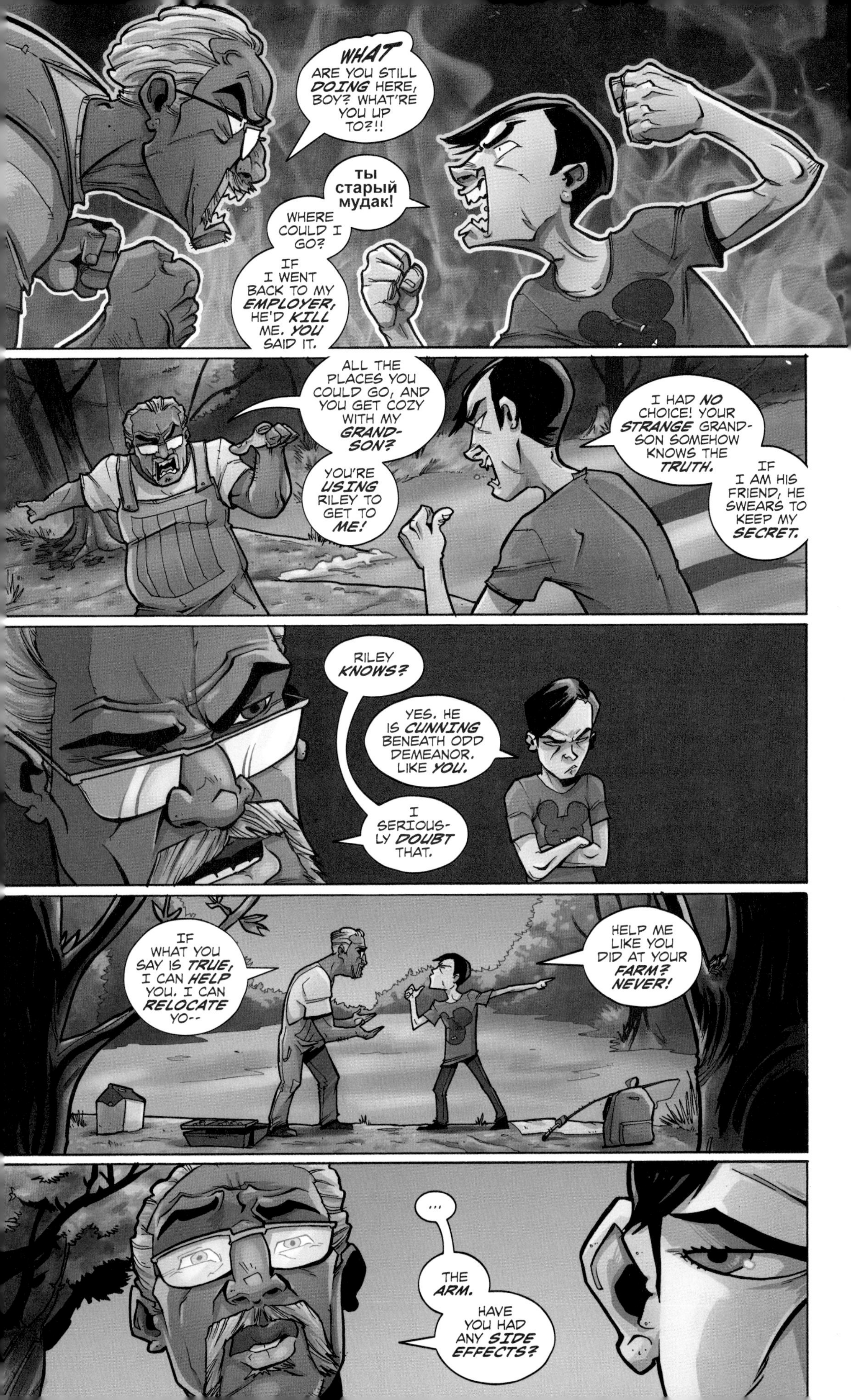
WHAT ARE YOU STILL DOING HERE, BOY? WHAT'RE YOU UP TO?!!
ты старый мудак!
WHERE COULD I GO?
IF I WENT BACK TO MY EMPLOYER, HE'D KILL ME. YOU SAID IT.
ALL THE PLACES YOU COULD GO, AND YOU GET COZY WITH MY GRANDSON?
YOU'RE USING RILEY TO GET TO ME!
I HAD NO CHOICE! YOUR STRANGE GRANDSON SOMEHOW KNOWS THE TRUTH.
IF I AM HIS FRIEND, HE SWEARS TO KEEP MY SECRET.
RILEY KNOWS?
YES. HE IS CUNNING BENEATH ODD DEMEANOR. LIKE YOU.
I SERIOUSLY DOUBT THAT.
IF WHAT YOU SAY IS TRUE, I CAN HELP YOU. I CAN RELOCATE YO--
HELP ME LIKE YOU DID AT YOUR FARM? NEVER!
...
THE ARM.
HAVE YOU HAD ANY SIDE EFFECTS?

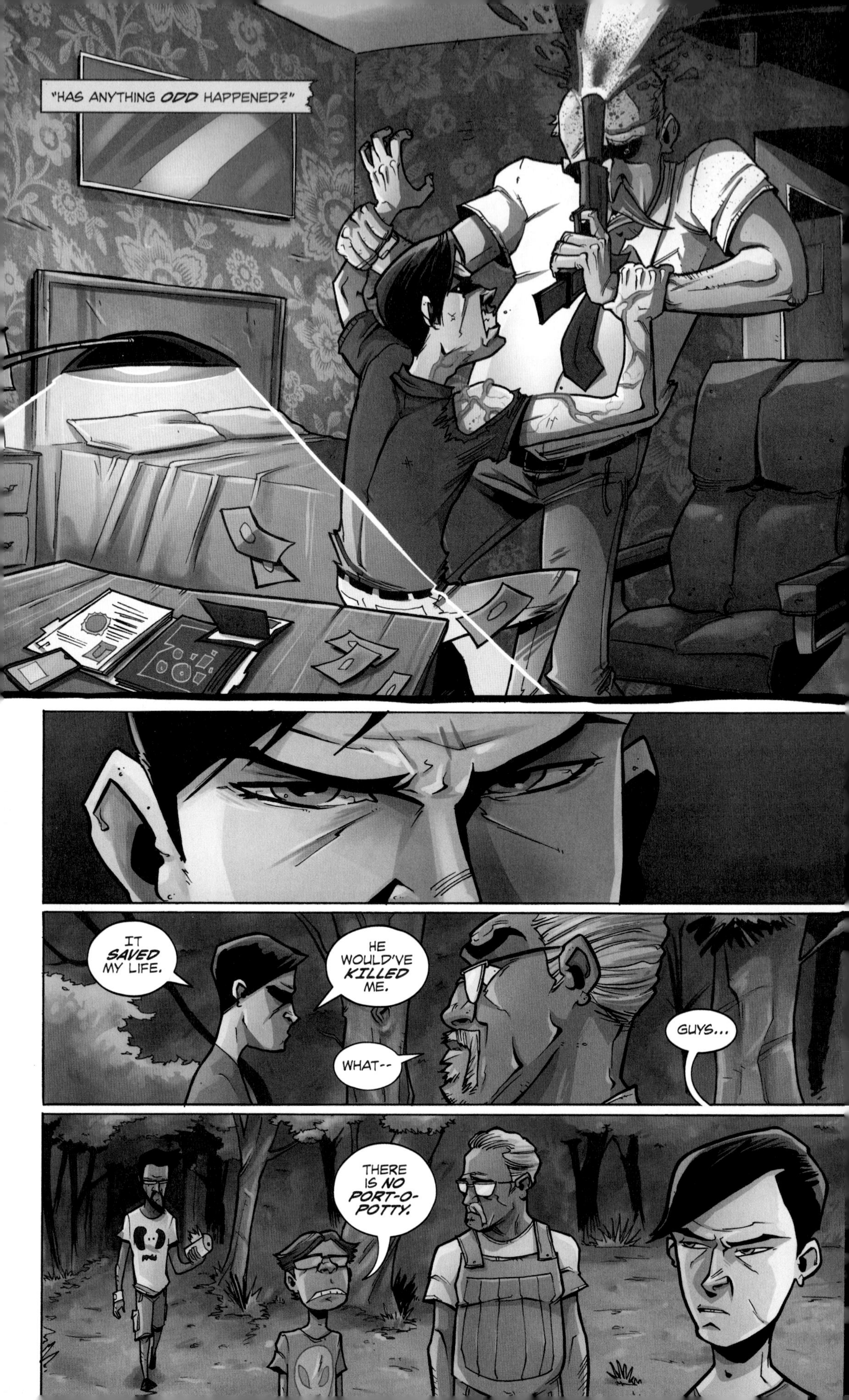
"HAS ANYTHING ODD HAPPENED?"
IT SAVED MY LIFE.
HE WOULD'VE KILLED ME.
WHAT--
GUYS...
THERE IS NO PORT-O-POTTY.

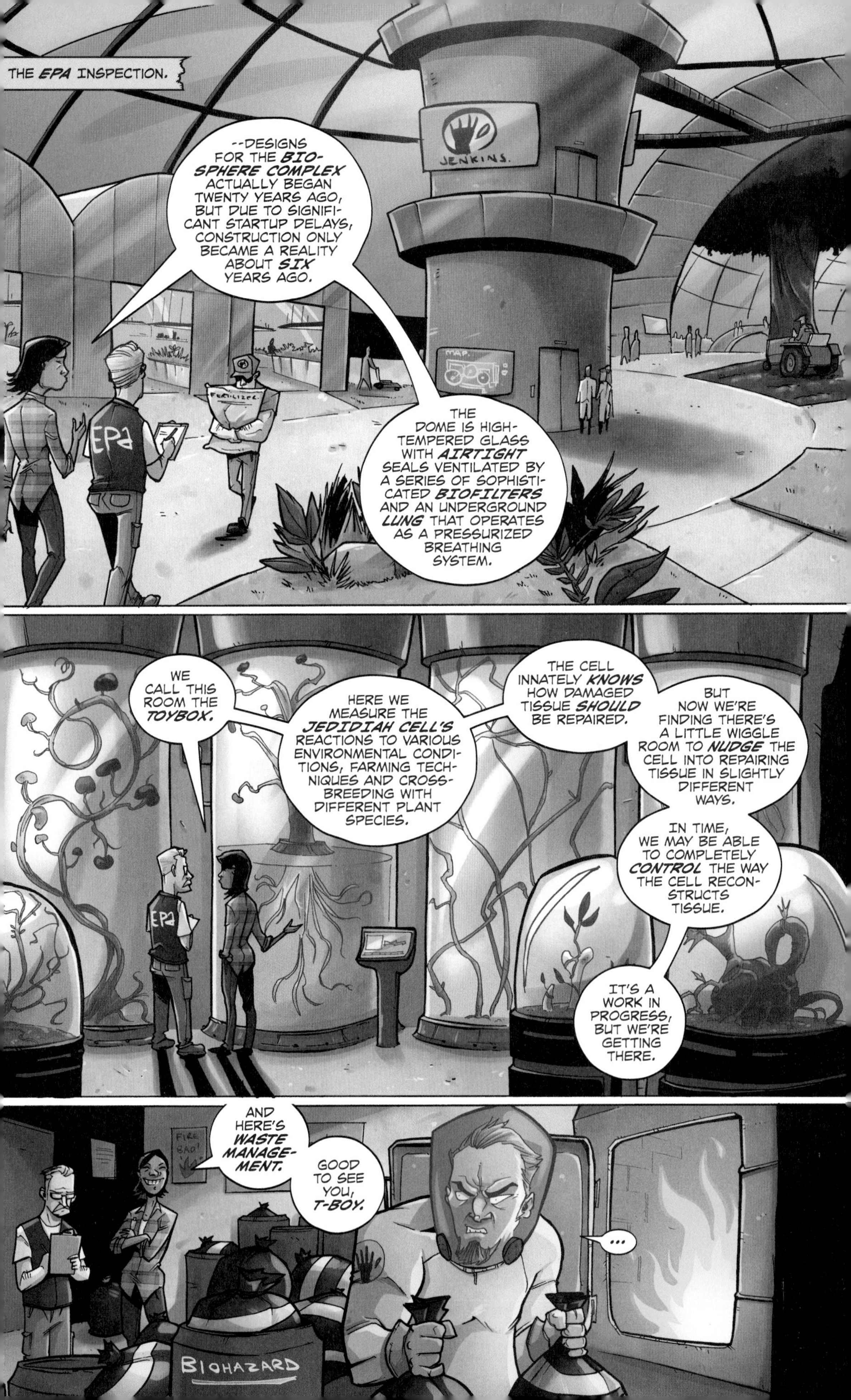
THE EPA INSPECTION.
--DESIGNS FOR THE BIO-SPHERE COMPLEX ACTUALLY BEGAN TWENTY YEARS AGO, BUT DUE TO SIGNIFI-CANT STARTUP DELAYS, CONSTRUCTION ONLY BECAME A REALITY ABOUT SIX YEARS AGO.
JENKINS.
MAP.
FERTILIZER
EPA
THE DOME IS HIGH-TEMPERED GLASS WITH AIRTIGHT SEALS VENTILATED BY A SERIES OF SOPHISTI-CATED BIOFILTERS AND AN UNDERGROUND LUNG THAT OPERATES AS A PRESSURIZED BREATHING SYSTEM.
WE CALL THIS ROOM THE TOYBOX.
HERE WE MEASURE THE JEDIDIAH CELL'S REACTIONS TO VARIOUS ENVIRONMENTAL CONDI-TIONS, FARMING TECH-NIQUES AND CROSS-BREEDING WITH DIFFERENT PLANT SPECIES.
THE CELL INNATELY KNOWS HOW DAMAGED TISSUE SHOULD BE REPAIRED.
BUT NOW WE'RE FINDING THERE'S A LITTLE WIGGLE ROOM TO NUDGE THE CELL INTO REPAIRING TISSUE IN SLIGHTLY DIFFERENT WAYS.
IN TIME, WE MAY BE ABLE TO COMPLETELY CONTROL THE WAY THE CELL RECON-STRUCTS TISSUE.
IT'S A WORK IN PROGRESS, BUT WE'RE GETTING THERE.
EPA
AND HERE'S WASTE MANAGE-MENT.
GOOD TO SEE YOU, T-BOY.
...
BIOHAZARD

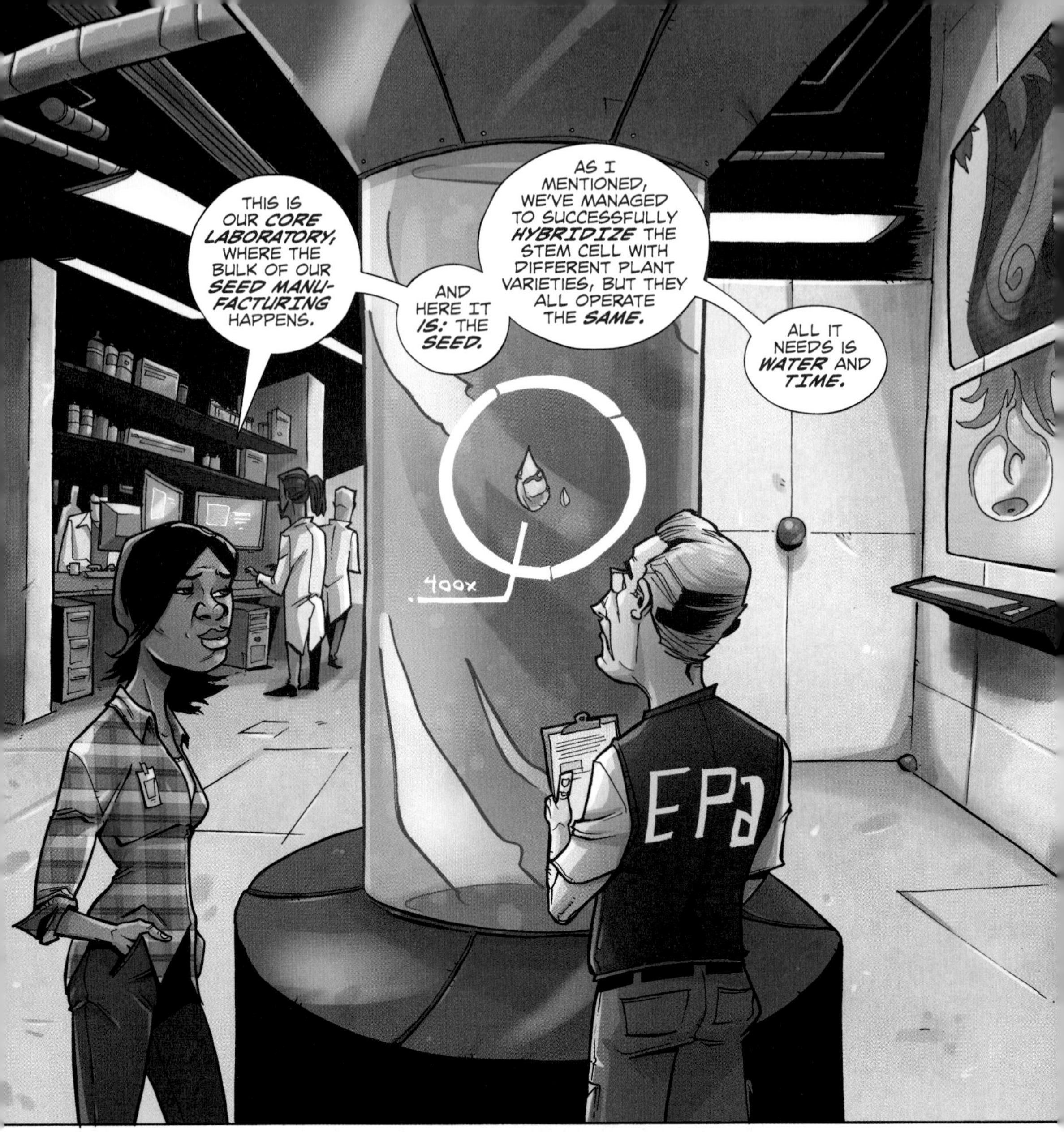
THIS IS OUR CORE LABORATORY, WHERE THE BULK OF OUR SEED MANUFACTURING HAPPENS.
AND HERE IT IS: THE SEED.
AS I MENTIONED, WE'VE MANAGED TO SUCCESSFULLY HYBRIDIZE THE STEM CELL WITH DIFFERENT PLANT VARIETIES, BUT THEY ALL OPERATE THE SAME.
ALL IT NEEDS IS WATER AND TIME.
400x
EPA

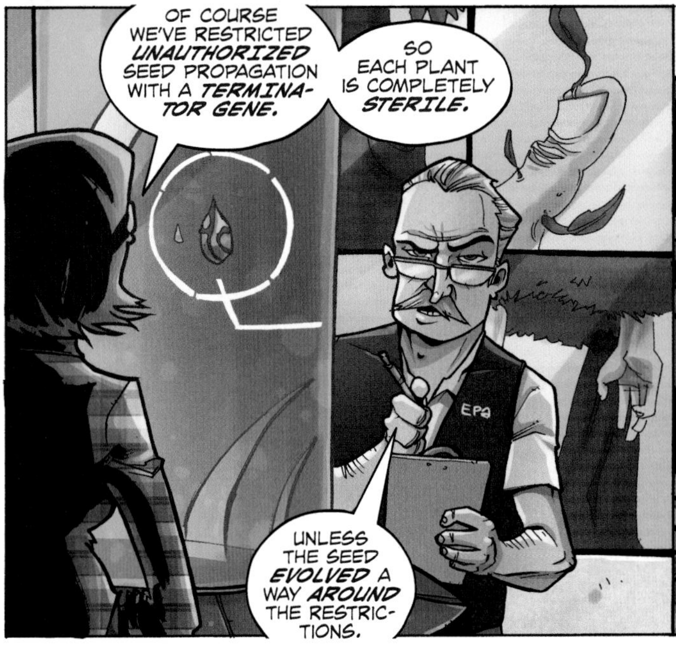
OF COURSE WE'VE RESTRICTED UNAUTHORIZED SEED PROPAGATION WITH A TERMINATOR GENE.
SO EACH PLANT IS COMPLETELY STERILE.
EPA
UNLESS THE SEED EVOLVED A WAY AROUND THE RESTRICTIONS.

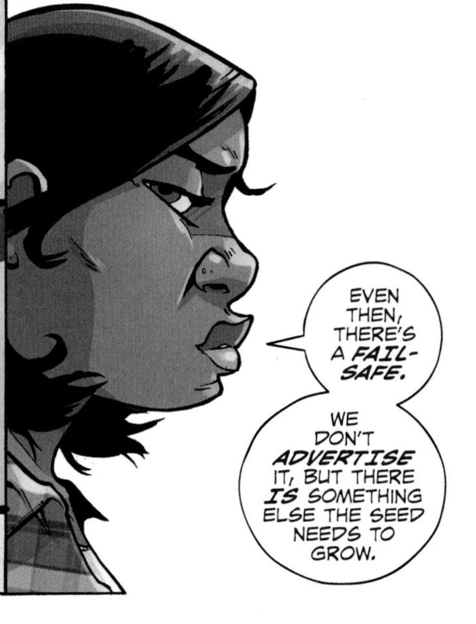
EVEN THEN, THERE'S A FAIL-SAFE.
WE DON'T ADVERTISE IT, BUT THERE IS SOMETHING ELSE THE SEED NEEDS TO GROW.

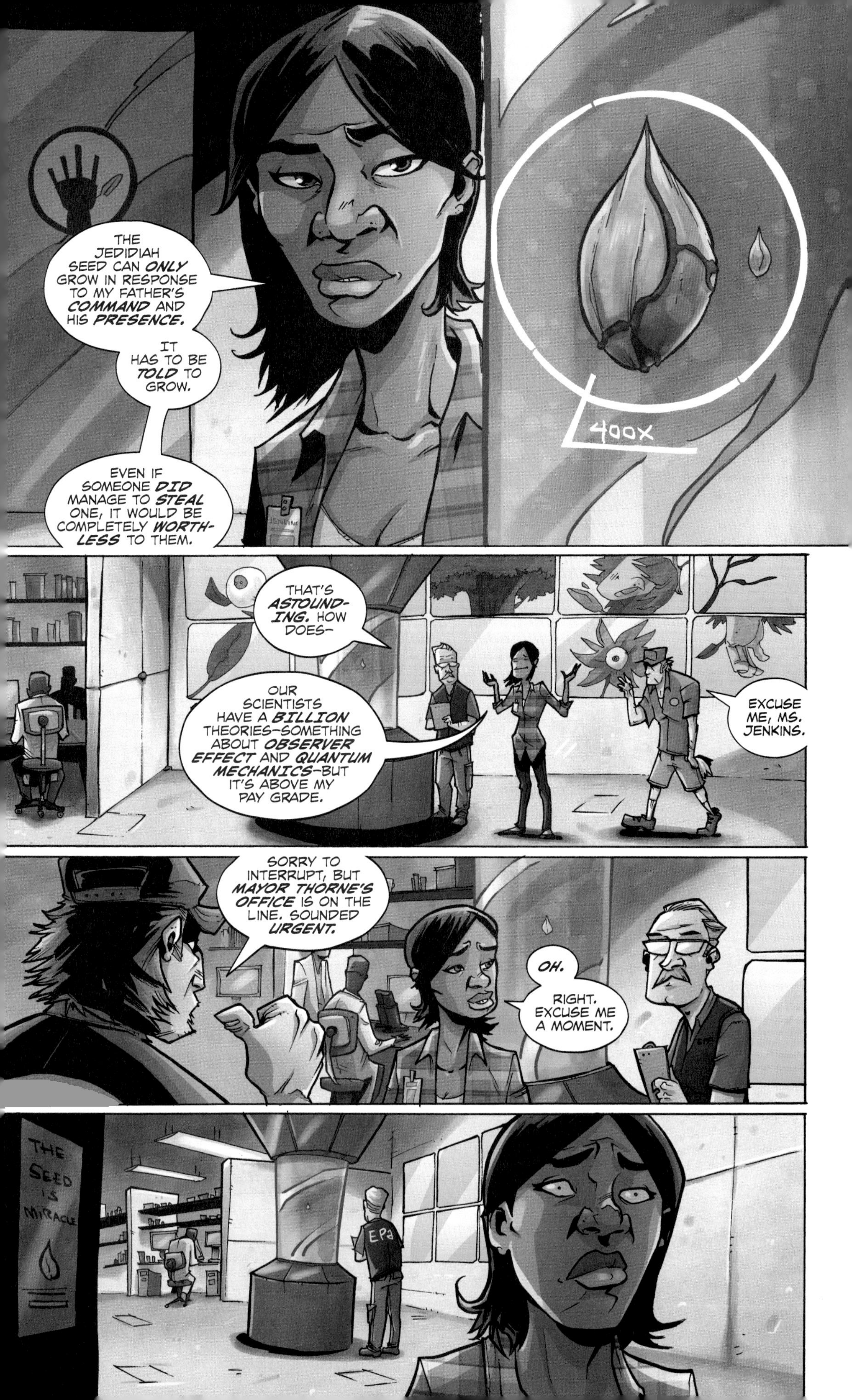
THE JEDIDIAH SEED CAN ONLY GROW IN RESPONSE TO MY FATHER'S COMMAND AND HIS PRESENCE.
IT HAS TO BE TOLD TO GROW.
EVEN IF SOMEONE DID MANAGE TO STEAL ONE, IT WOULD BE COMPLETELY WORTH-LESS TO THEM.
400X
THAT'S ASTOUND-ING. HOW DOES–
OUR SCIENTISTS HAVE A BILLION THEORIES–SOMETHING ABOUT OBSERVER EFFECT AND QUANTUM MECHANICS–BUT IT'S ABOVE MY PAY GRADE.
EXCUSE ME, MS. JENKINS.
SORRY TO INTERRUPT, BUT MAYOR THORNE'S OFFICE IS ON THE LINE. SOUNDED URGENT.
OH.
RIGHT. EXCUSE ME A MOMENT.
THE SEED IS MIRACLE
EPA

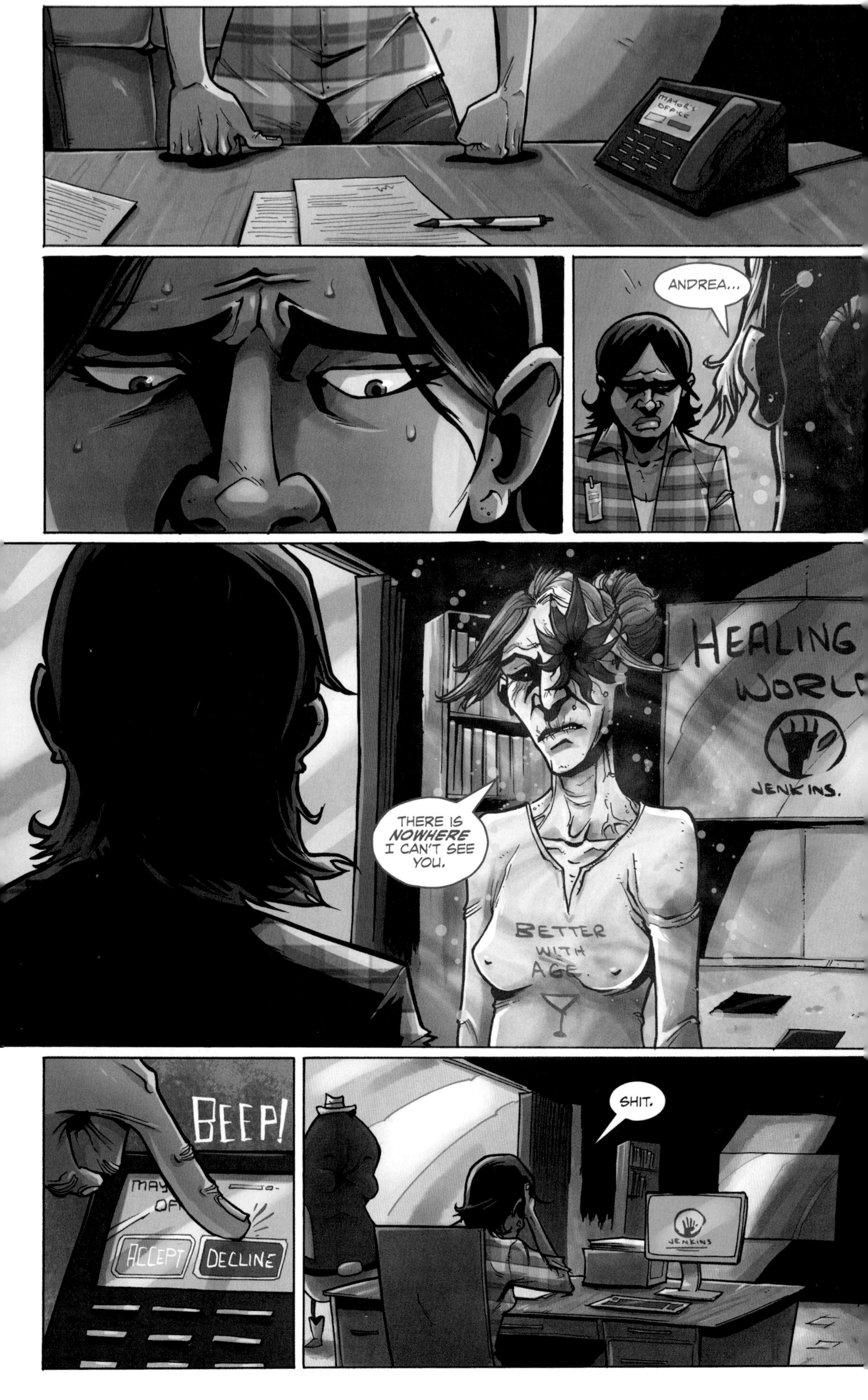
MAYOR'S OFFICE
ANDREA...
HEALING
JENKINS.
THERE IS *NOWHERE* I CAN'T SEE YOU.
BETTER WITH AGE
BEEP!
ACCEPT
DECLINE
SHIT.
JENKINS

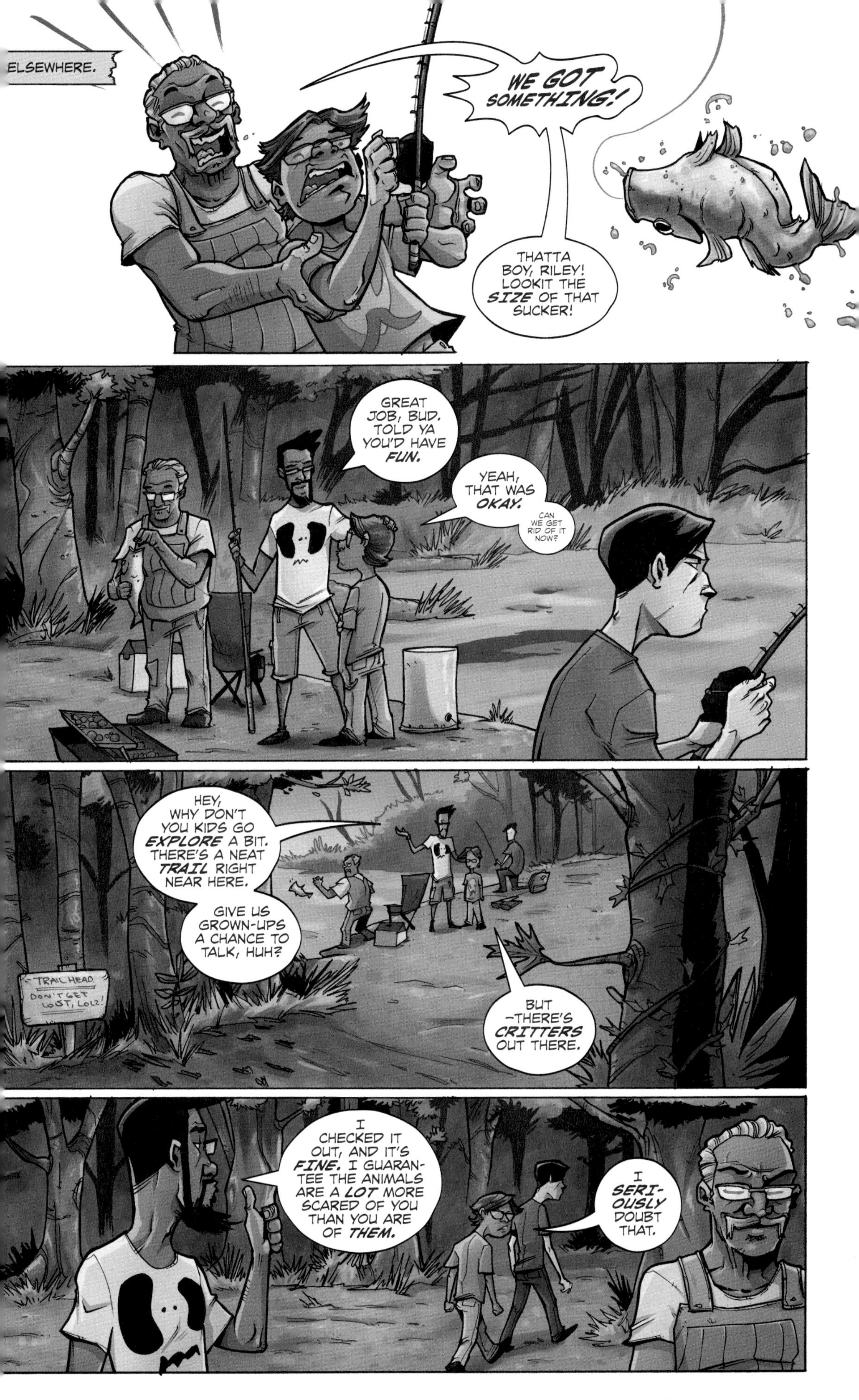
ELSEWHERE.
WE GOT SOMETHING!
THATTA BOY, RILEY! LOOKIT THE SIZE OF THAT SUCKER!
GREAT JOB, BUD. TOLD YA YOU'D HAVE FUN.
YEAH, THAT WAS OKAY.
CAN WE GET RID OF IT NOW?
HEY, WHY DON'T YOU KIDS GO EXPLORE A BIT. THERE'S A NEAT TRAIL RIGHT NEAR HERE.
GIVE US GROWN-UPS A CHANCE TO TALK, HUH?
TRAIL HEAD.
DON'T GET LOST, LOLZ!
BUT --THERE'S CRITTERS OUT THERE.
I CHECKED IT OUT, AND IT'S FINE. I GUARANTEE THE ANIMALS ARE A LOT MORE SCARED OF YOU THAN YOU ARE OF THEM.
I SERIOUSLY DOUBT THAT.

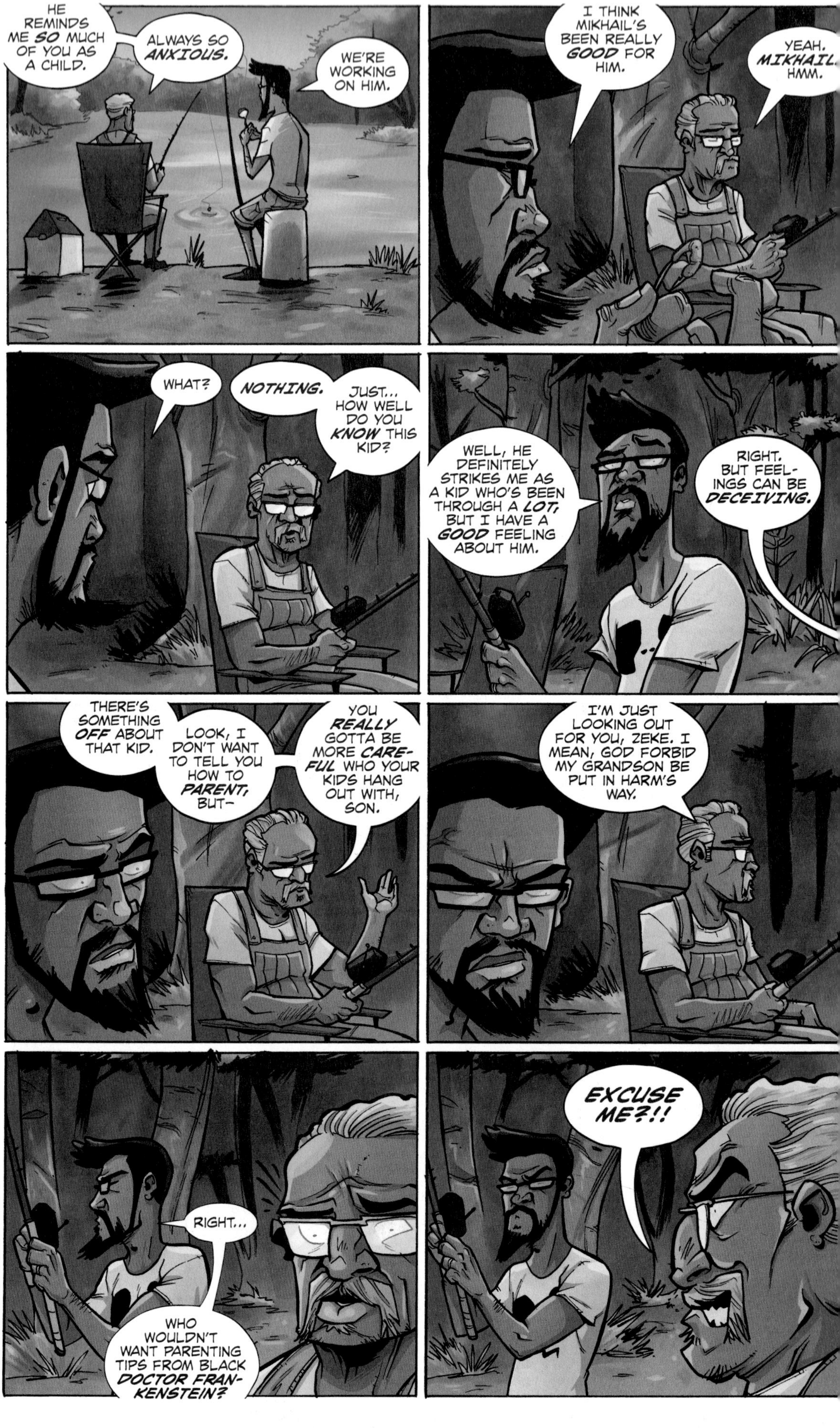
HE REMINDS ME SO MUCH OF YOU AS A CHILD.
ALWAYS SO ANXIOUS.
WE'RE WORKING ON HIM.
I THINK MIKHAIL'S BEEN REALLY GOOD FOR HIM.
YEAH. MIKHAIL. HMM.
WHAT?
NOTHING.
JUST... HOW WELL DO YOU KNOW THIS KID?
WELL, HE DEFINITELY STRIKES ME AS A KID WHO'S BEEN THROUGH A LOT, BUT I HAVE A GOOD FEELING ABOUT HIM.
RIGHT. BUT FEEL-INGS CAN BE DECEIVING.
THERE'S SOMETHING OFF ABOUT THAT KID.
LOOK, I DON'T WANT TO TELL YOU HOW TO PARENT, BUT-
YOU REALLY GOTTA BE MORE CARE-FUL WHO YOUR KIDS HANG OUT WITH, SON.
I'M JUST LOOKING OUT FOR YOU, ZEKE. I MEAN, GOD FORBID MY GRANDSON BE PUT IN HARM'S WAY.
RIGHT...
WHO WOULDN'T WANT PARENTING TIPS FROM BLACK DOCTOR FRAN-KENSTEIN?
EXCUSE ME?!!

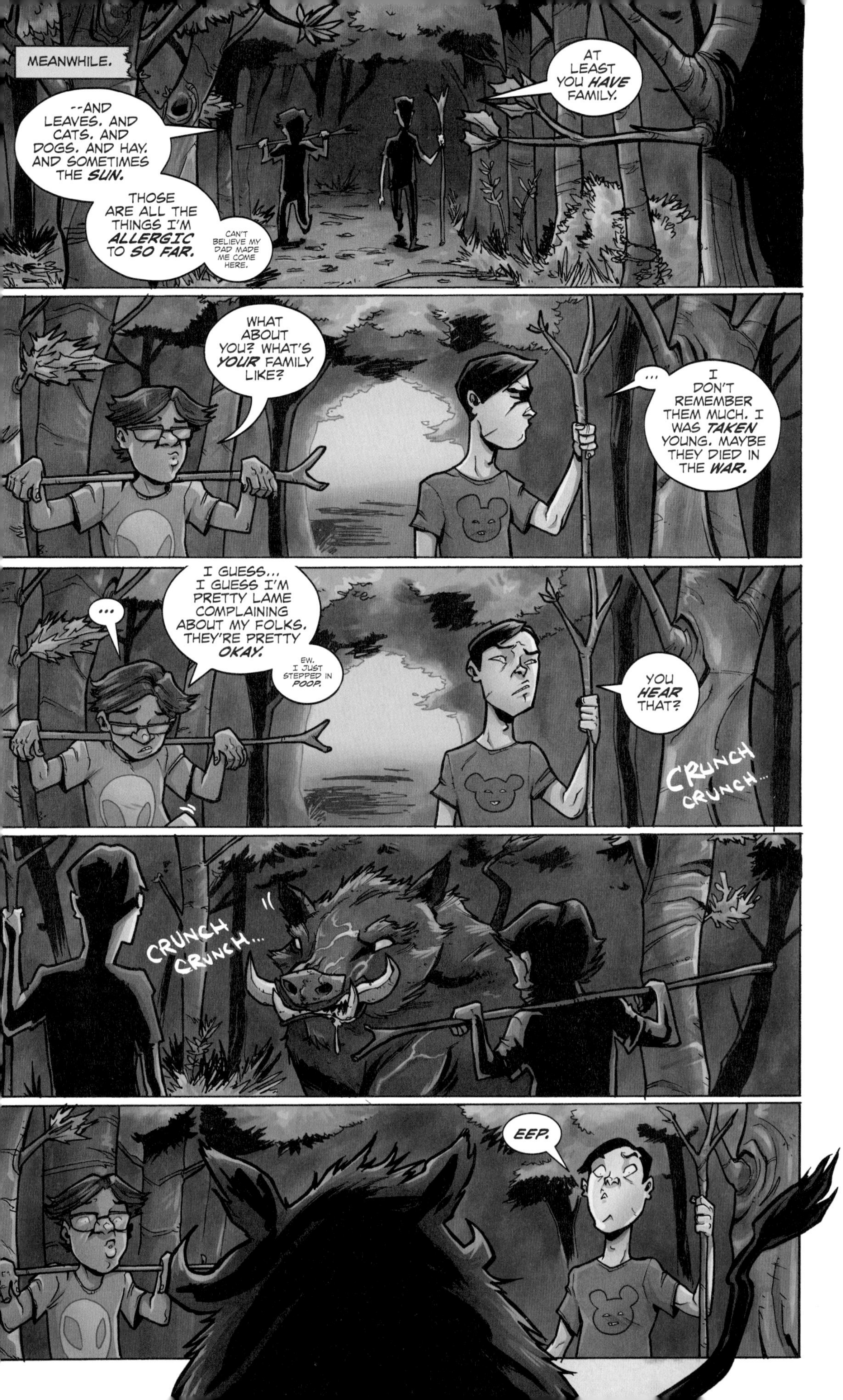
MEANWHILE.
--AND LEAVES. AND CATS. AND DOGS. AND HAY. AND SOMETIMES THE SUN.
THOSE ARE ALL THE THINGS I'M ALLERGIC TO SO FAR.
CAN'T BELIEVE MY DAD MADE ME COME HERE.
AT LEAST YOU HAVE FAMILY.
WHAT ABOUT YOU? WHAT'S YOUR FAMILY LIKE?
...
I DON'T REMEMBER THEM MUCH. I WAS TAKEN YOUNG. MAYBE THEY DIED IN THE WAR.
...
I GUESS... I GUESS I'M PRETTY LAME COMPLAINING ABOUT MY FOLKS. THEY'RE PRETTY OKAY.
EW. I JUST STEPPED IN POOP.
YOU HEAR THAT?
CRUNCH CRUNCH...
CRUNCH CRUNCH...
EEP.

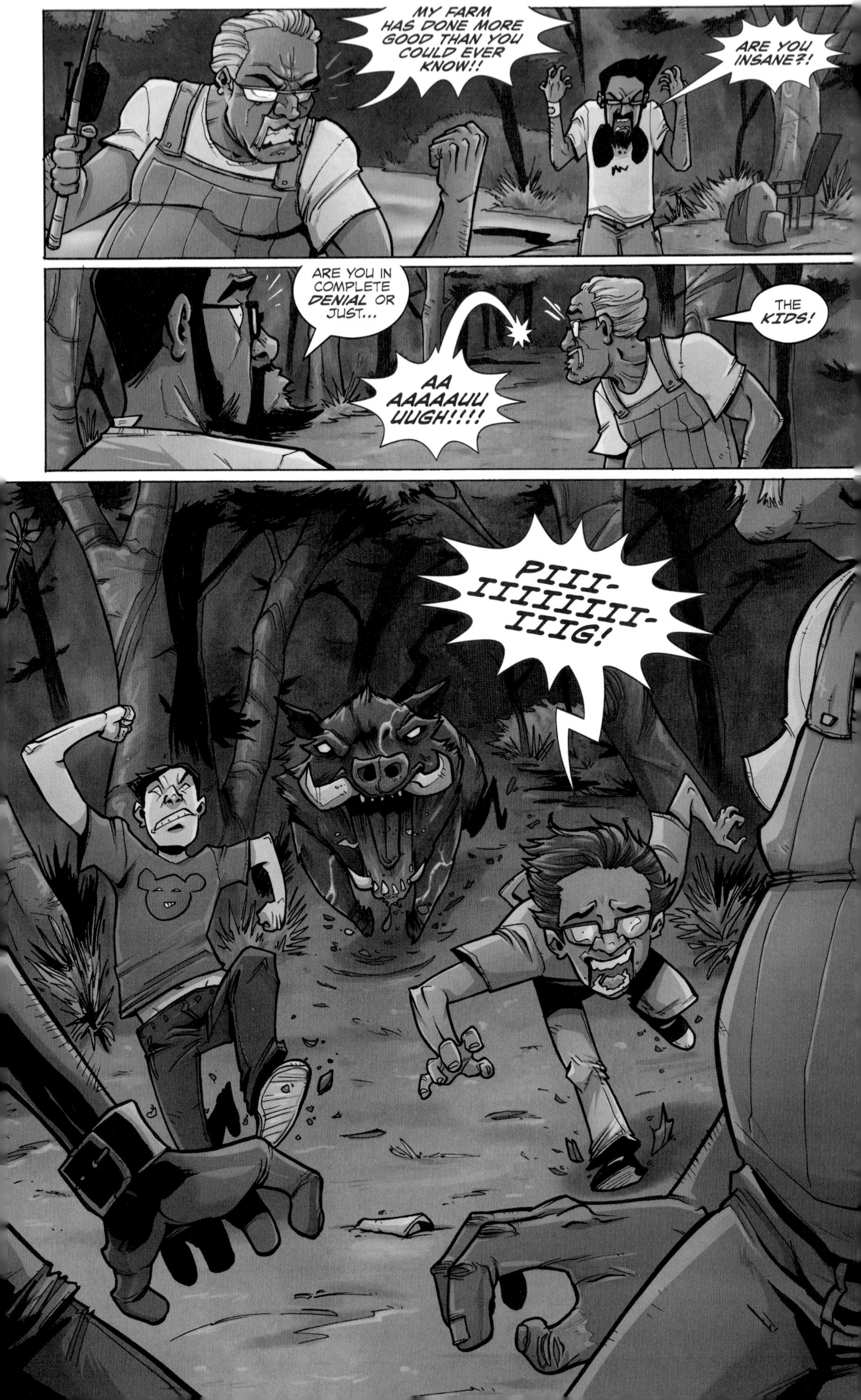
MY FARM HAS DONE MORE GOOD THAN YOU COULD EVER KNOW!!
ARE YOU INSANE?!
ARE YOU IN COMPLETE DENIAL OR JUST...
AA AAAAAAUU UUGH!!!!
THE KIDS!
PIII-IIIIIIII-IIIG!

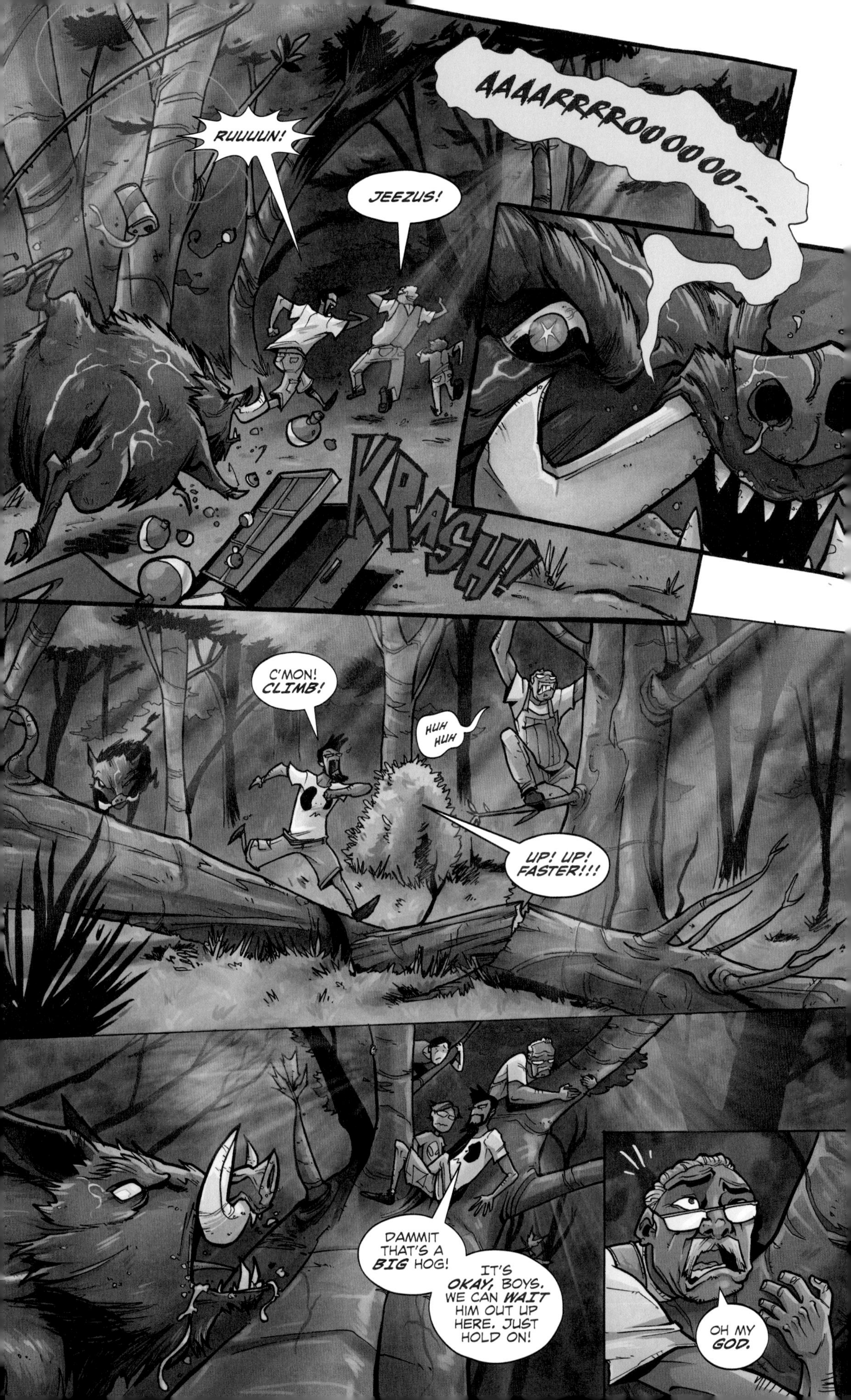
RUUUUN!
JEEZUS!
AAAARRRROOOOOO----
KRASH!
C'MON! CLIMB!
HUH HUH
UP! UP! FASTER!!!
DAMMIT THAT'S A BIG HOG!
IT'S OKAY, BOYS. WE CAN WAIT HIM OUT UP HERE. JUST HOLD ON!
OH MY GOD.

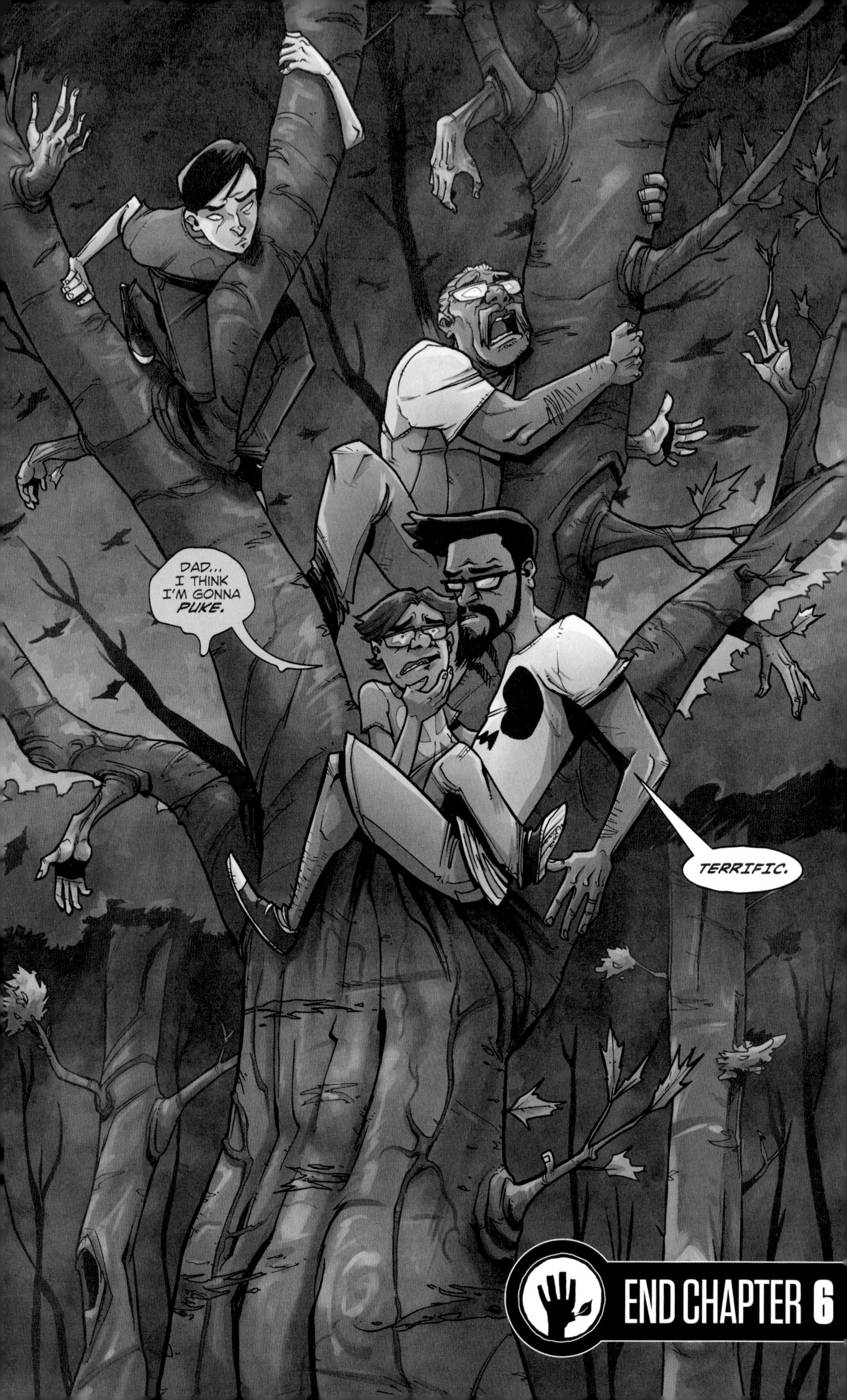
DAD... I THINK I'M GONNA PUKE.
TERRIFIC.
END CHAPTER 6

CHAPTER 7

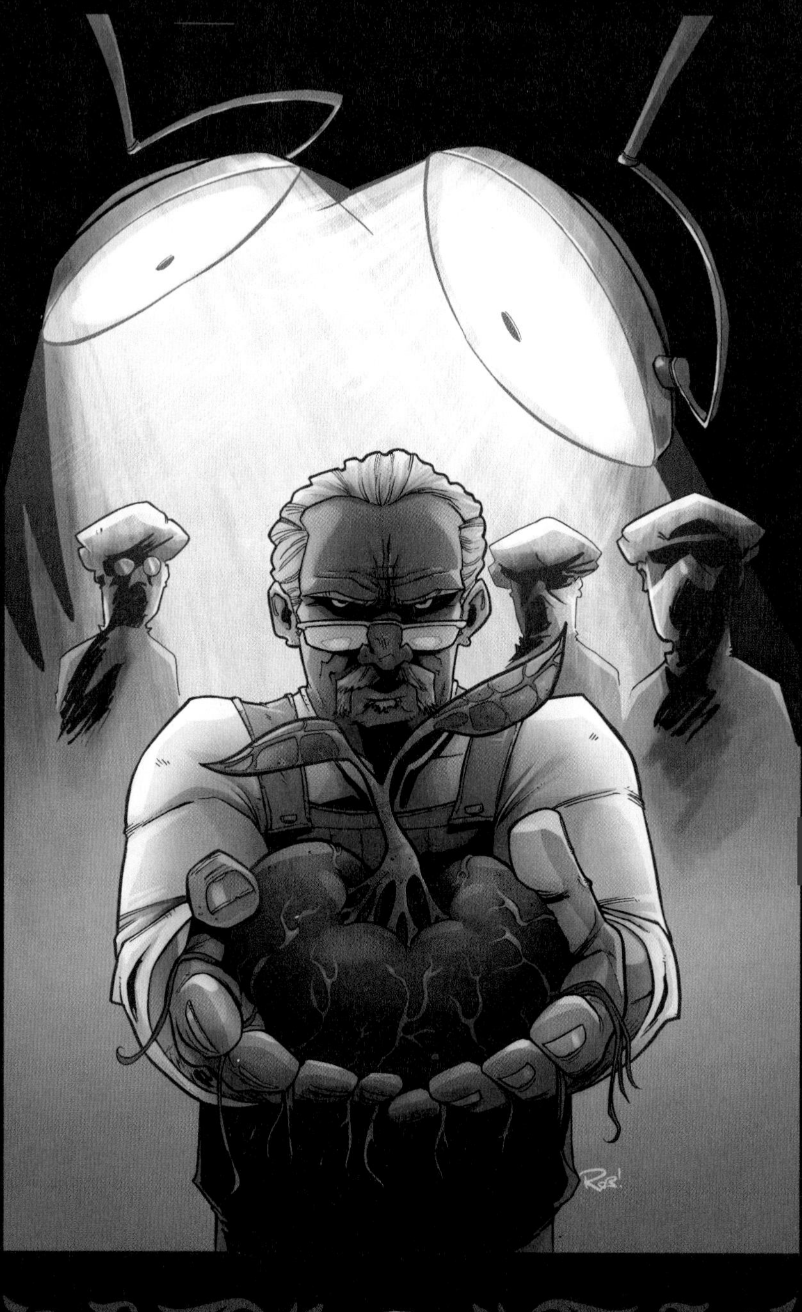

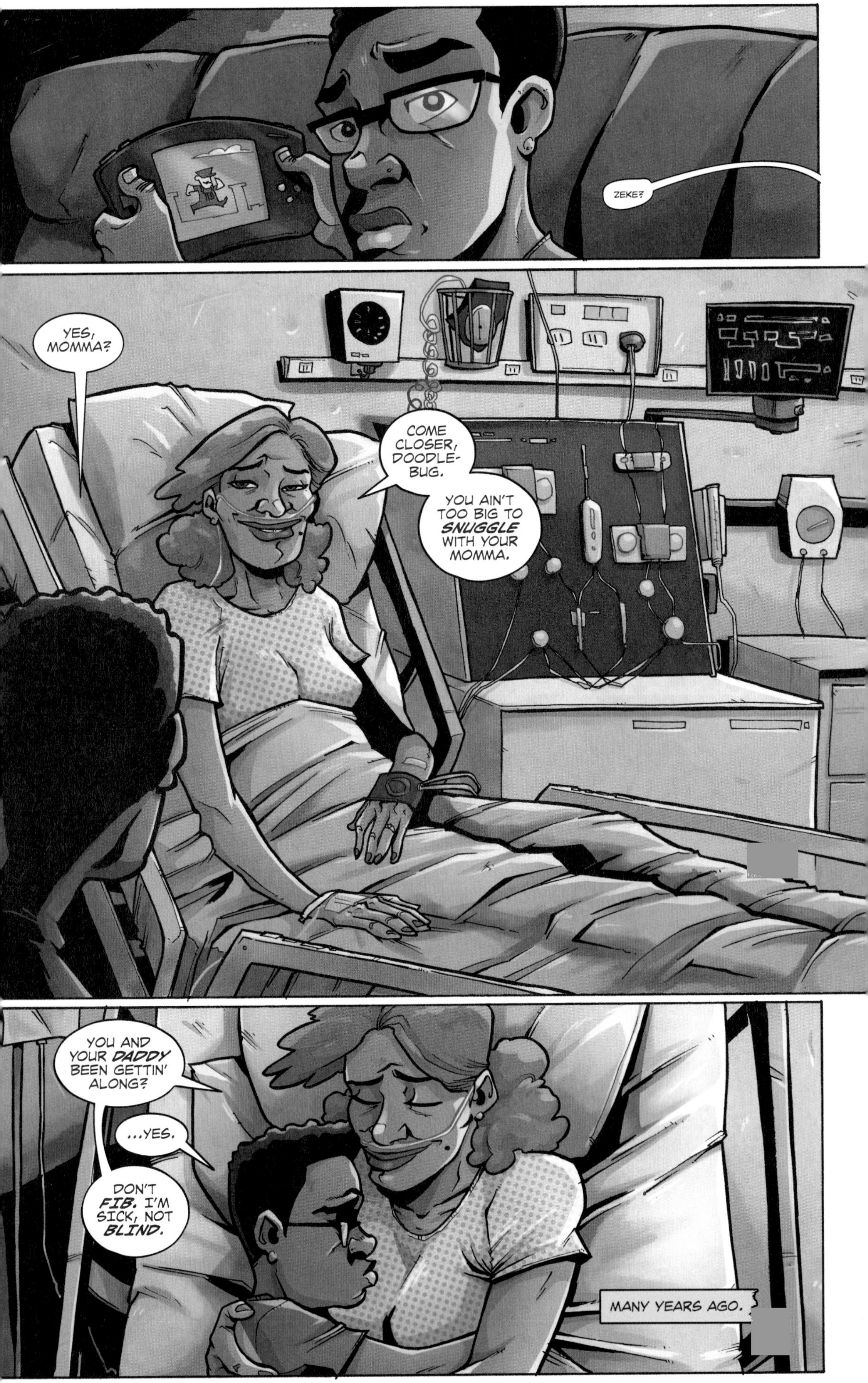
ZEKE?
YES, MOMMA?
COME CLOSER, DOODLE-BUG.
YOU AIN'T TOO BIG TO SNUGGLE WITH YOUR MOMMA.
YOU AND YOUR DADDY BEEN GETTIN' ALONG?
...YES.
DON'T FIB. I'M SICK, NOT BLIND.
MANY YEARS AGO.

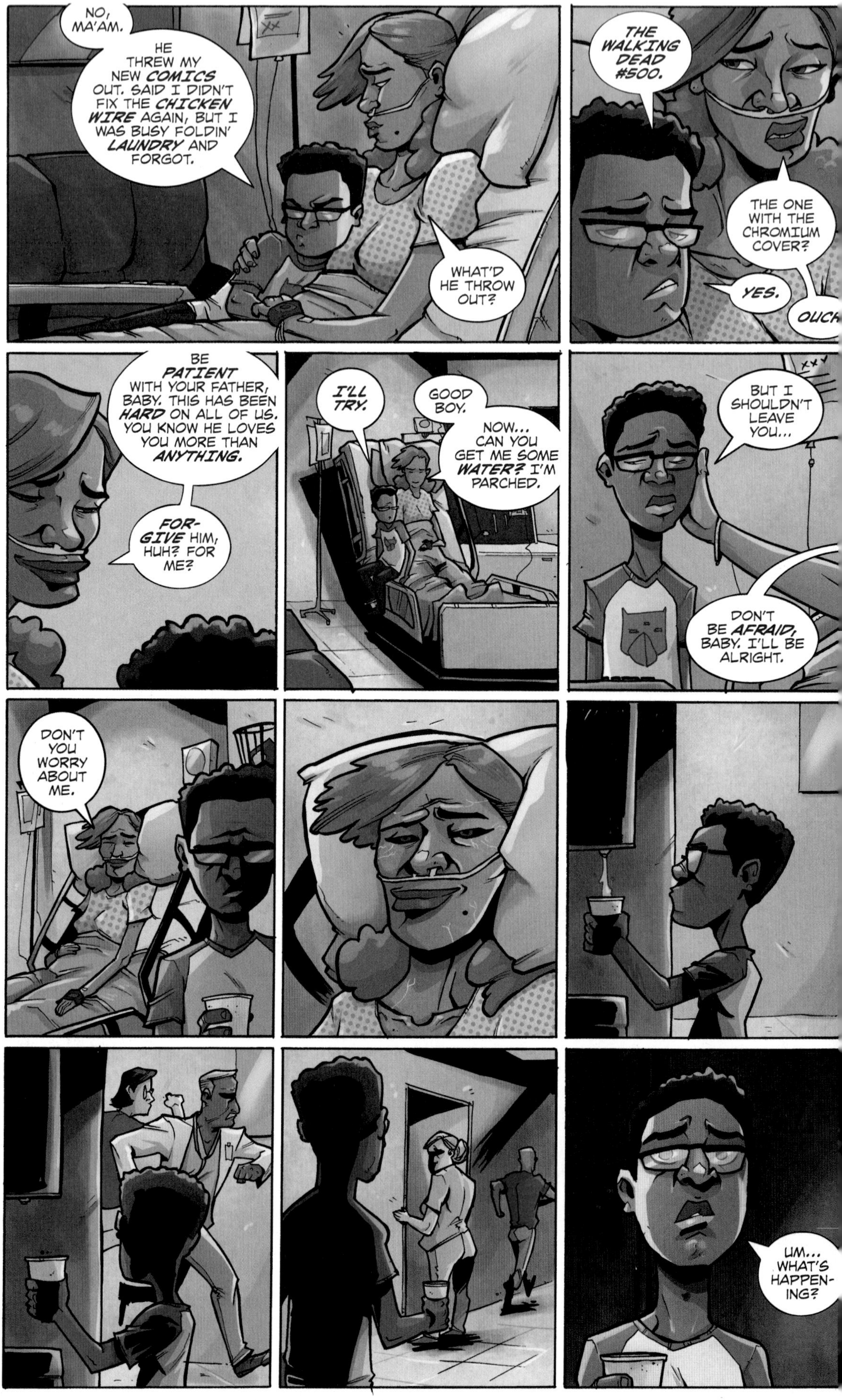
NO, MA'AM.
HE THREW MY NEW COMICS OUT. SAID I DIDN'T FIX THE CHICKEN WIRE AGAIN, BUT I WAS BUSY FOLDIN' LAUNDRY AND FORGOT.
WHAT'D HE THROW OUT?
THE WALKING DEAD #500.
THE ONE WITH THE CHROMIUM COVER?
YES.
OUCH
BE PATIENT WITH YOUR FATHER, BABY. THIS HAS BEEN HARD ON ALL OF US. YOU KNOW HE LOVES YOU MORE THAN ANYTHING.
FOR-GIVE HIM, HUH? FOR ME?
I'LL TRY.
GOOD BOY.
NOW... CAN YOU GET ME SOME WATER? I'M PARCHED.
BUT I SHOULDN'T LEAVE YOU...
DON'T BE AFRAID, BABY. I'LL BE ALRIGHT.
DON'T YOU WORRY ABOUT ME.
UM... WHAT'S HAPPEN-ING?

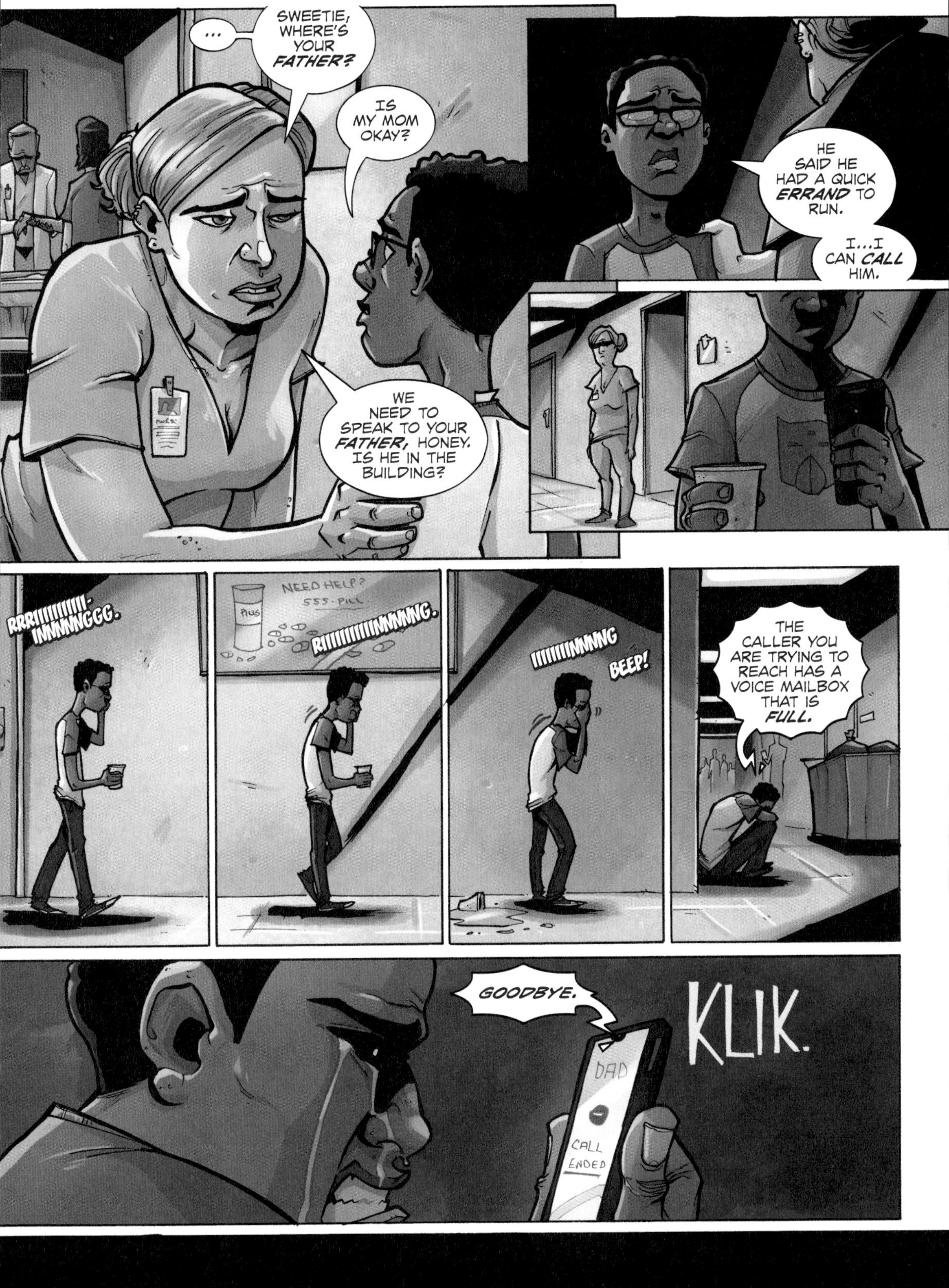
...
SWEETIE, WHERE'S YOUR FATHER?
IS MY MOM OKAY?
WE NEED TO SPEAK TO YOUR FATHER, HONEY. IS HE IN THE BUILDING?
HE SAID HE HAD A QUICK ERRAND TO RUN.
I...I CAN CALL HIM.
RRRIIIIIIIIIIII-INNNNNGGG.
NEED HELP? 555-PILL
PILLS
RIIIIIIIIIIIINNNNNG.
IIIIIIIINNNNG
BEEP!
THE CALLER YOU ARE TRYING TO REACH HAS A VOICE MAILBOX THAT IS FULL.
GOODBYE.
KLIK.
DAD
CALL ENDED

CHAPTER 7: **THE WOUND.**

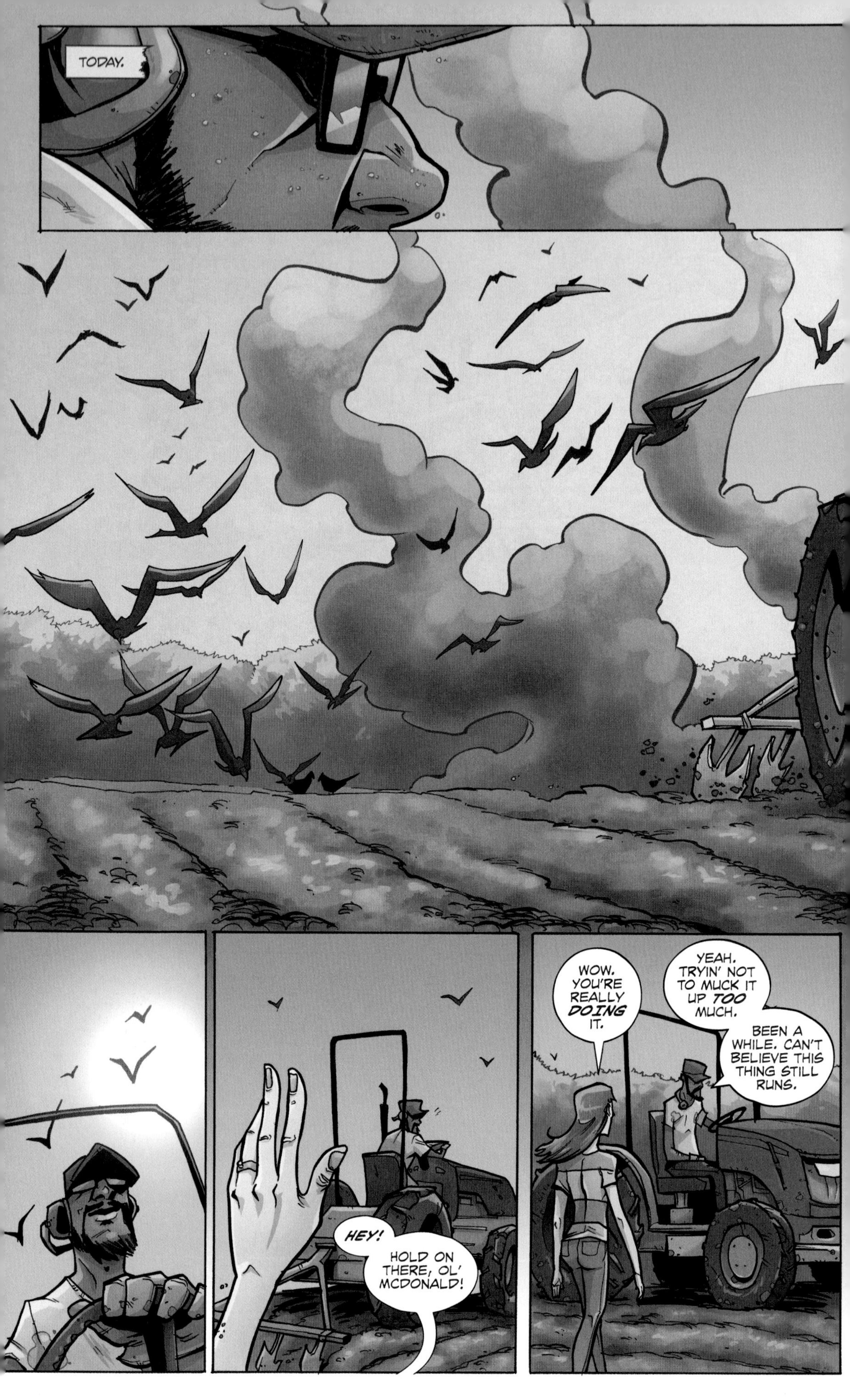
TODAY.
HEY!
HOLD ON THERE, OL' MCDONALD!
WOW. YOU'RE REALLY DOING IT.
YEAH. TRYIN' NOT TO MUCK IT UP TOO MUCH.
BEEN A WHILE. CAN'T BELIEVE THIS THING STILL RUNS.

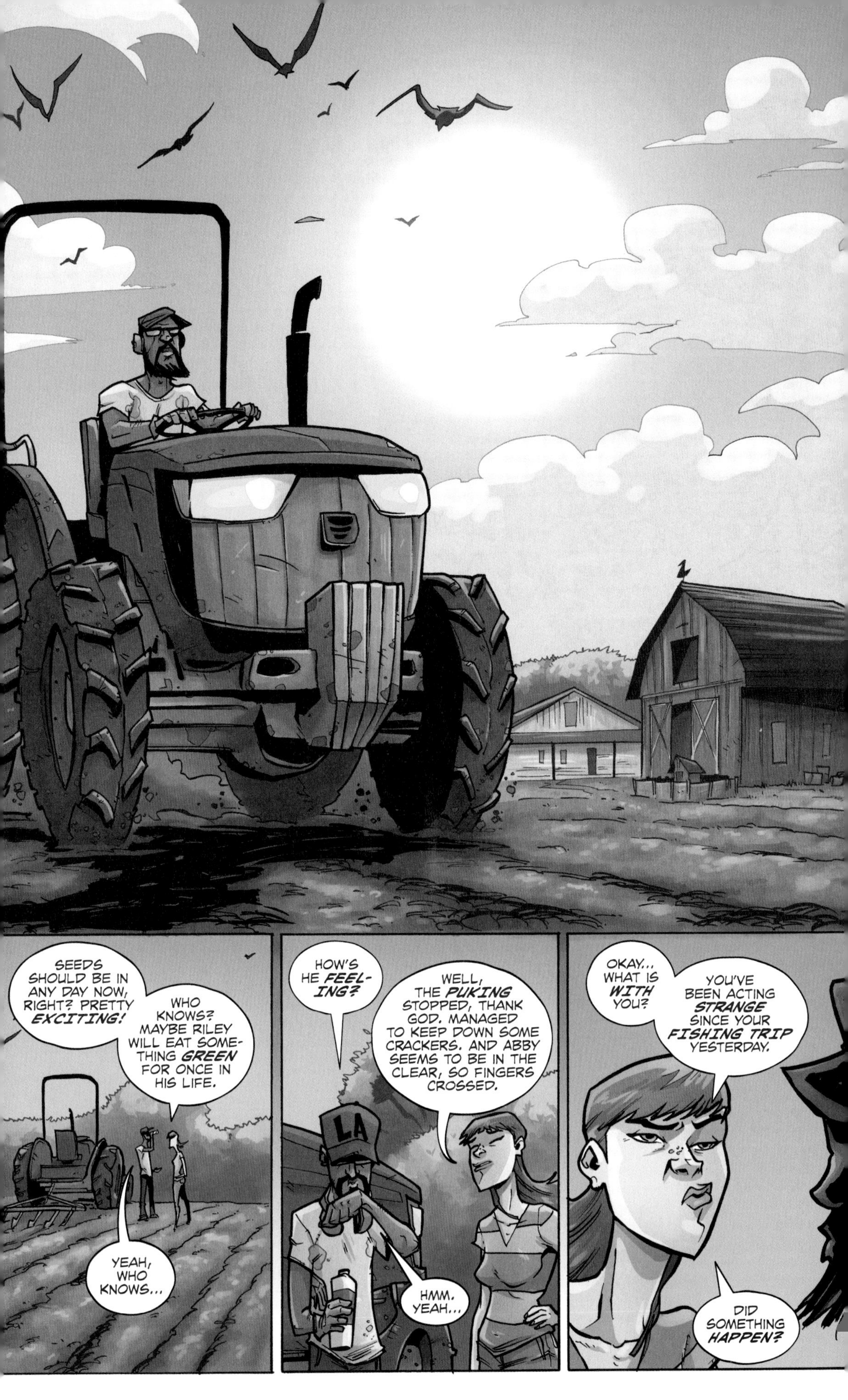
SEEDS SHOULD BE IN ANY DAY NOW, RIGHT? PRETTY EXCITING!
WHO KNOWS? MAYBE RILEY WILL EAT SOMETHING GREEN FOR ONCE IN HIS LIFE.
YEAH, WHO KNOWS...
HOW'S HE FEELING?
WELL, THE PUKING STOPPED, THANK GOD. MANAGED TO KEEP DOWN SOME CRACKERS. AND ABBY SEEMS TO BE IN THE CLEAR, SO FINGERS CROSSED.
HMM. YEAH...
OKAY... WHAT IS WITH YOU?
YOU'VE BEEN ACTING STRANGE SINCE YOUR FISHING TRIP YESTERDAY.
DID SOMETHING HAPPEN?
LA

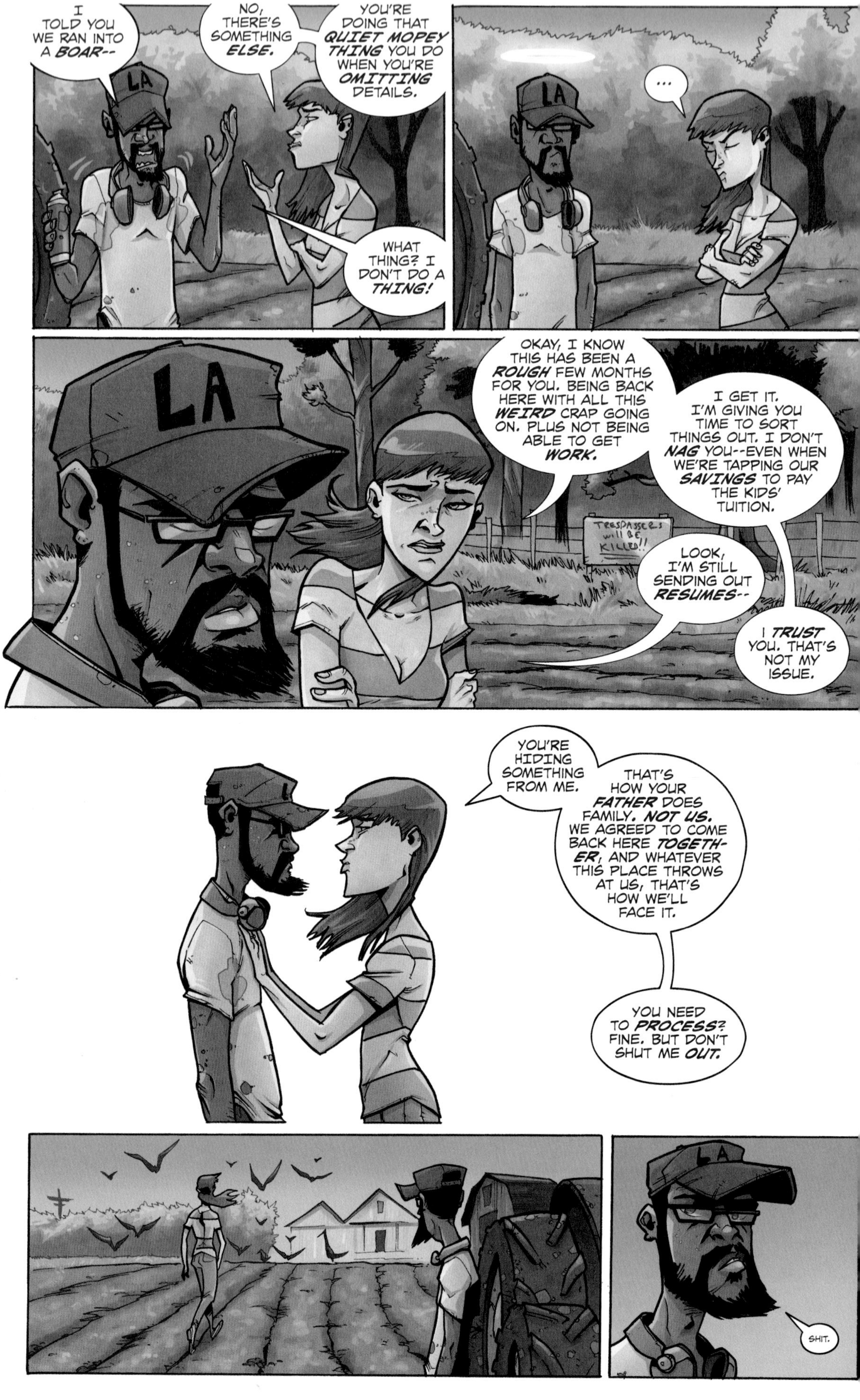
I TOLD YOU WE RAN INTO A BOAR--
NO, THERE'S SOMETHING ELSE.
YOU'RE DOING THAT QUIET MOPEY THING YOU DO WHEN YOU'RE OMITTING DETAILS.
WHAT THING? I DON'T DO A THING!
...
OKAY, I KNOW THIS HAS BEEN A ROUGH FEW MONTHS FOR YOU. BEING BACK HERE WITH ALL THIS WEIRD CRAP GOING ON. PLUS NOT BEING ABLE TO GET WORK.
I GET IT. I'M GIVING YOU TIME TO SORT THINGS OUT. I DON'T NAG YOU--EVEN WHEN WE'RE TAPPING OUR SAVINGS TO PAY THE KIDS' TUITION.
TRESPASSERS will BE KILLED!!
LOOK, I'M STILL SENDING OUT RESUMES--
I TRUST YOU. THAT'S NOT MY ISSUE.
YOU'RE HIDING SOMETHING FROM ME.
THAT'S HOW YOUR FATHER DOES FAMILY. NOT US. WE AGREED TO COME BACK HERE TOGETHER, AND WHATEVER THIS PLACE THROWS AT US, THAT'S HOW WE'LL FACE IT.
YOU NEED TO PROCESS? FINE. BUT DON'T SHUT ME OUT.
SHIT.

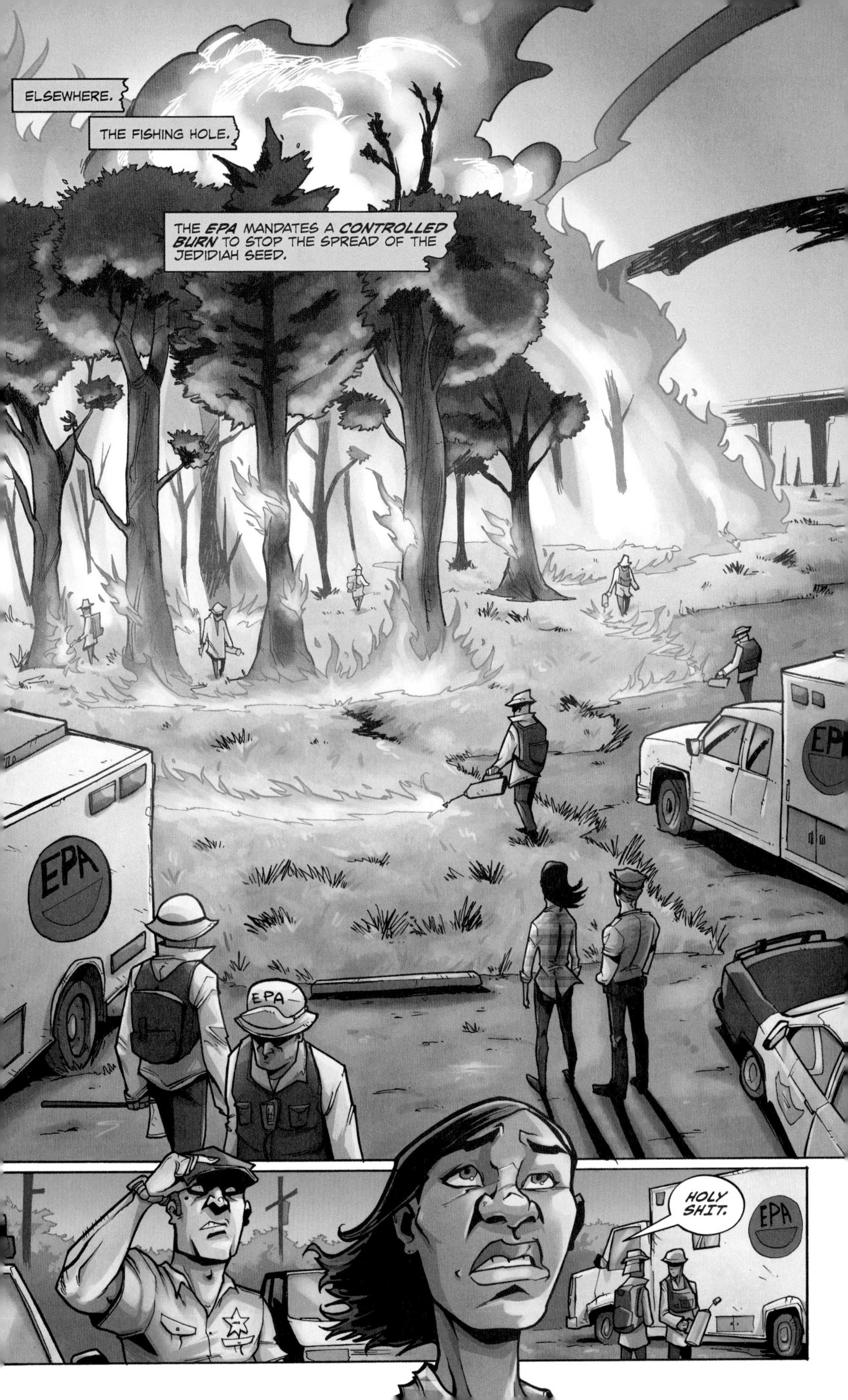
ELSEWHERE.
THE FISHING HOLE.
THE EPA MANDATES A CONTROLLED BURN TO STOP THE SPREAD OF THE JEDIDIAH SEED.
EPA
EPA
EPA
EPA
HOLY SHIT.
EPA

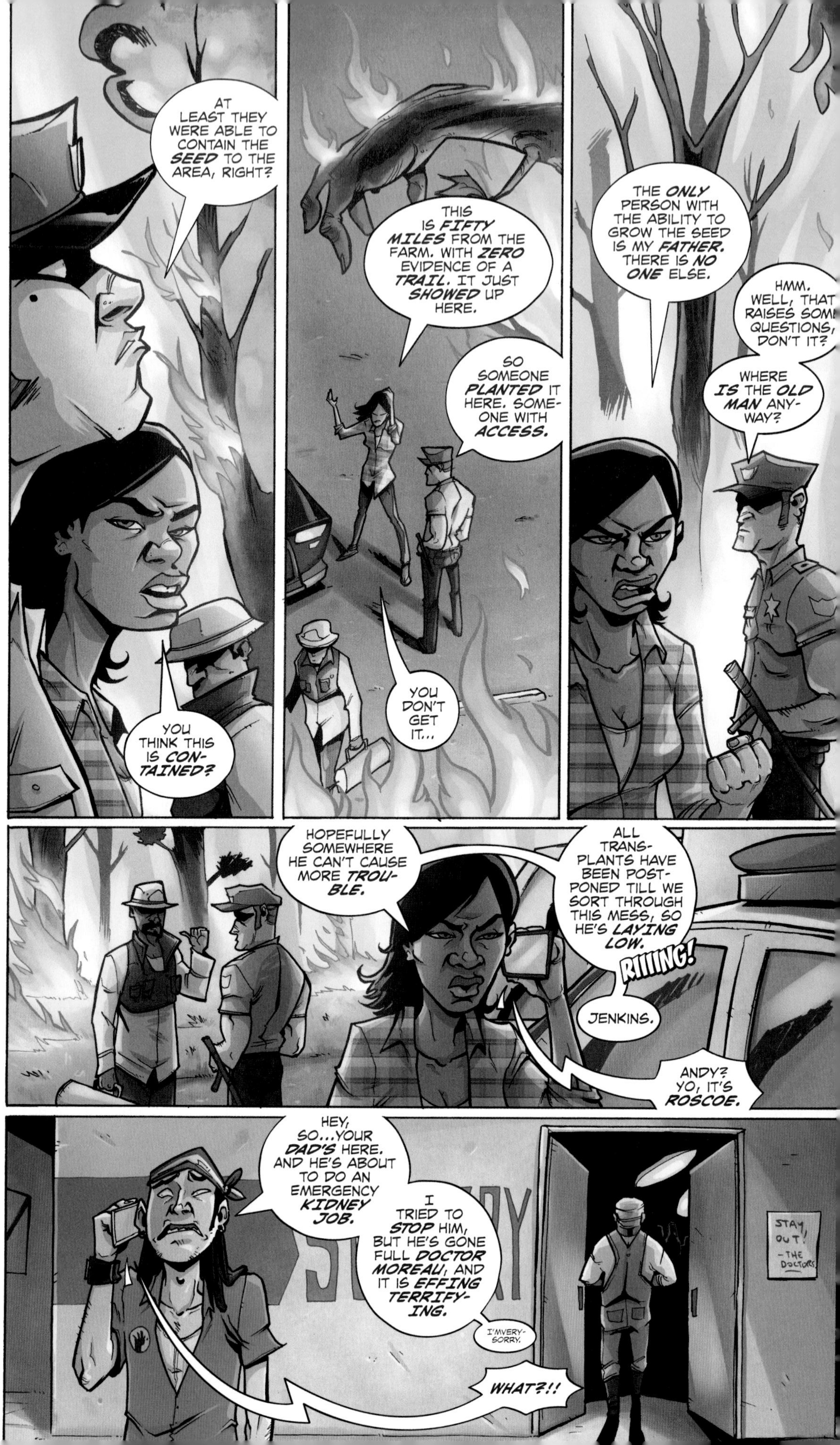
AT LEAST THEY WERE ABLE TO CONTAIN THE SEED TO THE AREA, RIGHT?
YOU THINK THIS IS CON-TAINED?
THIS IS FIFTY MILES FROM THE FARM. WITH ZERO EVIDENCE OF A TRAIL. IT JUST SHOWED UP HERE.
SO SOMEONE PLANTED IT HERE. SOME-ONE WITH ACCESS.
YOU DON'T GET IT...
THE ONLY PERSON WITH THE ABILITY TO GROW THE SEED IS MY FATHER. THERE IS NO ONE ELSE.
HMM. WELL, THAT RAISES SOM QUESTIONS, DON'T IT?
WHERE IS THE OLD MAN ANY-WAY?
HOPEFULLY SOMEWHERE HE CAN'T CAUSE MORE TROU-BLE.
ALL TRANS-PLANTS HAVE BEEN POST-PONED TILL WE SORT THROUGH THIS MESS, SO HE'S LAYING LOW.
RIIIING!
JENKINS.
ANDY? YO, IT'S ROSCOE.
HEY, SO...YOUR DAD'S HERE. AND HE'S ABOUT TO DO AN EMERGENCY KIDNEY JOB.
I TRIED TO STOP HIM, BUT HE'S GONE FULL DOCTOR MOREAU, AND IT IS EFFING TERRIFY-ING.
I'MVERY-SORRY.
WHAT?!!
STAY OUT! -THE DOCTORS

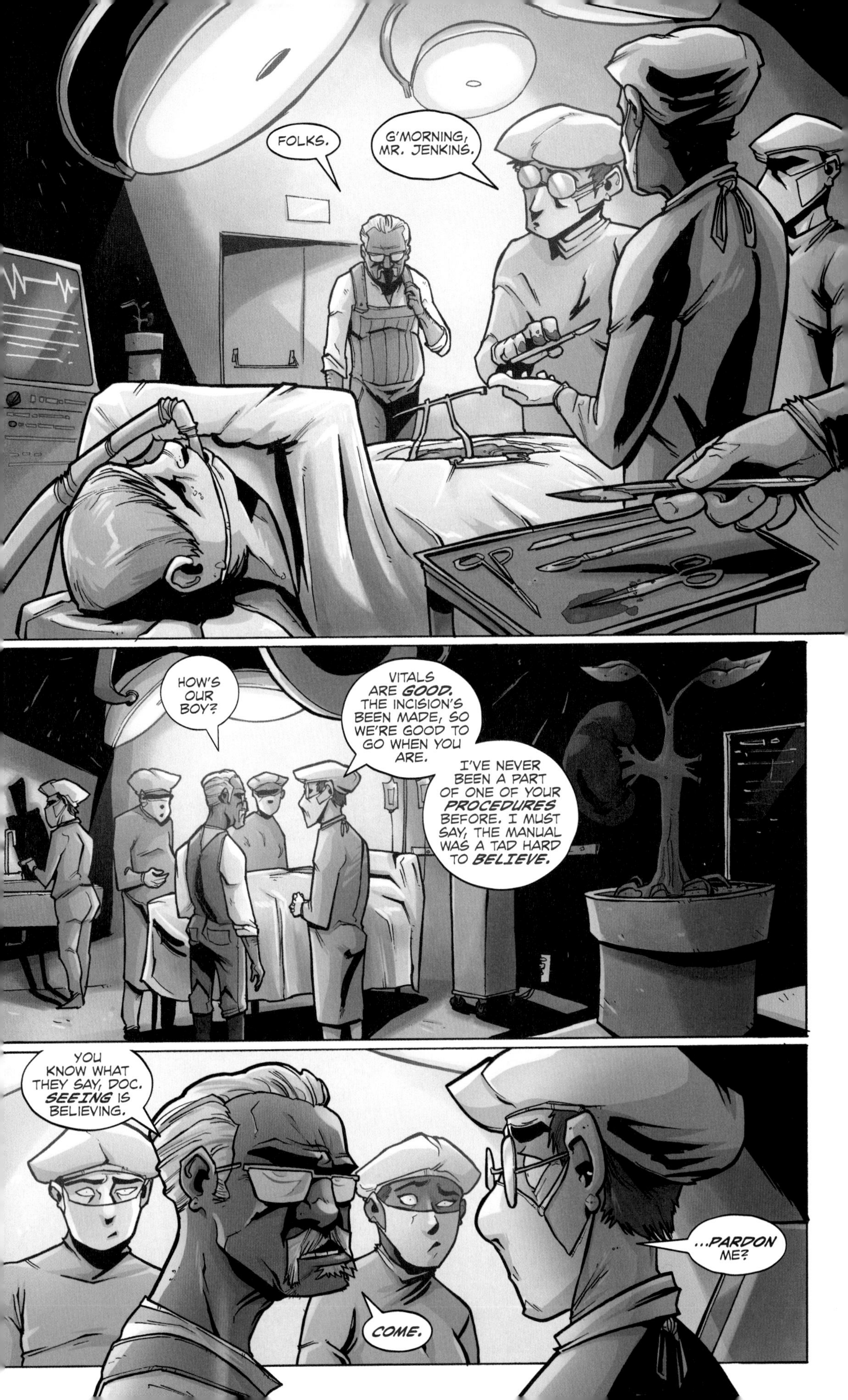
FOLKS.
G'MORNING, MR. JENKINS.
HOW'S OUR BOY?
VITALS ARE GOOD. THE INCISION'S BEEN MADE, SO WE'RE GOOD TO GO WHEN YOU ARE.
I'VE NEVER BEEN A PART OF ONE OF YOUR PROCEDURES BEFORE. I MUST SAY, THE MANUAL WAS A TAD HARD TO BELIEVE.
YOU KNOW WHAT THEY SAY, DOC. SEEING IS BELIEVING.
...PARDON ME?
COME.

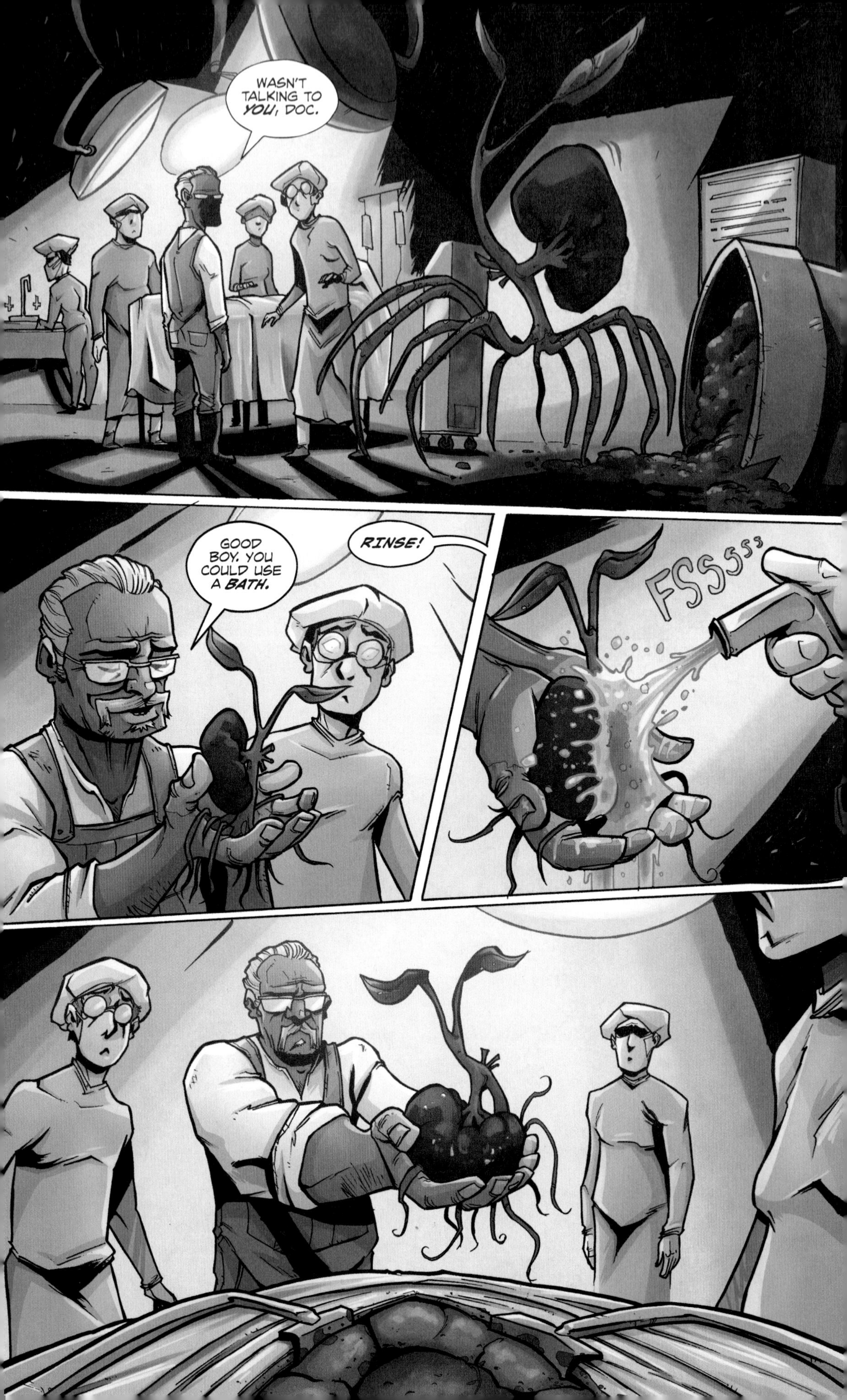
WASN'T TALKING TO *YOU*, DOC.
GOOD BOY. YOU COULD USE A *BATH*.
RINSE!
FSSsss

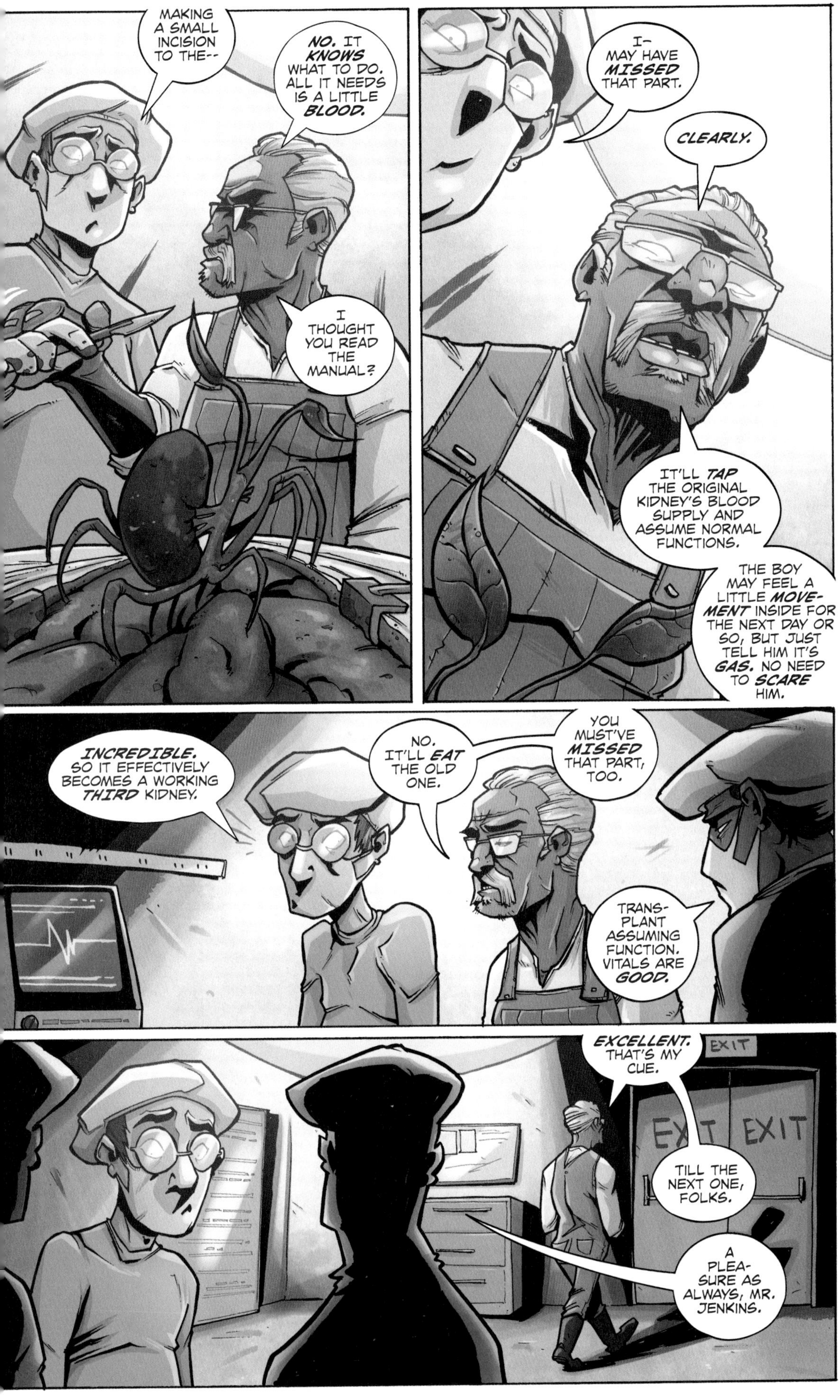
MAKING A SMALL INCISION TO THE--
NO. IT KNOWS WHAT TO DO. ALL IT NEEDS IS A LITTLE BLOOD.
I THOUGHT YOU READ THE MANUAL?
I— MAY HAVE MISSED THAT PART.
CLEARLY.
IT'LL TAP THE ORIGINAL KIDNEY'S BLOOD SUPPLY AND ASSUME NORMAL FUNCTIONS.
THE BOY MAY FEEL A LITTLE MOVE-MENT INSIDE FOR THE NEXT DAY OR SO, BUT JUST TELL HIM IT'S GAS. NO NEED TO SCARE HIM.
INCREDIBLE. SO IT EFFECTIVELY BECOMES A WORKING THIRD KIDNEY.
NO. IT'LL EAT THE OLD ONE.
YOU MUST'VE MISSED THAT PART, TOO.
TRANS-PLANT ASSUMING FUNCTION. VITALS ARE GOOD.
EXCELLENT. THAT'S MY CUE.
EXIT
EXIT EXIT
TILL THE NEXT ONE, FOLKS.
A PLEA-SURE AS ALWAYS, MR. JENKINS.

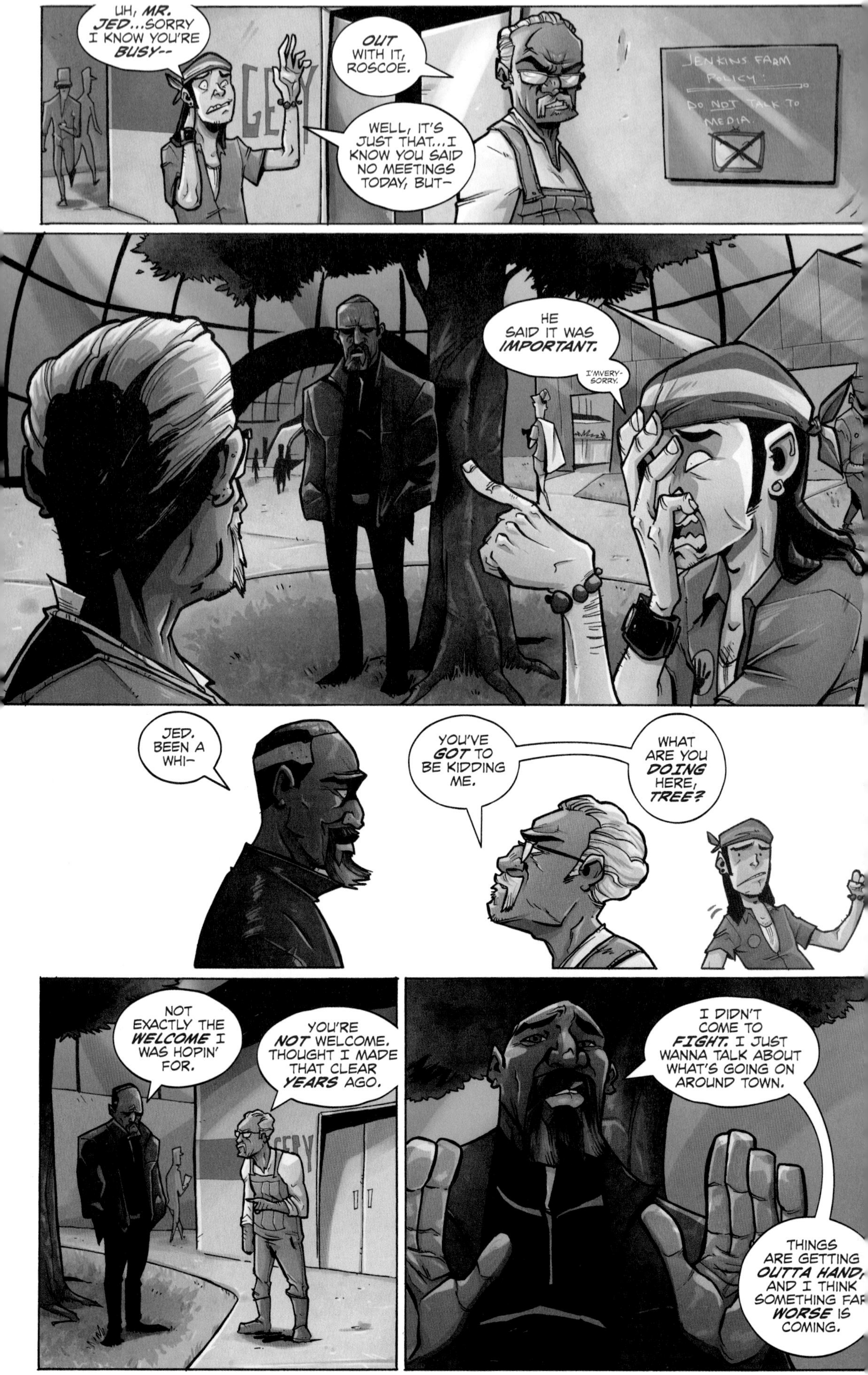

UH, MR. JED...SORRY I KNOW YOU'RE BUSY--
OUT WITH IT, ROSCOE.
WELL, IT'S JUST THAT...I KNOW YOU SAID NO MEETINGS TODAY, BUT-
JENKINS FARM POLICY: DO NOT TALK TO MEDIA.
HE SAID IT WAS IMPORTANT.
I'MVERY-SORRY.
JED. BEEN A WHI-
YOU'VE GOT TO BE KIDDING ME.
WHAT ARE YOU DOING HERE, TREE?
NOT EXACTLY THE WELCOME I WAS HOPIN' FOR.
YOU'RE NOT WELCOME. THOUGHT I MADE THAT CLEAR YEARS AGO.
I DIDN'T COME TO FIGHT. I JUST WANNA TALK ABOUT WHAT'S GOING ON AROUND TOWN.
THINGS ARE GETTING OUTTA HAND, AND I THINK SOMETHING FAR WORSE IS COMING.

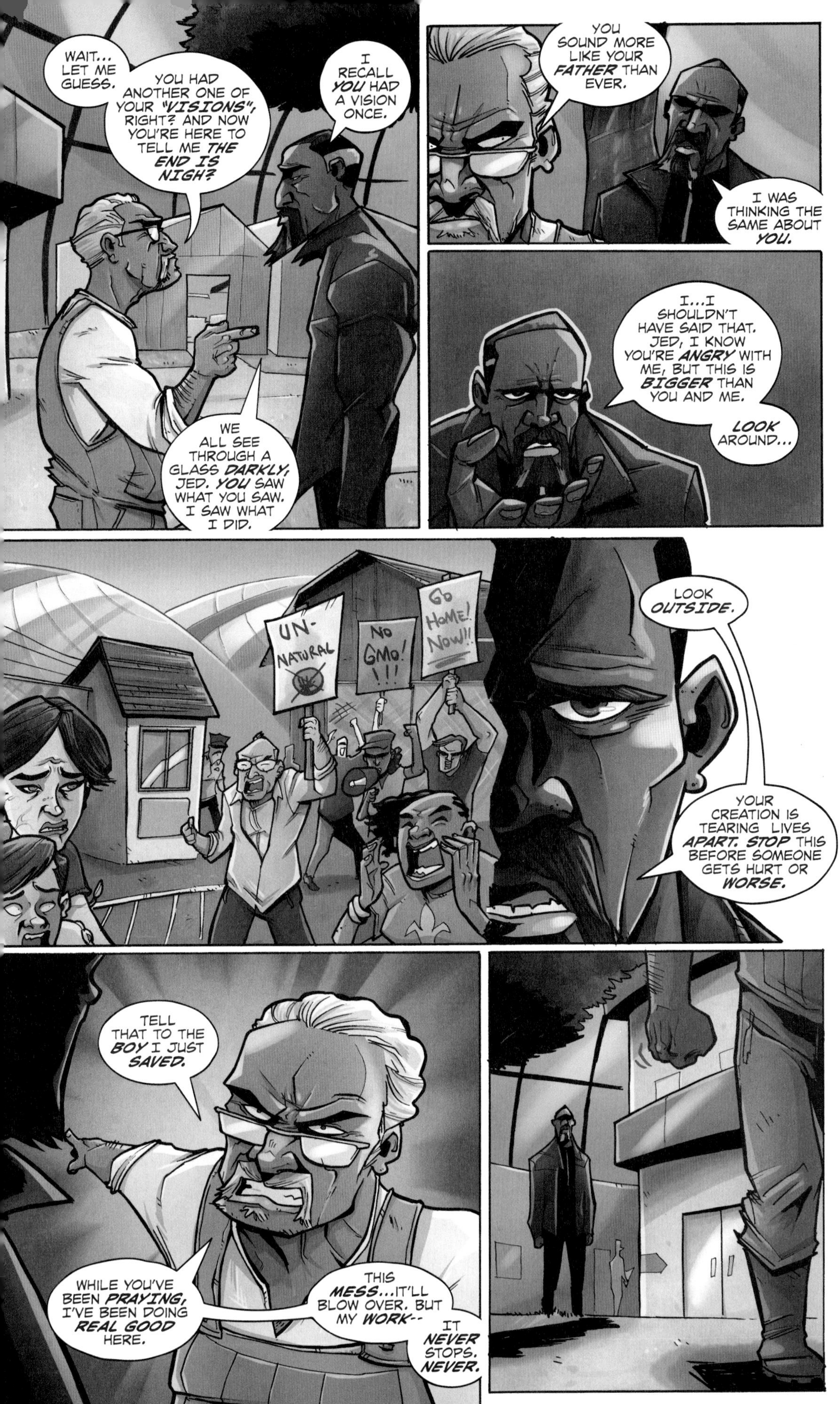
WAIT... LET ME GUESS.
YOU HAD ANOTHER ONE OF YOUR "VISIONS", RIGHT? AND NOW YOU'RE HERE TO TELL ME THE END IS NIGH?
I RECALL YOU HAD A VISION ONCE.
WE ALL SEE THROUGH A GLASS DARKLY, JED. YOU SAW WHAT YOU SAW. I SAW WHAT I DID.
YOU SOUND MORE LIKE YOUR FATHER THAN EVER.
I WAS THINKING THE SAME ABOUT YOU.
I...I SHOULDN'T HAVE SAID THAT. JED, I KNOW YOU'RE ANGRY WITH ME, BUT THIS IS BIGGER THAN YOU AND ME.
LOOK AROUND...
LOOK OUTSIDE.
UN-NATURAL
NO GMO! !!!
GO HOME! NOW!!
YOUR CREATION IS TEARING LIVES APART. STOP THIS BEFORE SOMEONE GETS HURT OR WORSE.
TELL THAT TO THE BOY I JUST SAVED.
WHILE YOU'VE BEEN PRAYING, I'VE BEEN DOING REAL GOOD HERE.
THIS MESS...IT'LL BLOW OVER. BUT MY WORK--
IT NEVER STOPS. NEVER.

ELSEWHERE.

HEY. GOT A SEC?

!!!

THAT'S HATS.com

SALE!! THE SEUSIS!

HOT MAMA

SURE... JUST DOING A LITTLE *PAPERWORK.* WH--WHAT'S UP?

SO...YOU WERE *RIGHT.* I HAVEN'T BEEN TOTALLY *HONEST* WITH YOU.

SOMETHING *DID* HAPPEN YESTERDAY. MORE THAN JUST A *BOAR...*

OUTER DARKNESS

SEW COOL

REMINDER: EMAIL THAT DUDE ABOUT THAT THING...

ORDER: $44.95

I WAS *GONNA* TELL YOU. I JUST NEEDED TO THINK IT THROUGH, I GUESS.

I STILL DON'T HAVE ALL THE ANSWERS, BUT I...I DON'T WANNA KEEP YOU IN THE DARK.

NO MORE SECRETS, RIGHT?

OUTER DARKNESS

RIGHT...

NO MORE SECRETS.

THAT'S H

THE KLONDIKE

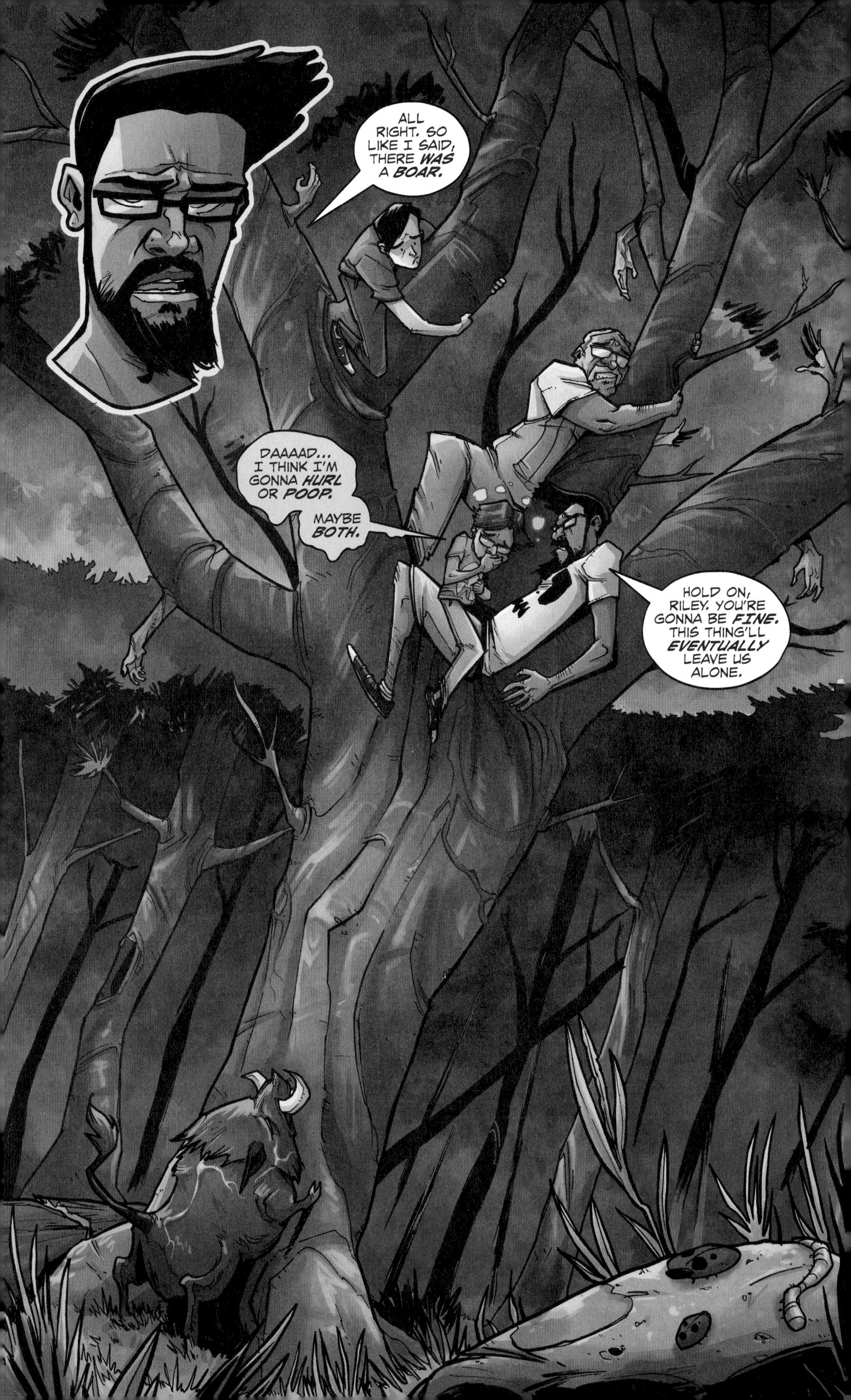
ALL RIGHT. SO LIKE I SAID, THERE *WAS* A *BOAR.*
DAAAAD... I THINK I'M GONNA *HURL* OR *POOP.*
MAYBE *BOTH.*
HOLD ON, RILEY. YOU'RE GONNA BE *FINE.* THIS THING'LL *EVENTUALLY* LEAVE US ALONE.

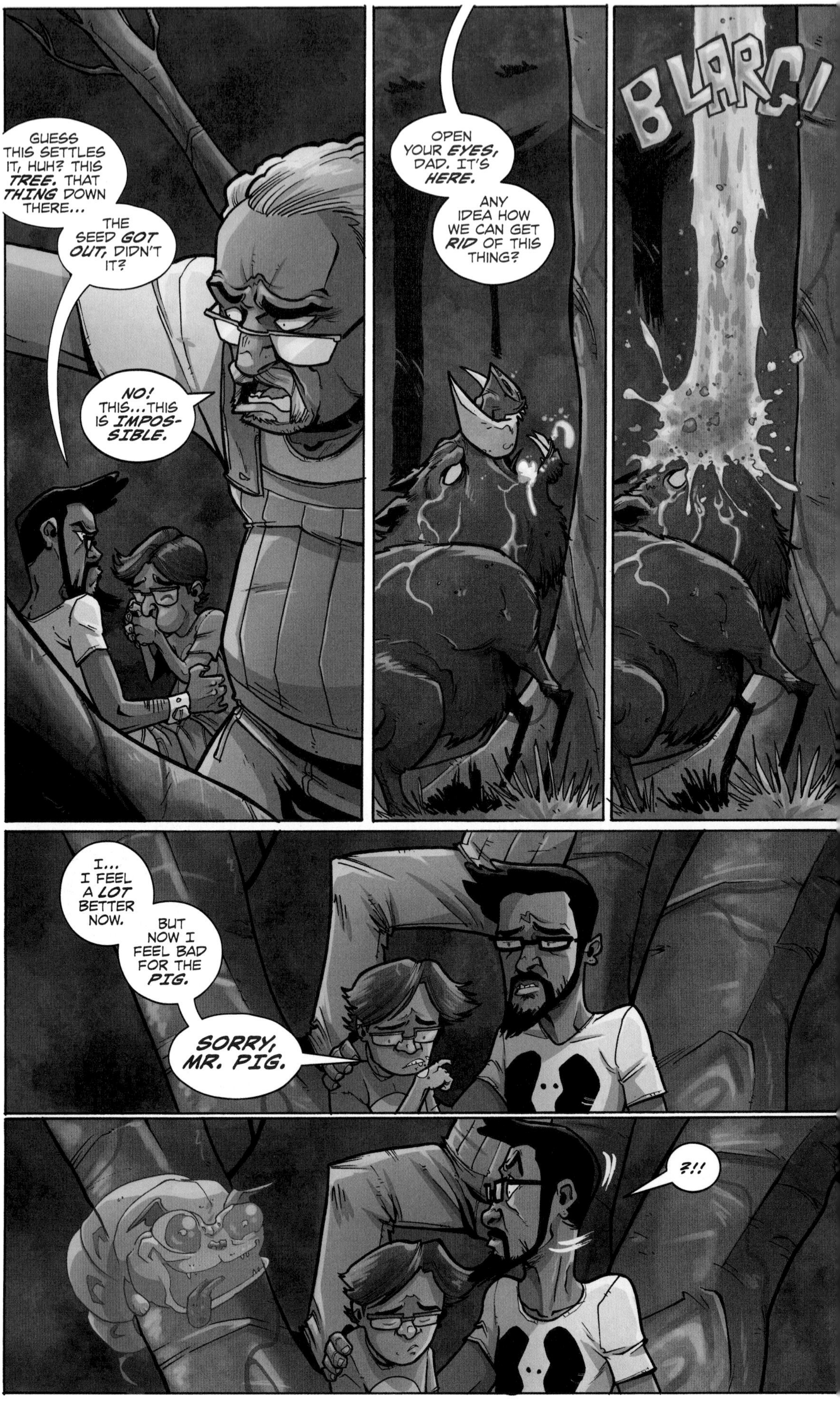
GUESS THIS SETTLES IT, HUH? THIS TREE. THAT THING DOWN THERE...
THE SEED GOT OUT, DIDN'T IT?
NO! THIS...THIS IS IMPOSSIBLE.
OPEN YOUR EYES, DAD. IT'S HERE.
ANY IDEA HOW WE CAN GET RID OF THIS THING?
BLARG!
I... I FEEL A LOT BETTER NOW.
BUT NOW I FEEL BAD FOR THE PIG.
SORRY, MR. PIG.
?!!

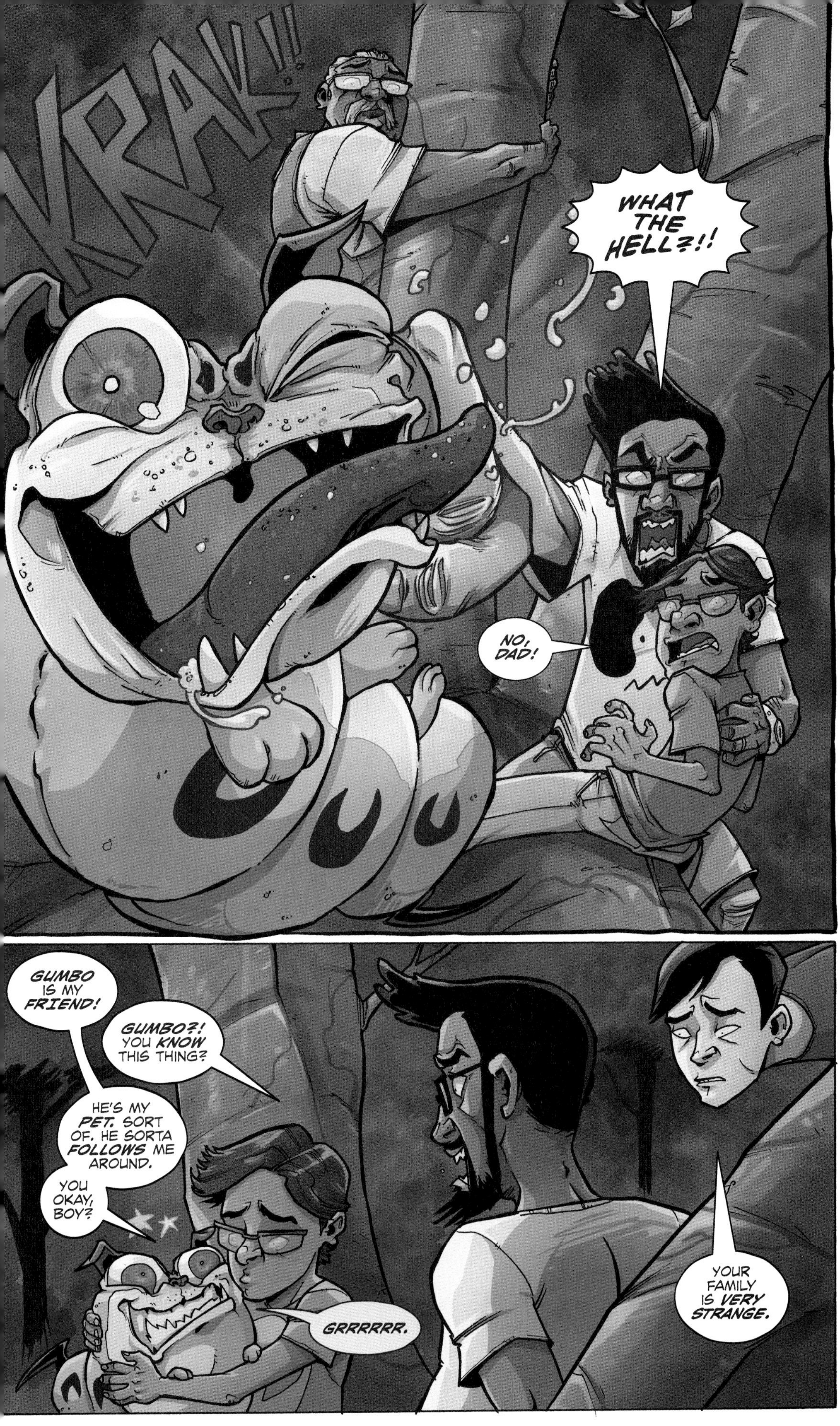
KRAK!!!
WHAT THE HELL?!!
NO, DAD!
GUMBO IS MY FRIEND!
GUMBO?! YOU KNOW THIS THING?
HE'S MY PET. SORT OF. HE SORTA FOLLOWS ME AROUND.
YOU OKAY, BOY?
GRRRRRR.
YOUR FAMILY IS VERY STRANGE.

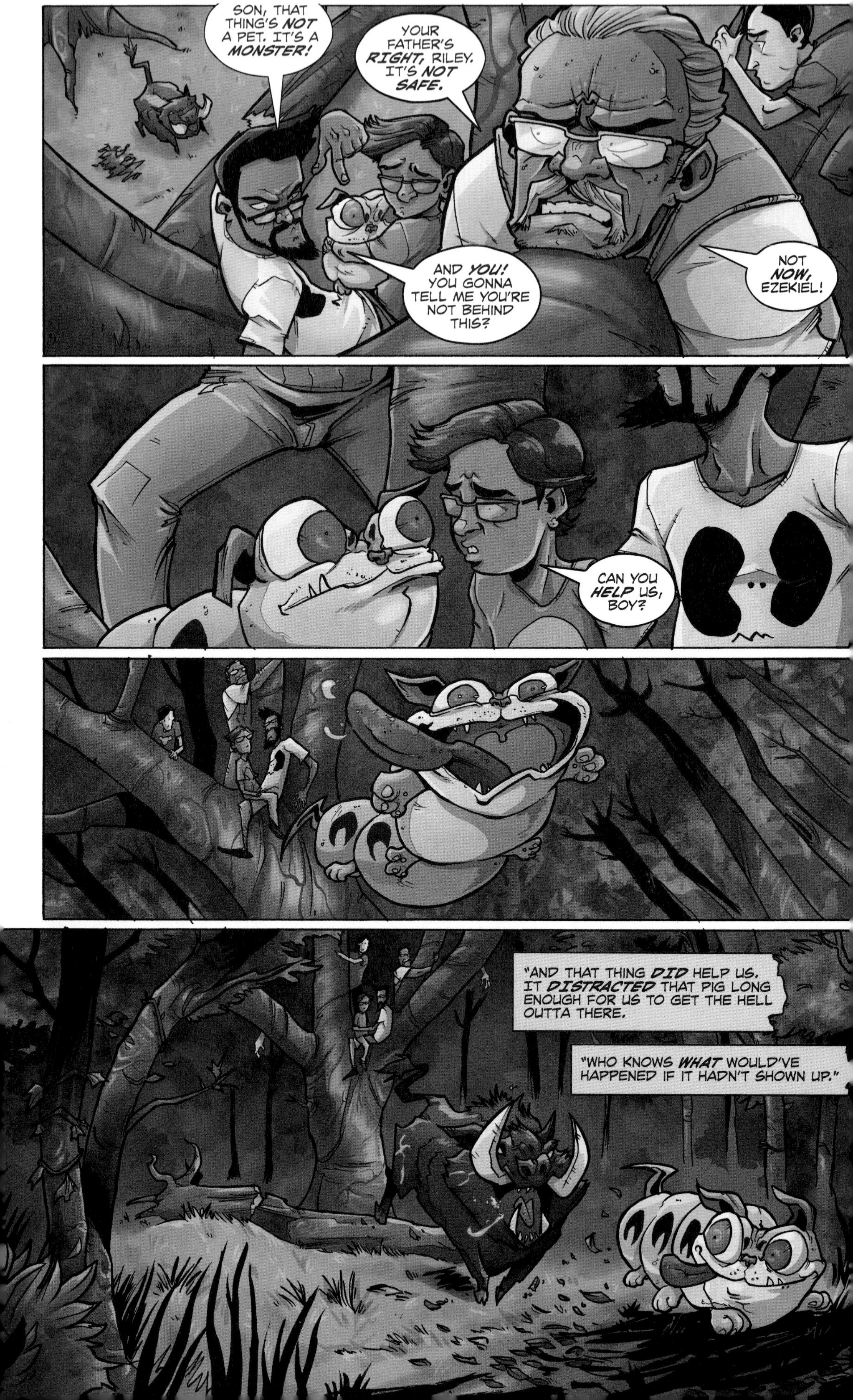
SON, THAT THING'S NOT A PET. IT'S A MONSTER!
YOUR FATHER'S RIGHT, RILEY. IT'S NOT SAFE.
AND YOU! YOU GONNA TELL ME YOU'RE NOT BEHIND THIS?
NOT NOW, EZEKIEL!
CAN YOU HELP US, BOY?
"AND THAT THING DID HELP US. IT DISTRACTED THAT PIG LONG ENOUGH FOR US TO GET THE HELL OUTTA THERE.
"WHO KNOWS WHAT WOULD'VE HAPPENED IF IT HADN'T SHOWN UP."

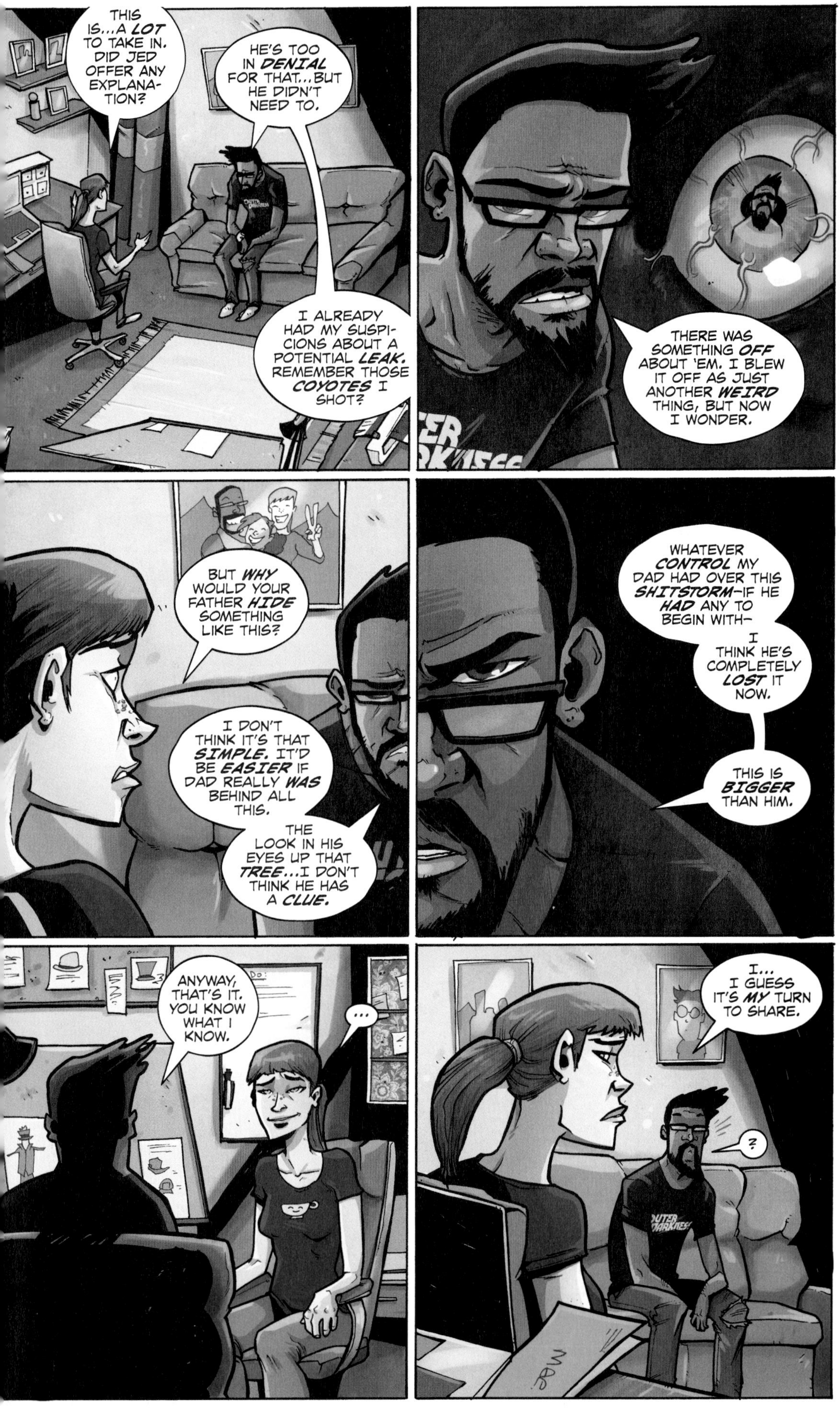
THIS IS...A LOT TO TAKE IN. DID JED OFFER ANY EXPLANATION?
HE'S TOO IN DENIAL FOR THAT...BUT HE DIDN'T NEED TO.
I ALREADY HAD MY SUSPICIONS ABOUT A POTENTIAL LEAK. REMEMBER THOSE COYOTES I SHOT?
THERE WAS SOMETHING OFF ABOUT 'EM. I BLEW IT OFF AS JUST ANOTHER WEIRD THING, BUT NOW I WONDER.
BUT WHY WOULD YOUR FATHER HIDE SOMETHING LIKE THIS?
I DON'T THINK IT'S THAT SIMPLE. IT'D BE EASIER IF DAD REALLY WAS BEHIND ALL THIS.
THE LOOK IN HIS EYES UP THAT TREE...I DON'T THINK HE HAS A CLUE.
WHATEVER CONTROL MY DAD HAD OVER THIS SHITSTORM—IF HE HAD ANY TO BEGIN WITH—
I THINK HE'S COMPLETELY LOST IT NOW.
THIS IS BIGGER THAN HIM.
ANYWAY, THAT'S IT. YOU KNOW WHAT I KNOW.
...
I... I GUESS IT'S MY TURN TO SHARE.
?

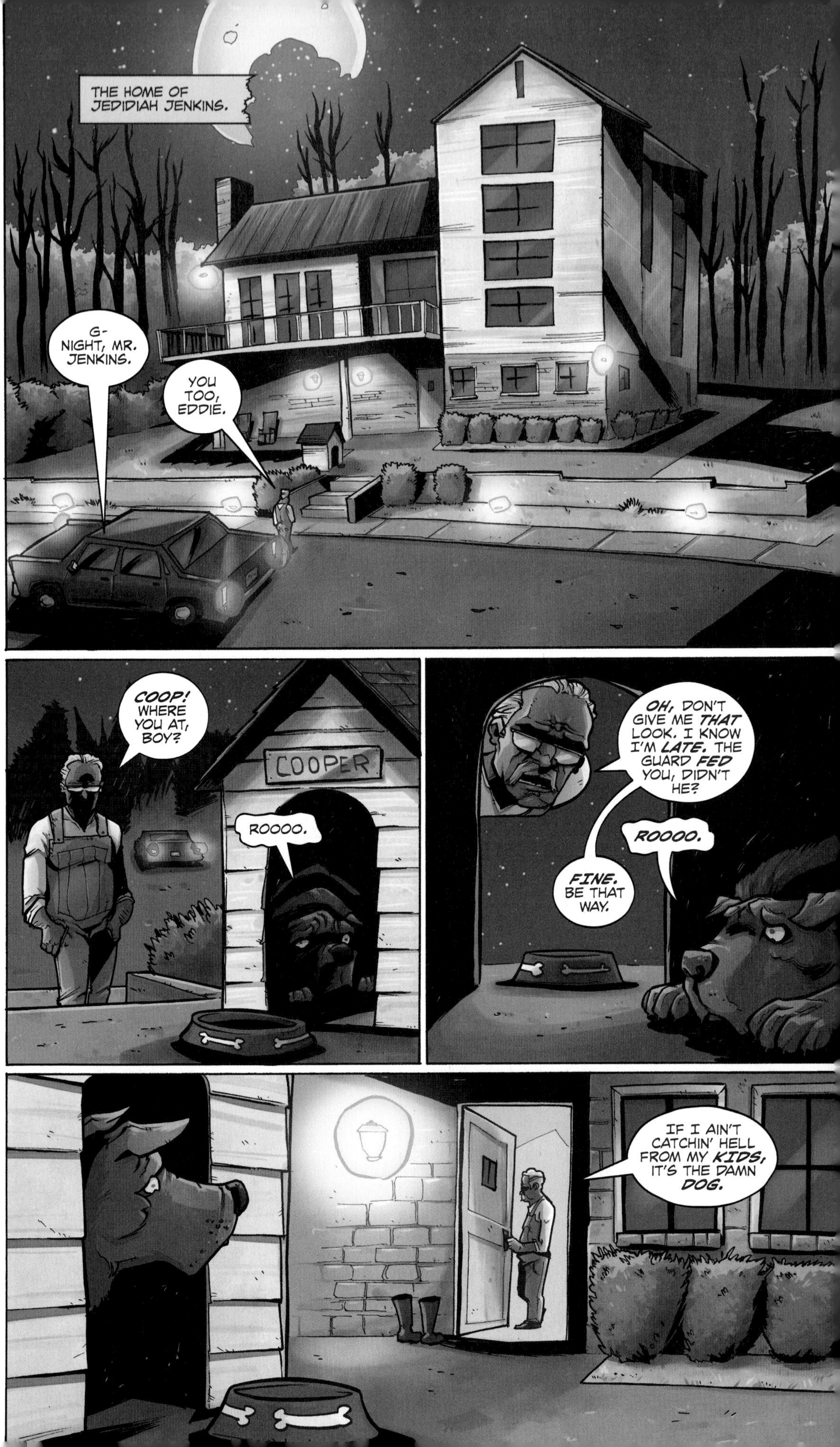
THE HOME OF JEDIDIAH JENKINS.
G-NIGHT, MR. JENKINS.
YOU TOO, EDDIE.
COOP! WHERE YOU AT, BOY?
COOPER
ROOOO.
OH, DON'T GIVE ME THAT LOOK. I KNOW I'M LATE. THE GUARD FED YOU, DIDN'T HE?
ROOOO.
FINE. BE THAT WAY.
IF I AIN'T CATCHIN' HELL FROM MY KIDS, IT'S THE DAMN DOG.

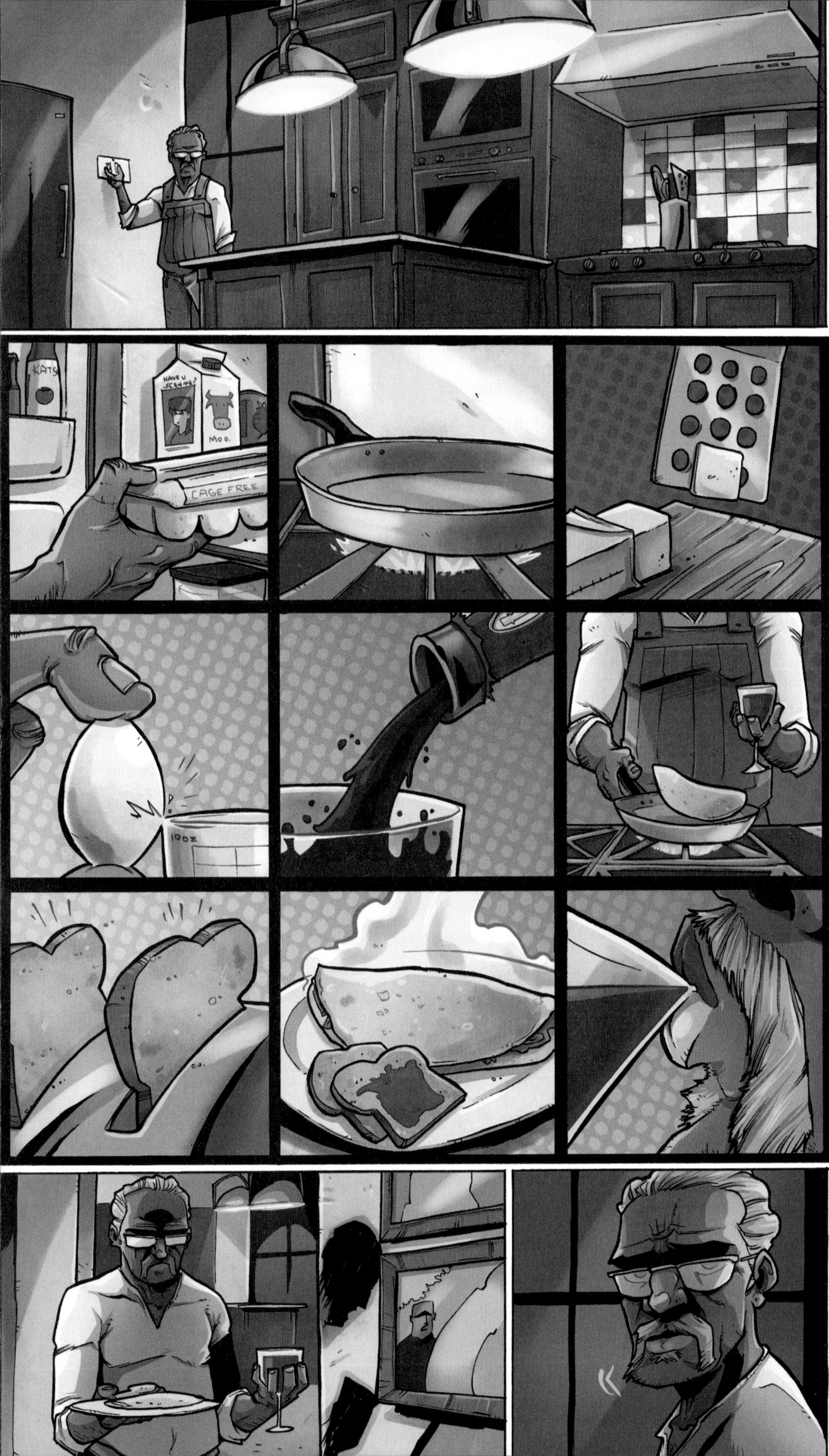
KATS
HAVE U SEEN ME?
MOO.
CAGE FREE
10OZ

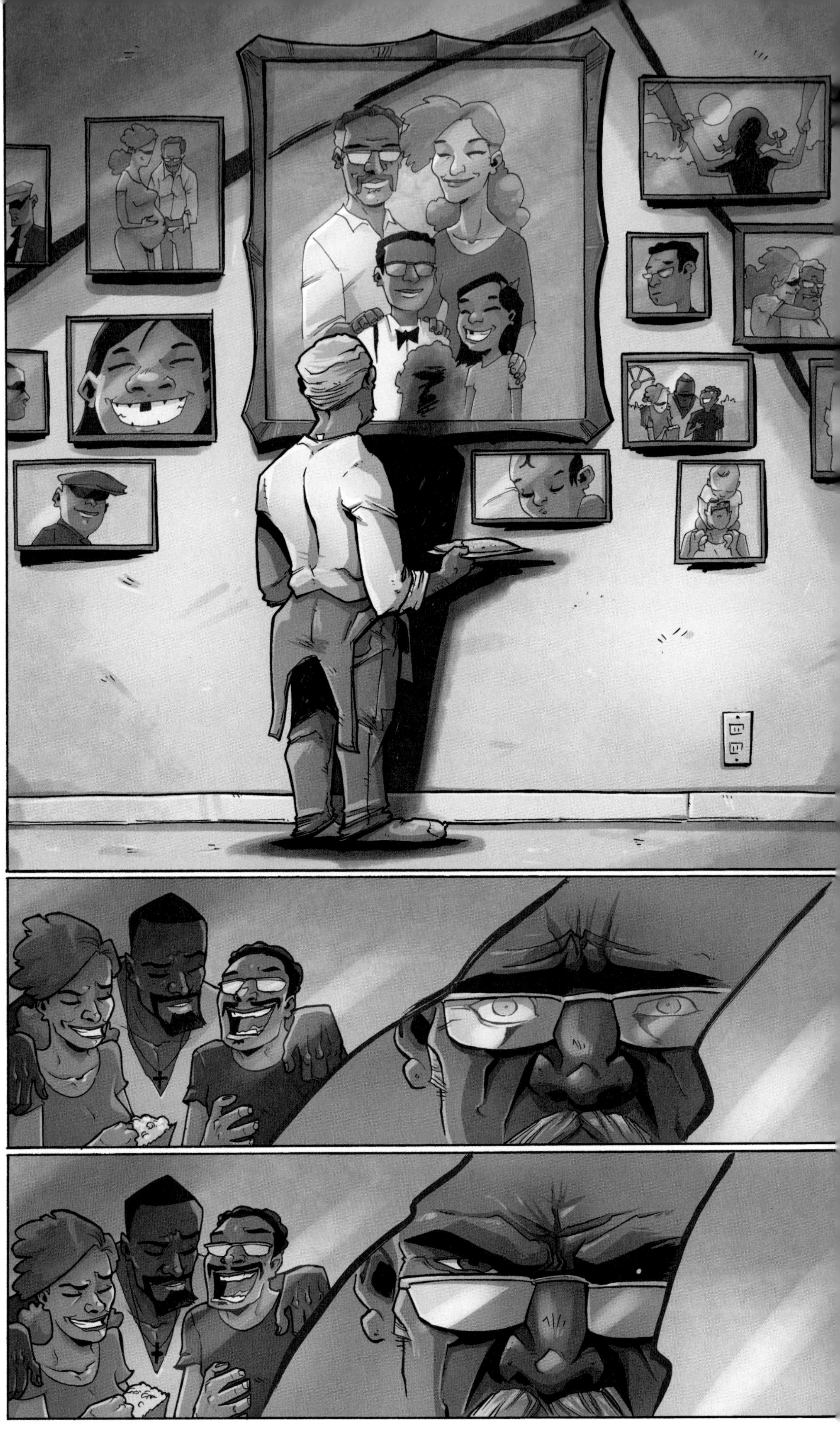

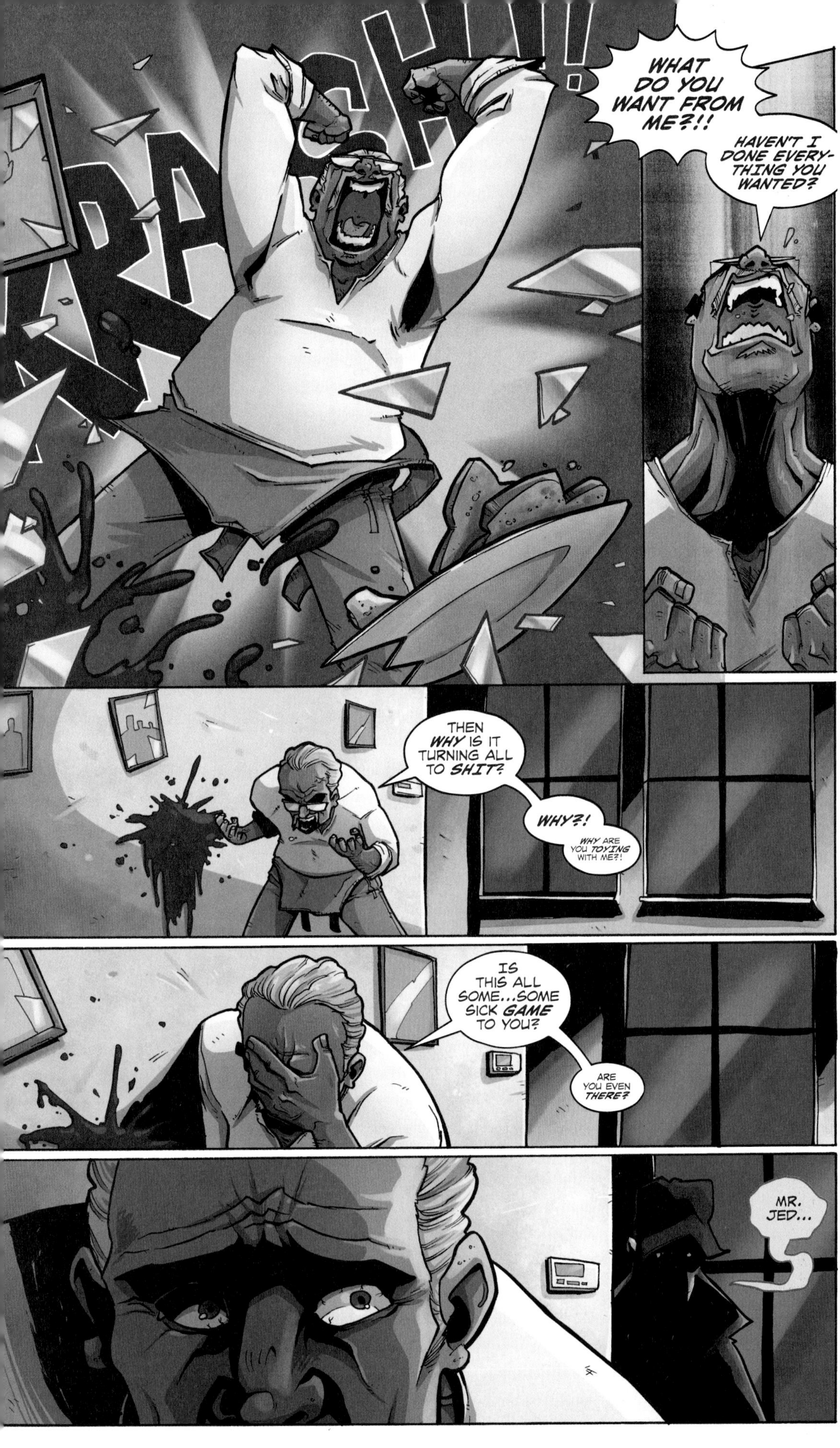

WHAT DO YOU WANT FROM ME?!!
HAVEN'T I DONE EVERYTHING YOU WANTED?
THEN *WHY* IS IT TURNING ALL TO *SHIT*?
WHY?!
WHY ARE YOU *TOYING* WITH ME?!
IS THIS ALL SOME...SOME SICK *GAME* TO YOU?
ARE YOU EVEN *THERE?*
MR. JED...

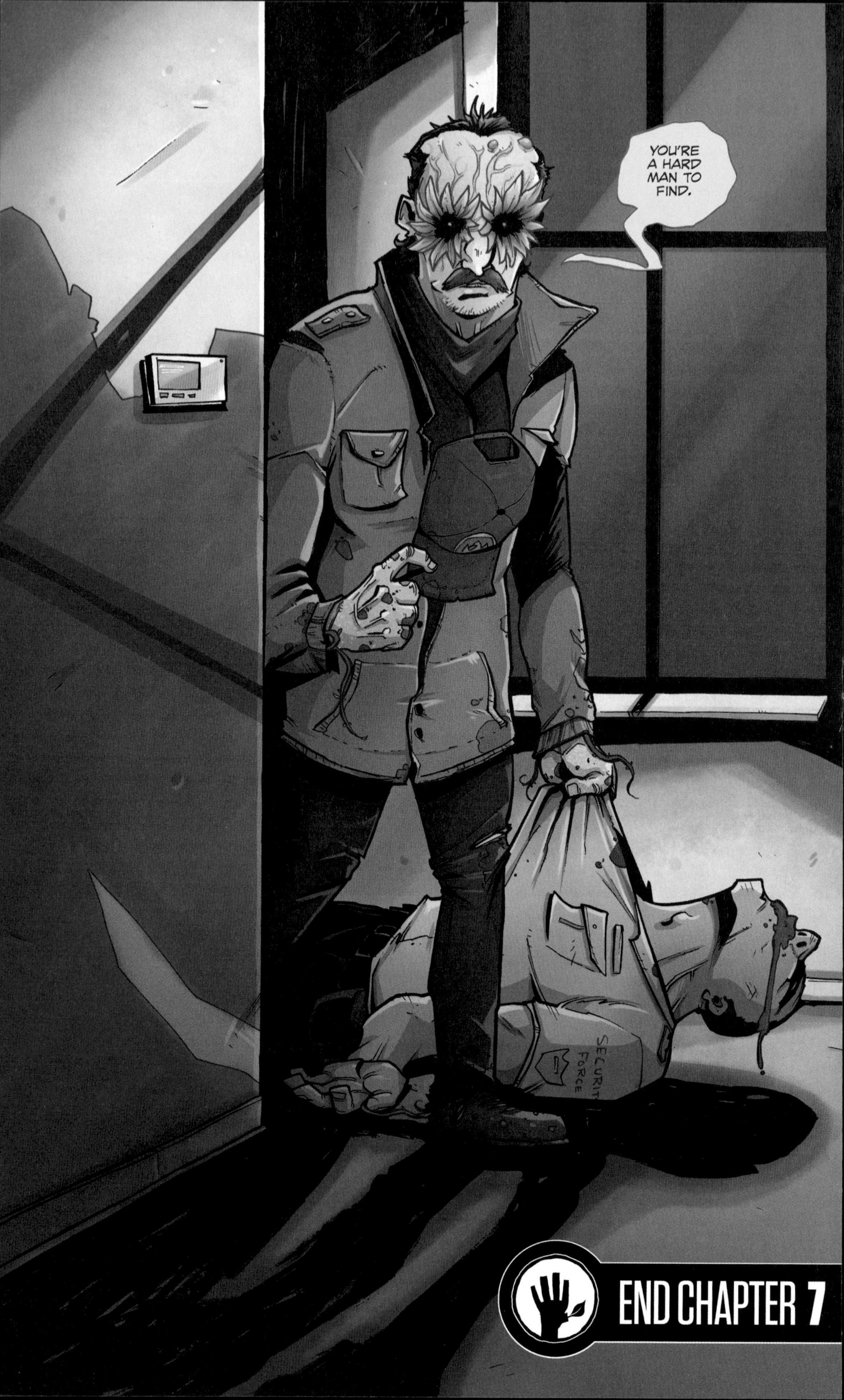

YOU'RE A HARD MAN TO FIND.
SECURITY FORCE
END CHAPTER 7

CHAPTER 8

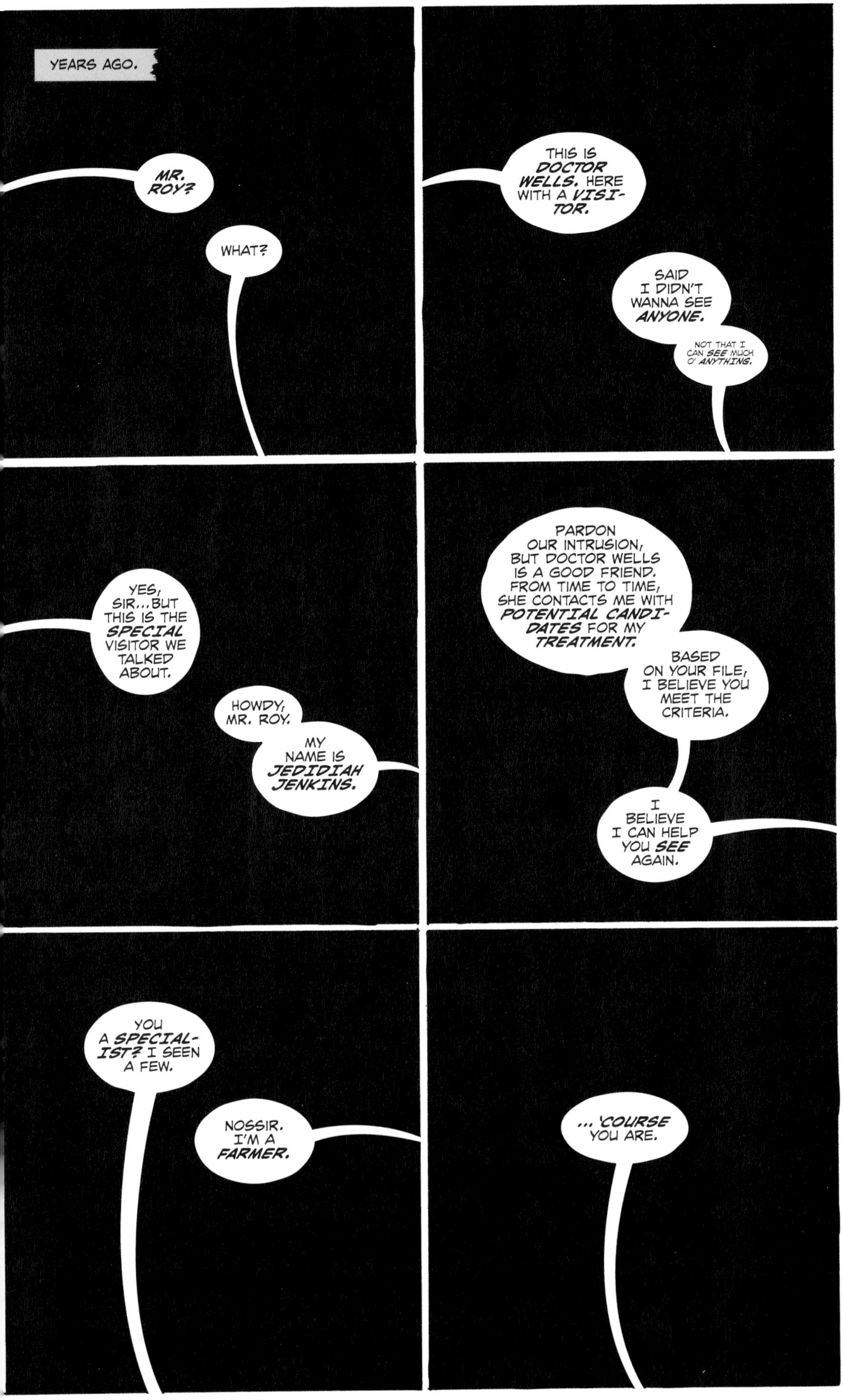
YEARS AGO.
MR. ROY?
WHAT?
THIS IS DOCTOR WELLS. HERE WITH A VISI- TOR.
SAID I DIDN'T WANNA SEE ANYONE.
NOT THAT I CAN SEE MUCH O' ANYTHING.
YES, SIR... BUT THIS IS THE SPECIAL VISITOR WE TALKED ABOUT.
HOWDY, MR. ROY.
MY NAME IS JEDIDIAH JENKINS.
PARDON OUR INTRUSION, BUT DOCTOR WELLS IS A GOOD FRIEND. FROM TIME TO TIME, SHE CONTACTS ME WITH POTENTIAL CANDI- DATES FOR MY TREATMENT.
BASED ON YOUR FILE, I BELIEVE YOU MEET THE CRITERIA.
I BELIEVE I CAN HELP YOU SEE AGAIN.
YOU A SPECIAL- IST? I SEEN A FEW.
NOSSIR. I'M A FARMER.
...'COURSE YOU ARE.

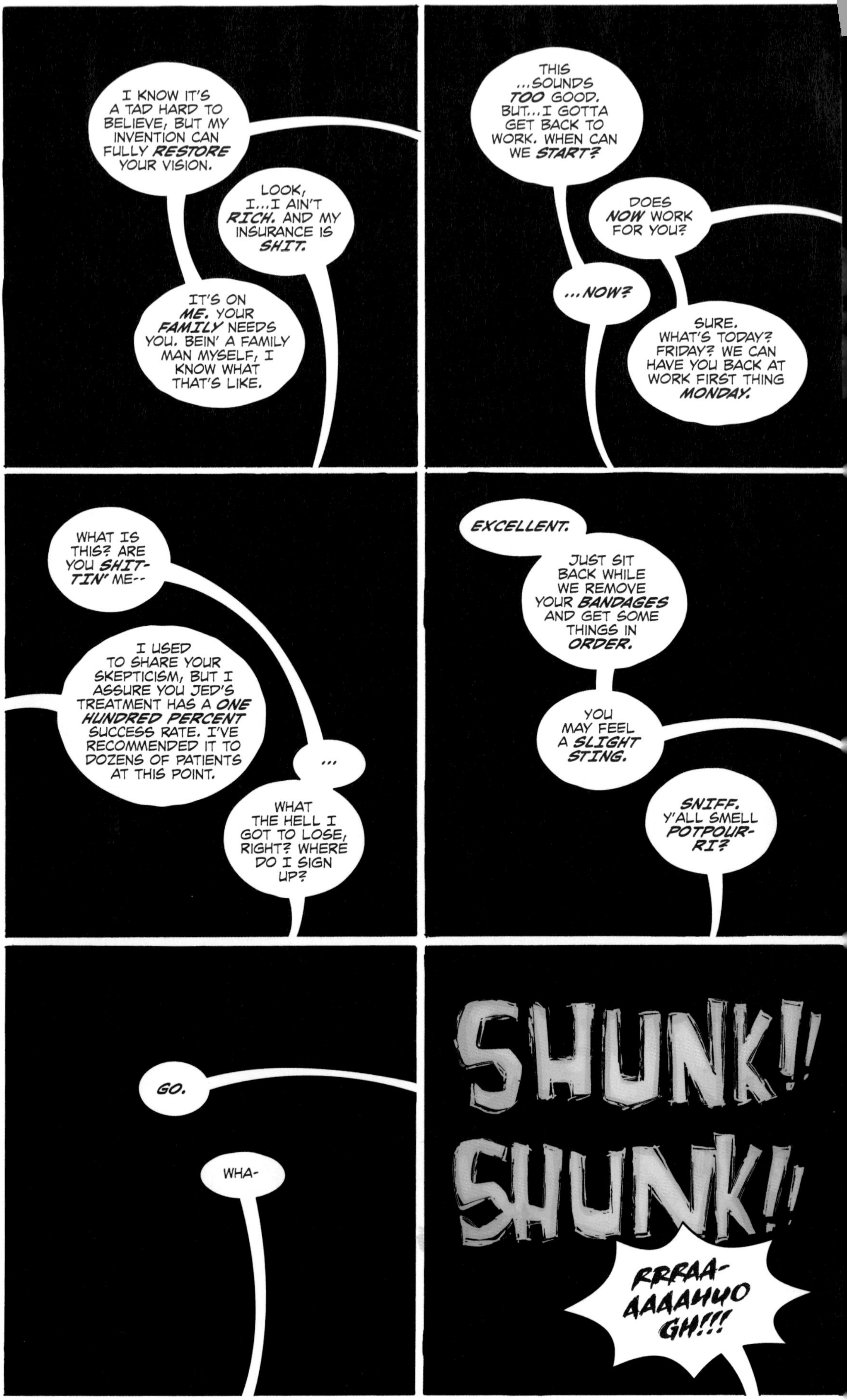

I KNOW IT'S A TAD HARD TO BELIEVE, BUT MY INVENTION CAN FULLY RESTORE YOUR VISION.
LOOK, I...I AIN'T RICH. AND MY INSURANCE IS SHIT.
IT'S ON ME. YOUR FAMILY NEEDS YOU. BEIN' A FAMILY MAN MYSELF, I KNOW WHAT THAT'S LIKE.
THIS ...SOUNDS TOO GOOD. BUT...I GOTTA GET BACK TO WORK. WHEN CAN WE START?
DOES NOW WORK FOR YOU?
...NOW?
SURE. WHAT'S TODAY? FRIDAY? WE CAN HAVE YOU BACK AT WORK FIRST THING MONDAY.
WHAT IS THIS? ARE YOU SHIT-TIN' ME--
I USED TO SHARE YOUR SKEPTICISM, BUT I ASSURE YOU JED'S TREATMENT HAS A ONE HUNDRED PERCENT SUCCESS RATE. I'VE RECOMMENDED IT TO DOZENS OF PATIENTS AT THIS POINT.
...
WHAT THE HELL I GOT TO LOSE, RIGHT? WHERE DO I SIGN UP?
EXCELLENT.
JUST SIT BACK WHILE WE REMOVE YOUR BANDAGES AND GET SOME THINGS IN ORDER.
YOU MAY FEEL A SLIGHT STING.
SNIFF. Y'ALL SMELL POTPOUR-RI?
GO.
WHA-
SHUNK!!
SHUNK!!
RRRAA-AAAAHUO GH!!!

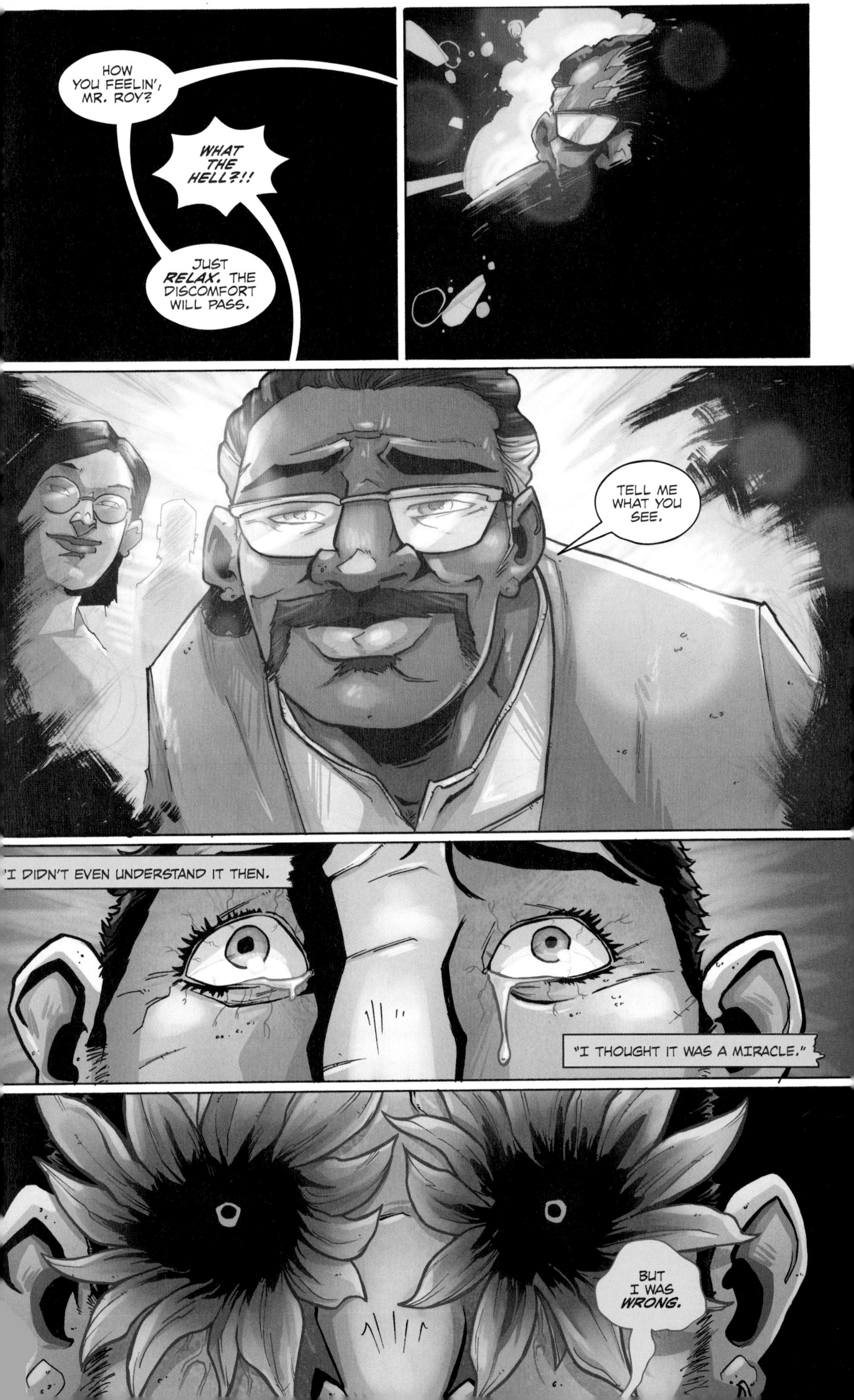
HOW YOU FEELIN', MR. ROY?
WHAT THE HELL?!!
JUST RELAX. THE DISCOMFORT WILL PASS.
TELL ME WHAT YOU SEE.
"I DIDN'T EVEN UNDERSTAND IT THEN.
"I THOUGHT IT WAS A MIRACLE."
BUT I WAS WRONG.

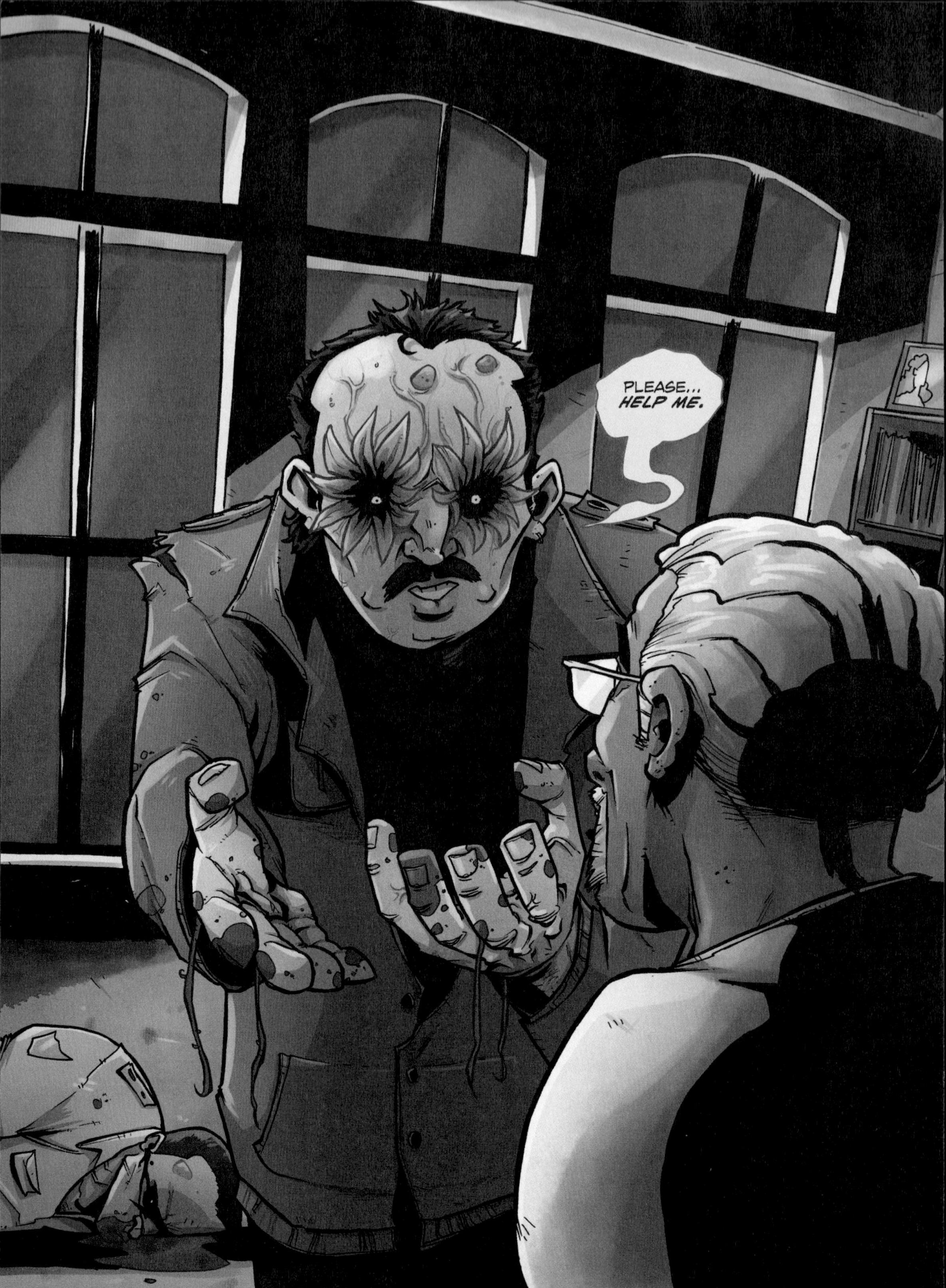
PLEASE... *HELP ME.*

CHAPTER 8: **A TIME TO REAP.**

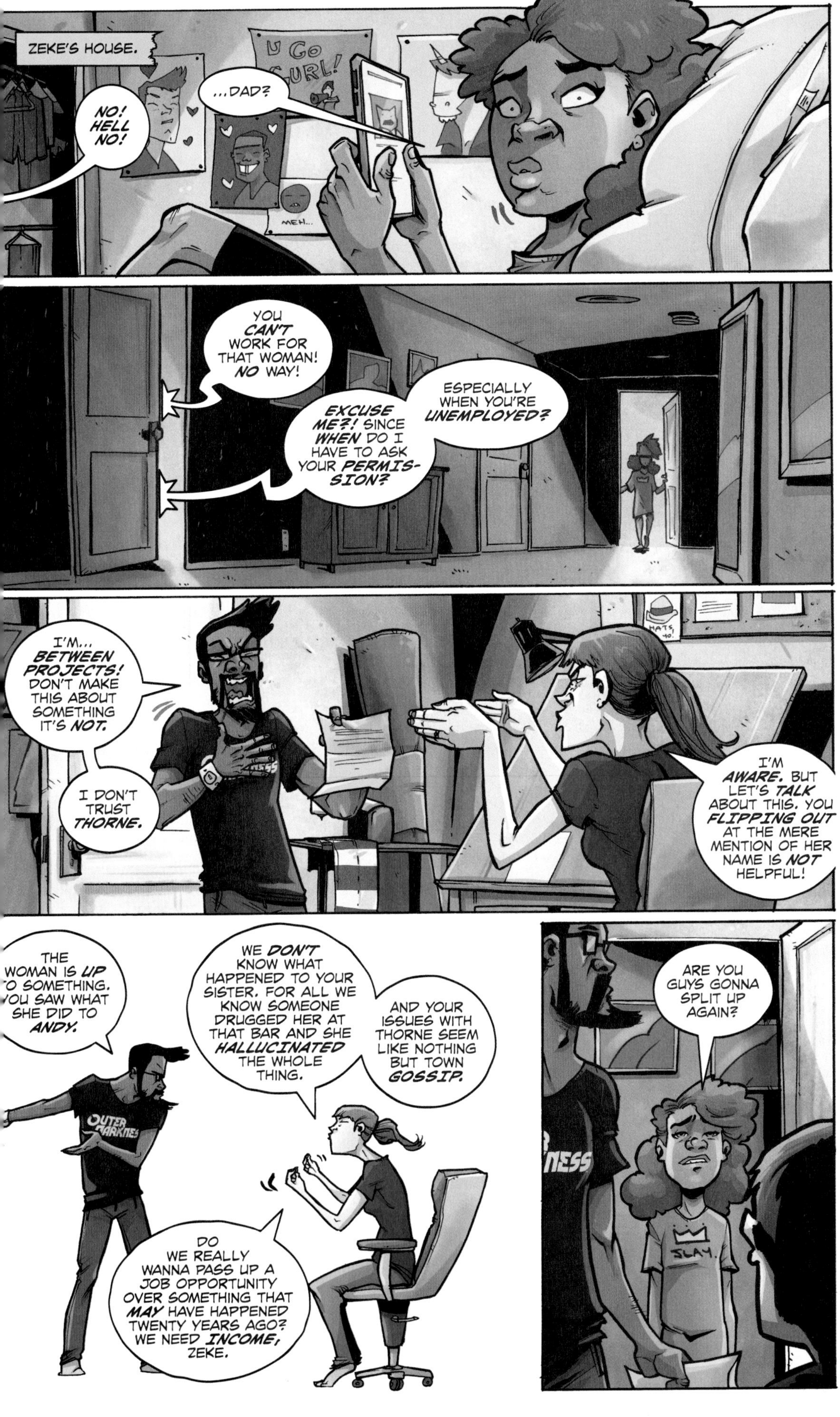
ZEKE'S HOUSE.
...DAD?
U GO GURL!
NO! HELL NO!
MEH...
YOU CAN'T WORK FOR THAT WOMAN! NO WAY!
EXCUSE ME?! SINCE WHEN DO I HAVE TO ASK YOUR PERMISSION?
ESPECIALLY WHEN YOU'RE UNEMPLOYED?
I'M... BETWEEN PROJECTS! DON'T MAKE THIS ABOUT SOMETHING IT'S NOT.
I DON'T TRUST THORNE.
HATS, YO!
I'M AWARE. BUT LET'S TALK ABOUT THIS. YOU FLIPPING OUT AT THE MERE MENTION OF HER NAME IS NOT HELPFUL!
THE WOMAN IS UP TO SOMETHING. YOU SAW WHAT SHE DID TO ANDY.
WE DON'T KNOW WHAT HAPPENED TO YOUR SISTER. FOR ALL WE KNOW SOMEONE DRUGGED HER AT THAT BAR AND SHE HALLUCINATED THE WHOLE THING.
AND YOUR ISSUES WITH THORNE SEEM LIKE NOTHING BUT TOWN GOSSIP.
DO WE REALLY WANNA PASS UP A JOB OPPORTUNITY OVER SOMETHING THAT MAY HAVE HAPPENED TWENTY YEARS AGO? WE NEED INCOME, ZEKE.
ARE YOU GUYS GONNA SPLIT UP AGAIN?
SLAY.

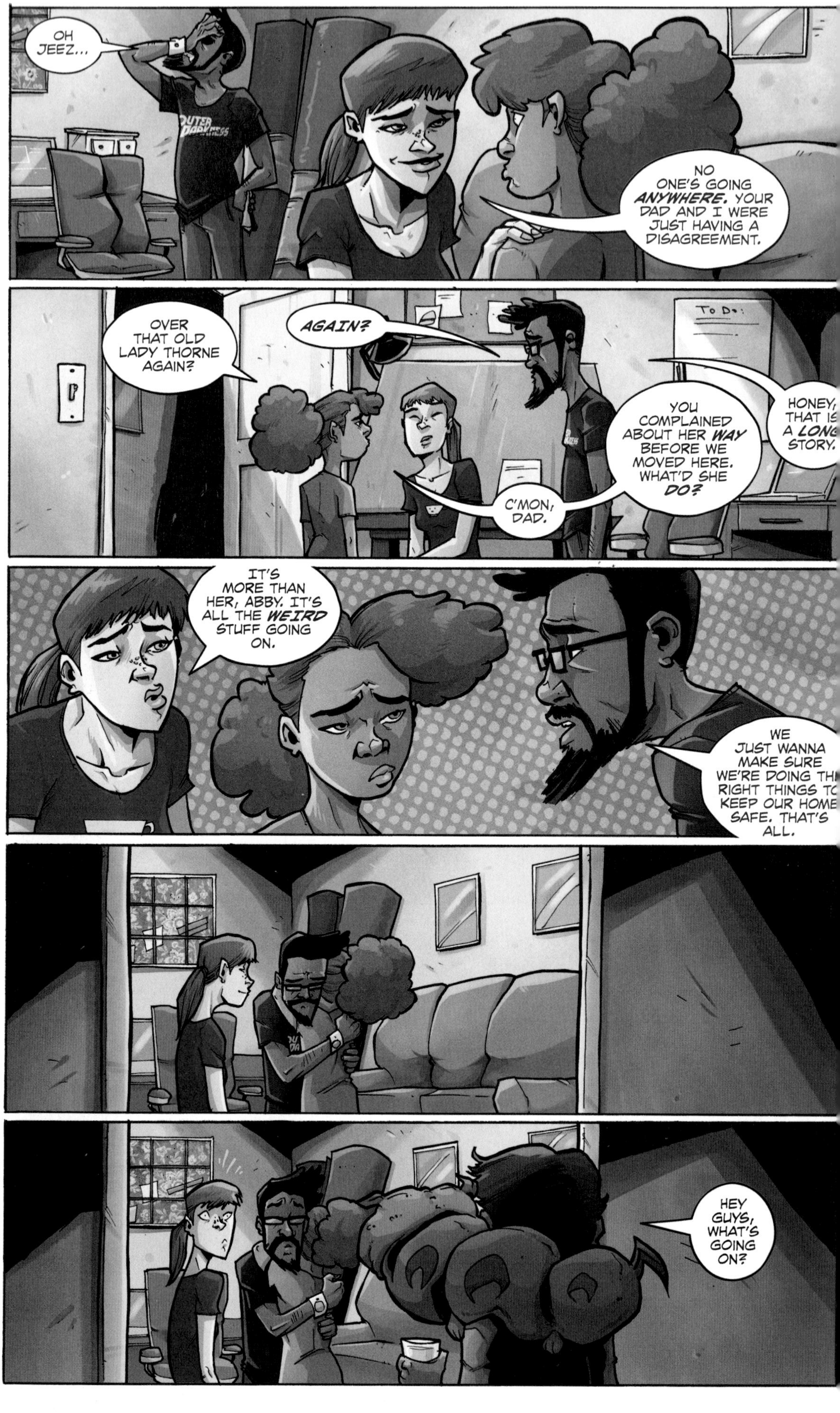
OH JEEZ...
NO ONE'S GOING ANYWHERE. YOUR DAD AND I WERE JUST HAVING A DISAGREEMENT.
OVER THAT OLD LADY THORNE AGAIN?
AGAIN?
YOU COMPLAINED ABOUT HER WAY BEFORE WE MOVED HERE. WHAT'D SHE DO?
C'MON, DAD.
HONEY, THAT IS A LONG STORY.
IT'S MORE THAN HER, ABBY. IT'S ALL THE WEIRD STUFF GOING ON.
WE JUST WANNA MAKE SURE WE'RE DOING THE RIGHT THINGS TO KEEP OUR HOME SAFE. THAT'S ALL.
HEY GUYS, WHAT'S GOING ON?

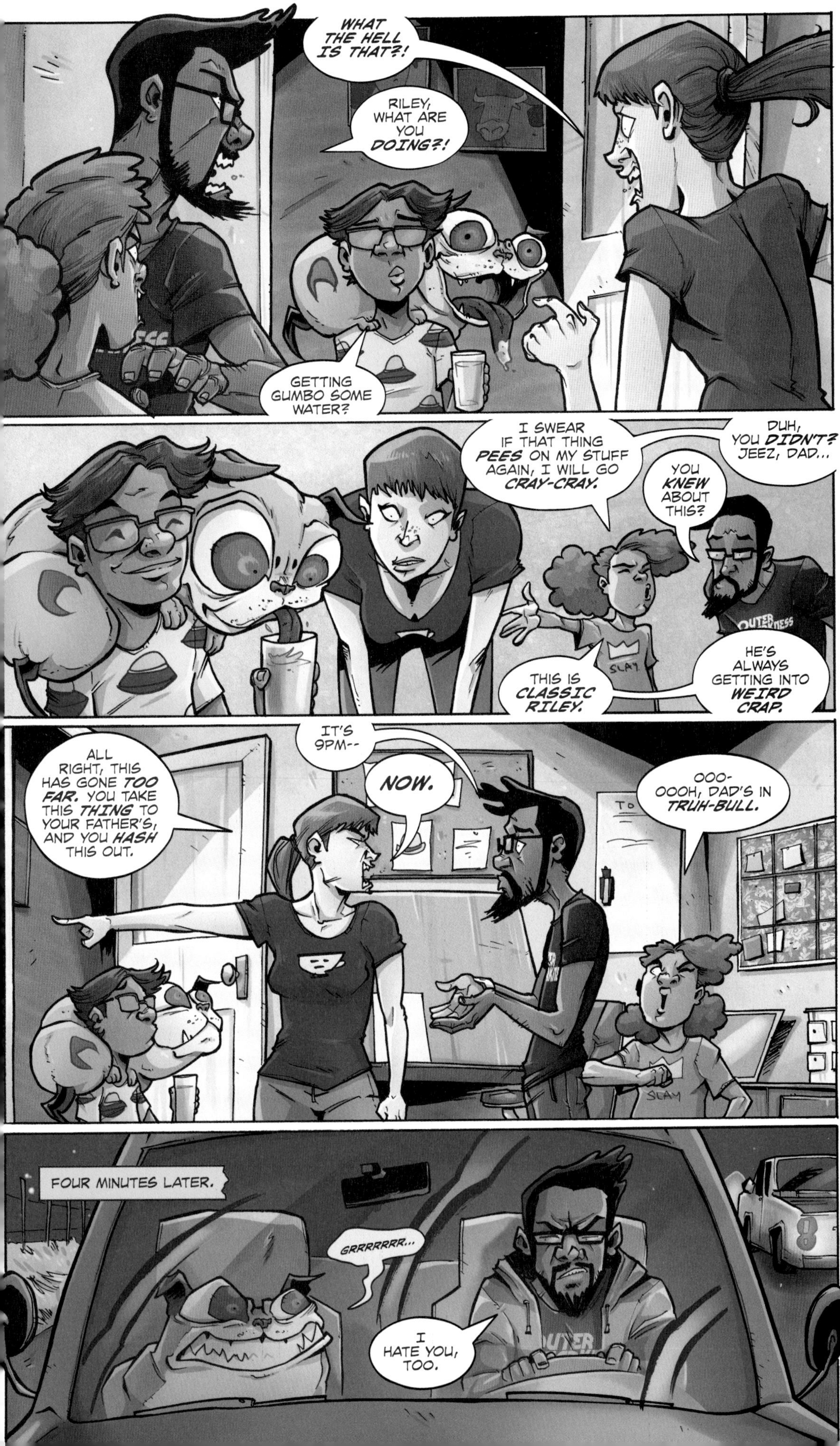

WHAT THE HELL IS THAT?!
RILEY, WHAT ARE YOU DOING?!
GETTING GUMBO SOME WATER?
I SWEAR IF THAT THING PEES ON MY STUFF AGAIN, I WILL GO CRAY-CRAY.
YOU KNEW ABOUT THIS?
DUH, YOU DIDN'T? JEEZ, DAD...
THIS IS CLASSIC RILEY.
HE'S ALWAYS GETTING INTO WEIRD CRAP.
ALL RIGHT, THIS HAS GONE TOO FAR. YOU TAKE THIS THING TO YOUR FATHER'S, AND YOU HASH THIS OUT.
IT'S 9PM--
NOW.
OOO-OOOH, DAD'S IN TRUH-BULL.
FOUR MINUTES LATER.
GRRRRRRR...
I HATE YOU, TOO.

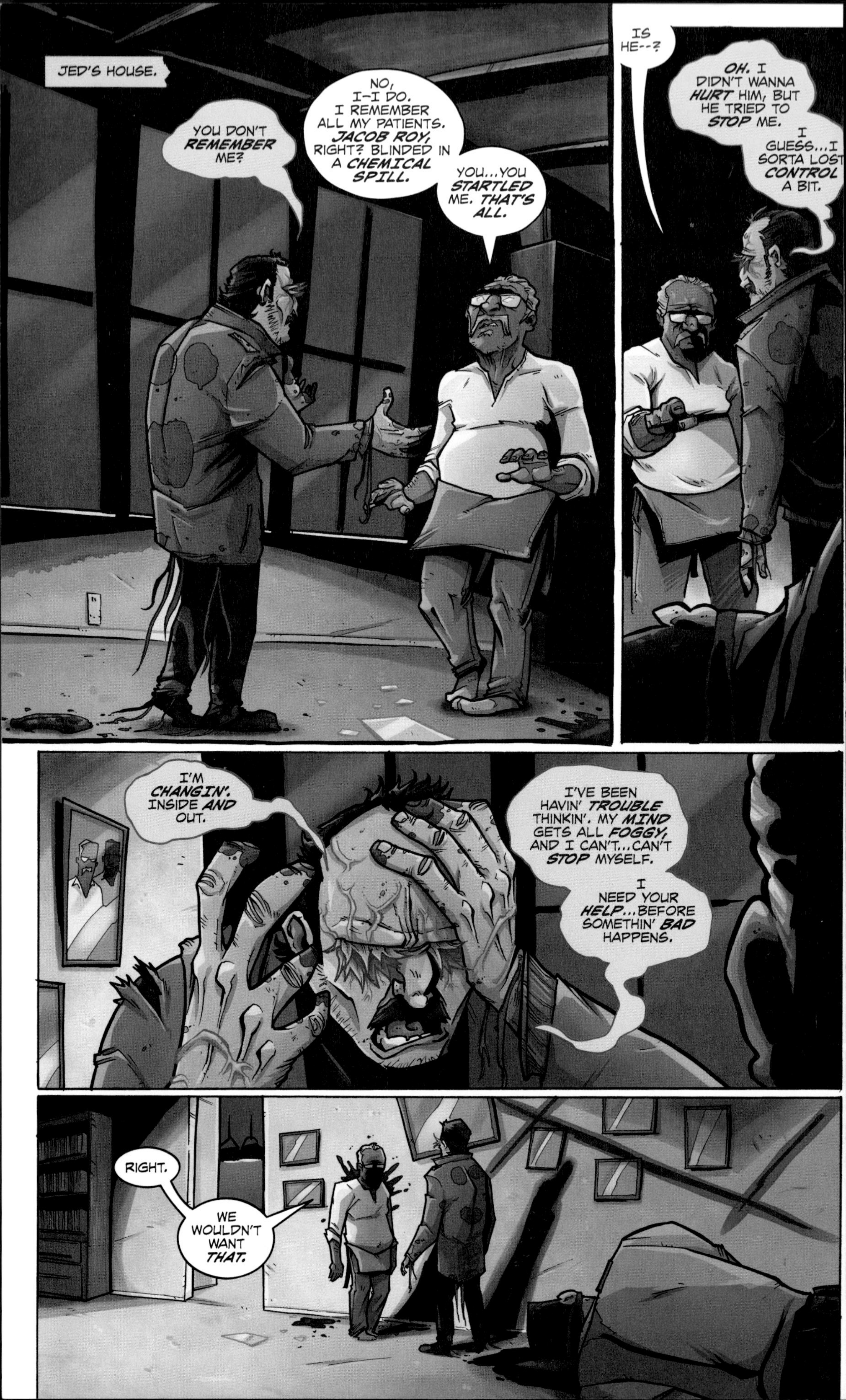
JED'S HOUSE.
YOU DON'T REMEMBER ME?
NO, I-I DO. I REMEMBER ALL MY PATIENTS. JACOB ROY, RIGHT? BLINDED IN A CHEMICAL SPILL.
YOU...YOU STARTLED ME. THAT'S ALL.
IS HE--?
OH. I DIDN'T WANNA HURT HIM, BUT HE TRIED TO STOP ME.
I GUESS...I SORTA LOST CONTROL A BIT.
I'M CHANGIN'. INSIDE AND OUT.
I'VE BEEN HAVIN' TROUBLE THINKIN'. MY MIND GETS ALL FOGGY, AND I CAN'T...CAN'T STOP MYSELF.
I NEED YOUR HELP...BEFORE SOMETHIN' BAD HAPPENS.
RIGHT.
WE WOULDN'T WANT THAT.

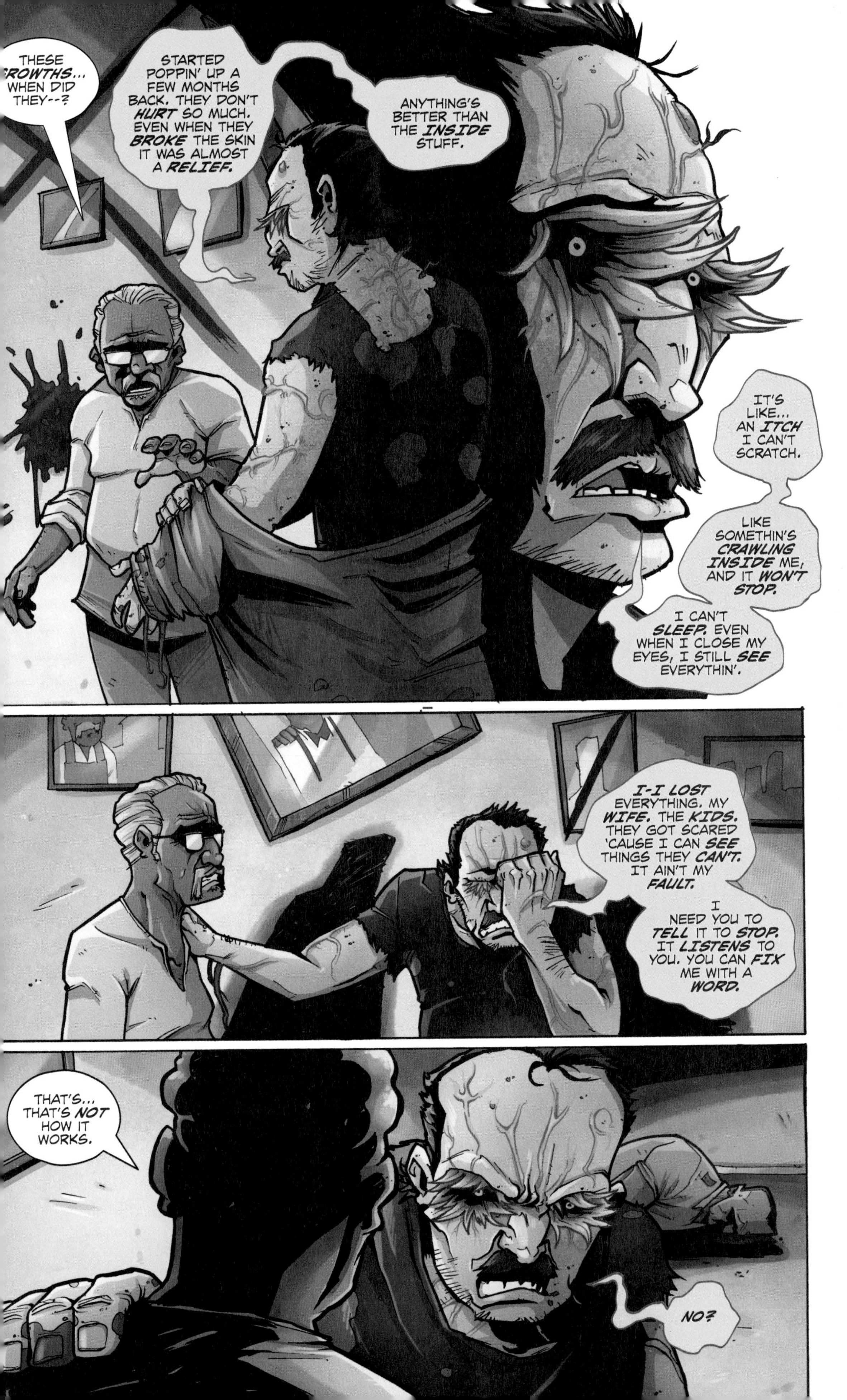
THESE GROWTHS... WHEN DID THEY--?
STARTED POPPIN' UP A FEW MONTHS BACK. THEY DON'T HURT SO MUCH. EVEN WHEN THEY BROKE THE SKIN IT WAS ALMOST A RELIEF.
ANYTHING'S BETTER THAN THE INSIDE STUFF.
IT'S LIKE... AN ITCH I CAN'T SCRATCH.
LIKE SOMETHIN'S CRAWLING INSIDE ME, AND IT WON'T STOP.
I CAN'T SLEEP. EVEN WHEN I CLOSE MY EYES, I STILL SEE EVERYTHIN'.
I-I LOST EVERYTHING. MY WIFE. THE KIDS. THEY GOT SCARED 'CAUSE I CAN SEE THINGS THEY CAN'T. IT AIN'T MY FAULT.
I NEED YOU TO TELL IT TO STOP. IT LISTENS TO YOU. YOU CAN FIX ME WITH A WORD.
THAT'S... THAT'S NOT HOW IT WORKS.
NO?

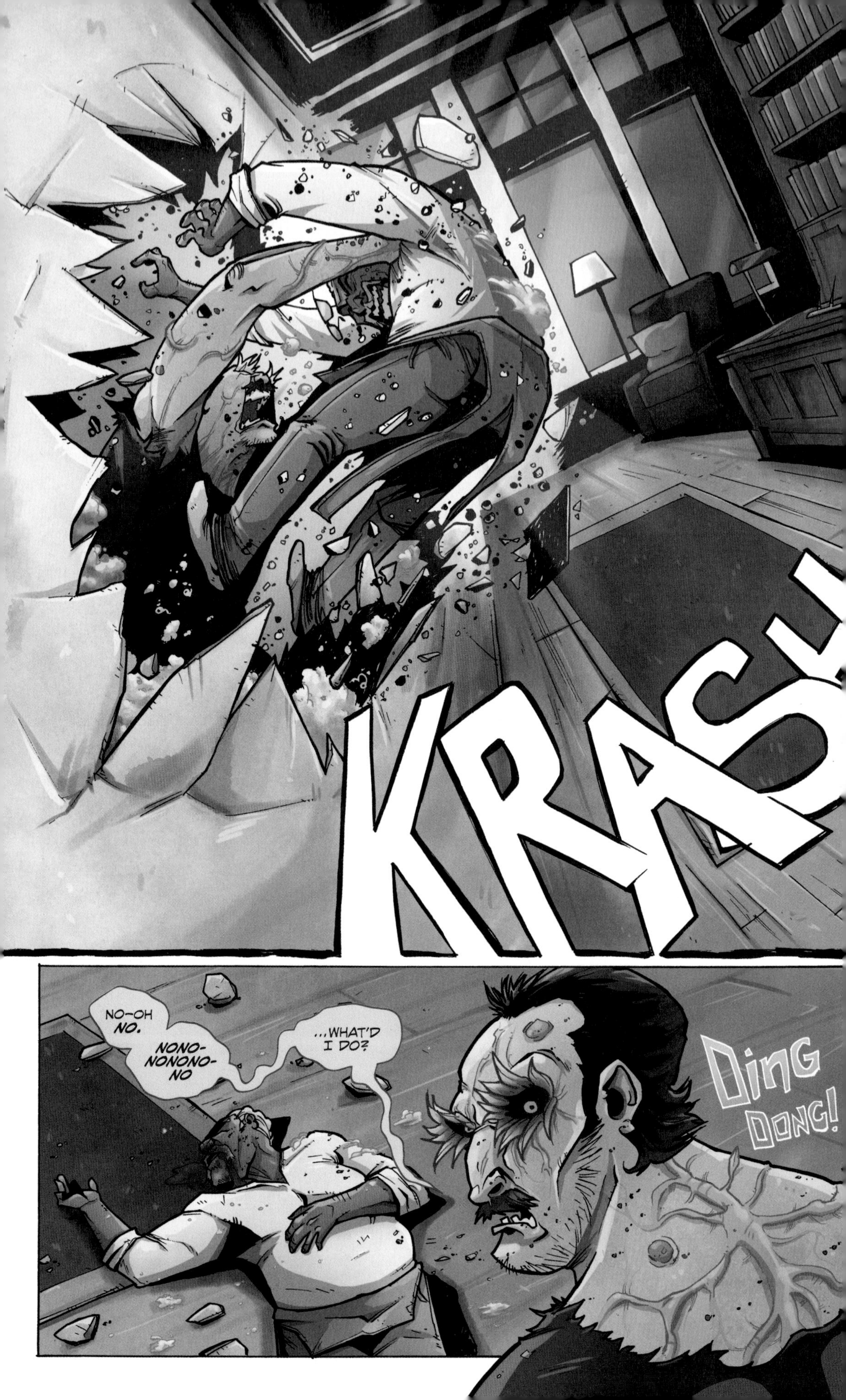
KRAS
NO-OH *NO.*
NONO-NONONO-NO
...WHAT'D I DO?
DING DONG!

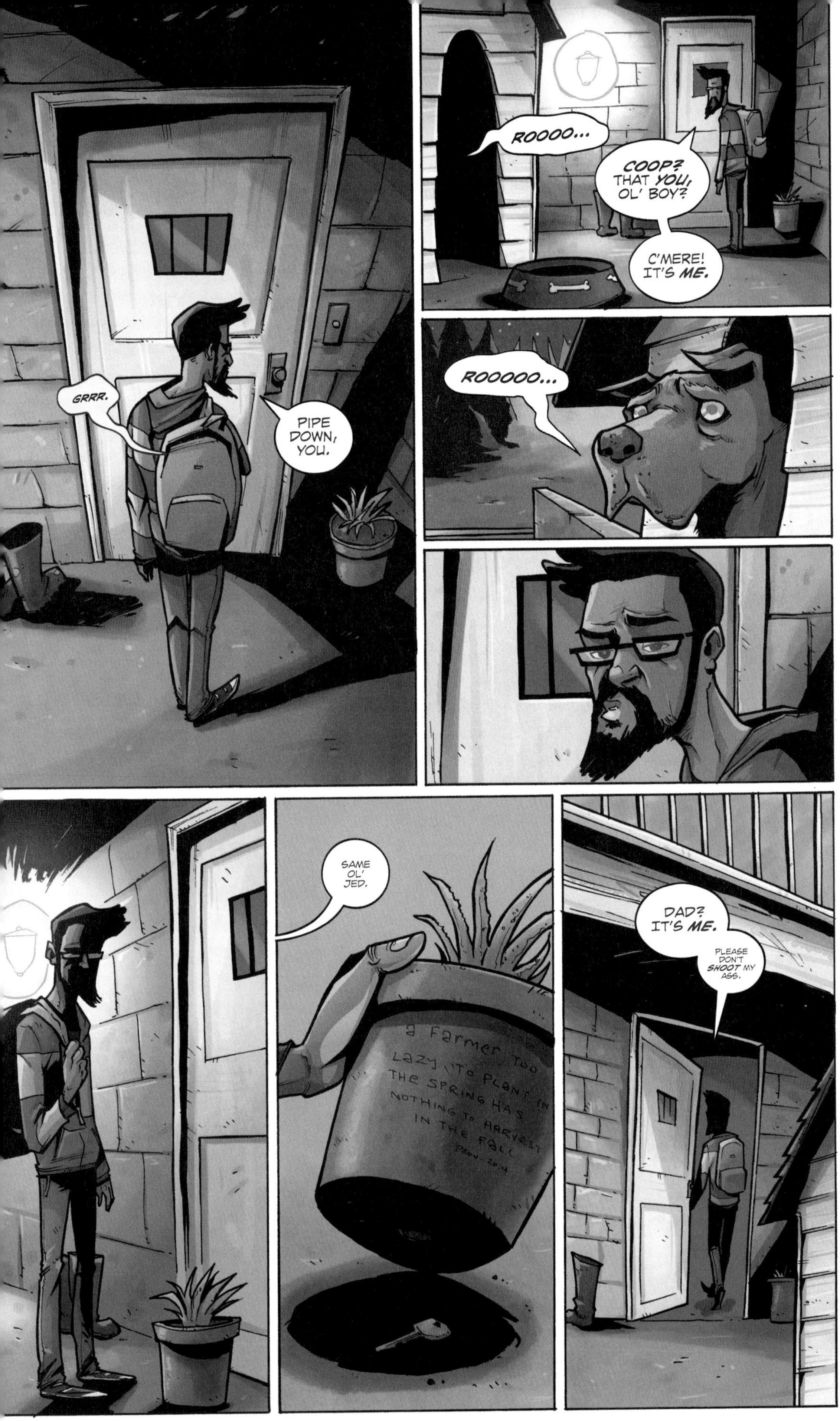
GRRR.
PIPE DOWN, YOU.
ROOOO...
COOP? THAT YOU, OL' BOY?
C'MERE! IT'S ME.
ROOOOO...
SAME OL' JED.
A FARMER TOO LAZY TO PLANT IN THE SPRING HAS NOTHING TO HARVEST IN THE FALL
PROV. 20:4
DAD? IT'S ME.
PLEASE DON'T SHOOT MY ASS.

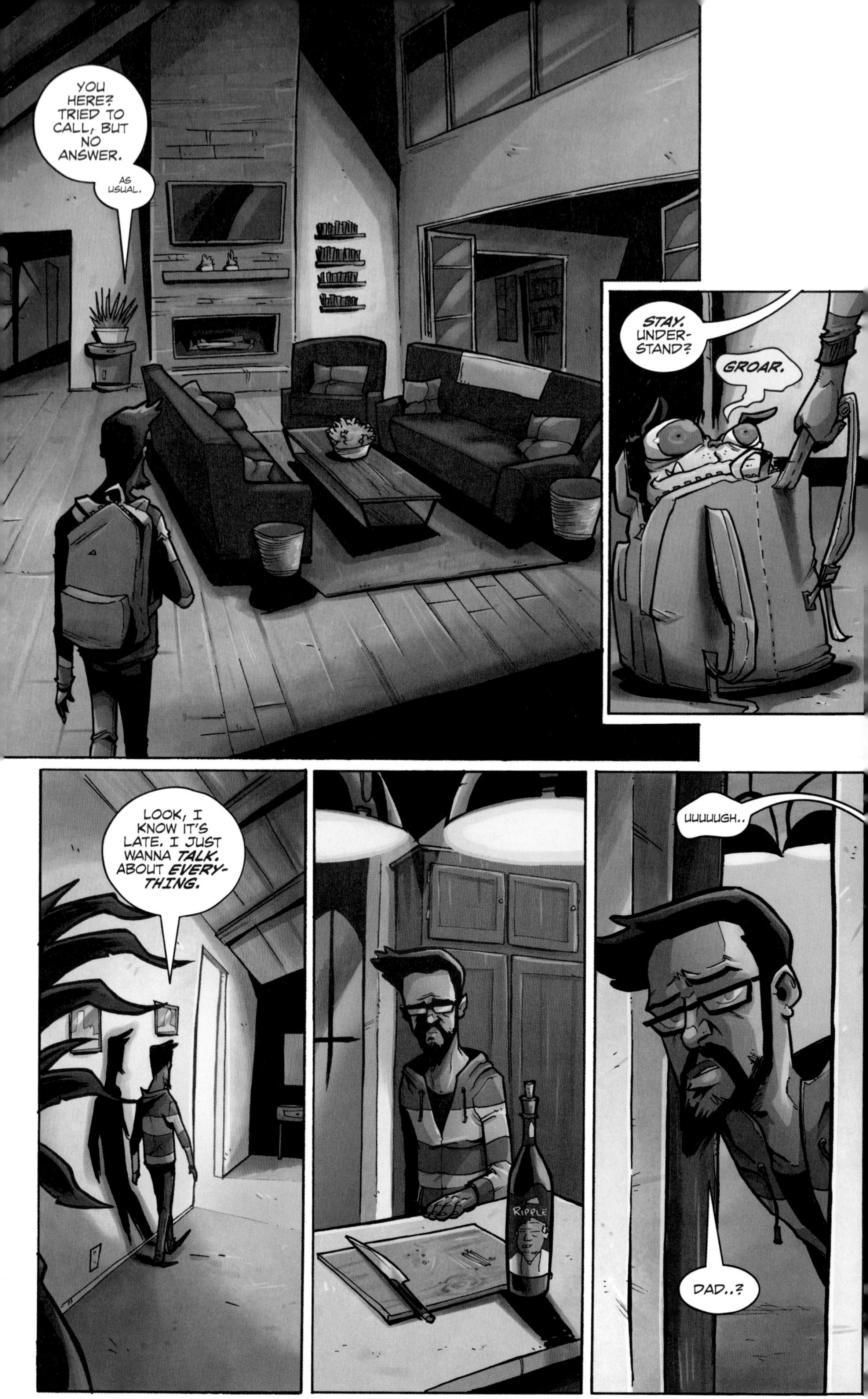
YOU HERE? TRIED TO CALL, BUT NO ANSWER.
AS USUAL.
STAY. UNDER-STAND?
GROAR.
LOOK, I KNOW IT'S LATE. I JUST WANNA TALK. ABOUT EVERY-THING.
RIPPLE
UUUUUGH..
DAD..?

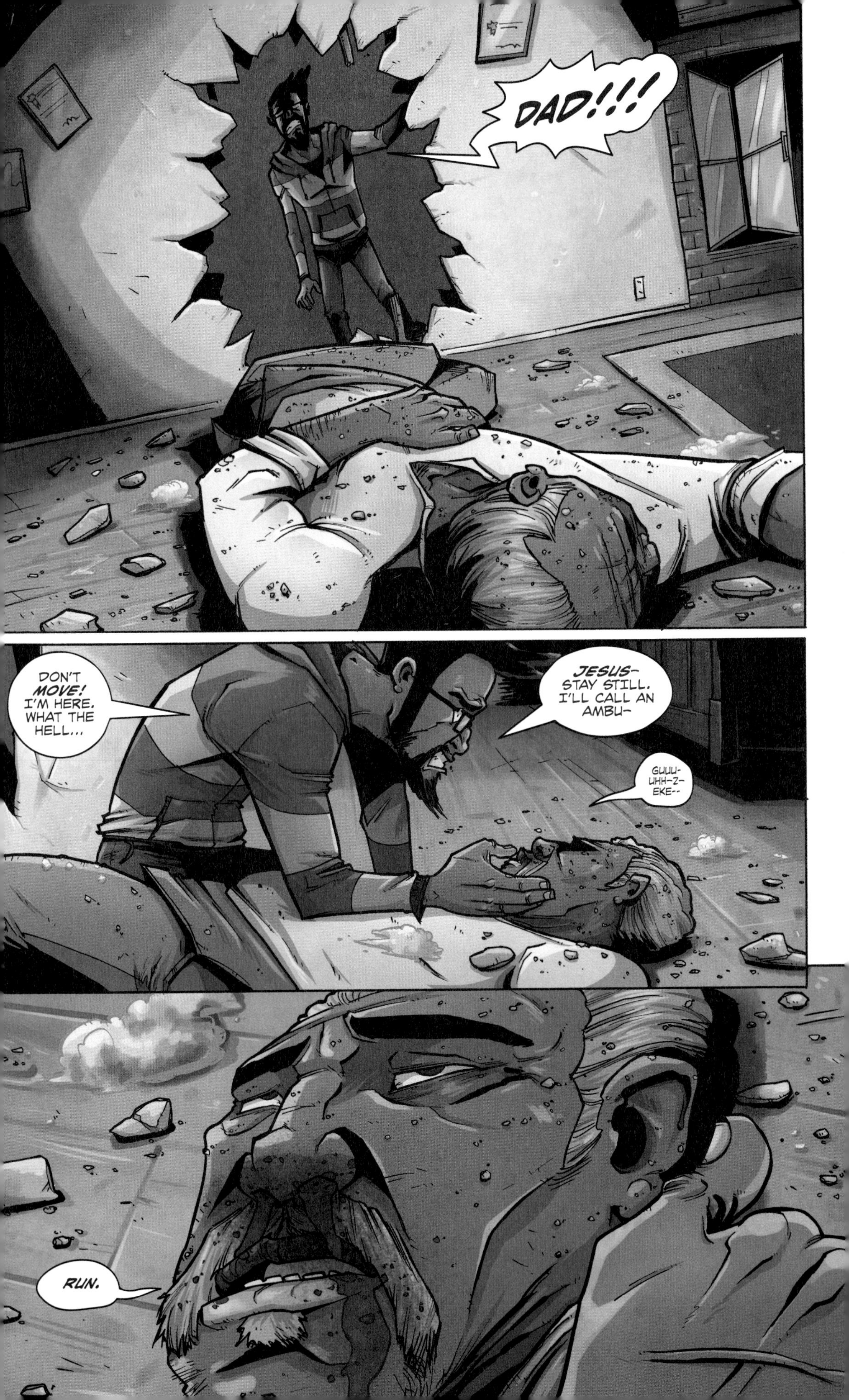
DAD!!!
DON'T *MOVE!* I'M HERE. WHAT THE HELL...
JESUS- STAY STILL. I'LL CALL AN AMBU-
GUUU-UHH-Z-EKE--
RUN.

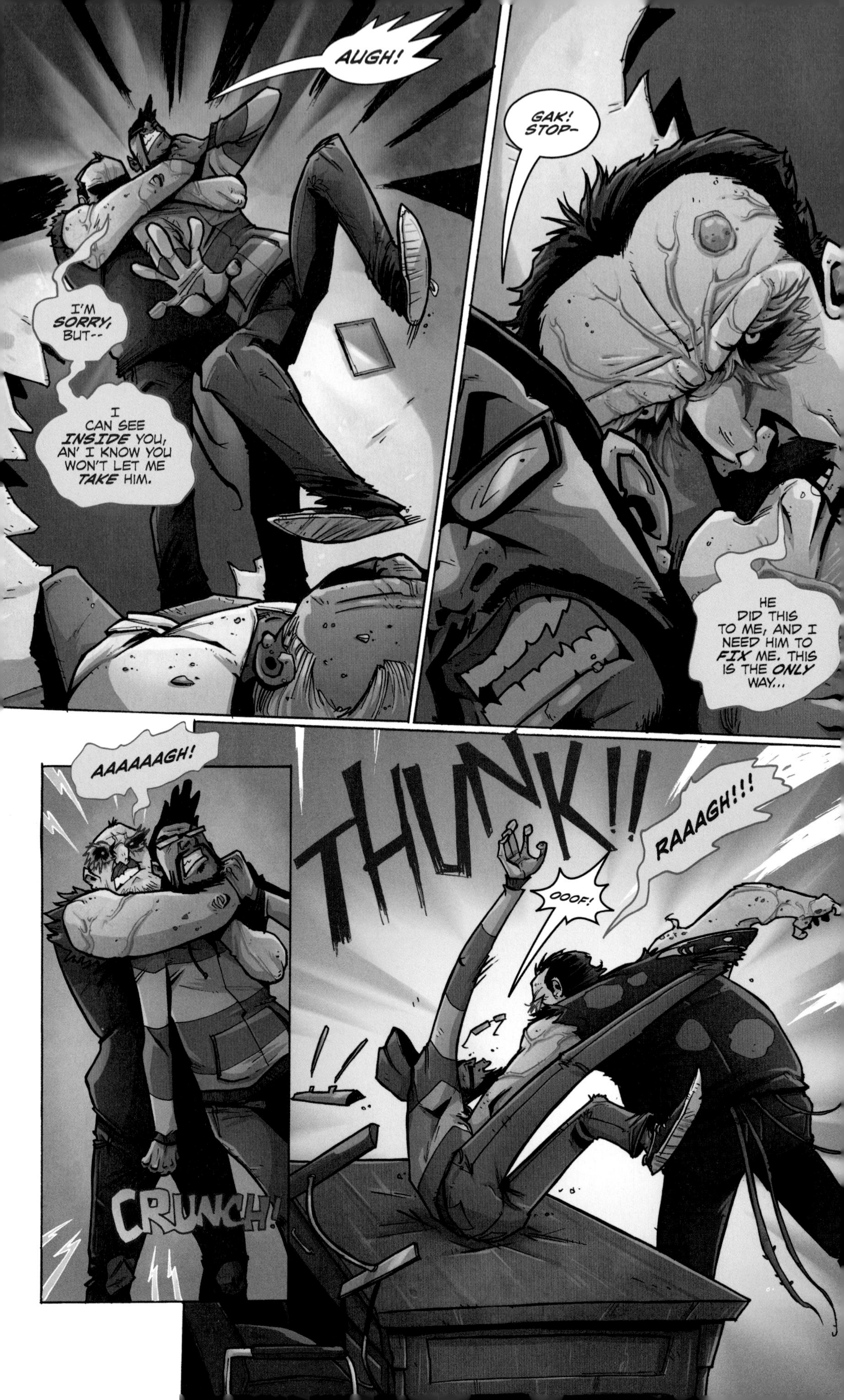
AUGH!
I'M SORRY, BUT--
I CAN SEE INSIDE YOU, AN' I KNOW YOU WON'T LET ME TAKE HIM.
GAK! STOP-
HE DID THIS TO ME, AND I NEED HIM TO FIX ME. THIS IS THE ONLY WAY...
AAAAAAGH!
CRUNCH!
THUNK!!
OOOF!
RAAAGH!!!

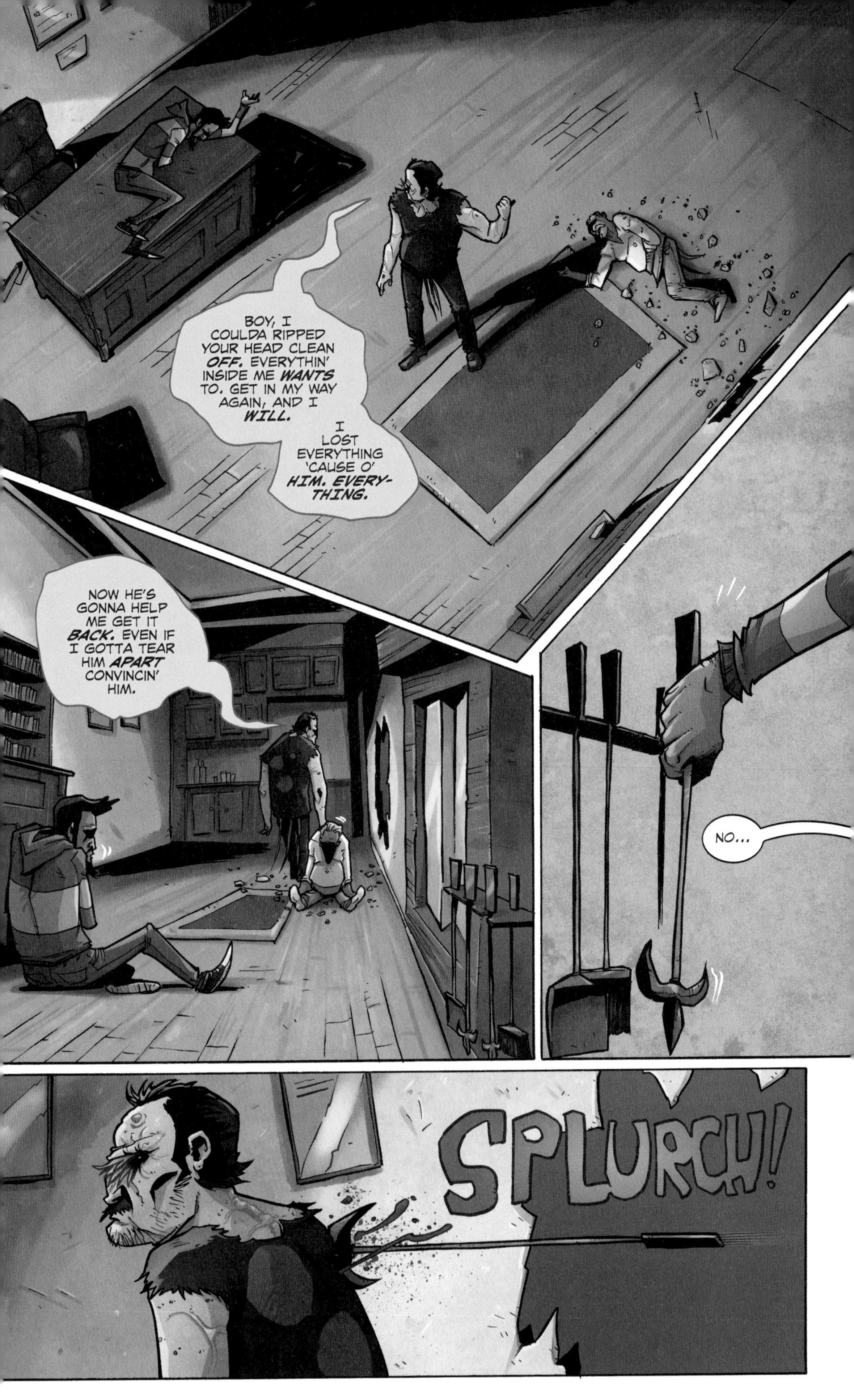
BOY, I COULDA RIPPED YOUR HEAD CLEAN OFF. EVERYTHIN' INSIDE ME WANTS TO. GET IN MY WAY AGAIN, AND I WILL.
I LOST EVERYTHING 'CAUSE O' HIM. EVERY-THING.
NOW HE'S GONNA HELP ME GET IT BACK. EVEN IF I GOTTA TEAR HIM APART CONVINCIN' HIM.
NO...
SPLURCH!

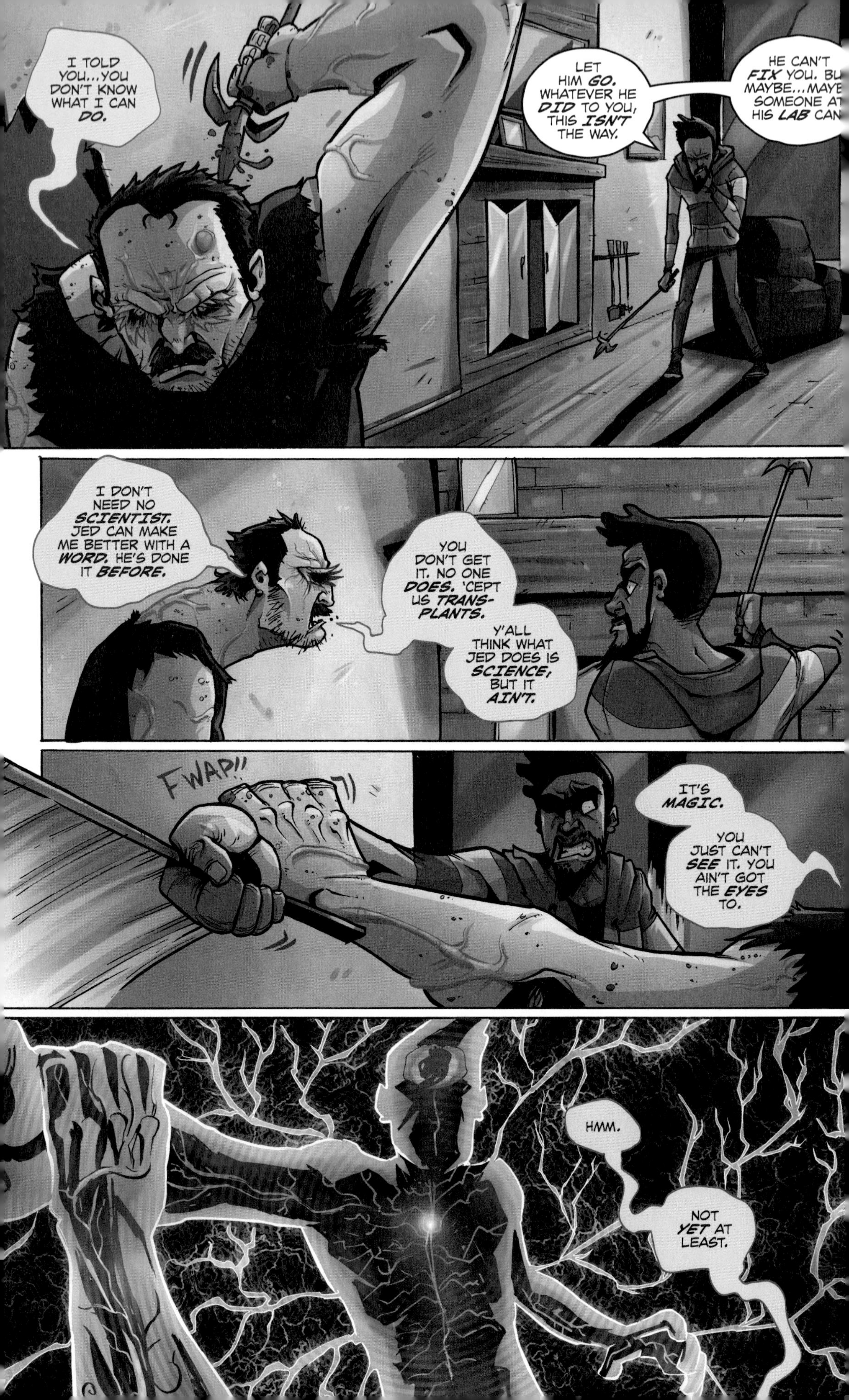

I TOLD YOU...YOU DON'T KNOW WHAT I CAN DO.
LET HIM GO. WHATEVER HE DID TO YOU, THIS ISN'T THE WAY.
HE CAN'T FIX YOU. BU MAYBE...MAYB SOMEONE AT HIS LAB CAN
I DON'T NEED NO SCIENTIST. JED CAN MAKE ME BETTER WITH A WORD. HE'S DONE IT BEFORE.
YOU DON'T GET IT. NO ONE DOES. 'CEPT US TRANS-PLANTS.
Y'ALL THINK WHAT JED DOES IS SCIENCE, BUT IT AIN'T.
FWAP!!
IT'S MAGIC.
YOU JUST CAN'T SEE IT. YOU AIN'T GOT THE EYES TO.
HMM.
NOT YET AT LEAST.

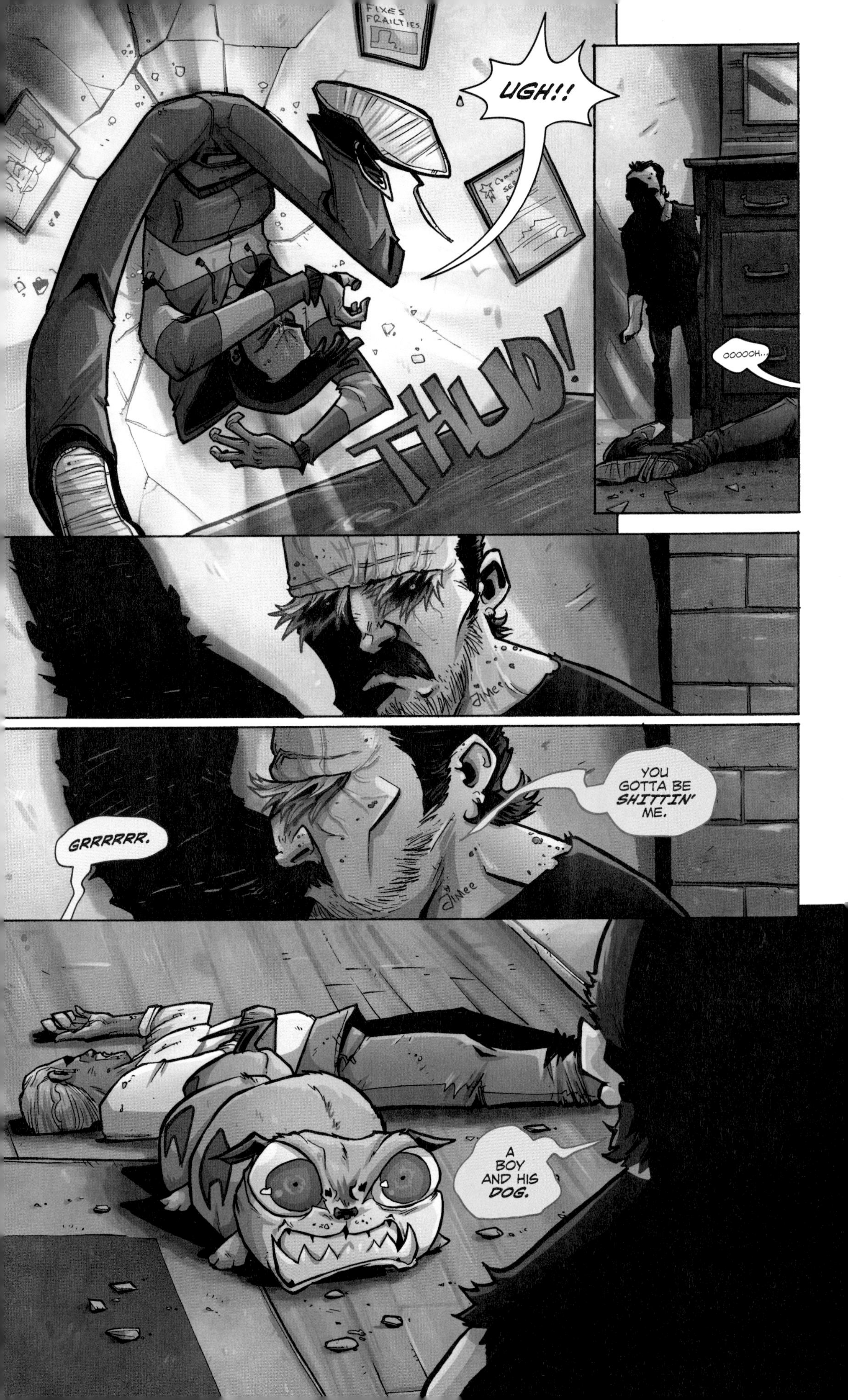
FIXES FRAILTIES.
UGH!!
THUD!
OOOOOH...
GRRRRRR.
YOU GOTTA BE SHITTIN' ME.
A BOY AND HIS DOG.

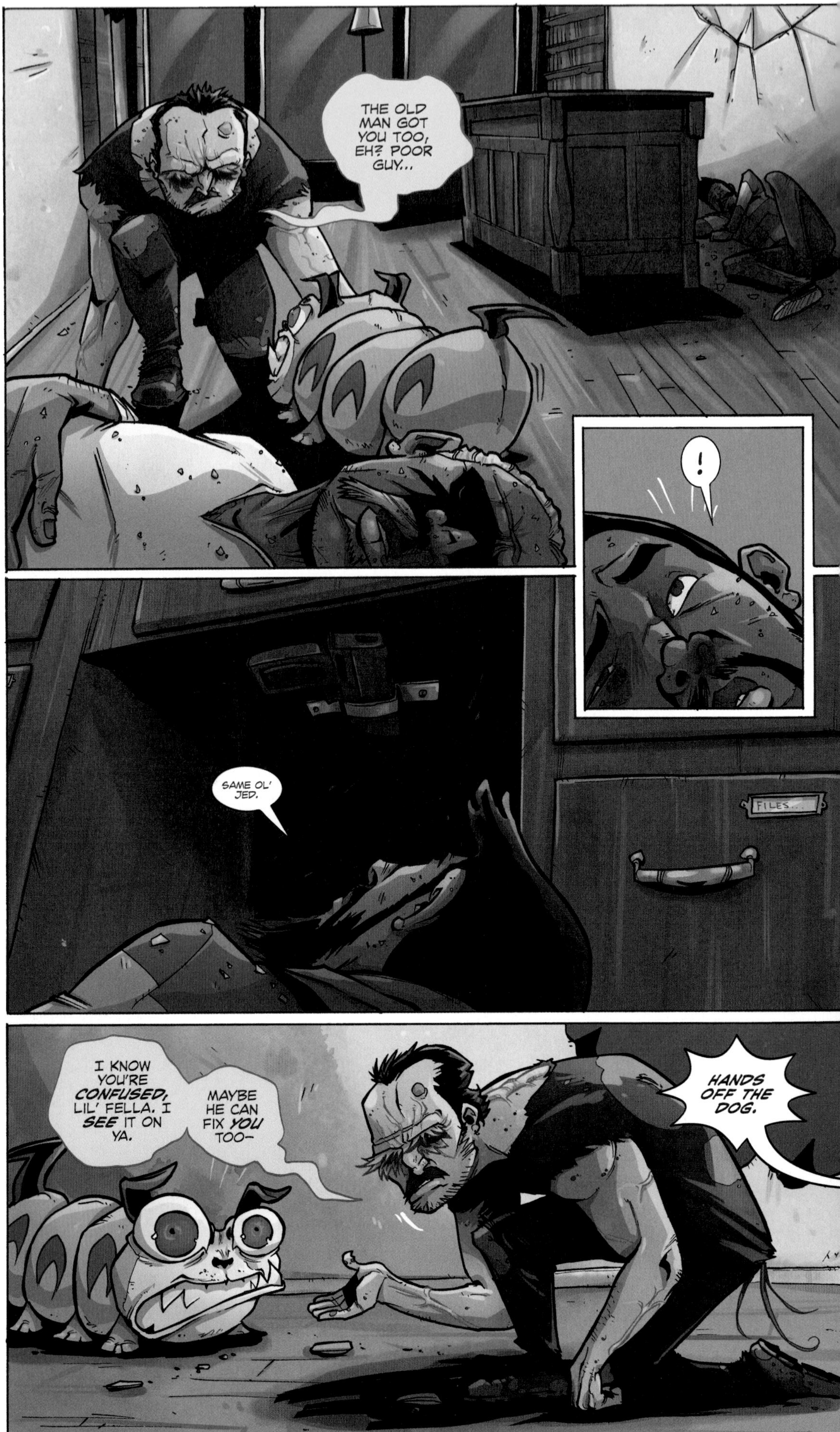
THE OLD MAN GOT YOU TOO, EH? POOR GUY...
!
SAME OL' JED.
FILES...
I KNOW YOU'RE CONFUSED, LIL' FELLA. I SEE IT ON YA.
MAYBE HE CAN FIX YOU TOO—
HANDS OFF THE DOG.

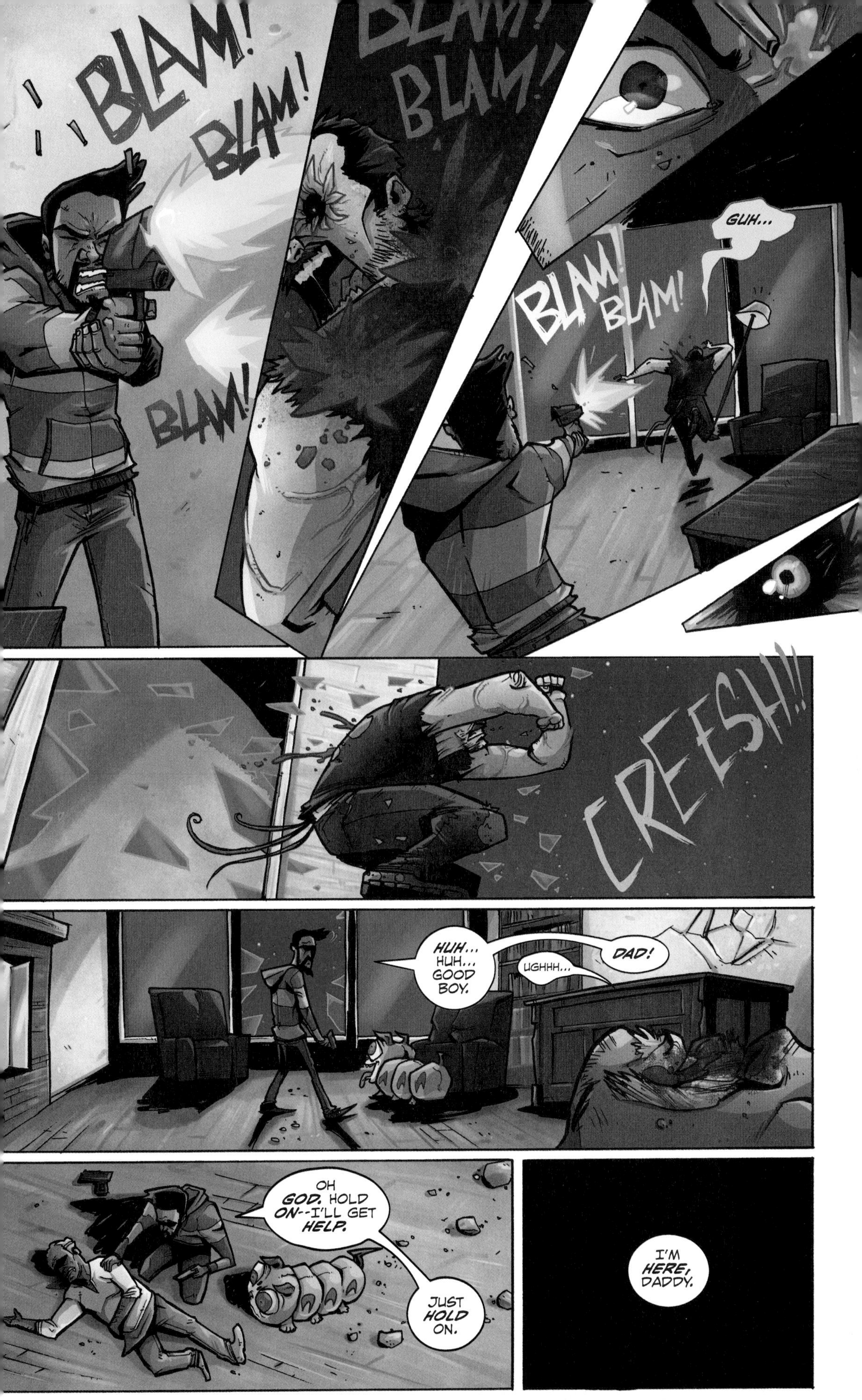
BLAM!
BLAM!
BLAM!
BLAM!
BLAM!
GUH...
BLAM!
BLAM!
CREESH!!
HUH... HUH... GOOD BOY.
UGHHH...
DAD!
OH GOD. HOLD ON--I'LL GET HELP.
JUST HOLD ON.
I'M HERE, DADDY.

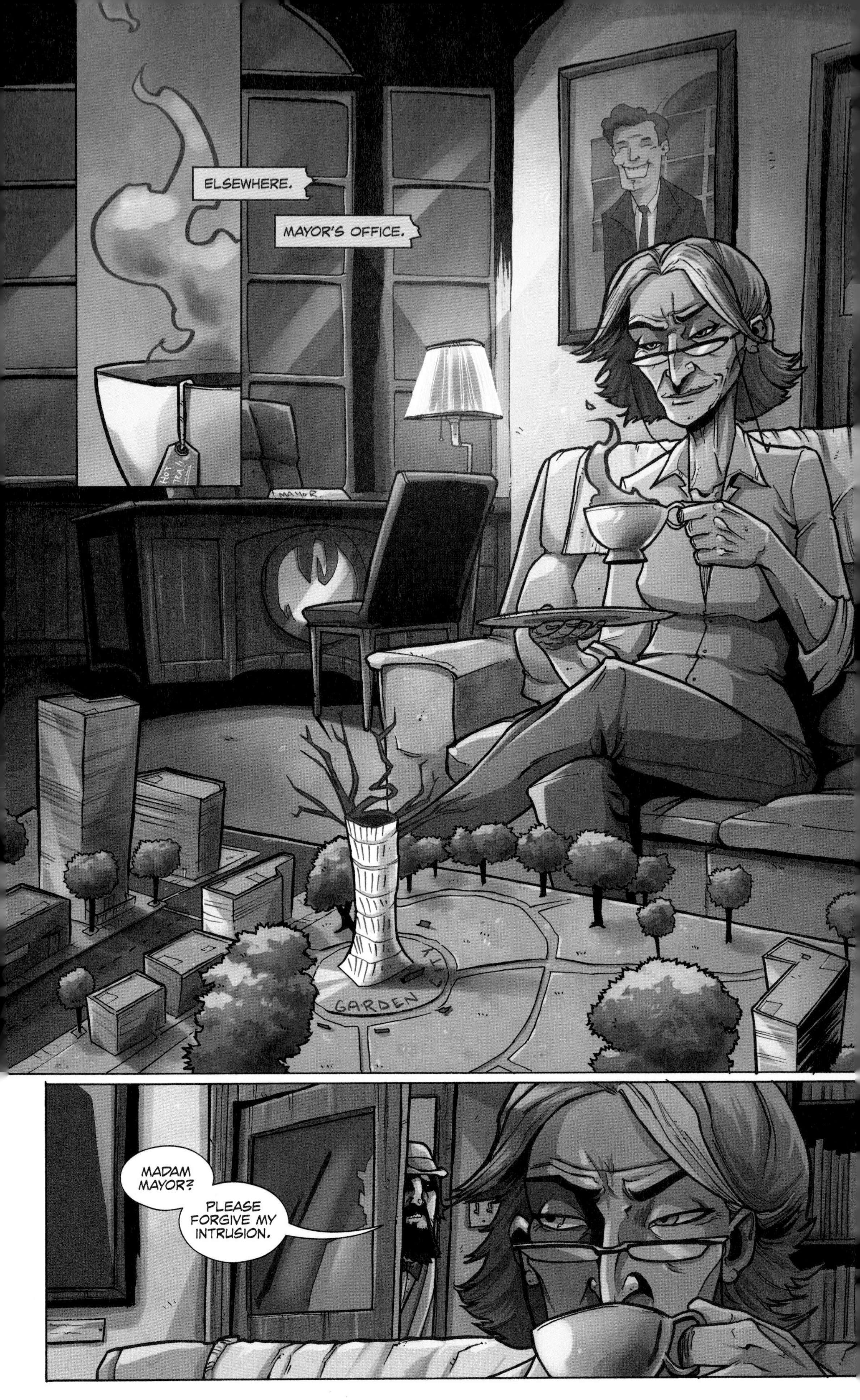
ELSEWHERE.
MAYOR'S OFFICE.
HOT TEA!!
MAYOR
GARDEN
MADAM MAYOR?
PLEASE FORGIVE MY INTRUSION.

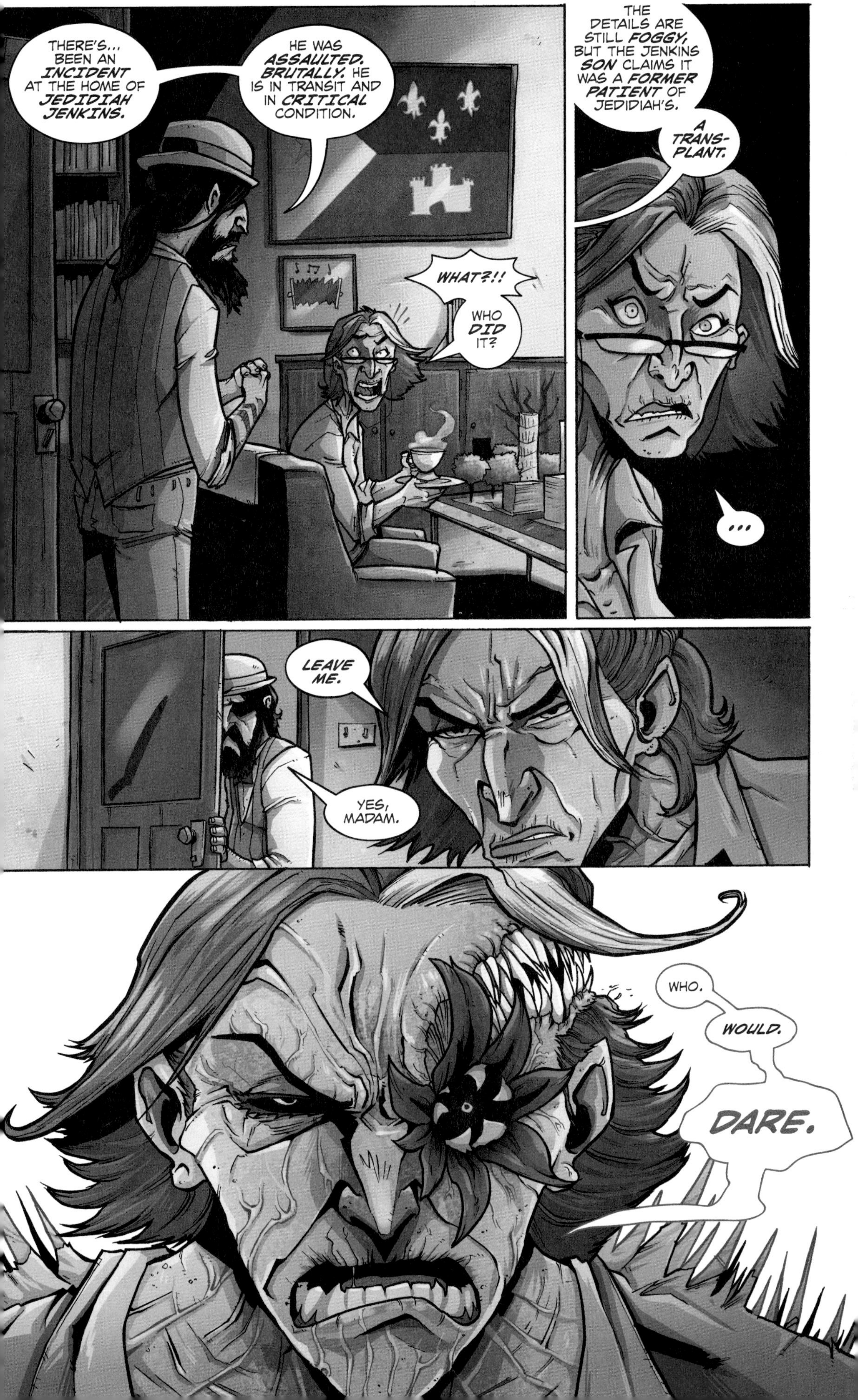

THERE'S... BEEN AN *INCIDENT* AT THE HOME OF *JEDIDIAH JENKINS.*
HE WAS *ASSAULTED. BRUTALLY.* HE IS IN TRANSIT AND IN *CRITICAL* CONDITION.
WHAT?!!
WHO *DID* IT?
THE DETAILS ARE STILL *FOGGY,* BUT THE JENKINS *SON* CLAIMS IT WAS A *FORMER PATIENT* OF JEDIDIAH'S.
A TRANS-PLANT.
...
LEAVE ME.
YES, MADAM.
WHO.
WOULD.
DARE.

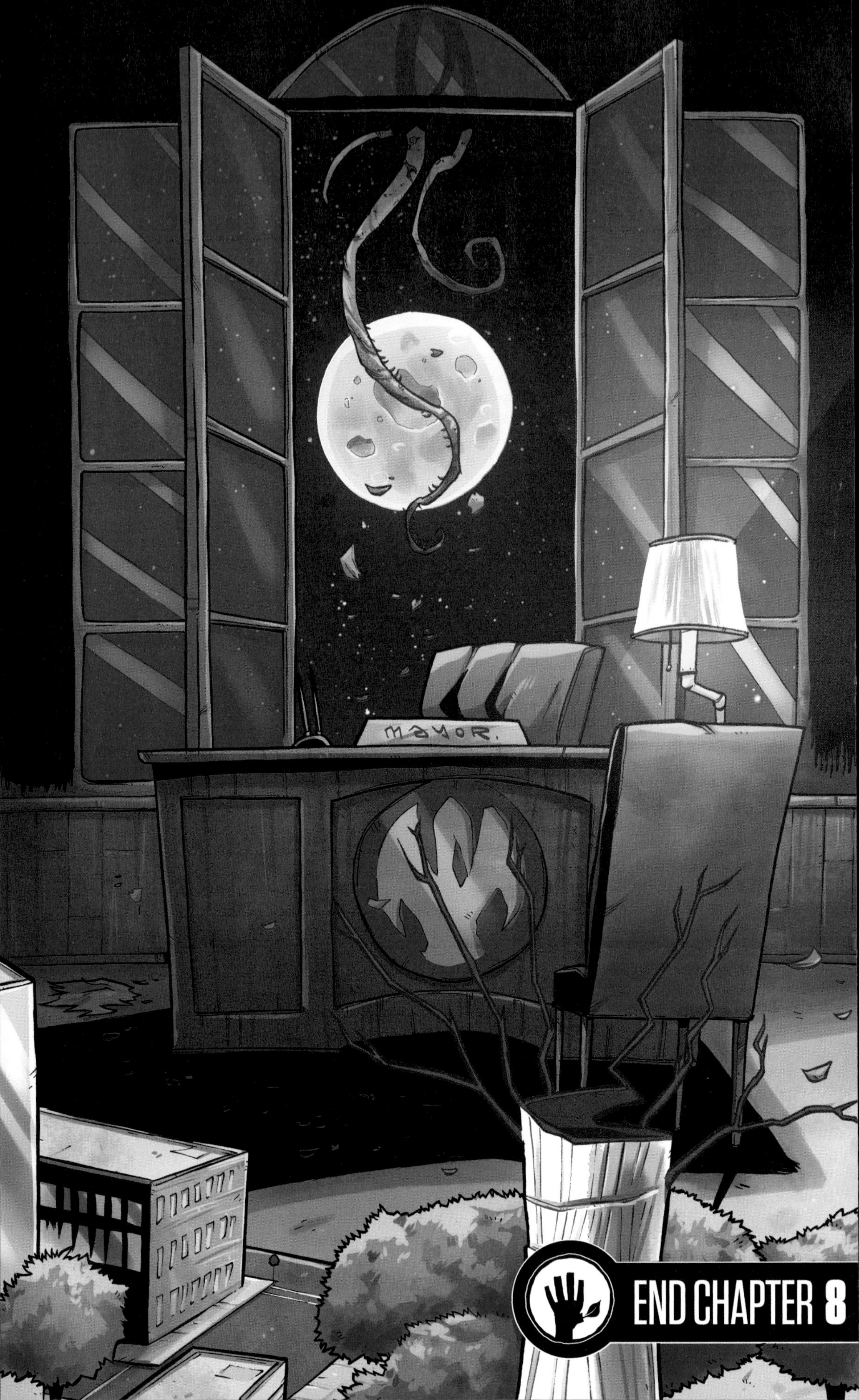
MAYOR.
END CHAPTER 8

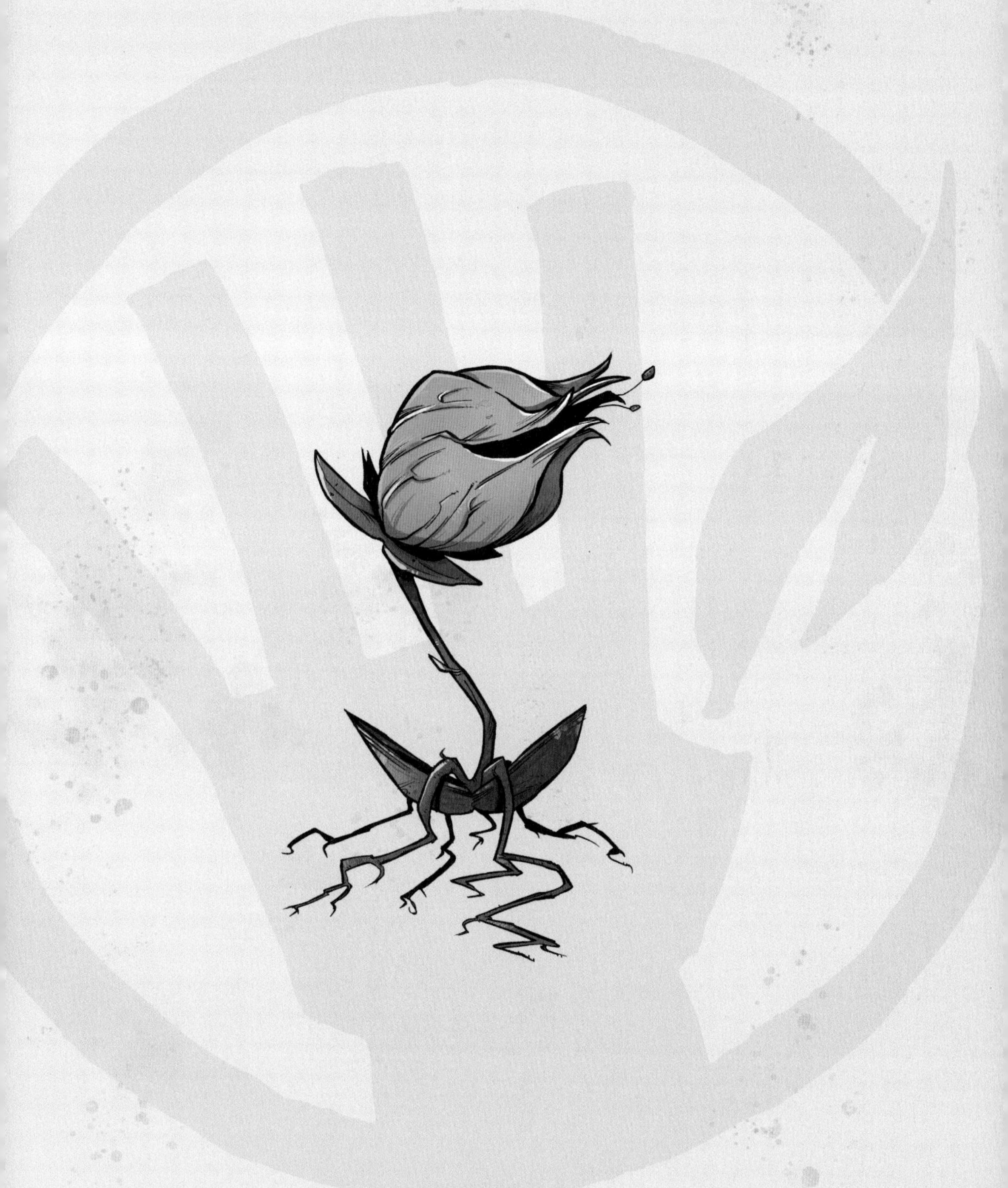

CHAPTER 9

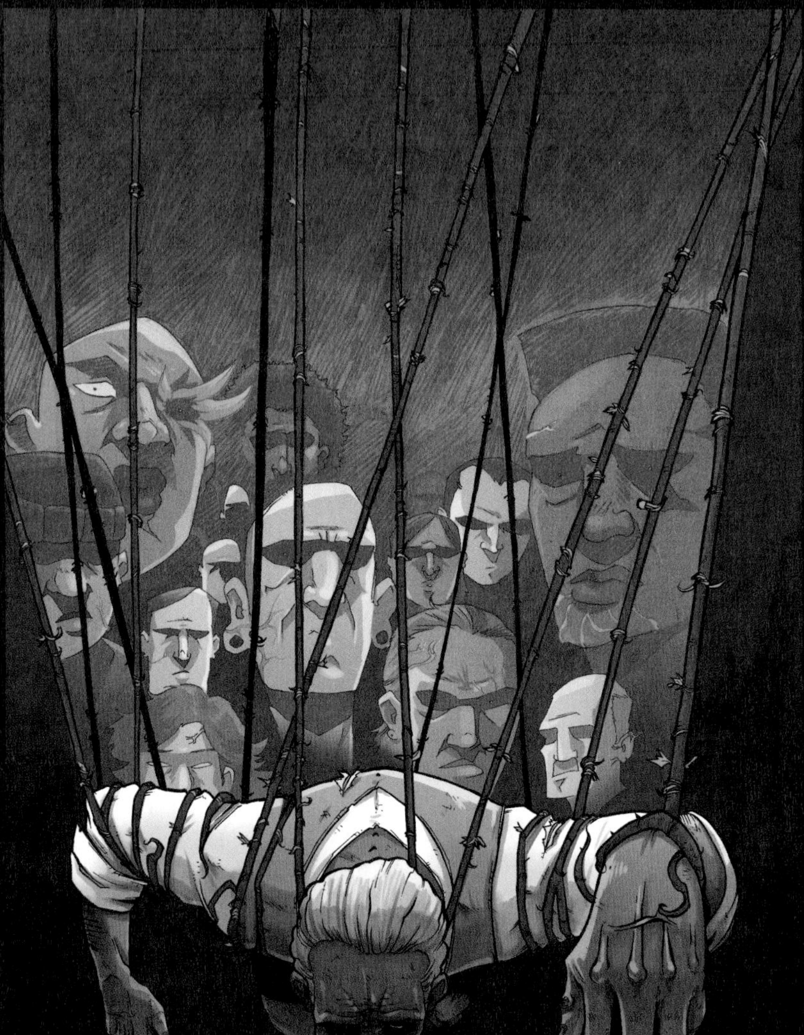

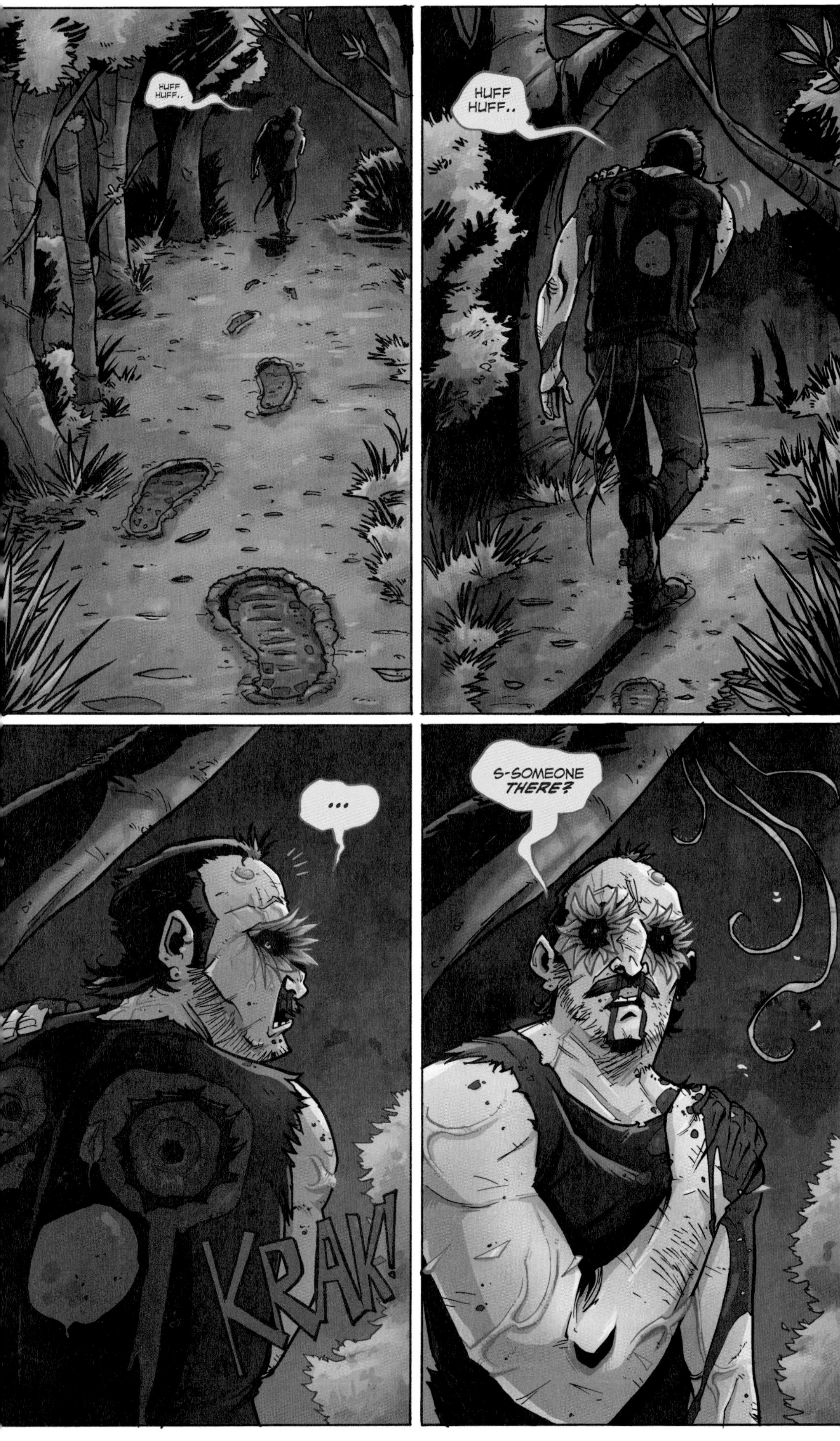
HUFF HUFF..
HUFF HUFF..
...
KRAK!
S-SOMEONE THERE?

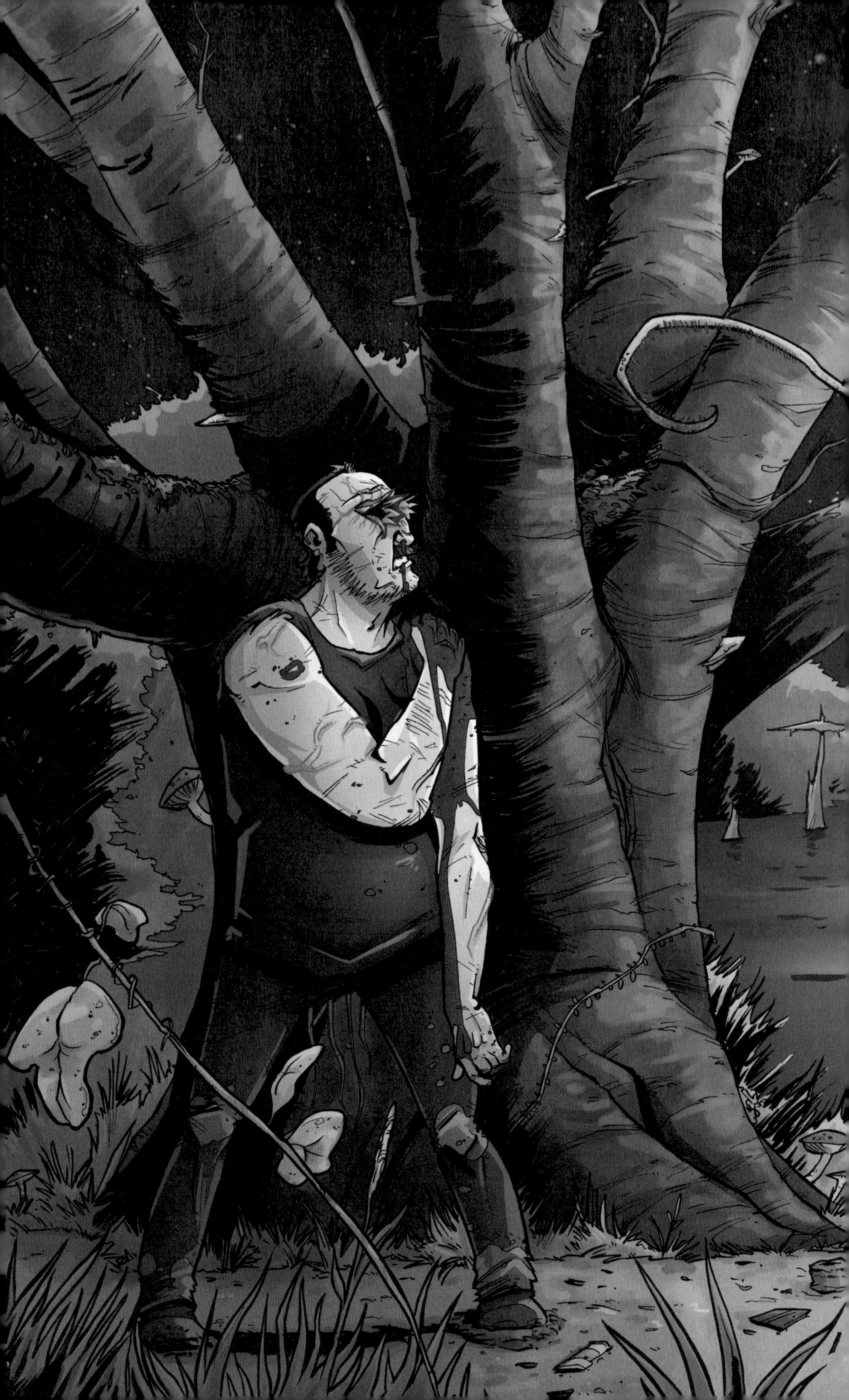

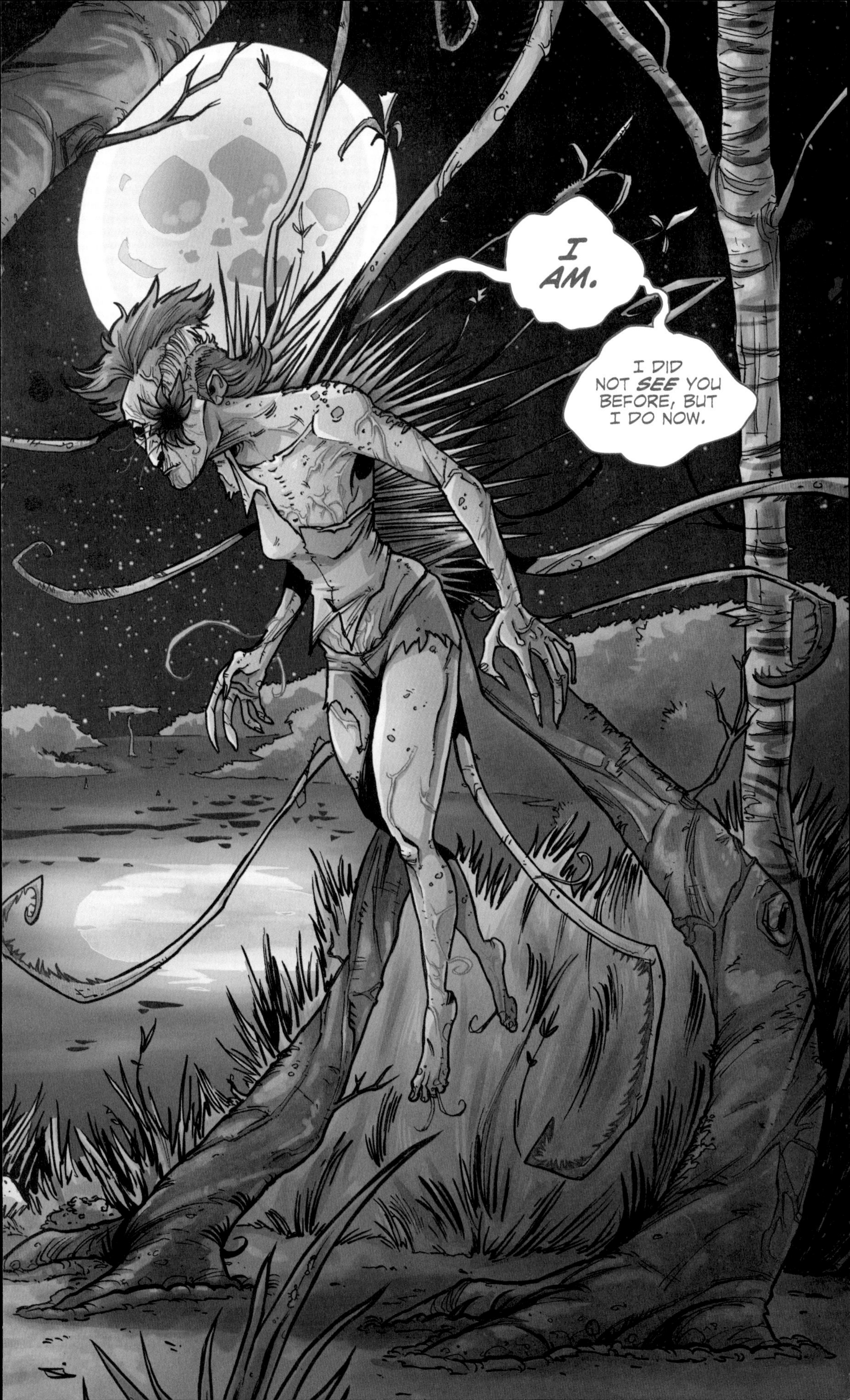
I AM.
I DID NOT SEE YOU BEFORE, BUT I DO NOW.

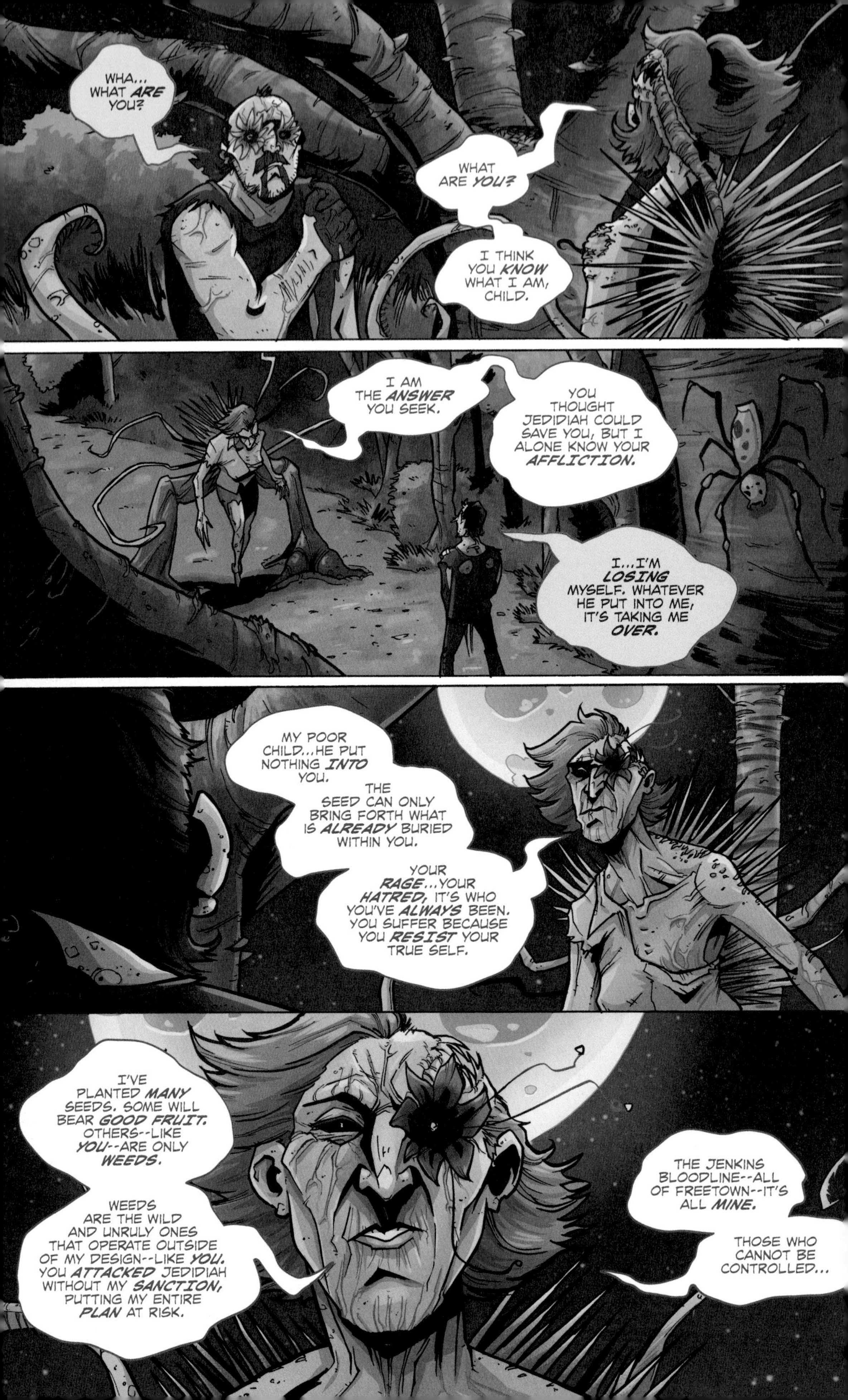
WHA... WHAT ARE YOU?
WHAT ARE YOU?
I THINK YOU KNOW WHAT I AM, CHILD.
I AM THE ANSWER YOU SEEK.
YOU THOUGHT JEDIDIAH COULD SAVE YOU, BUT I ALONE KNOW YOUR AFFLICTION.
I...I'M LOSING MYSELF. WHATEVER HE PUT INTO ME, IT'S TAKING ME OVER.
MY POOR CHILD...HE PUT NOTHING INTO YOU.
THE SEED CAN ONLY BRING FORTH WHAT IS ALREADY BURIED WITHIN YOU.
YOUR RAGE...YOUR HATRED, IT'S WHO YOU'VE ALWAYS BEEN. YOU SUFFER BECAUSE YOU RESIST YOUR TRUE SELF.
I'VE PLANTED MANY SEEDS. SOME WILL BEAR GOOD FRUIT. OTHERS--LIKE YOU--ARE ONLY WEEDS.
WEEDS ARE THE WILD AND UNRULY ONES THAT OPERATE OUTSIDE OF MY DESIGN--LIKE YOU. YOU ATTACKED JEDIDIAH WITHOUT MY SANCTION, PUTTING MY ENTIRE PLAN AT RISK.
THE JENKINS BLOODLINE--ALL OF FREETOWN--IT'S ALL MINE.
THOSE WHO CANNOT BE CONTROLLED...

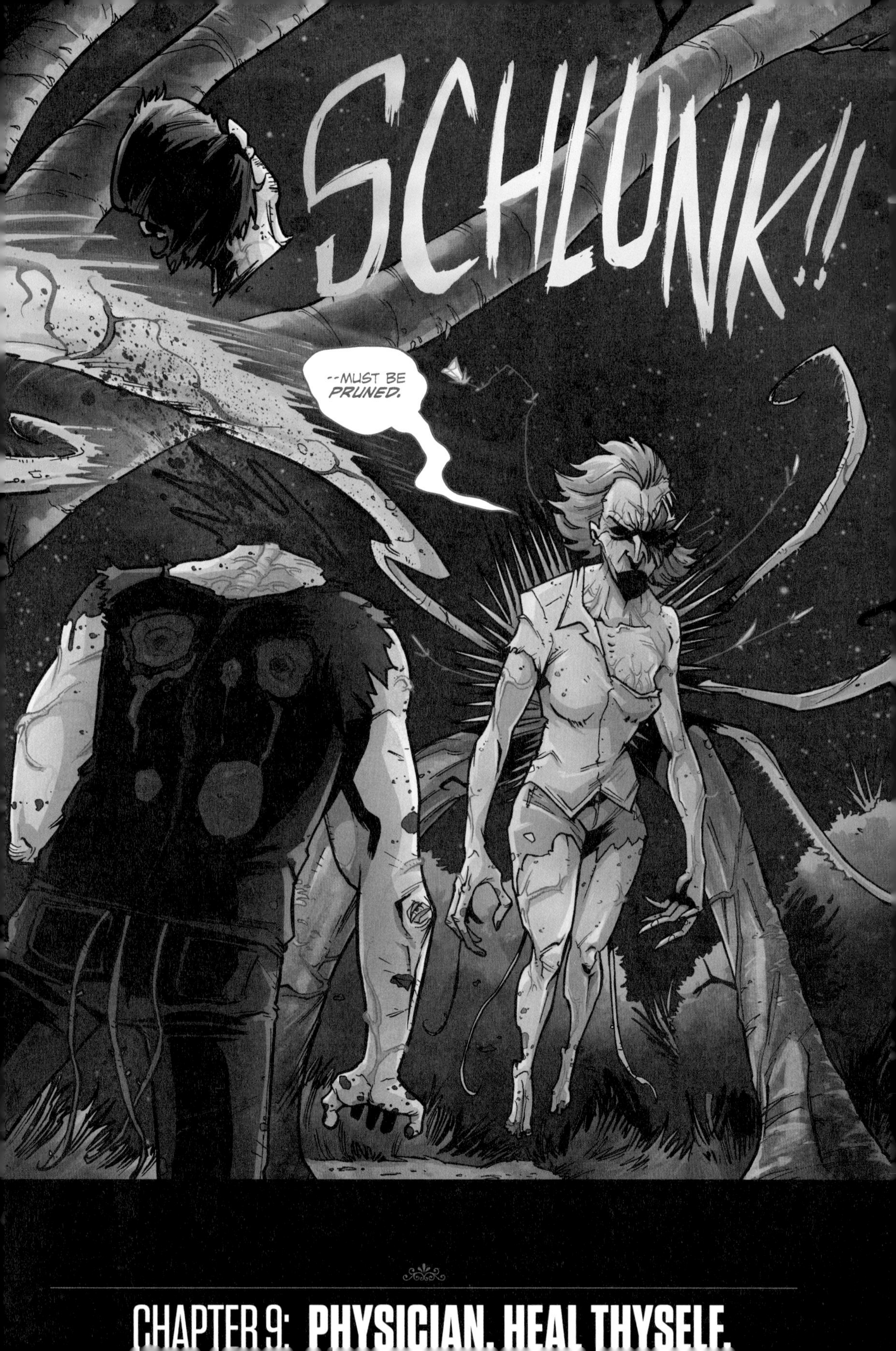
SCHLUNK!!
--MUST BE PRUNED.

CHAPTER 9: PHYSICIAN, HEAL THYSELF.

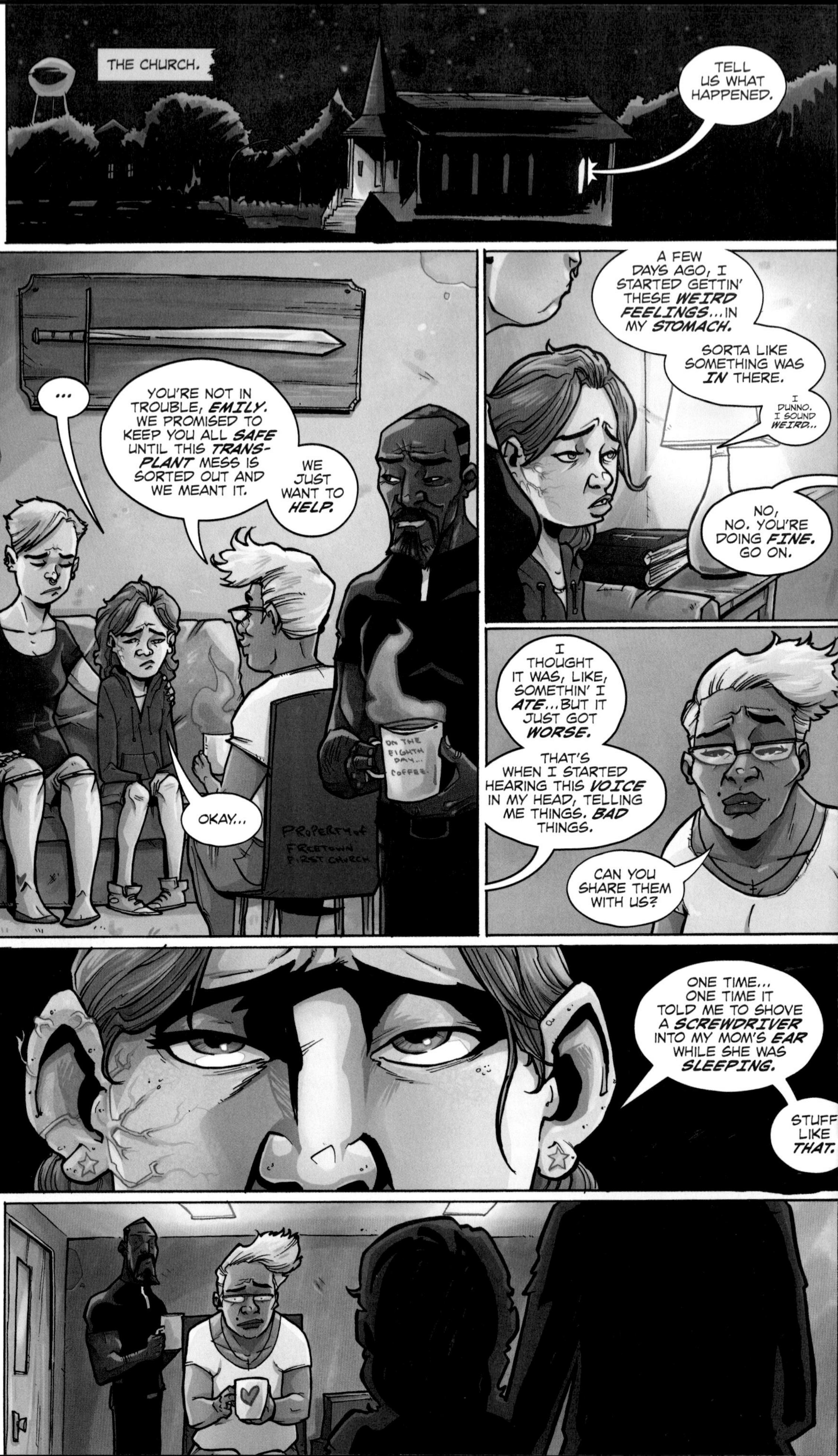
THE CHURCH.
TELL US WHAT HAPPENED.
...
YOU'RE NOT IN TROUBLE, EMILY. WE PROMISED TO KEEP YOU ALL SAFE UNTIL THIS TRANS-PLANT MESS IS SORTED OUT AND WE MEANT IT.
WE JUST WANT TO HELP.
OKAY...
ON THE EIGHTH DAY... COFFEE.
PROPERTY of FREETOWN FIRST CHURCH
A FEW DAYS AGO, I STARTED GETTIN' THESE WEIRD FEELINGS... IN MY STOMACH.
SORTA LIKE SOMETHING WAS IN THERE.
I DUNNO. I SOUND WEIRD...
NO, NO. YOU'RE DOING FINE. GO ON.
I THOUGHT IT WAS, LIKE, SOMETHIN' I ATE... BUT IT JUST GOT WORSE.
THAT'S WHEN I STARTED HEARING THIS VOICE IN MY HEAD, TELLING ME THINGS. BAD THINGS.
CAN YOU SHARE THEM WITH US?
ONE TIME... ONE TIME IT TOLD ME TO SHOVE A SCREWDRIVER INTO MY MOM'S EAR WHILE SHE WAS SLEEPING.
STUFF LIKE THAT.

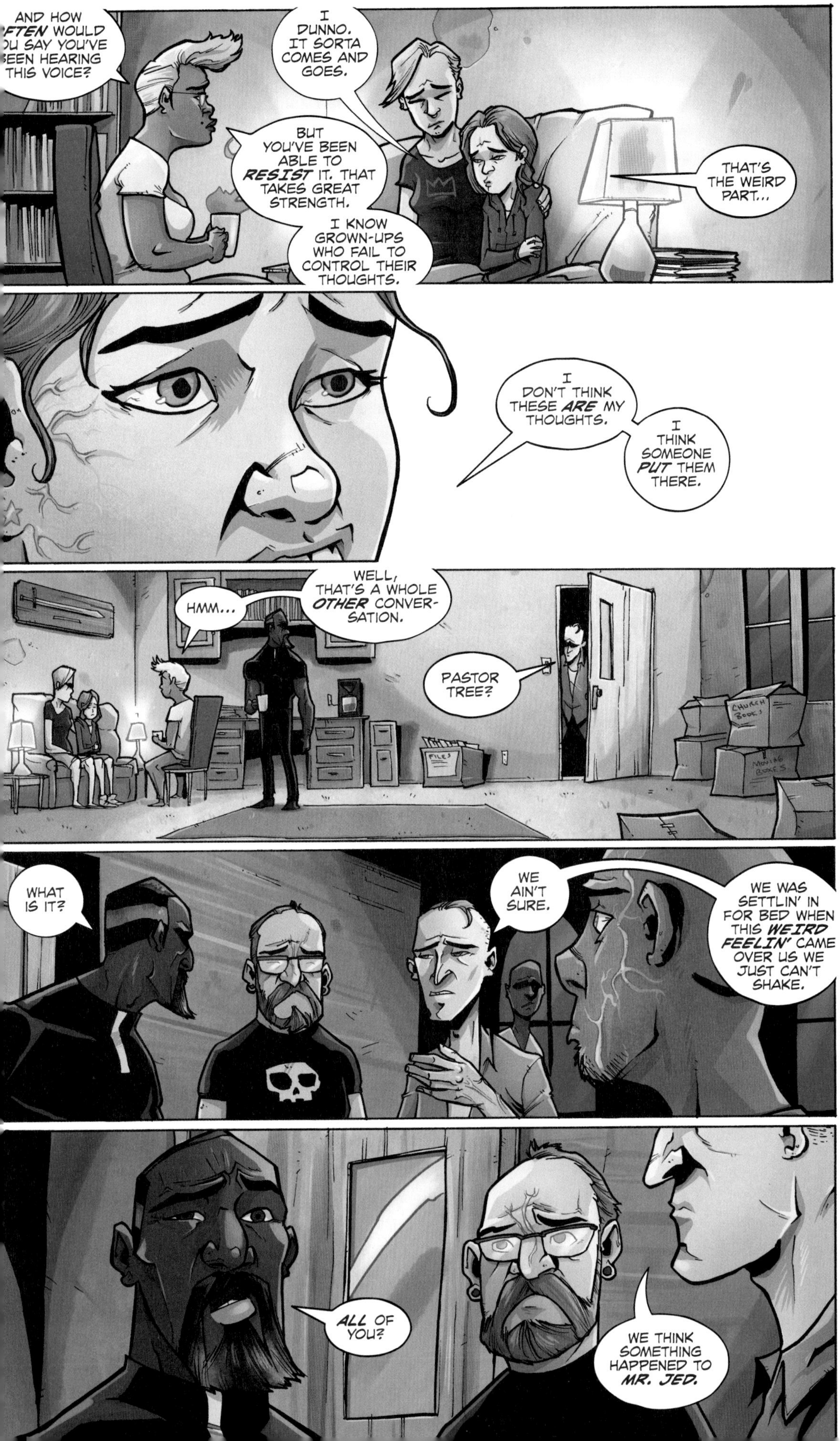
AND HOW OFTEN WOULD YOU SAY YOU'VE BEEN HEARING THIS VOICE?
I DUNNO. IT SORTA COMES AND GOES.
BUT YOU'VE BEEN ABLE TO RESIST IT. THAT TAKES GREAT STRENGTH.
I KNOW GROWN-UPS WHO FAIL TO CONTROL THEIR THOUGHTS.
THAT'S THE WEIRD PART...
I DON'T THINK THESE ARE MY THOUGHTS.
I THINK SOMEONE PUT THEM THERE.
HMM...
WELL, THAT'S A WHOLE OTHER CONVERSATION.
PASTOR TREE?
CHURCH BOOKS
FILES
MOVING BOXES
WHAT IS IT?
WE AIN'T SURE.
WE WAS SETTLIN' IN FOR BED WHEN THIS WEIRD FEELIN' CAME OVER US WE JUST CAN'T SHAKE.
ALL OF YOU?
WE THINK SOMETHING HAPPENED TO MR. JED.

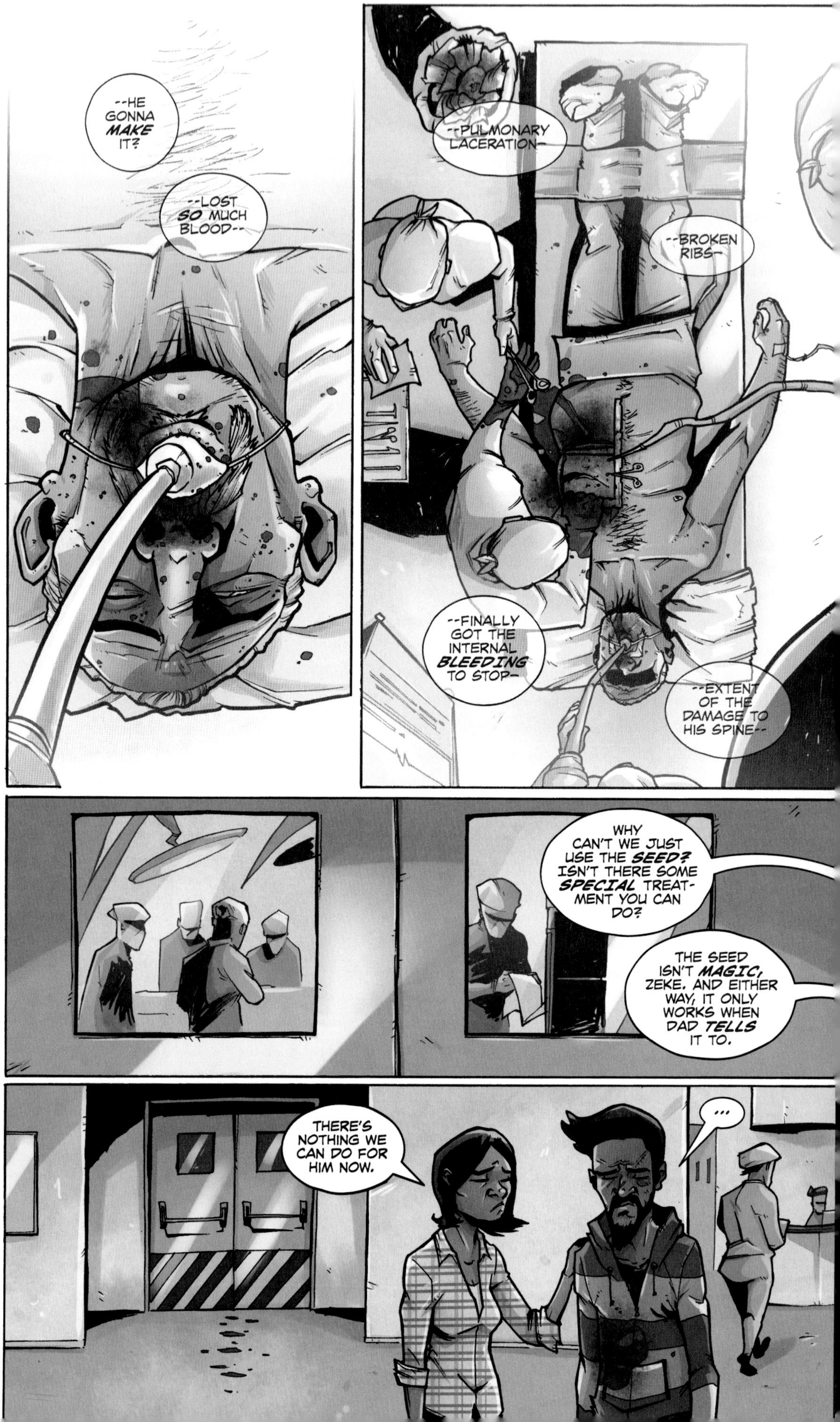

--HE GONNA MAKE IT?
--LOST SO MUCH BLOOD--
--PULMONARY LACERATION--
--BROKEN RIBS--
--FINALLY GOT THE INTERNAL BLEEDING TO STOP--
--EXTENT OF THE DAMAGE TO HIS SPINE--
WHY CAN'T WE JUST USE THE SEED? ISN'T THERE SOME SPECIAL TREAT-MENT YOU CAN DO?
THE SEED ISN'T MAGIC, ZEKE. AND EITHER WAY, IT ONLY WORKS WHEN DAD TELLS IT TO.
THERE'S NOTHING WE CAN DO FOR HIM NOW.
...

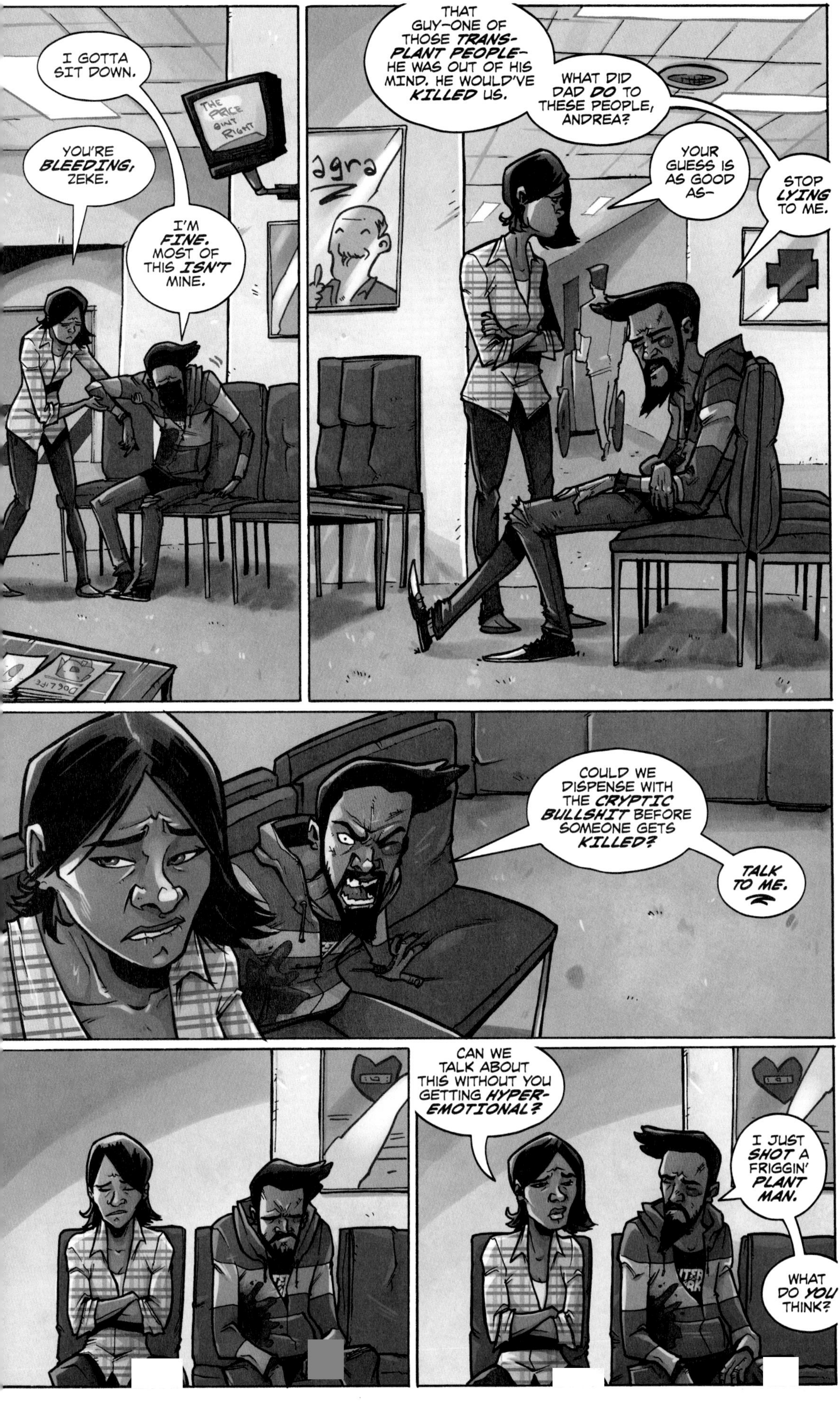
I GOTTA SIT DOWN.
YOU'RE *BLEEDING*, ZEKE.
I'M *FINE*. MOST OF THIS *ISN'T* MINE.
THAT GUY—ONE OF THOSE *TRANS-PLANT PEOPLE*—HE WAS OUT OF HIS MIND. HE WOULD'VE *KILLED* US.
WHAT DID DAD *DO* TO THESE PEOPLE, ANDREA?
YOUR GUESS IS AS GOOD AS—
STOP *LYING* TO ME.
COULD WE DISPENSE WITH THE *CRYPTIC BULLSHIT* BEFORE SOMEONE GETS *KILLED?*
TALK TO ME.
CAN WE TALK ABOUT THIS WITHOUT YOU GETTING *HYPER-EMOTIONAL?*
I JUST *SHOT* A FRIGGIN' *PLANT MAN.*
WHAT DO *YOU* THINK?

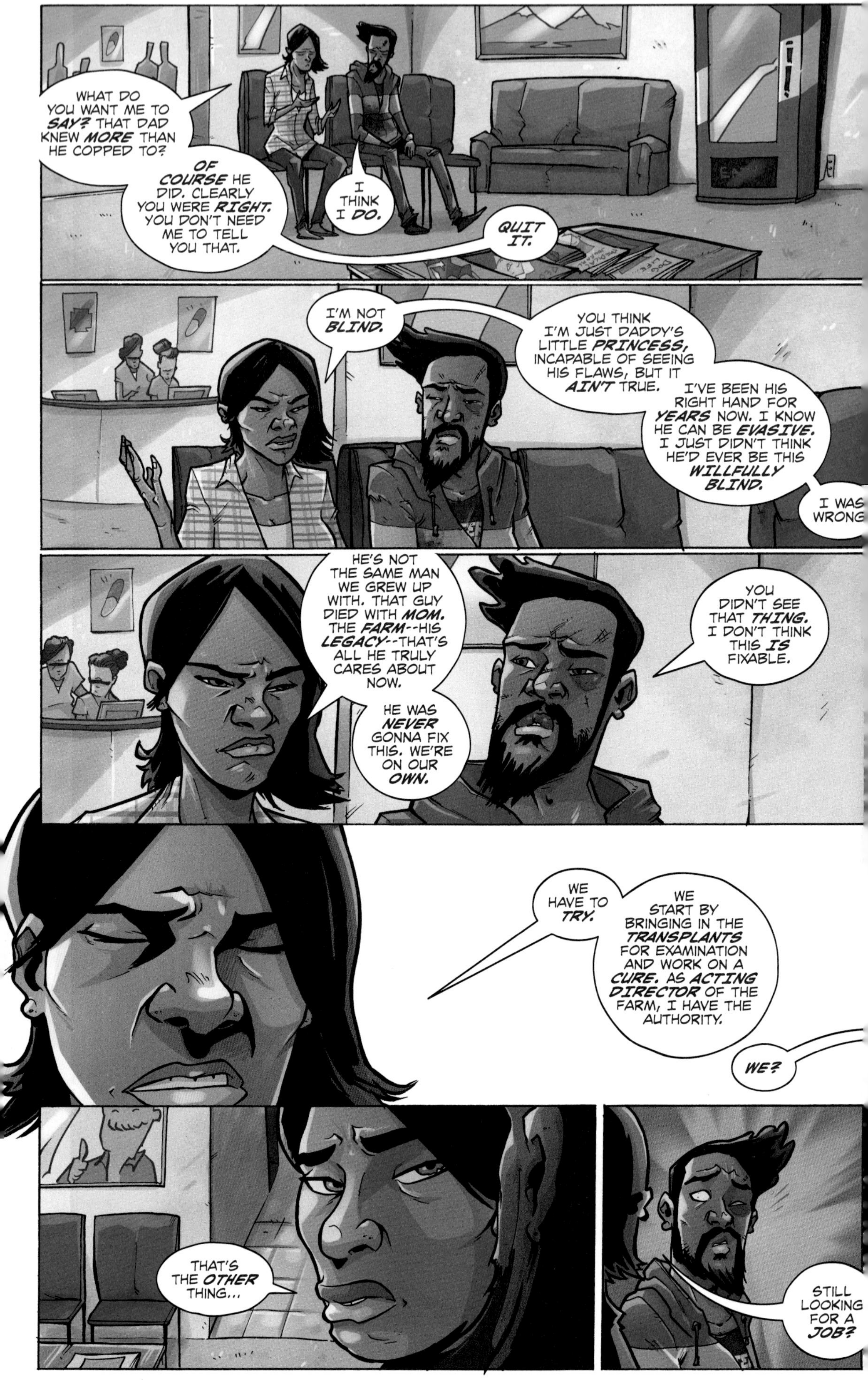

WHAT DO YOU WANT ME TO SAY? THAT DAD KNEW MORE THAN HE COPPED TO?
OF COURSE HE DID. CLEARLY YOU WERE RIGHT. YOU DON'T NEED ME TO TELL YOU THAT.
I THINK I DO.
QUIT IT.
DOG LIFE
I'M NOT BLIND.
YOU THINK I'M JUST DADDY'S LITTLE PRINCESS, INCAPABLE OF SEEING HIS FLAWS, BUT IT AIN'T TRUE.
I'VE BEEN HIS RIGHT HAND FOR YEARS NOW. I KNOW HE CAN BE EVASIVE. I JUST DIDN'T THINK HE'D EVER BE THIS WILLFULLY BLIND.
I WAS WRONG
HE'S NOT THE SAME MAN WE GREW UP WITH. THAT GUY DIED WITH MOM. THE FARM--HIS LEGACY--THAT'S ALL HE TRULY CARES ABOUT NOW.
HE WAS NEVER GONNA FIX THIS. WE'RE ON OUR OWN.
YOU DIDN'T SEE THAT THING. I DON'T THINK THIS IS FIXABLE.
WE HAVE TO TRY.
WE START BY BRINGING IN THE TRANSPLANTS FOR EXAMINATION AND WORK ON A CURE. AS ACTING DIRECTOR OF THE FARM, I HAVE THE AUTHORITY.
WE?
THAT'S THE OTHER THING...
STILL LOOKING FOR A JOB?

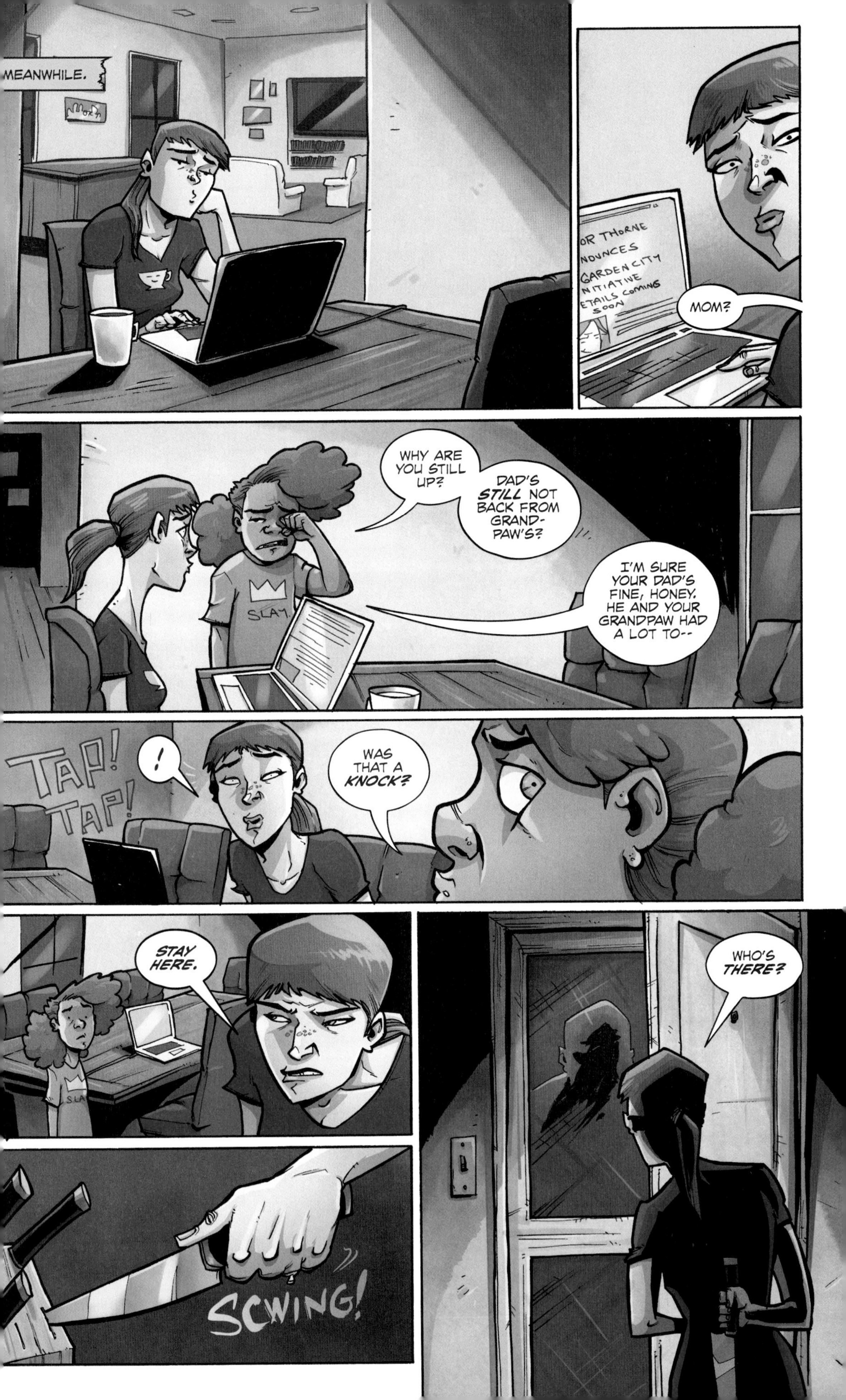
MEANWHILE.
OR THORNE
NOUNCES
GARDEN CITY
NITIATIVE
ETAILS COMING
SOON
MOM?
WHY ARE YOU STILL UP?
DAD'S STILL NOT BACK FROM GRAND-PAW'S?
I'M SURE YOUR DAD'S FINE, HONEY. HE AND YOUR GRANDPAW HAD A LOT TO--
TAP! TAP!
!
WAS THAT A KNOCK?
STAY HERE.
SCWING!
WHO'S THERE?

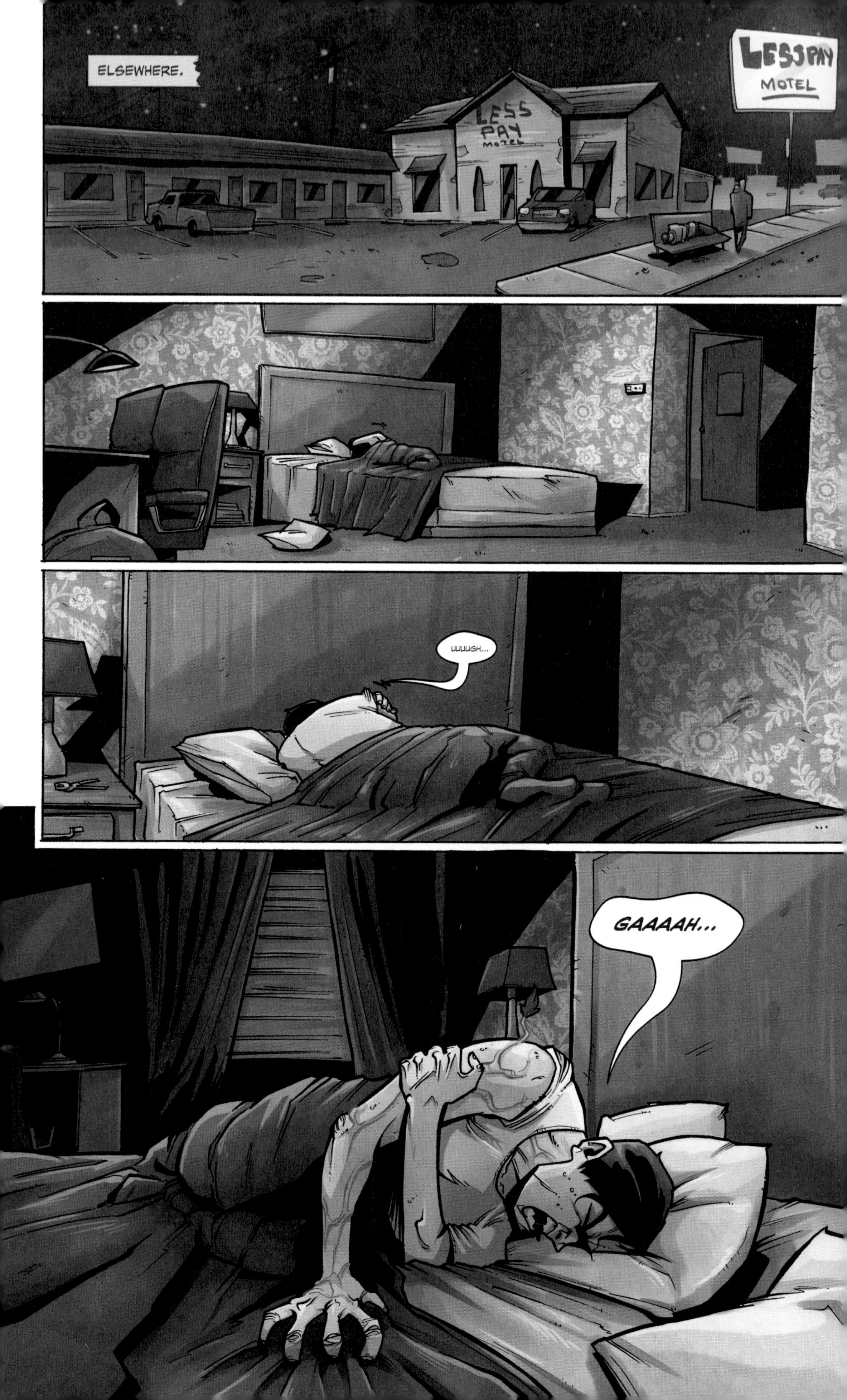
ELSEWHERE.
LESS PAY MOTEL
LESS PAY MOTEL
UUUUGH...
GAAAAH...

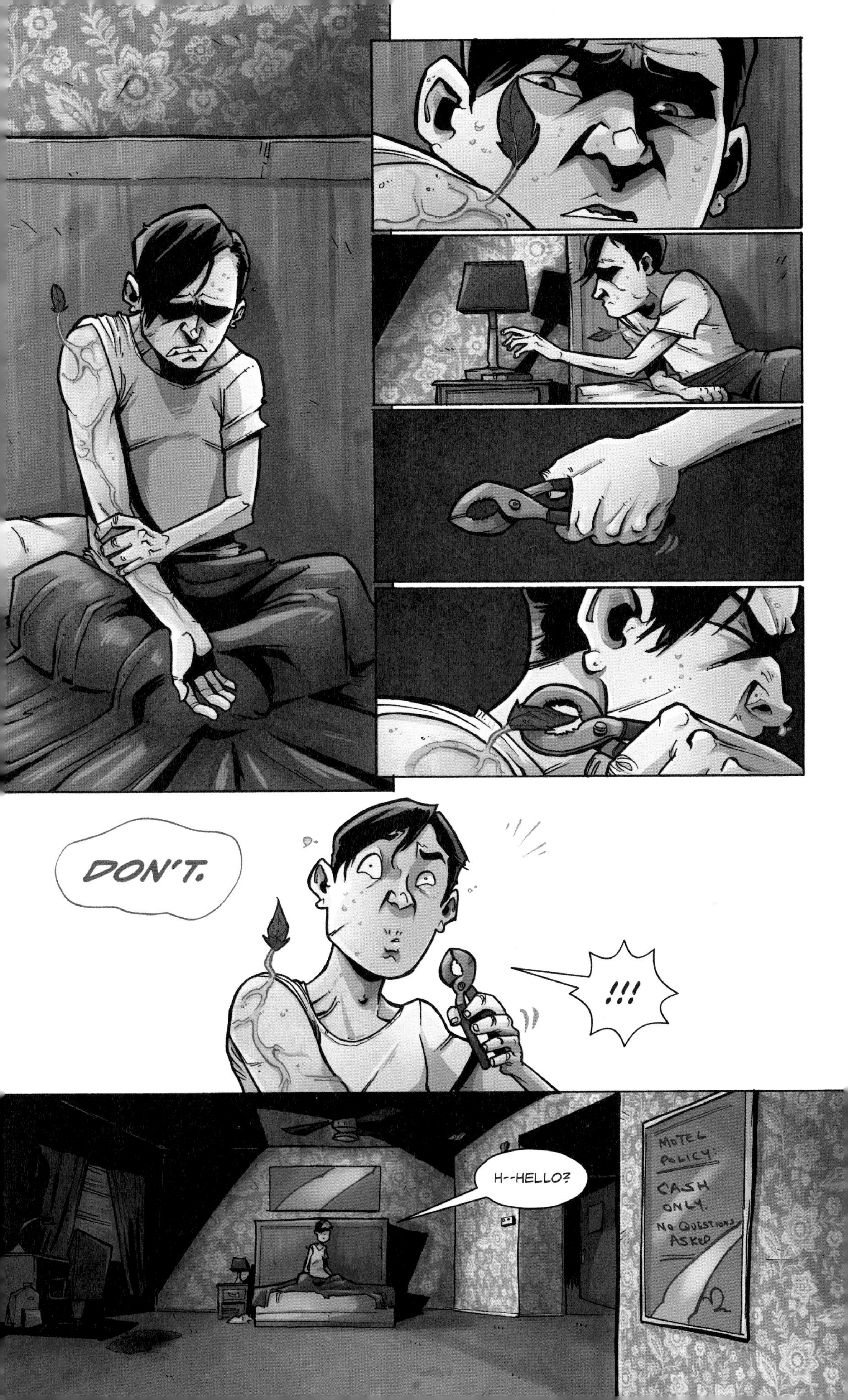
DON'T.
!!!
H--HELLO?
MOTEL POLICY:
CASH ONLY.
NO QUESTIONS ASKED

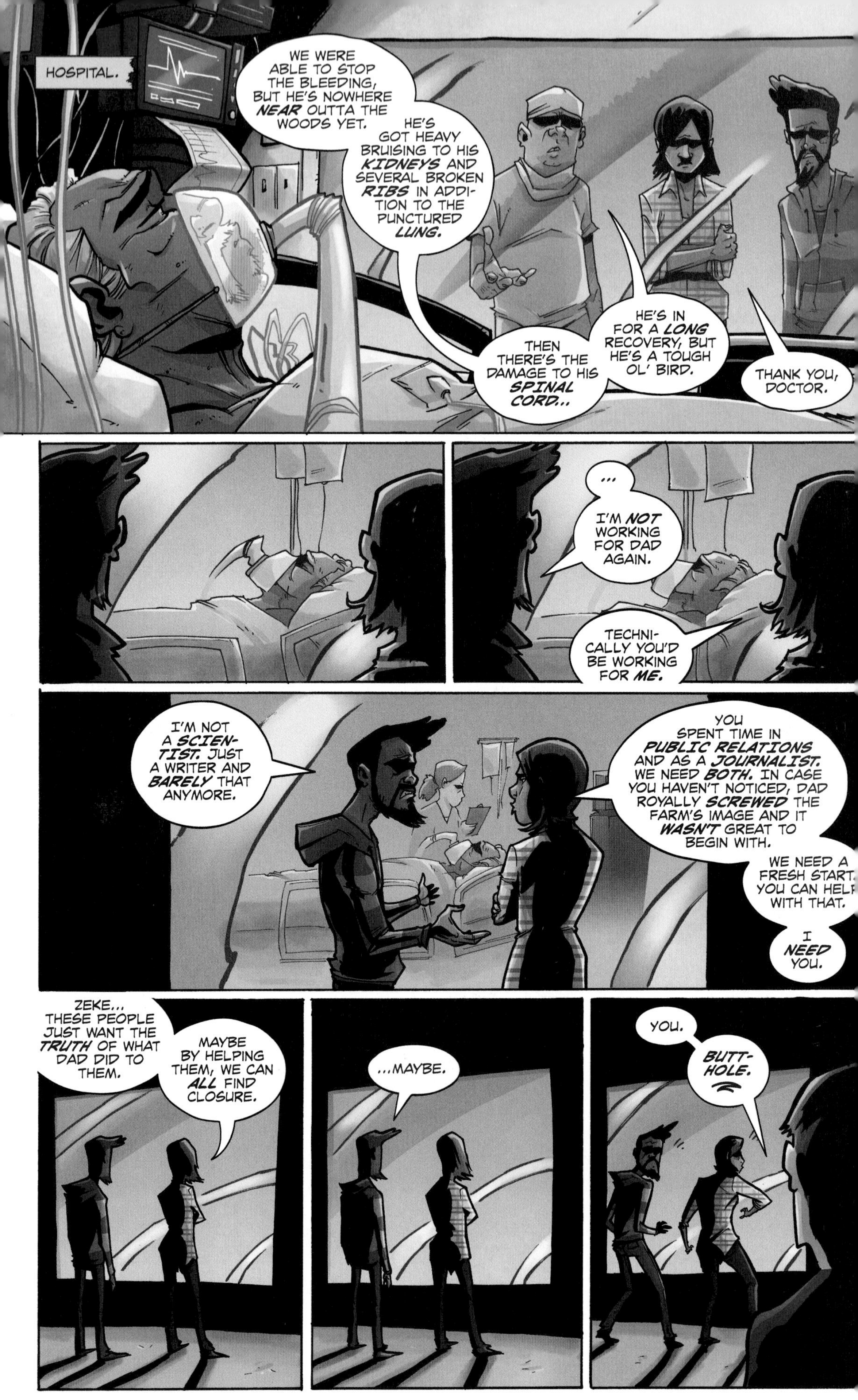
HOSPITAL.
WE WERE ABLE TO STOP THE BLEEDING, BUT HE'S NOWHERE NEAR OUTTA THE WOODS YET.
HE'S GOT HEAVY BRUISING TO HIS KIDNEYS AND SEVERAL BROKEN RIBS IN ADDITION TO THE PUNCTURED LUNG.
THEN THERE'S THE DAMAGE TO HIS SPINAL CORD...
HE'S IN FOR A LONG RECOVERY, BUT HE'S A TOUGH OL' BIRD.
THANK YOU, DOCTOR.
...
I'M NOT WORKING FOR DAD AGAIN.
TECHNICALLY YOU'D BE WORKING FOR ME.
I'M NOT A SCIENTIST. JUST A WRITER AND BARELY THAT ANYMORE.
YOU SPENT TIME IN PUBLIC RELATIONS AND AS A JOURNALIST. WE NEED BOTH. IN CASE YOU HAVEN'T NOTICED, DAD ROYALLY SCREWED THE FARM'S IMAGE AND IT WASN'T GREAT TO BEGIN WITH.
WE NEED A FRESH START. YOU CAN HELP WITH THAT.
I NEED YOU.
ZEKE... THESE PEOPLE JUST WANT THE TRUTH OF WHAT DAD DID TO THEM.
MAYBE BY HELPING THEM, WE CAN ALL FIND CLOSURE.
...MAYBE.
YOU.
BUTT-HOLE.

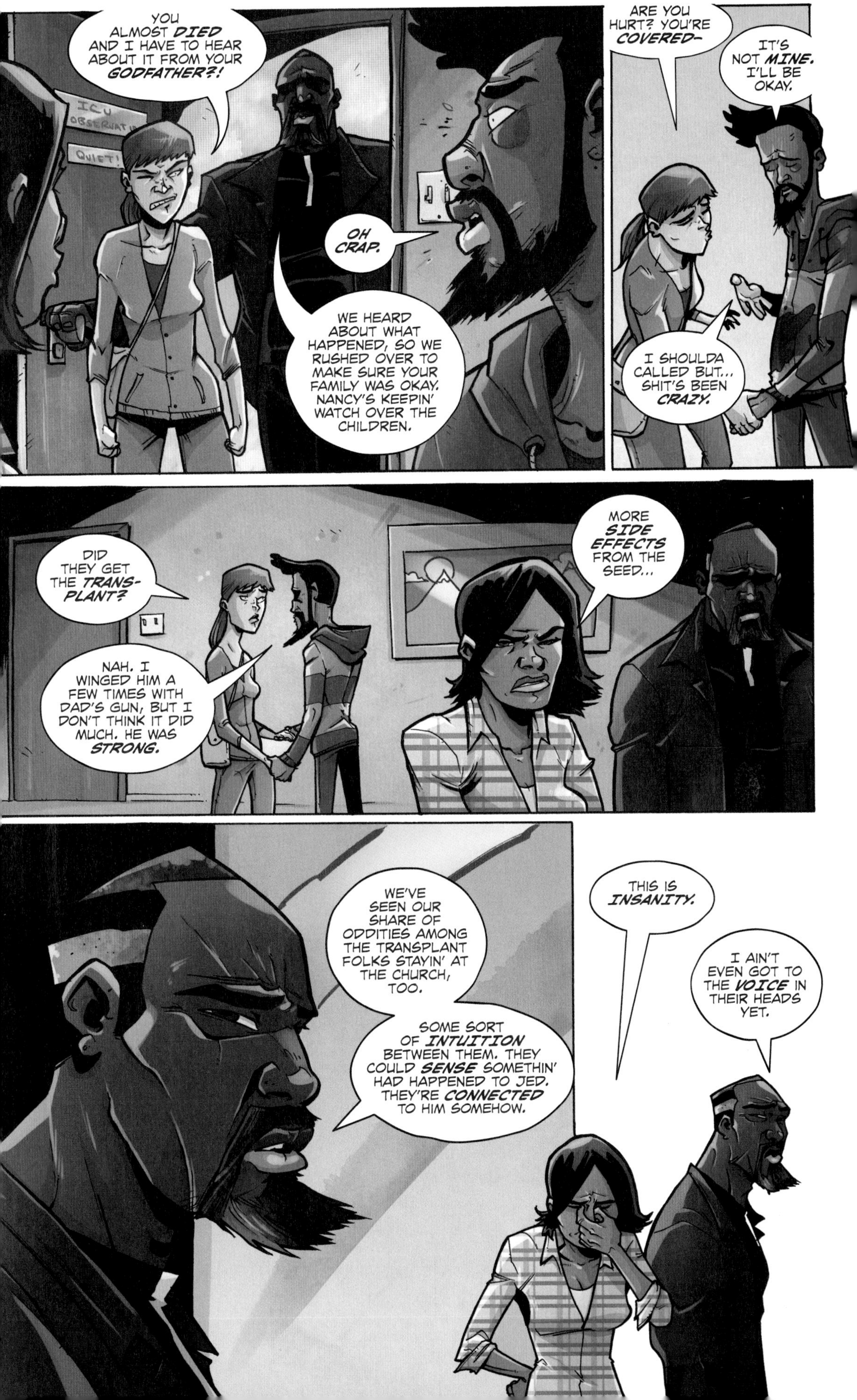
YOU ALMOST DIED AND I HAVE TO HEAR ABOUT IT FROM YOUR GODFATHER?!
ICU OBSERVATI
QUIET!
OH CRAP.
WE HEARD ABOUT WHAT HAPPENED, SO WE RUSHED OVER TO MAKE SURE YOUR FAMILY WAS OKAY. NANCY'S KEEPIN' WATCH OVER THE CHILDREN.
ARE YOU HURT? YOU'RE COVERED–
IT'S NOT MINE. I'LL BE OKAY.
I SHOULDA CALLED BUT... SHIT'S BEEN CRAZY.
DID THEY GET THE TRANS-PLANT?
NAH. I WINGED HIM A FEW TIMES WITH DAD'S GUN, BUT I DON'T THINK IT DID MUCH. HE WAS STRONG.
MORE SIDE EFFECTS FROM THE SEED...
WE'VE SEEN OUR SHARE OF ODDITIES AMONG THE TRANSPLANT FOLKS STAYIN' AT THE CHURCH, TOO.
SOME SORT OF INTUITION BETWEEN THEM. THEY COULD SENSE SOMETHIN' HAD HAPPENED TO JED. THEY'RE CONNECTED TO HIM SOMEHOW.
THIS IS INSANITY.
I AIN'T EVEN GOT TO THE VOICE IN THEIR HEADS YET.

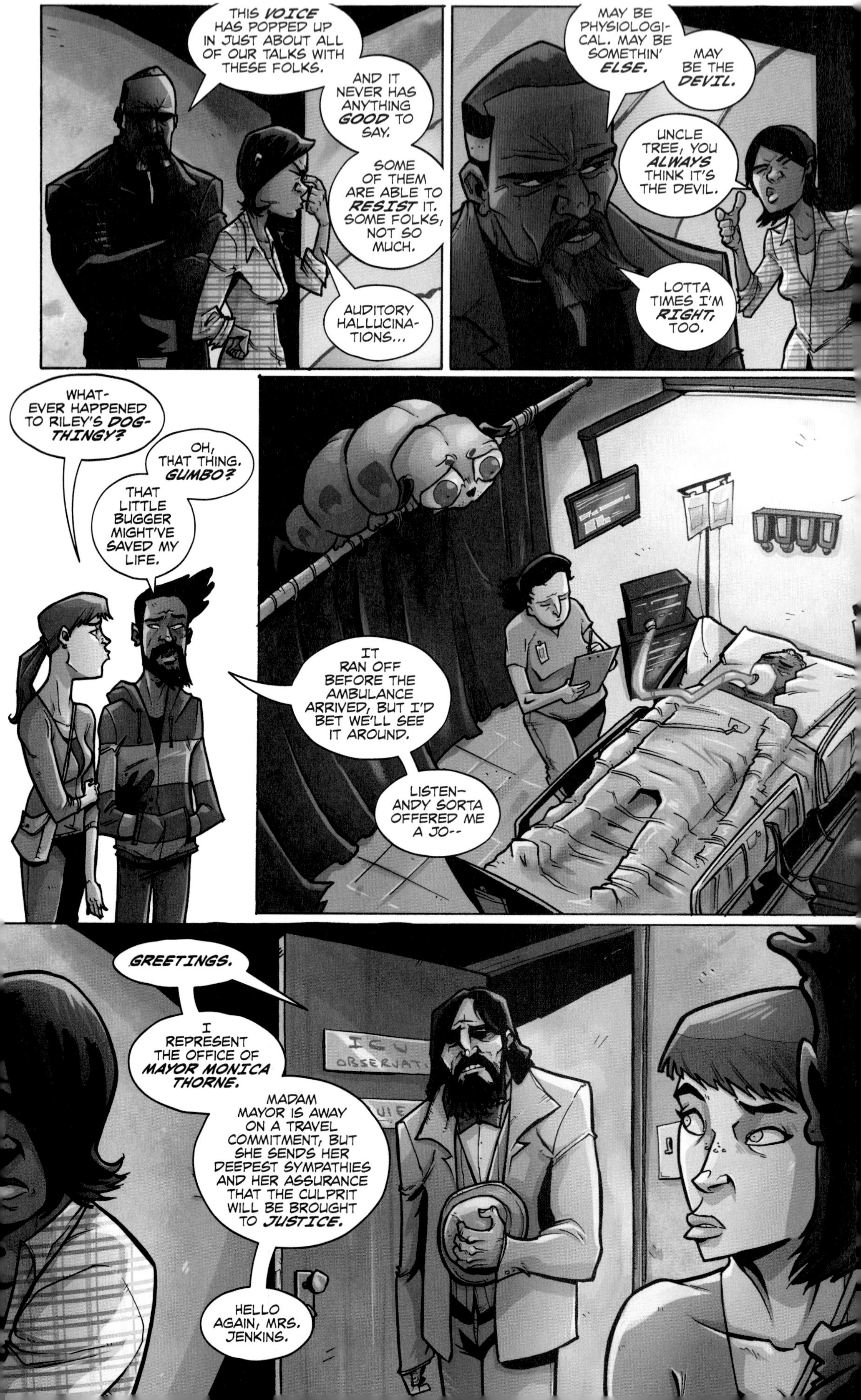
THIS VOICE HAS POPPED UP IN JUST ABOUT ALL OF OUR TALKS WITH THESE FOLKS.
AND IT NEVER HAS ANYTHING GOOD TO SAY.
SOME OF THEM ARE ABLE TO RESIST IT. SOME FOLKS, NOT SO MUCH.
AUDITORY HALLUCINA-TIONS...
MAY BE PHYSIOLOGI-CAL. MAY BE SOMETHIN' ELSE.
MAY BE THE DEVIL.
UNCLE TREE, YOU ALWAYS THINK IT'S THE DEVIL.
LOTTA TIMES I'M RIGHT, TOO.
WHAT-EVER HAPPENED TO RILEY'S DOG-THINGY?
OH, THAT THING. GUMBO?
THAT LITTLE BUGGER MIGHT'VE SAVED MY LIFE.
IT RAN OFF BEFORE THE AMBULANCE ARRIVED, BUT I'D BET WE'LL SEE IT AROUND.
LISTEN-ANDY SORTA OFFERED ME A JO--
GREETINGS.
I REPRESENT THE OFFICE OF MAYOR MONICA THORNE.
MADAM MAYOR IS AWAY ON A TRAVEL COMMITMENT, BUT SHE SENDS HER DEEPEST SYMPATHIES AND HER ASSURANCE THAT THE CULPRIT WILL BE BROUGHT TO JUSTICE.
HELLO AGAIN, MRS. JENKINS.

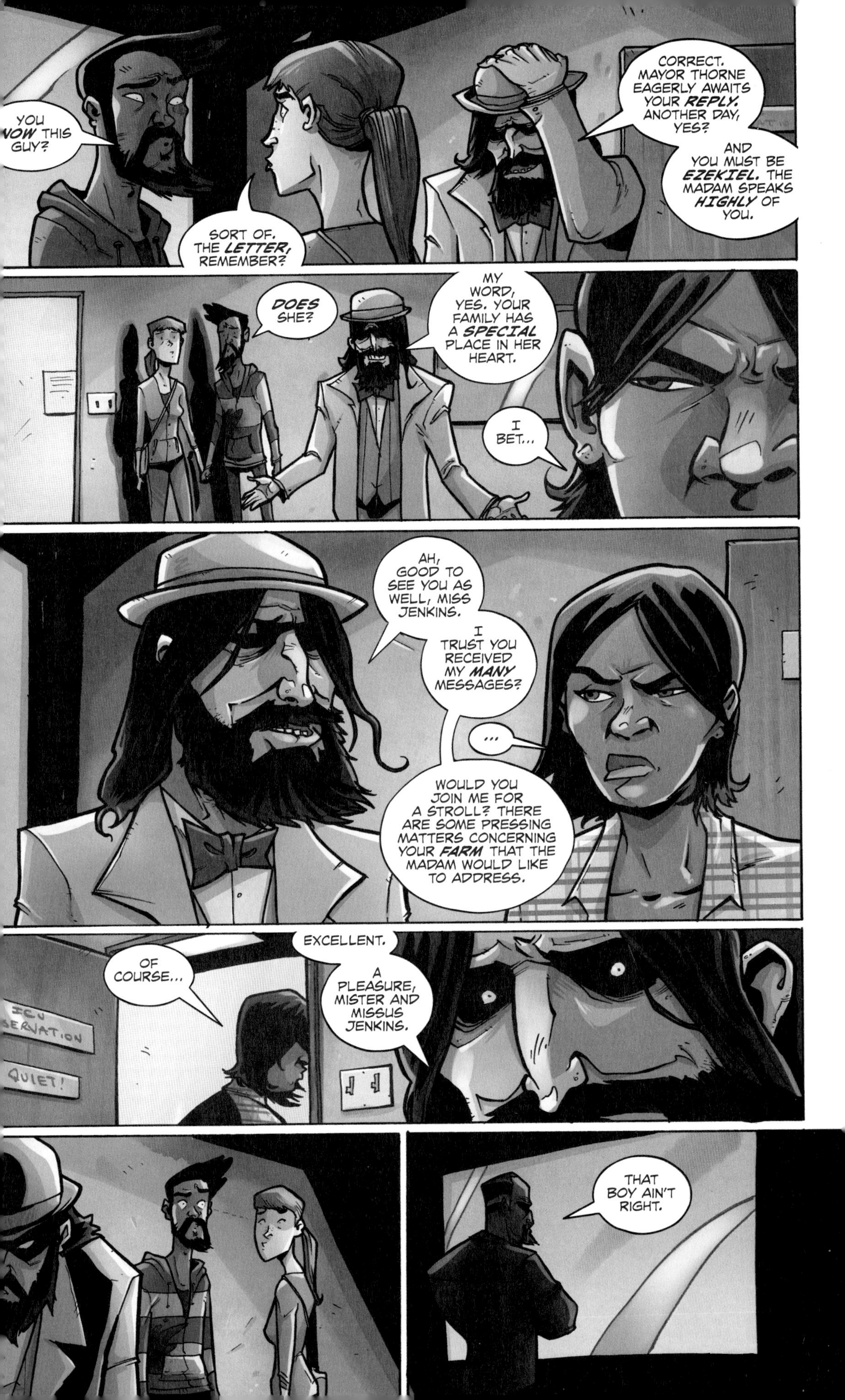
YOU NOW THIS GUY?
SORT OF. THE LETTER, REMEMBER?
CORRECT. MAYOR THORNE EAGERLY AWAITS YOUR REPLY. ANOTHER DAY, YES?
AND YOU MUST BE EZEKIEL. THE MADAM SPEAKS HIGHLY OF YOU.
DOES SHE?
MY WORD, YES. YOUR FAMILY HAS A SPECIAL PLACE IN HER HEART.
I BET...
AH, GOOD TO SEE YOU AS WELL, MISS JENKINS.
I TRUST YOU RECEIVED MY MANY MESSAGES?
...
WOULD YOU JOIN ME FOR A STROLL? THERE ARE SOME PRESSING MATTERS CONCERNING YOUR FARM THAT THE MADAM WOULD LIKE TO ADDRESS.
OF COURSE...
EXCELLENT.
A PLEASURE, MISTER AND MISSUS JENKINS.
QUIET!
THAT BOY AIN'T RIGHT.

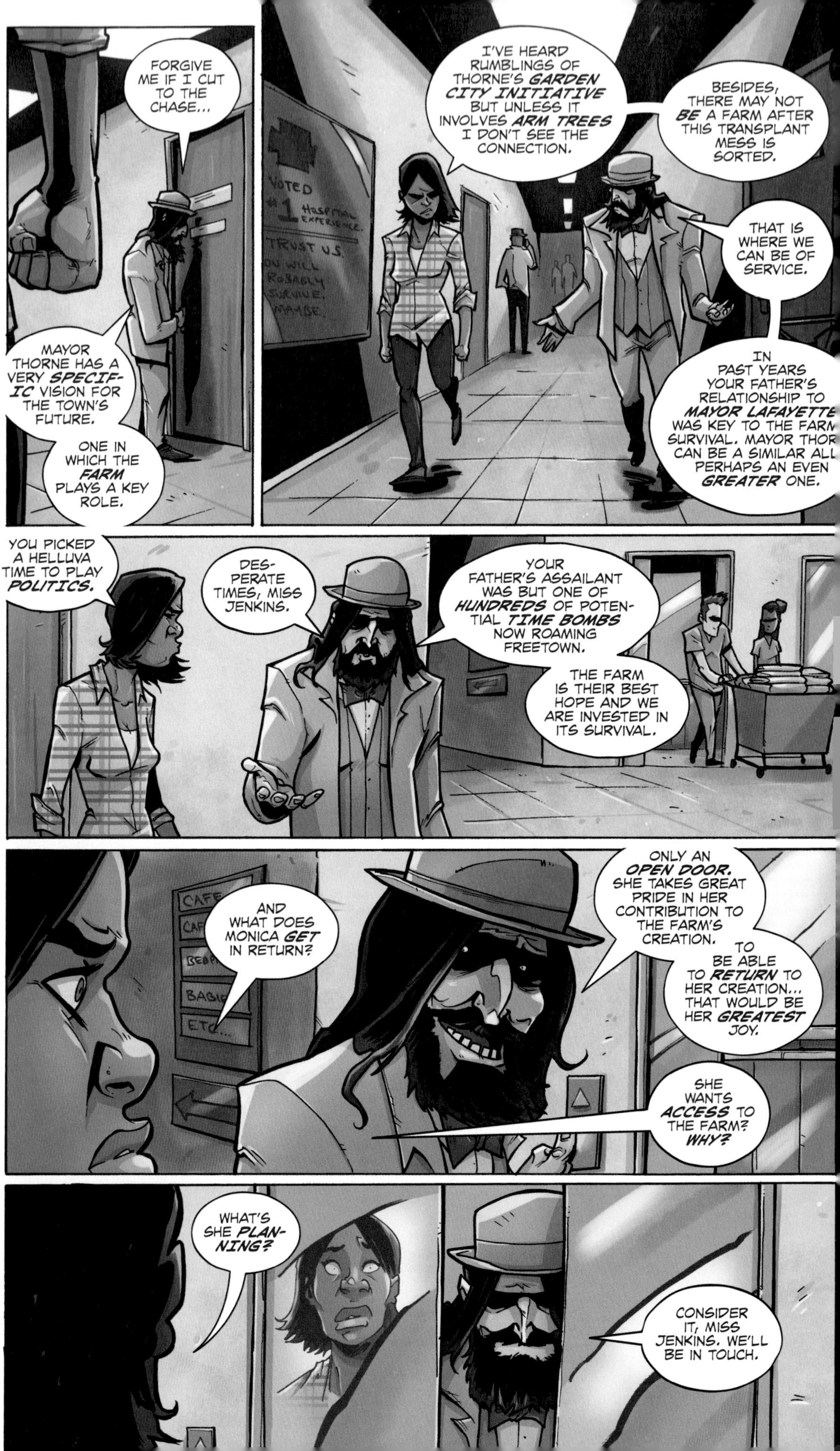
FORGIVE ME IF I CUT TO THE CHASE...
MAYOR THORNE HAS A VERY SPECIFIC VISION FOR THE TOWN'S FUTURE.
ONE IN WHICH THE FARM PLAYS A KEY ROLE.
VOTED #1 HOSPITAL EXPERIENCE.
TRUST US. YOU WILL PROBABLY SURVIVE. MAYBE.
I'VE HEARD RUMBLINGS OF THORNE'S GARDEN CITY INITIATIVE BUT UNLESS IT INVOLVES ARM TREES I DON'T SEE THE CONNECTION.
BESIDES, THERE MAY NOT BE A FARM AFTER THIS TRANSPLANT MESS IS SORTED.
THAT IS WHERE WE CAN BE OF SERVICE.
IN PAST YEARS YOUR FATHER'S RELATIONSHIP TO MAYOR LAFAYETTE WAS KEY TO THE FARM SURVIVAL. MAYOR THOR CAN BE A SIMILAR ALL PERHAPS AN EVEN GREATER ONE.
YOU PICKED A HELLUVA TIME TO PLAY POLITICS.
DESPERATE TIMES, MISS JENKINS.
YOUR FATHER'S ASSAILANT WAS BUT ONE OF HUNDREDS OF POTENTIAL TIME BOMBS NOW ROAMING FREETOWN.
THE FARM IS THEIR BEST HOPE AND WE ARE INVESTED IN ITS SURVIVAL.
AND WHAT DOES MONICA GET IN RETURN?
ONLY AN OPEN DOOR. SHE TAKES GREAT PRIDE IN HER CONTRIBUTION TO THE FARM'S CREATION.
TO BE ABLE TO RETURN TO HER CREATION... THAT WOULD BE HER GREATEST JOY.
SHE WANTS ACCESS TO THE FARM? WHY?
WHAT'S SHE PLANNING?
CONSIDER IT, MISS JENKINS. WE'LL BE IN TOUCH.

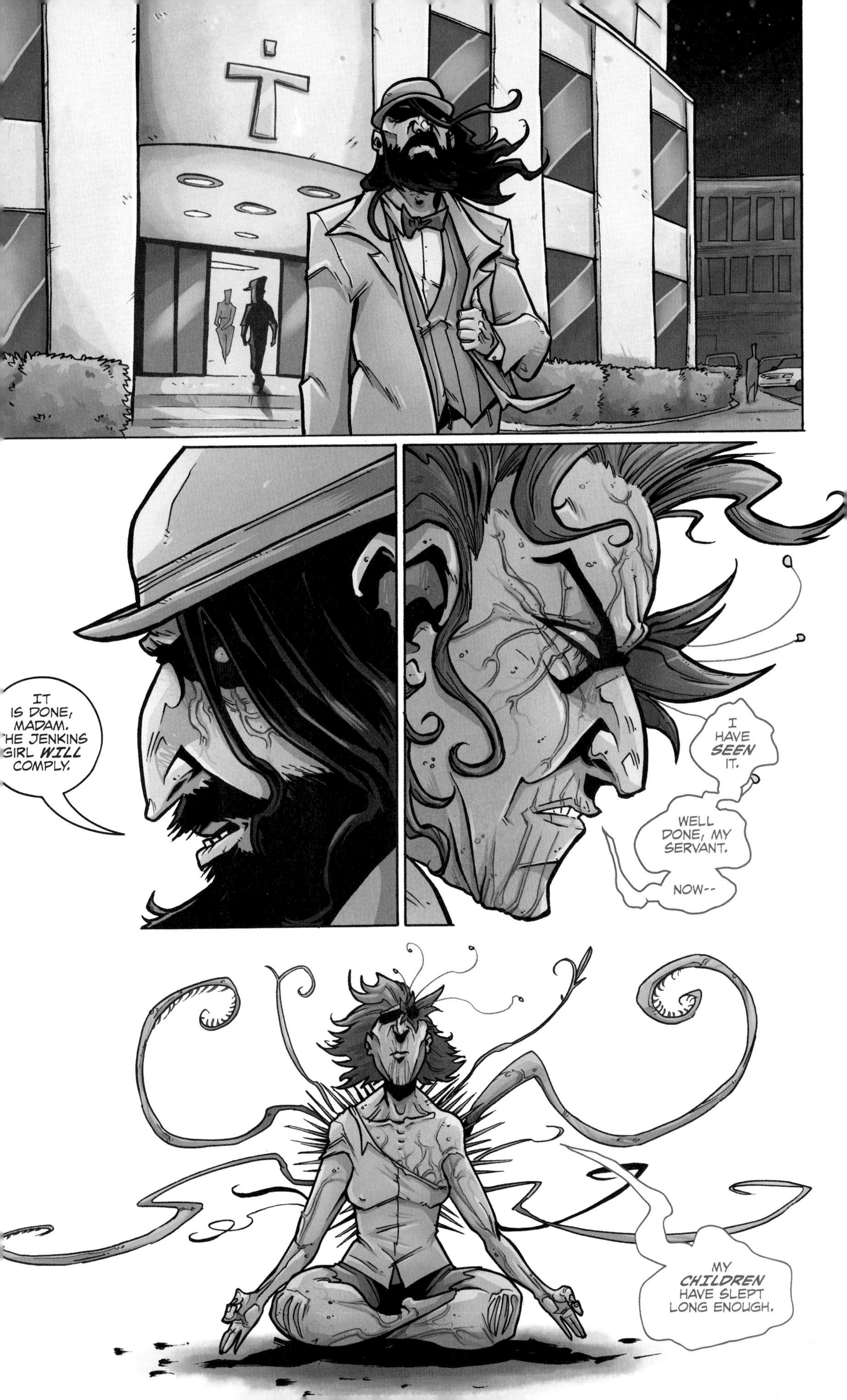

IT IS DONE, MADAM. THE JENKINS GIRL *WILL* COMPLY.
I HAVE *SEEN* IT.
WELL DONE, MY SERVANT.
NOW--
MY *CHILDREN* HAVE SLEPT LONG ENOUGH.

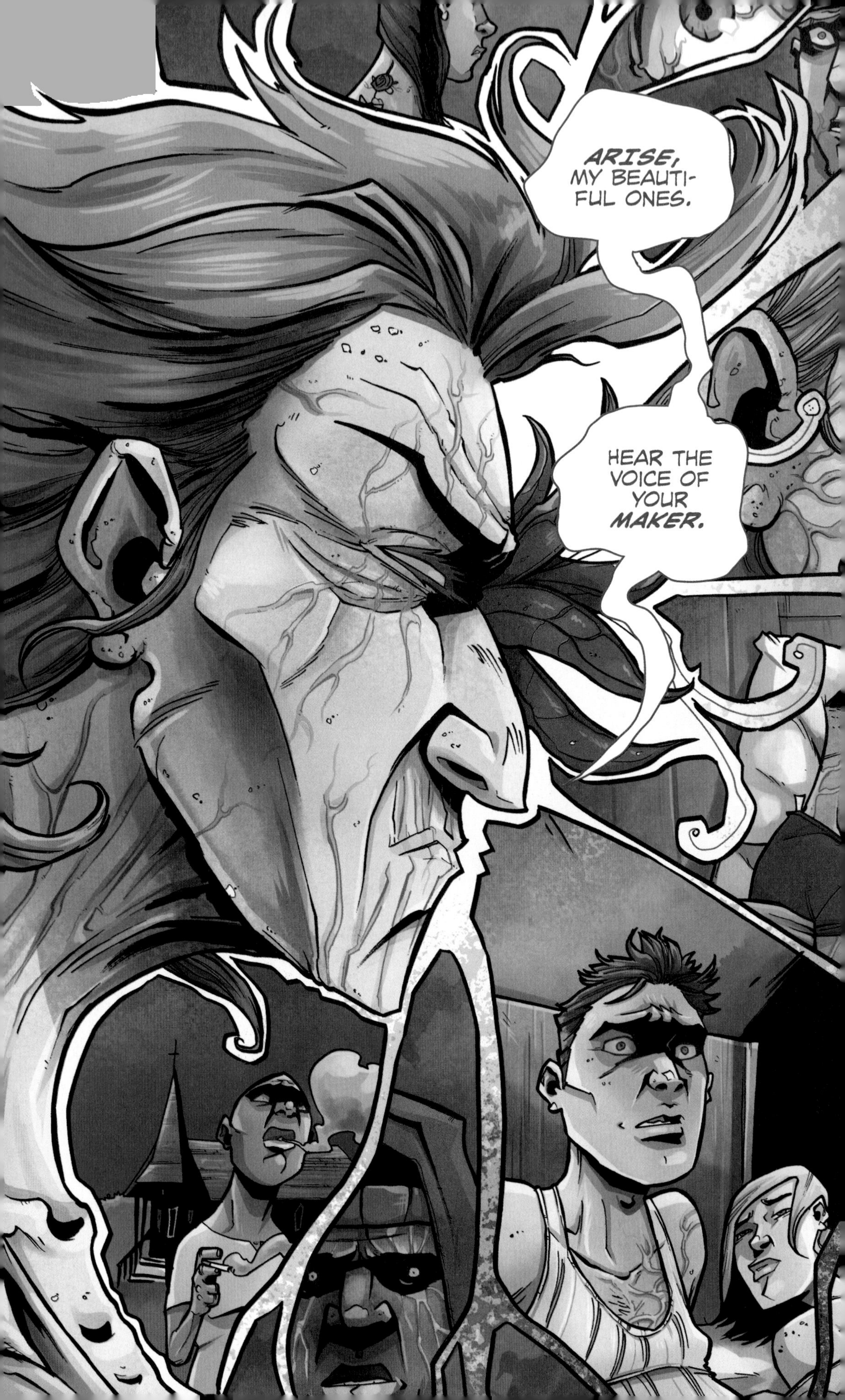
ARISE, MY BEAUTIFUL ONES.
HEAR THE VOICE OF YOUR MAKER.

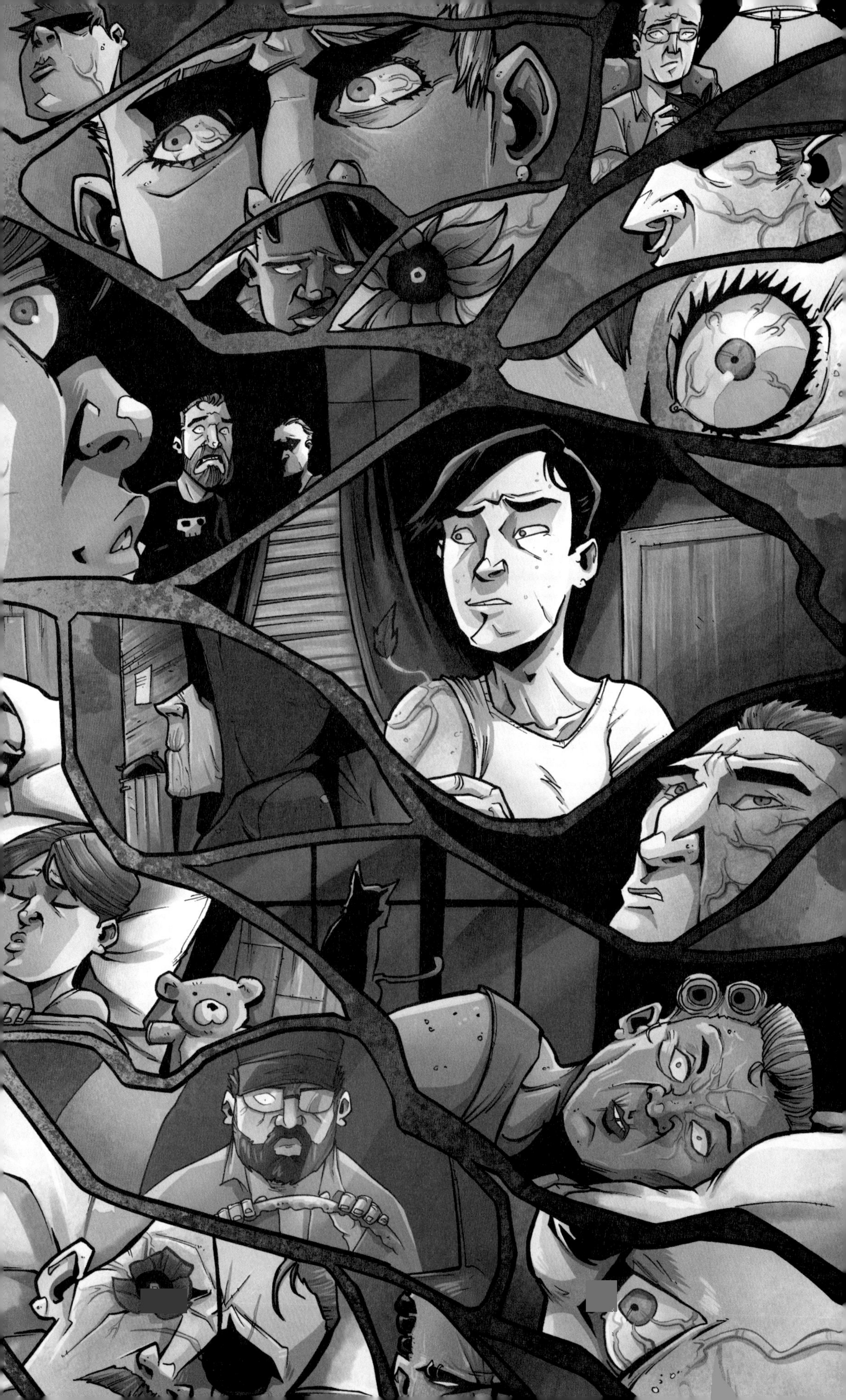

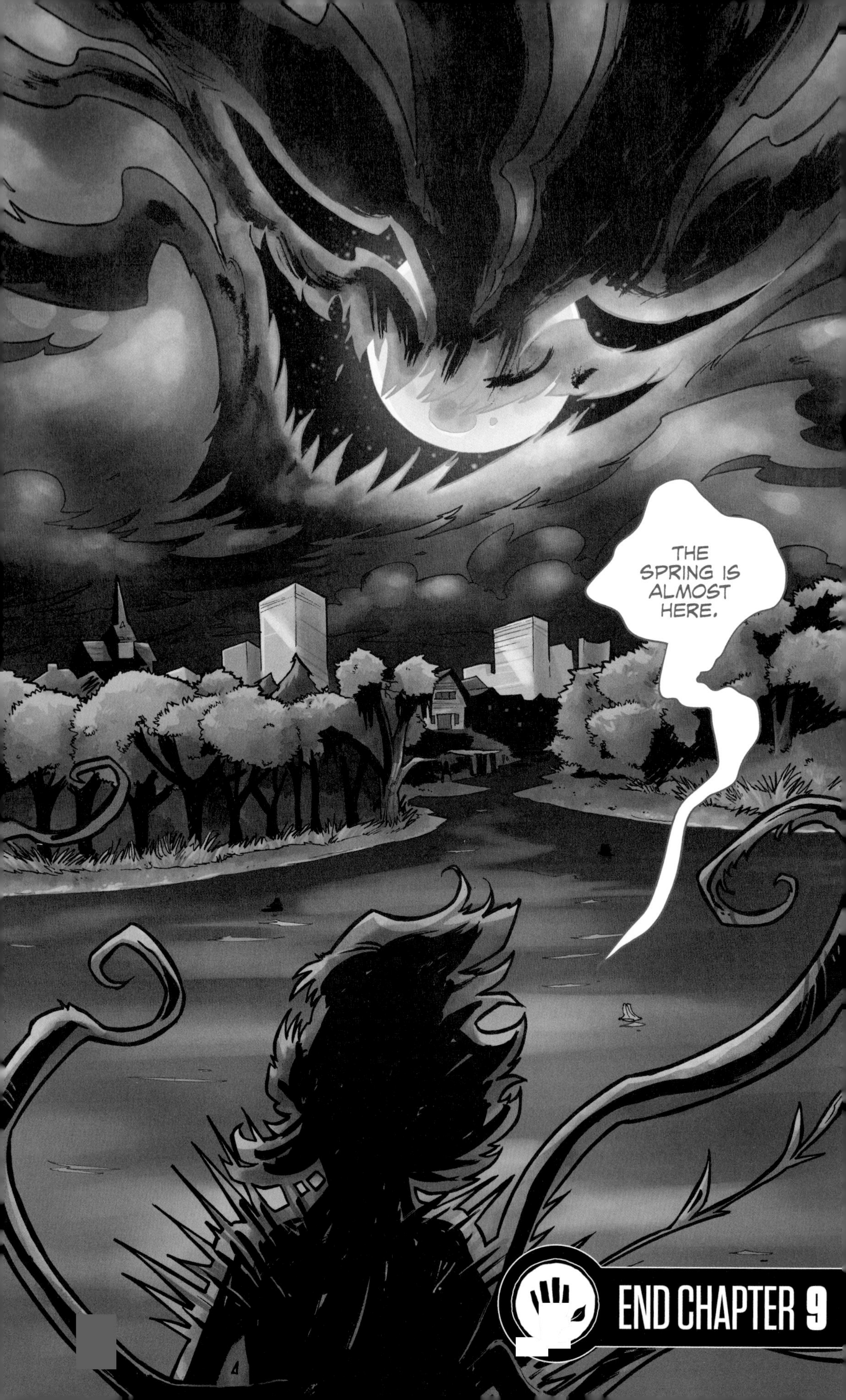
THE SPRING IS ALMOST HERE.
END CHAPTER 9

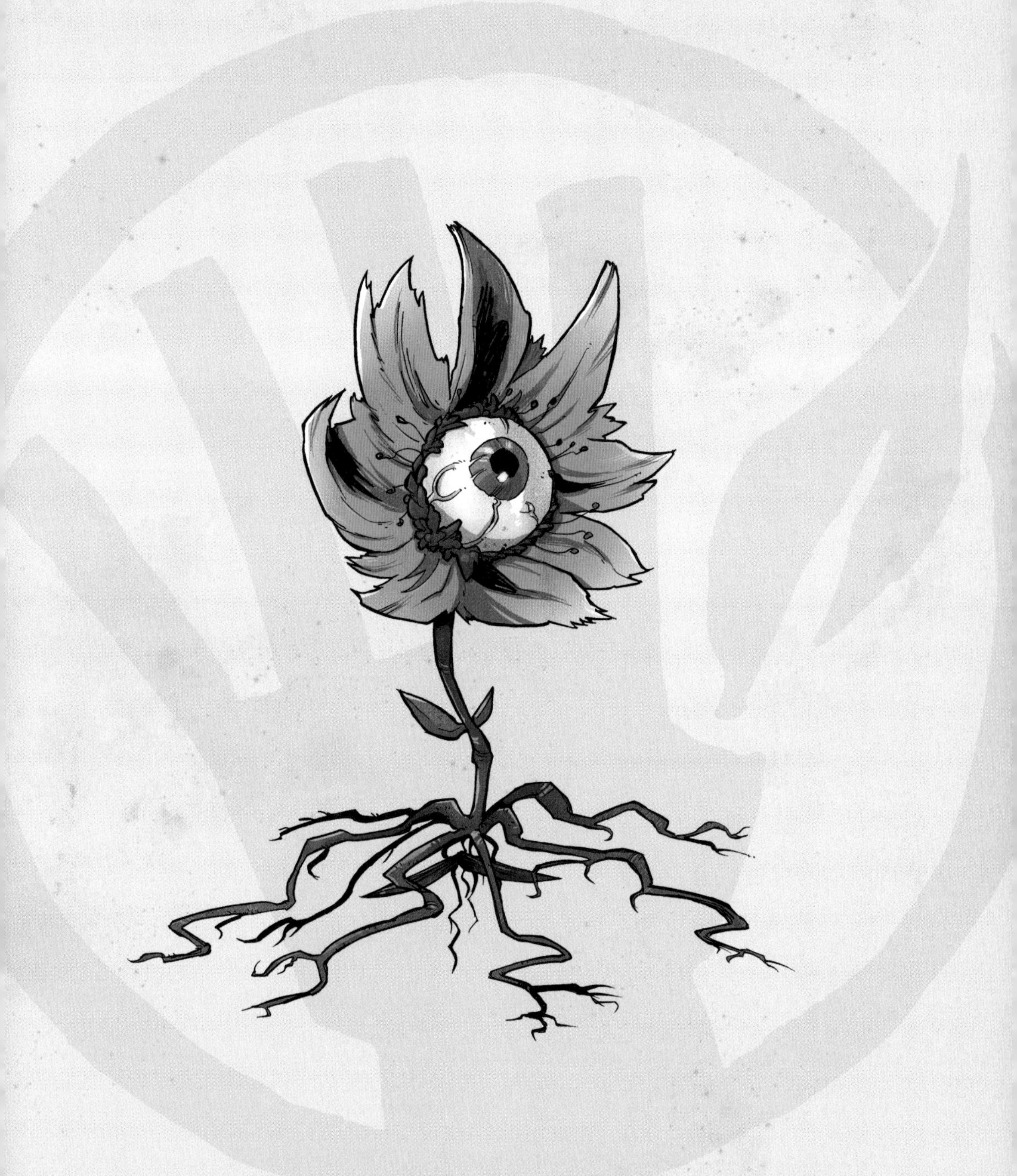

CHAPTER 10

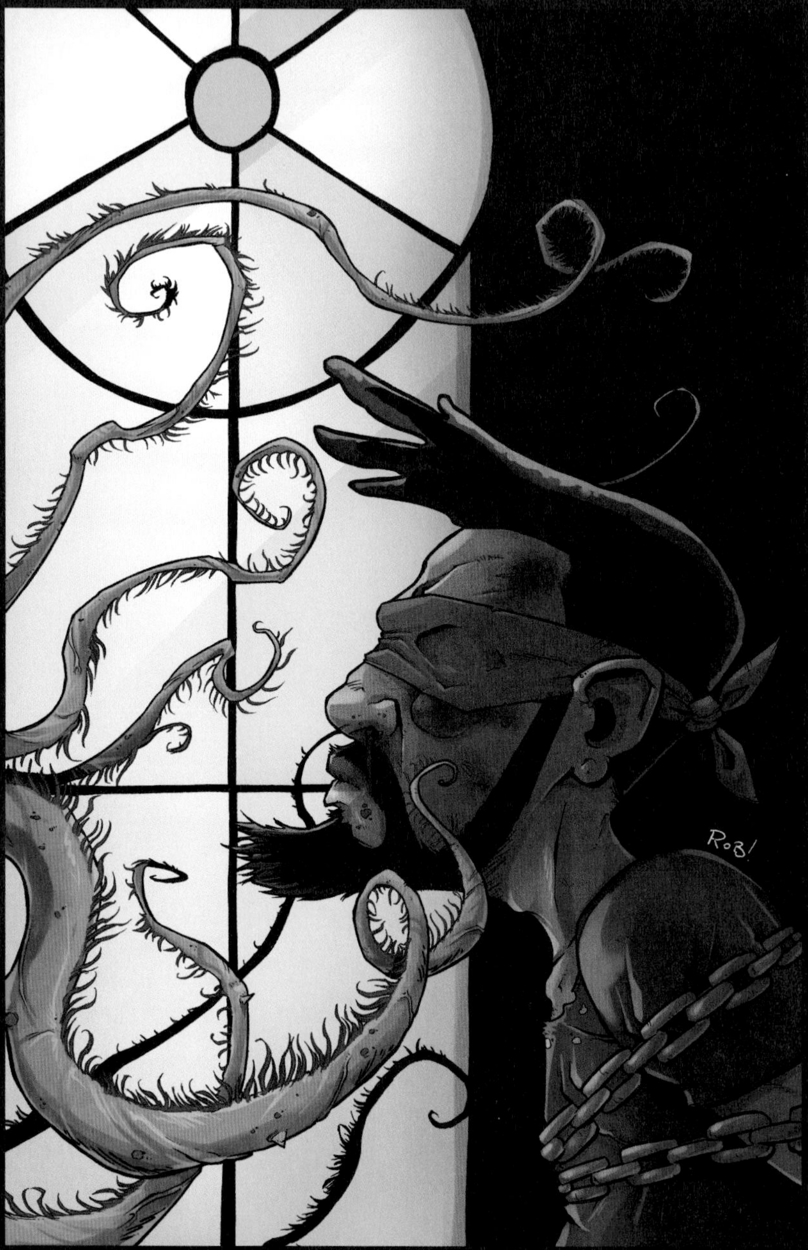
ROB!

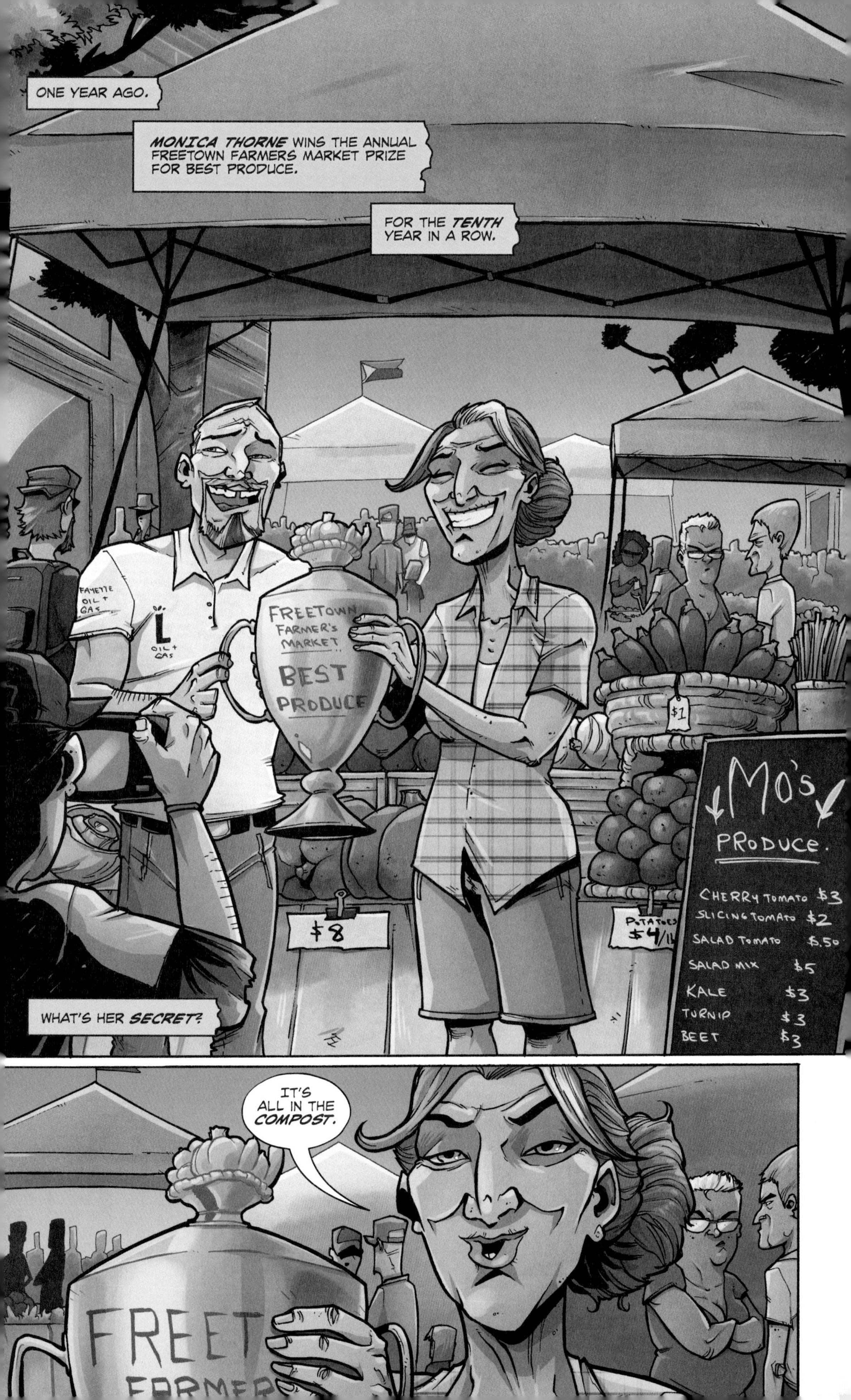

ONE YEAR AGO.
MONICA THORNE WINS THE ANNUAL FREETOWN FARMERS MARKET PRIZE FOR BEST PRODUCE.
FOR THE TENTH YEAR IN A ROW.
FAYETTE OIL + GAS
L OIL + GAS
FREETOWN FARMER'S MARKET BEST PRODUCE
$1
MO'S PRODUCE.
CHERRY TOMATO $3
SLICING TOMATO $2
SALAD TOMATO $.50
SALAD MIX $5
KALE $3
TURNIP $3
BEET $3
$8
POTATOES
WHAT'S HER SECRET?
IT'S ALL IN THE COMPOST.
FREET

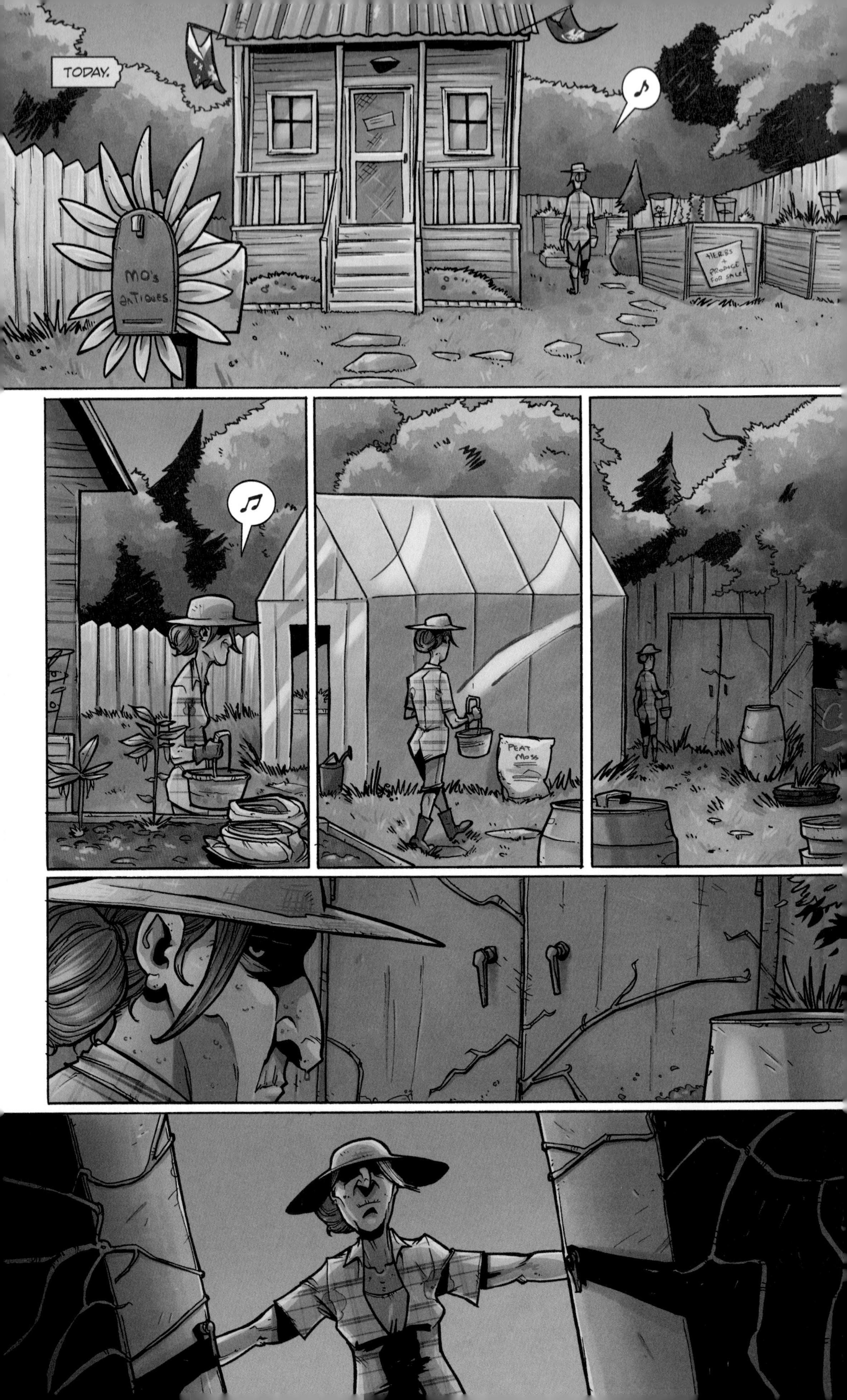
TODAY.
♪
MO's antiques.
HERBS + PRODUCE FOR SALE!
♫
PEAT MOSS

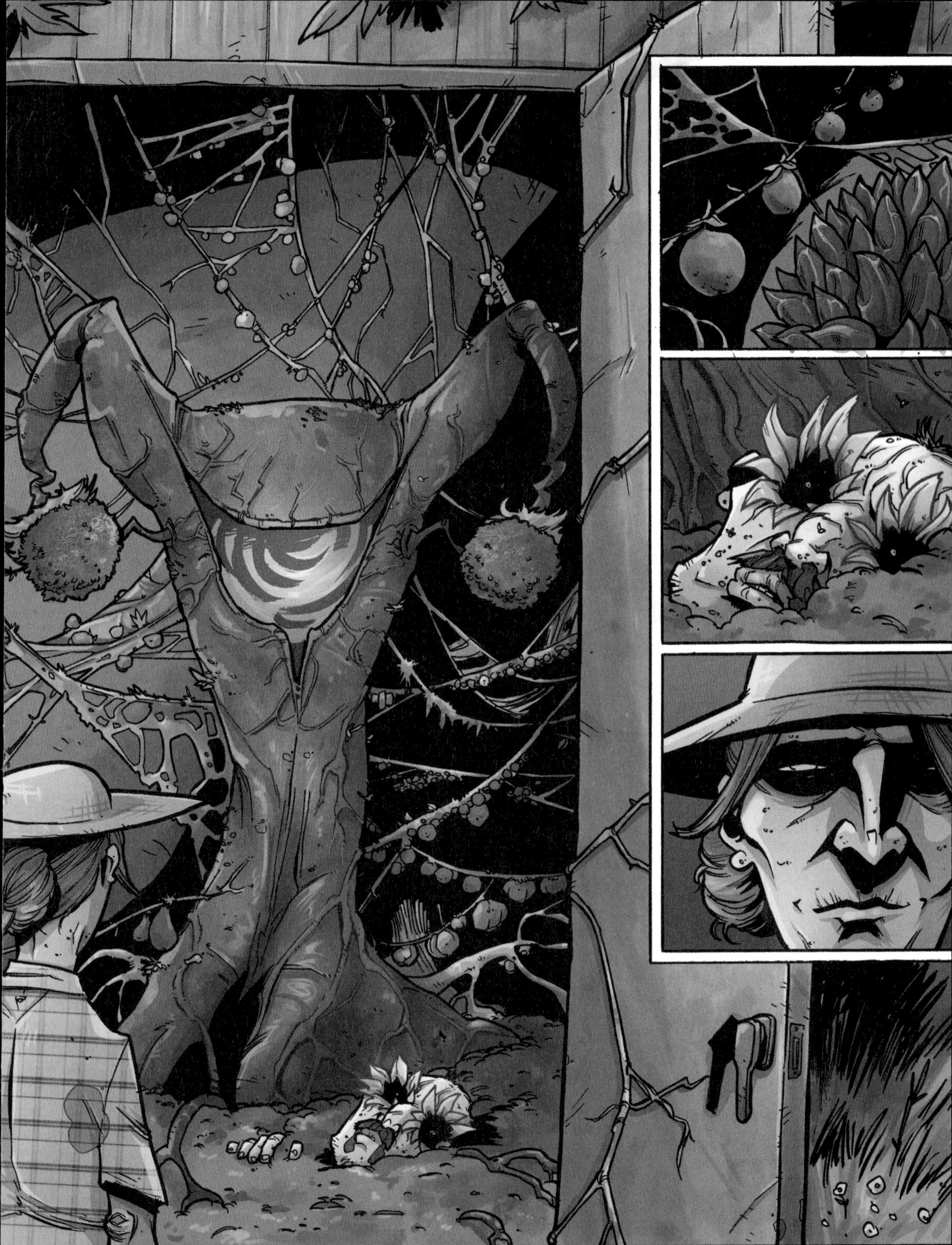

CHAPTER 10: **IN VOCATION.**

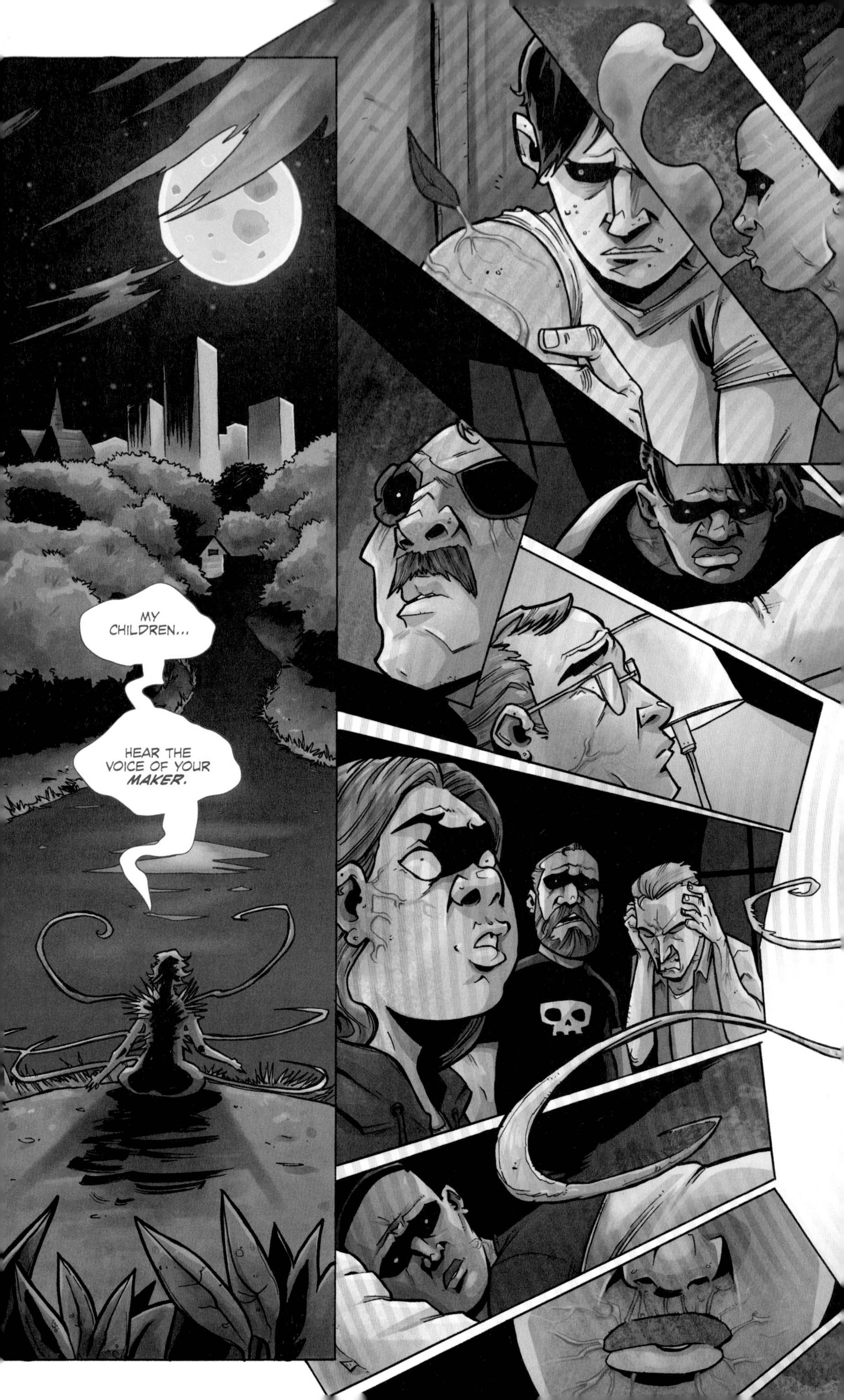
MY CHILDREN...
HEAR THE VOICE OF YOUR *MAKER.*

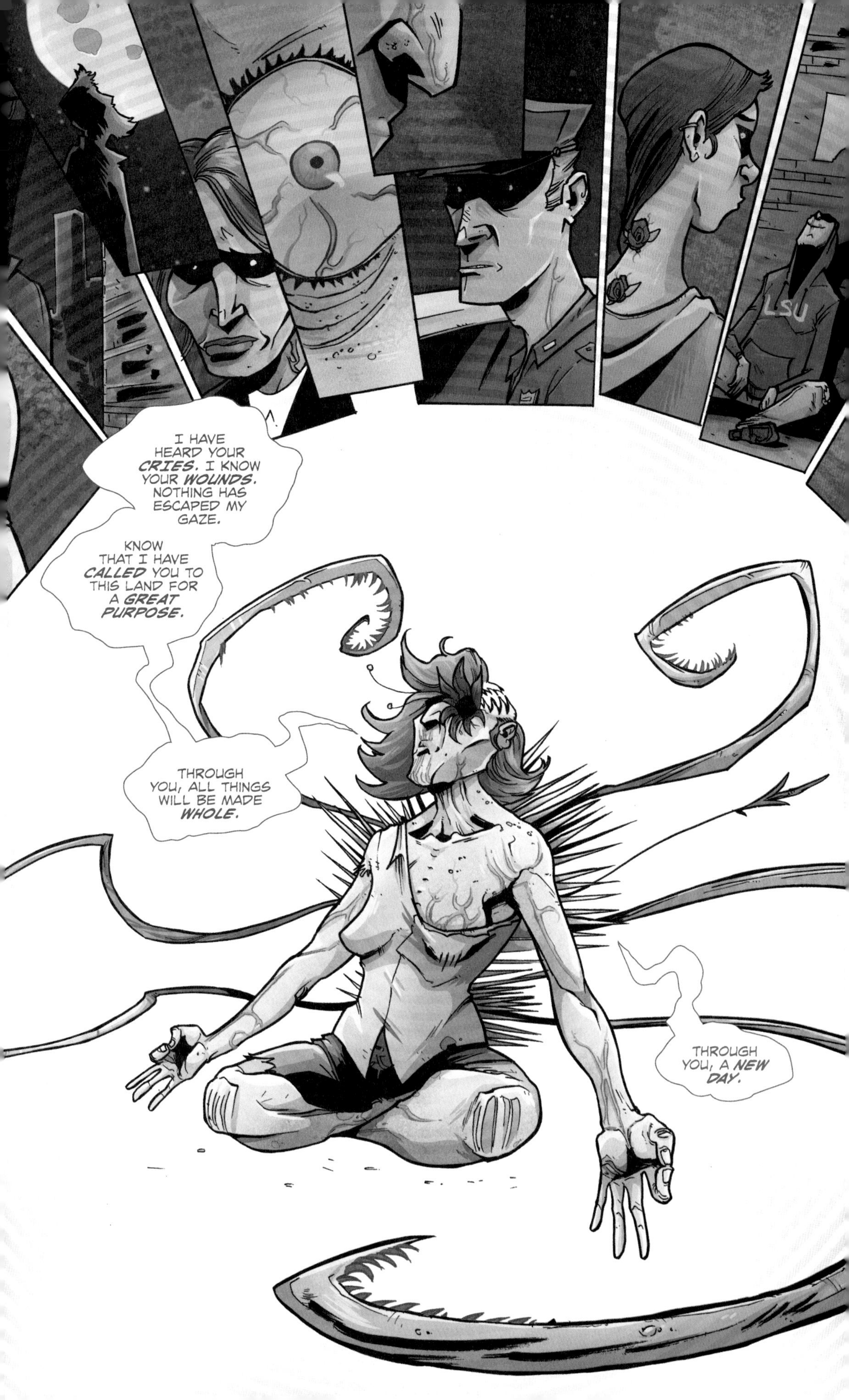
I HAVE HEARD YOUR CRIES. I KNOW YOUR WOUNDS. NOTHING HAS ESCAPED MY GAZE.
KNOW THAT I HAVE CALLED YOU TO THIS LAND FOR A GREAT PURPOSE.
THROUGH YOU, ALL THINGS WILL BE MADE WHOLE.
THROUGH YOU, A NEW DAY.
LSU

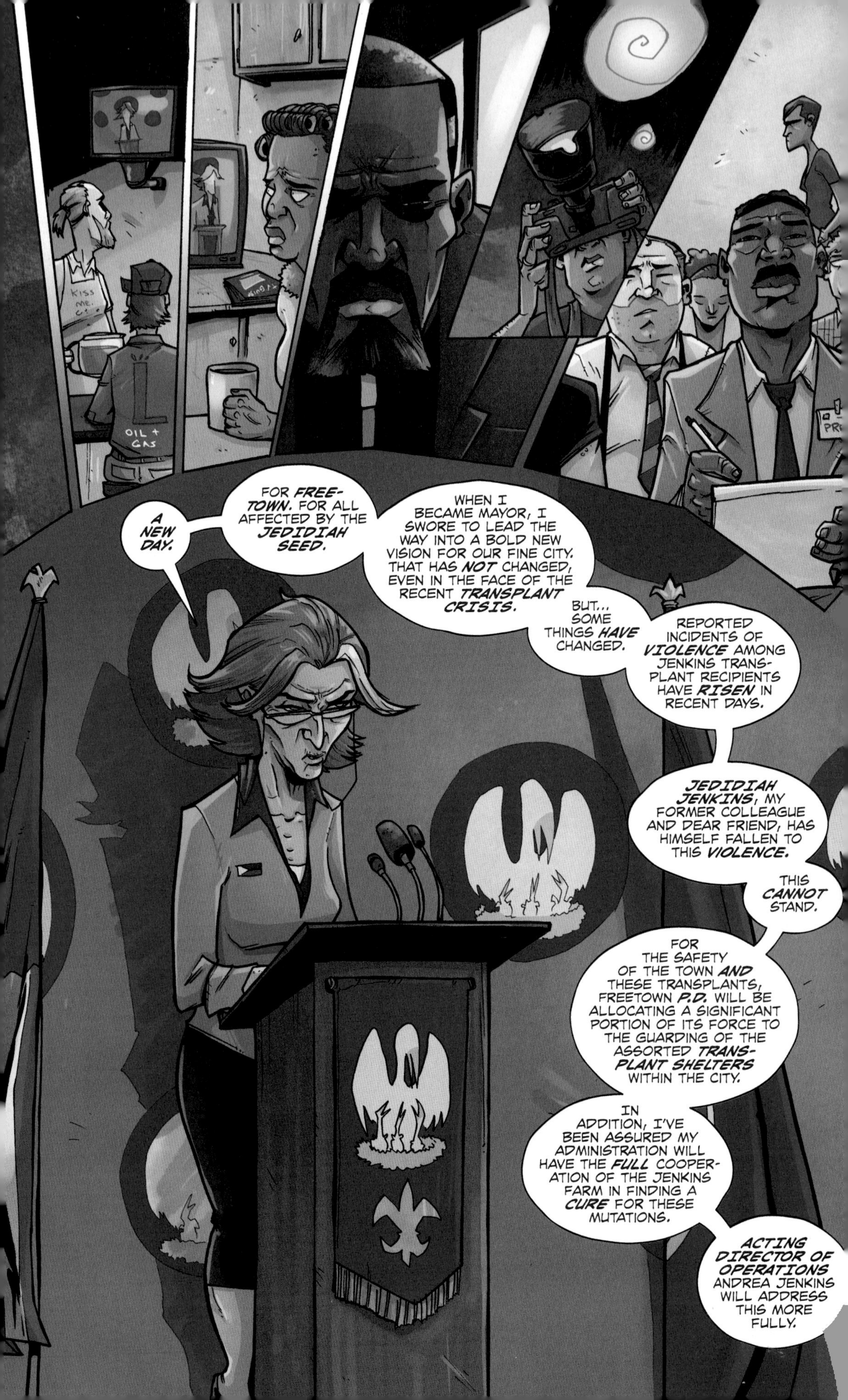

A NEW DAY.
FOR FREETOWN. FOR ALL AFFECTED BY THE JEDIDIAH SEED.
WHEN I BECAME MAYOR, I SWORE TO LEAD THE WAY INTO A BOLD NEW VISION FOR OUR FINE CITY. THAT HAS NOT CHANGED, EVEN IN THE FACE OF THE RECENT TRANSPLANT CRISIS.
BUT... SOME THINGS HAVE CHANGED.
REPORTED INCIDENTS OF VIOLENCE AMONG JENKINS TRANSPLANT RECIPIENTS HAVE RISEN IN RECENT DAYS.
JEDIDIAH JENKINS, MY FORMER COLLEAGUE AND DEAR FRIEND, HAS HIMSELF FALLEN TO THIS VIOLENCE.
THIS CANNOT STAND.
FOR THE SAFETY OF THE TOWN AND THESE TRANSPLANTS, FREETOWN P.D. WILL BE ALLOCATING A SIGNIFICANT PORTION OF ITS FORCE TO THE GUARDING OF THE ASSORTED TRANSPLANT SHELTERS WITHIN THE CITY.
IN ADDITION, I'VE BEEN ASSURED MY ADMINISTRATION WILL HAVE THE FULL COOPERATION OF THE JENKINS FARM IN FINDING A CURE FOR THESE MUTATIONS.
ACTING DIRECTOR OF OPERATIONS ANDREA JENKINS WILL ADDRESS THIS MORE FULLY.

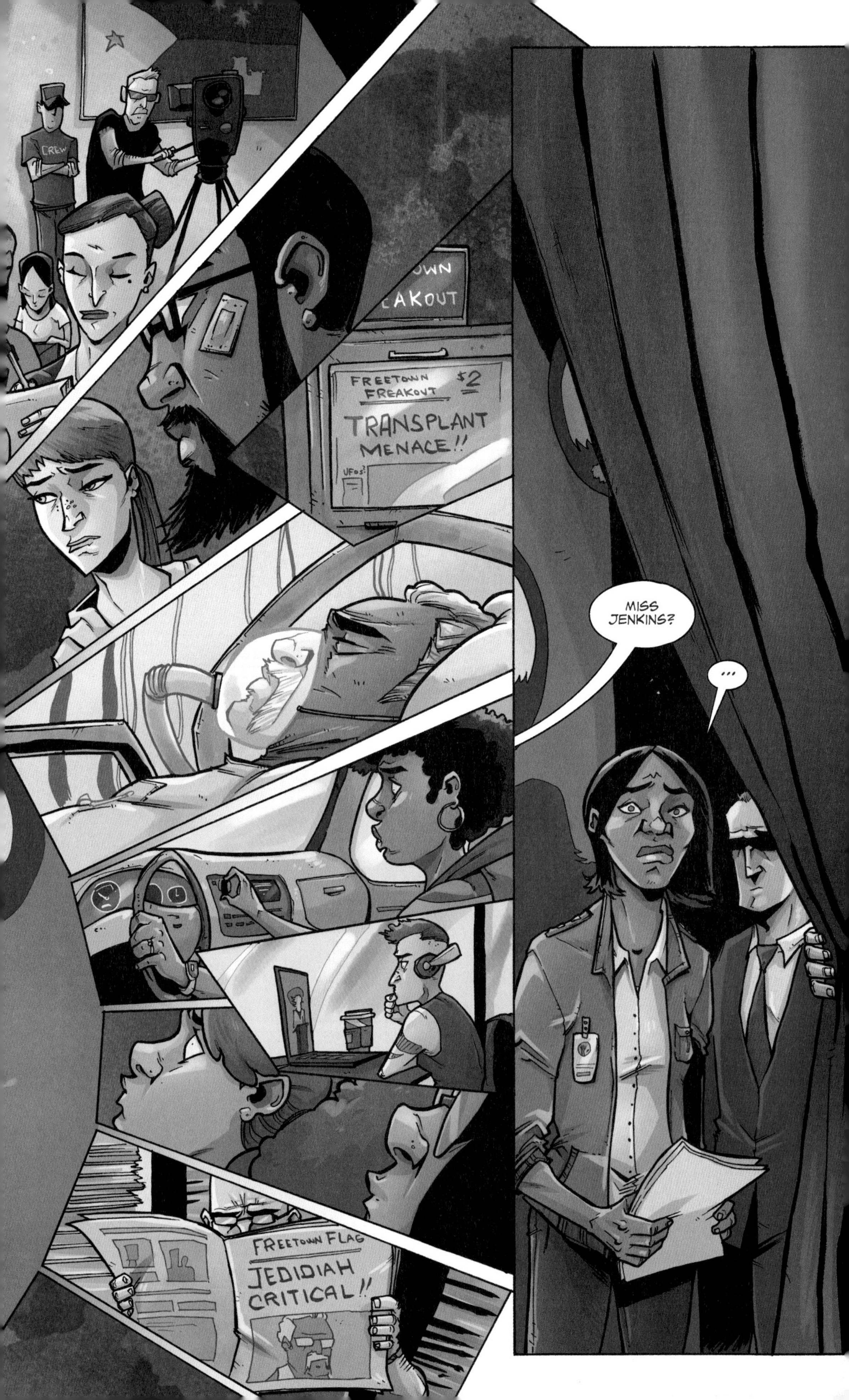
CREW
FREETOWN FREAKOUT $2
TRANSPLANT MENACE!!
UFOs?
FREETOWN FLAG
JEDIDIAH CRITICAL!!
MISS JENKINS?
...

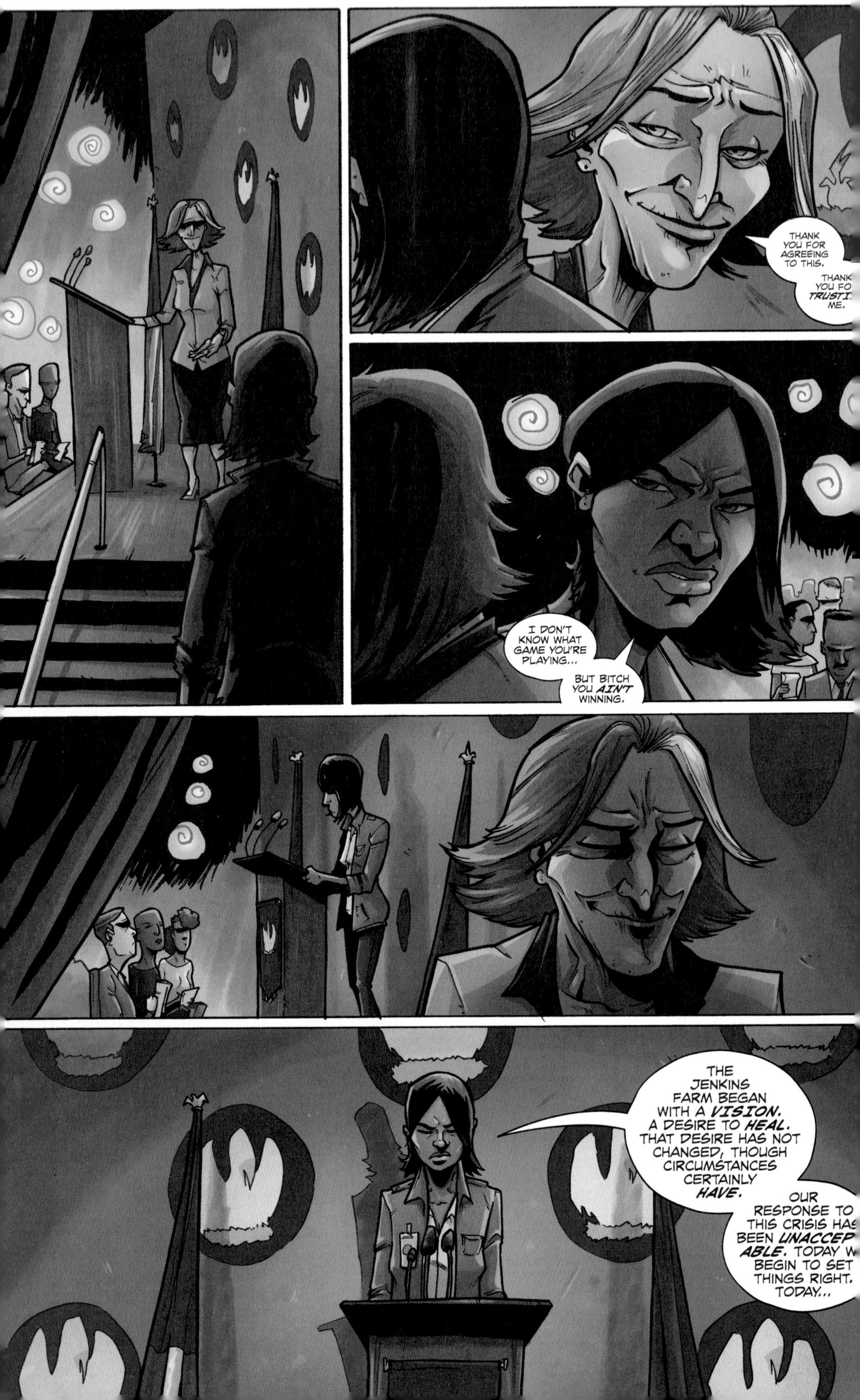
THANK YOU FOR AGREEING TO THIS.
THANK YOU FO TRUSTI ME.
I DON'T KNOW WHAT GAME YOU'RE PLAYING...
BUT BITCH YOU AIN'T WINNING.
THE JENKINS FARM BEGAN WITH A VISION. A DESIRE TO HEAL. THAT DESIRE HAS NOT CHANGED, THOUGH CIRCUMSTANCES CERTAINLY HAVE.
OUR RESPONSE TO THIS CRISIS HAS BEEN UNACCEP ABLE. TODAY W BEGIN TO SET THINGS RIGHT. TODAY...

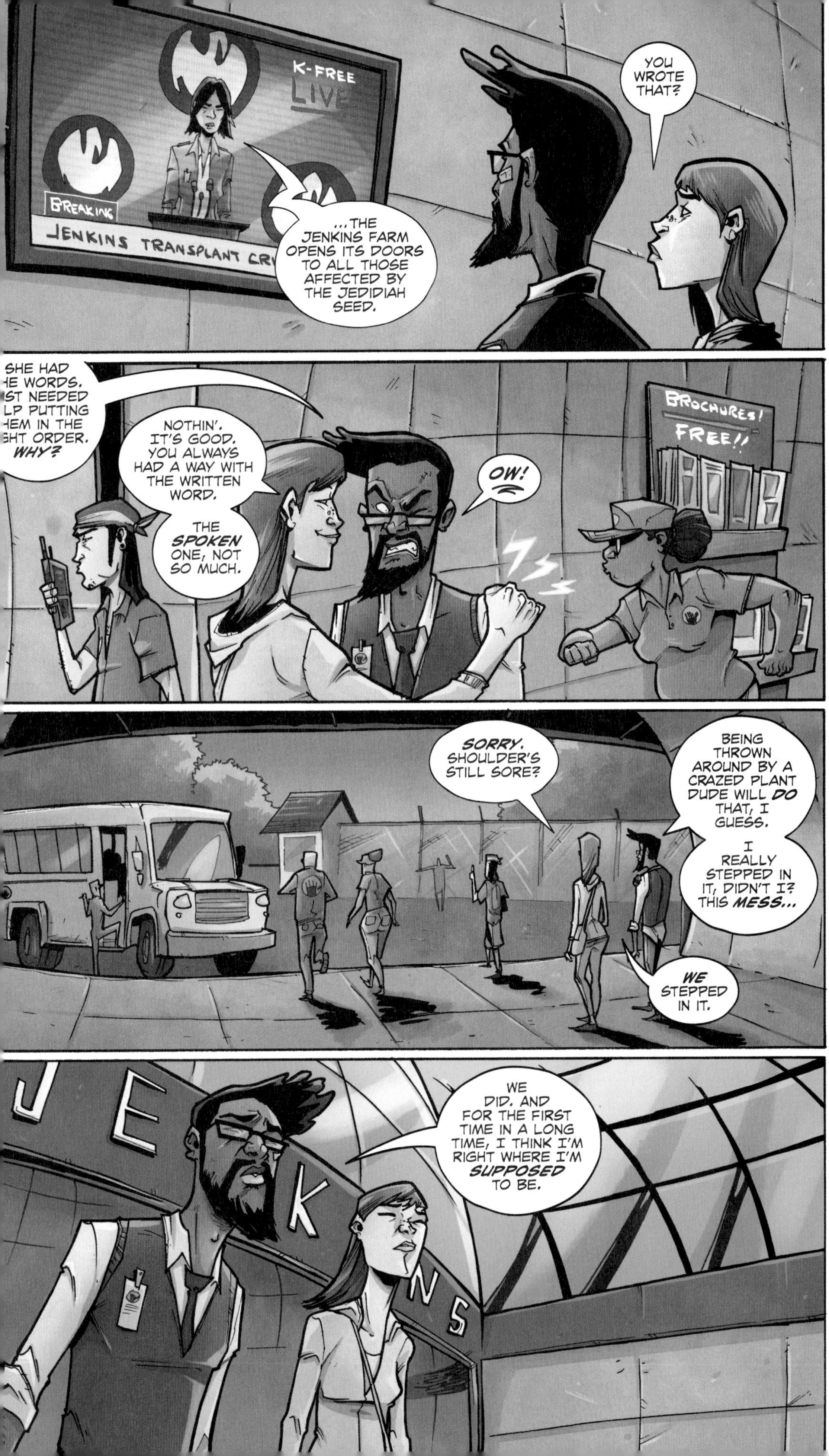
K-FREE
LIVE
BREAKING
JENKINS TRANSPLANT CRI
YOU WROTE THAT?
...THE JENKINS FARM OPENS ITS DOORS TO ALL THOSE AFFECTED BY THE JEDIDIAH SEED.
SHE HAD HE WORDS. IST NEEDED LP PUTTING HEM IN THE GHT ORDER. WHY?
NOTHIN'. IT'S GOOD. YOU ALWAYS HAD A WAY WITH THE WRITTEN WORD.
THE SPOKEN ONE, NOT SO MUCH.
OW!
BROCHURES! FREE!!
SORRY. SHOULDER'S STILL SORE?
BEING THROWN AROUND BY A CRAZED PLANT DUDE WILL DO THAT, I GUESS.
I REALLY STEPPED IN IT, DIDN'T I? THIS MESS...
WE STEPPED IN IT.
WE DID. AND FOR THE FIRST TIME IN A LONG TIME, I THINK I'M RIGHT WHERE I'M SUPPOSED TO BE.
J E K N S

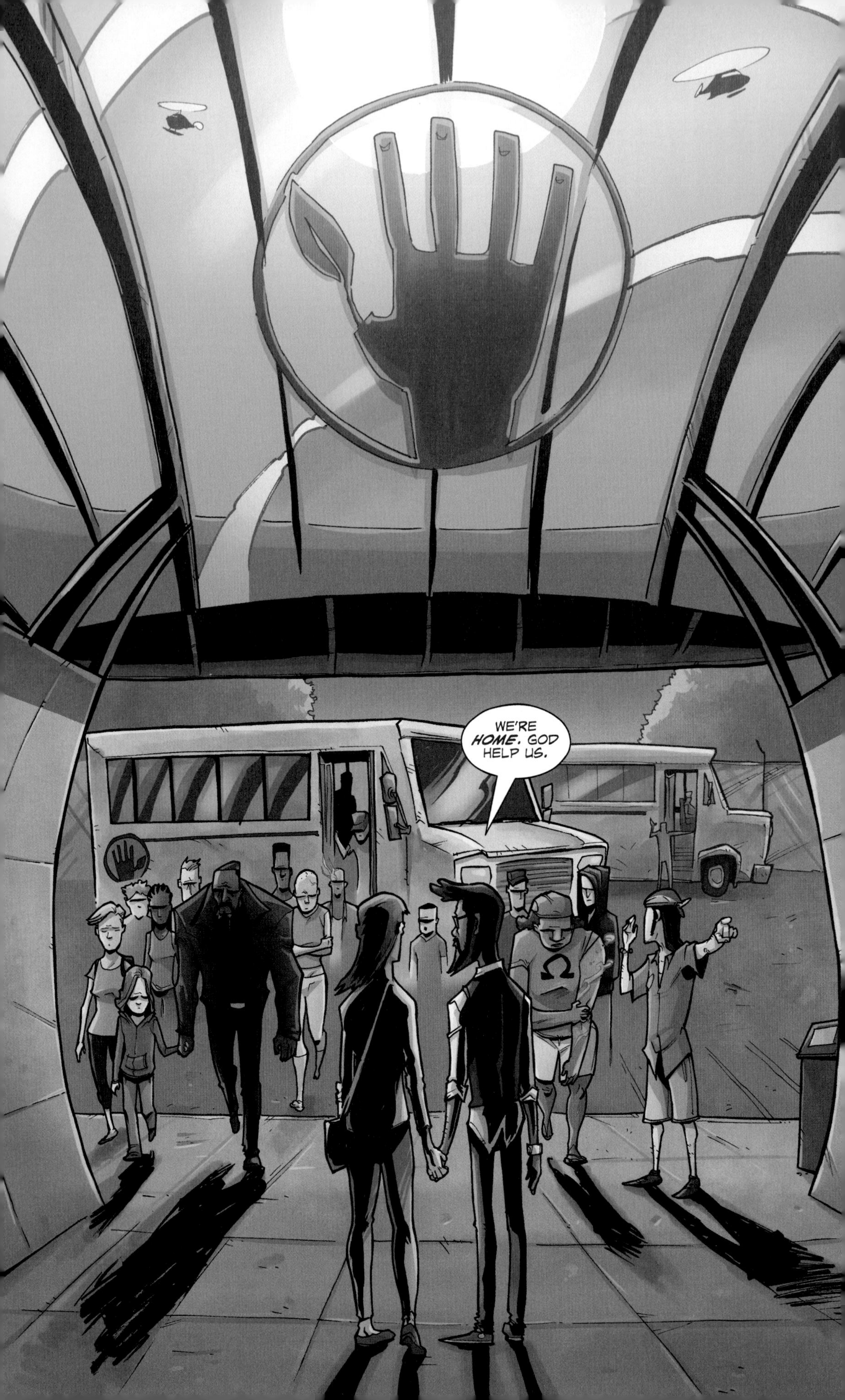
WE'RE HOME. GOD HELP US.

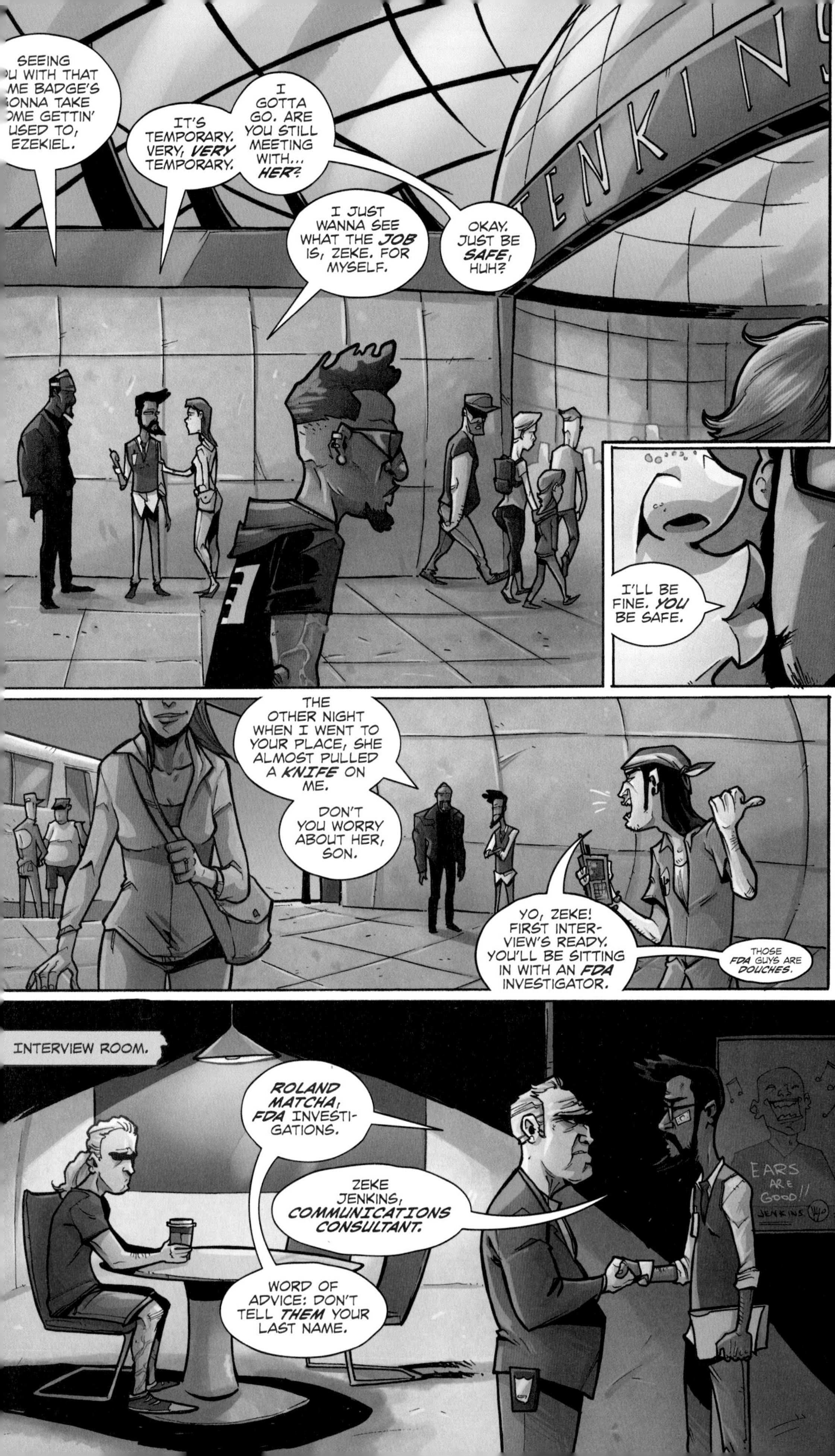

SEEING ...U WITH THAT ...ME BADGE'S ...ONNA TAKE ...OME GETTIN' USED TO, EZEKIEL.
IT'S TEMPORARY. VERY, VERY TEMPORARY.
I GOTTA GO. ARE YOU STILL MEETING WITH... HER?
I JUST WANNA SEE WHAT THE JOB IS, ZEKE. FOR MYSELF.
OKAY. JUST BE SAFE, HUH?
JENKIN
I'LL BE FINE. YOU BE SAFE.
THE OTHER NIGHT WHEN I WENT TO YOUR PLACE, SHE ALMOST PULLED A KNIFE ON ME.
DON'T YOU WORRY ABOUT HER, SON.
YO, ZEKE! FIRST INTER-VIEW'S READY. YOU'LL BE SITTING IN WITH AN FDA INVESTIGATOR.
THOSE FDA GUYS ARE DOUCHES.
INTERVIEW ROOM.
ROLAND MATCHA, FDA INVESTI-GATIONS.
ZEKE JENKINS, COMMUNICATIONS CONSULTANT.
EARS ARE GOOD!!
JENKINS
WORD OF ADVICE: DON'T TELL THEM YOUR LAST NAME.

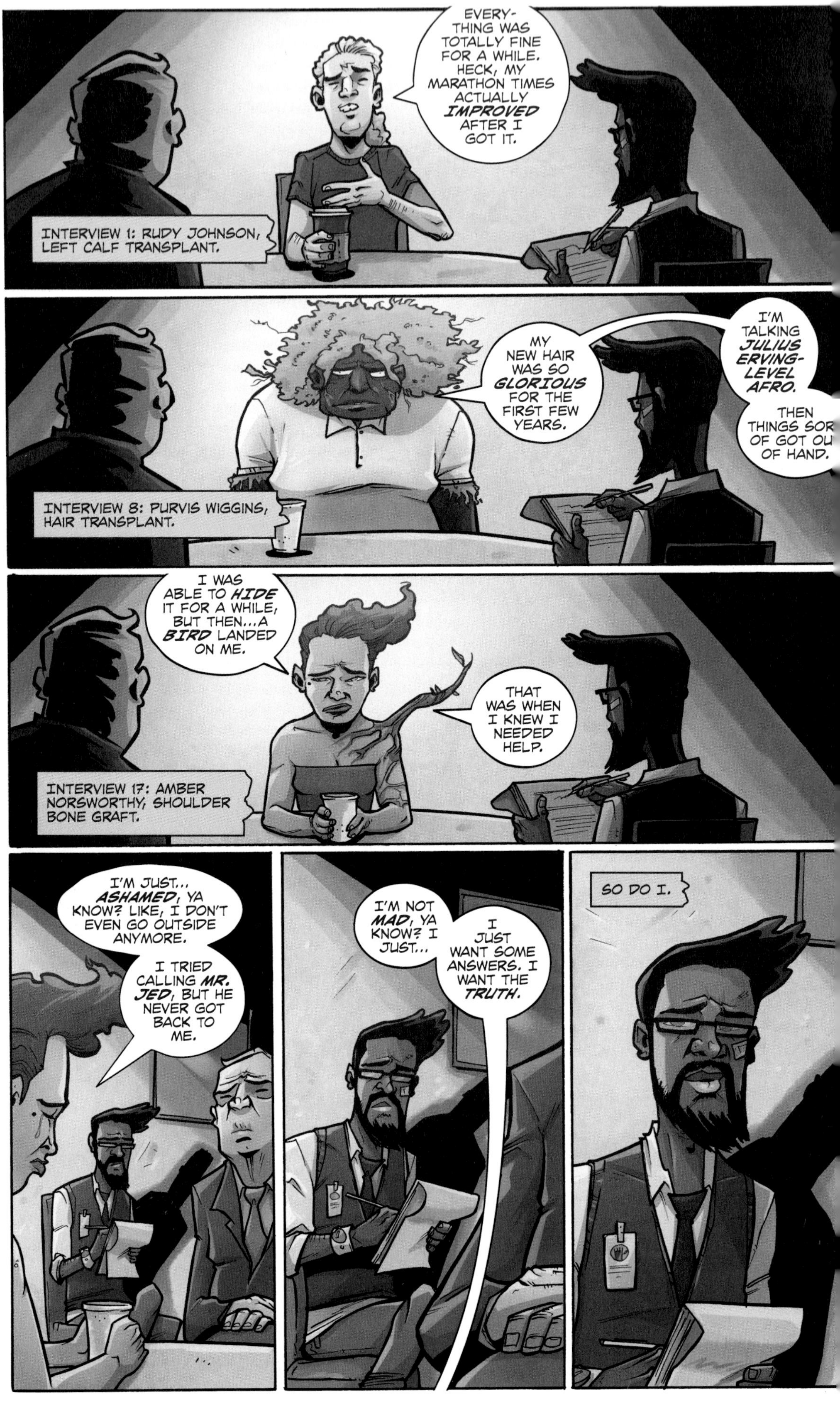

EVERY-THING WAS TOTALLY FINE FOR A WHILE. HECK, MY MARATHON TIMES ACTUALLY IMPROVED AFTER I GOT IT.
INTERVIEW 1: RUDY JOHNSON, LEFT CALF TRANSPLANT.
MY NEW HAIR WAS SO GLORIOUS FOR THE FIRST FEW YEARS.
I'M TALKING JULIUS ERVING-LEVEL AFRO.
THEN THINGS SOR OF GOT OU OF HAND.
INTERVIEW 8: PURVIS WIGGINS, HAIR TRANSPLANT.
I WAS ABLE TO HIDE IT FOR A WHILE, BUT THEN...A BIRD LANDED ON ME.
THAT WAS WHEN I KNEW I NEEDED HELP.
INTERVIEW 17: AMBER NORSWORTHY, SHOULDER BONE GRAFT.
I'M JUST... ASHAMED, YA KNOW? LIKE, I DON'T EVEN GO OUTSIDE ANYMORE.
I TRIED CALLING MR. JED, BUT HE NEVER GOT BACK TO ME.
I'M NOT MAD, YA KNOW? I JUST...
I JUST WANT SOME ANSWERS. I WANT THE TRUTH.
SO DO I.

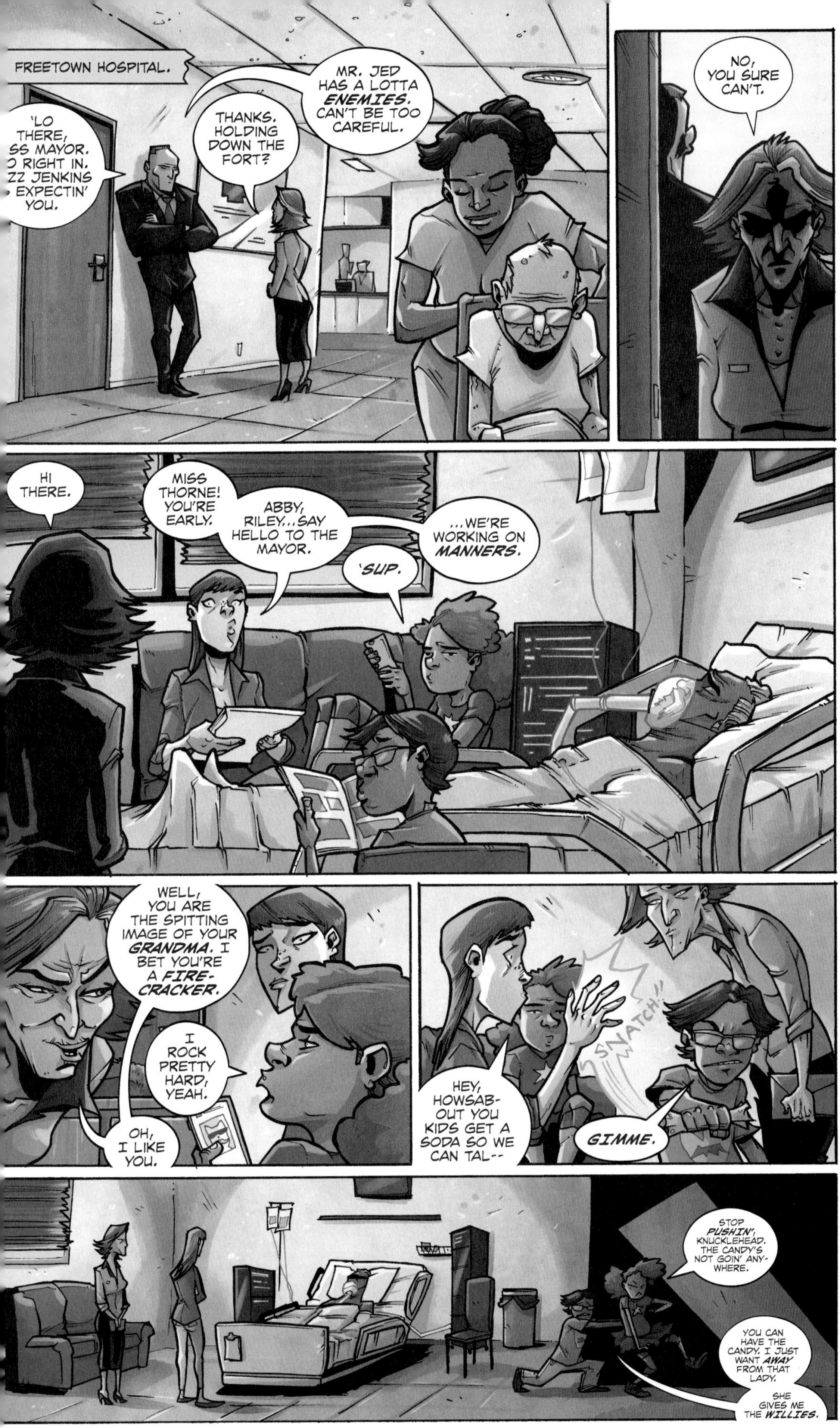
FREETOWN HOSPITAL.
'LO THERE, SS MAYOR. O RIGHT IN. ZZ JENKINS EXPECTIN' YOU.
THANKS. HOLDING DOWN THE FORT?
MR. JED HAS A LOTTA ENEMIES. CAN'T BE TOO CAREFUL.
NO, YOU SURE CAN'T.
HI THERE.
MISS THORNE! YOU'RE EARLY.
ABBY, RILEY...SAY HELLO TO THE MAYOR.
...WE'RE WORKING ON MANNERS.
'SUP.
WELL, YOU ARE THE SPITTING IMAGE OF YOUR GRANDMA. I BET YOU'RE A FIRE-CRACKER.
I ROCK PRETTY HARD, YEAH.
OH, I LIKE YOU.
HEY, HOWSAB-OUT YOU KIDS GET A SODA SO WE CAN TAL--
SNATCH!!
GIMME.
STOP PUSHIN', KNUCKLEHEAD. THE CANDY'S NOT GOIN' ANY-WHERE.
YOU CAN HAVE THE CANDY. I JUST WANT AWAY FROM THAT LADY.
SHE GIVES ME THE WILLIES.

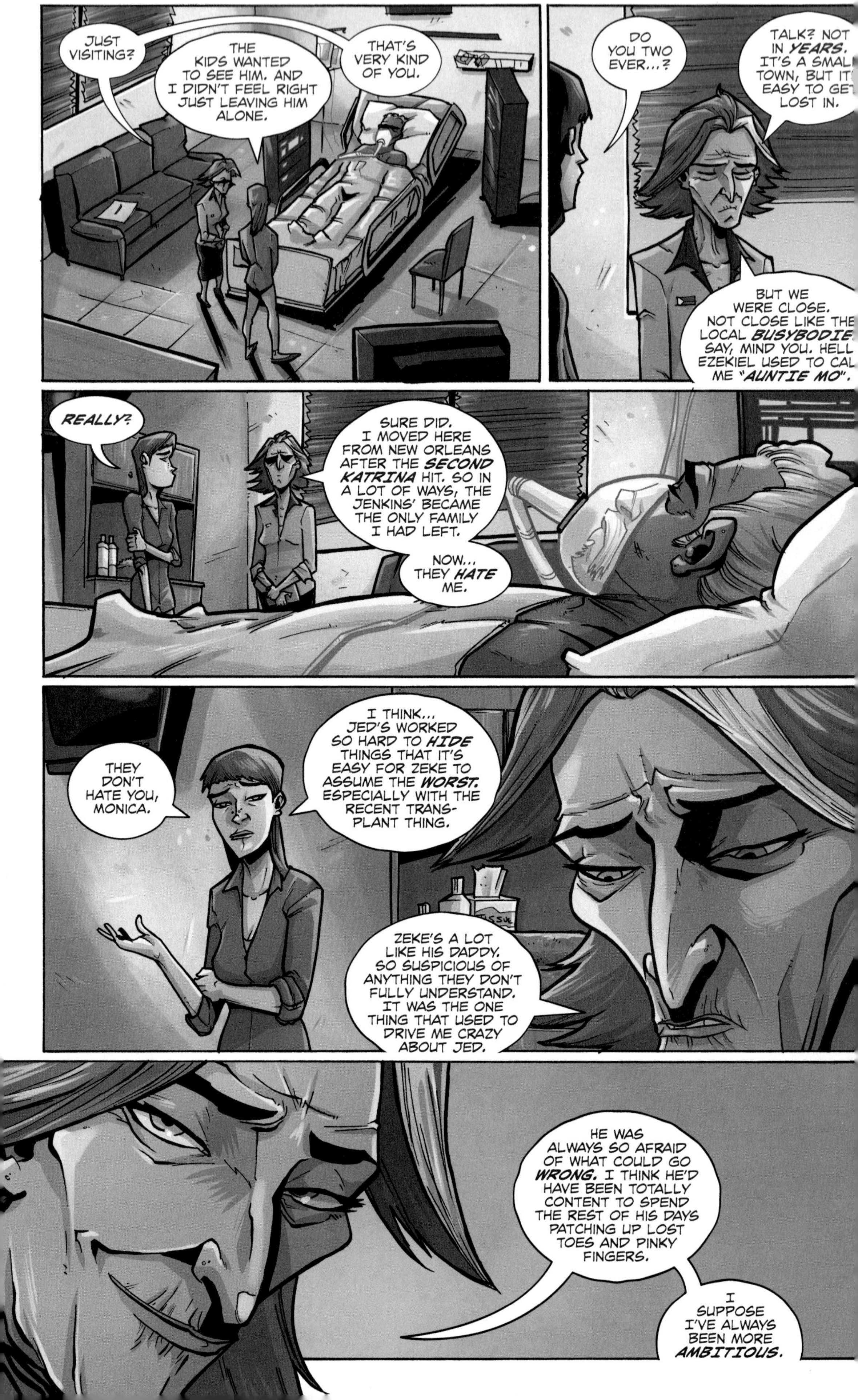

JUST VISITING?
THE KIDS WANTED TO SEE HIM. AND I DIDN'T FEEL RIGHT JUST LEAVING HIM ALONE.
THAT'S VERY KIND OF YOU.
DO YOU TWO EVER...?
TALK? NOT IN YEARS. IT'S A SMAL TOWN, BUT IT EASY TO GET LOST IN.
BUT WE WERE CLOSE. NOT CLOSE LIKE THE LOCAL BUSYBODIE SAY, MIND YOU. HELL EZEKIEL USED TO CAL ME "AUNTIE MO".
REALLY?
SURE DID. I MOVED HERE FROM NEW ORLEANS AFTER THE SECOND KATRINA HIT. SO IN A LOT OF WAYS, THE JENKINS' BECAME THE ONLY FAMILY I HAD LEFT.
NOW... THEY HATE ME.
THEY DON'T HATE YOU, MONICA.
I THINK... JED'S WORKED SO HARD TO HIDE THINGS THAT IT'S EASY FOR ZEKE TO ASSUME THE WORST. ESPECIALLY WITH THE RECENT TRANS-PLANT THING.
ZEKE'S A LOT LIKE HIS DADDY. SO SUSPICIOUS OF ANYTHING THEY DON'T FULLY UNDERSTAND. IT WAS THE ONE THING THAT USED TO DRIVE ME CRAZY ABOUT JED.
HE WAS ALWAYS SO AFRAID OF WHAT COULD GO WRONG. I THINK HE'D HAVE BEEN TOTALLY CONTENT TO SPEND THE REST OF HIS DAYS PATCHING UP LOST TOES AND PINKY FINGERS.
I SUPPOSE I'VE ALWAYS BEEN MORE AMBITIOUS.

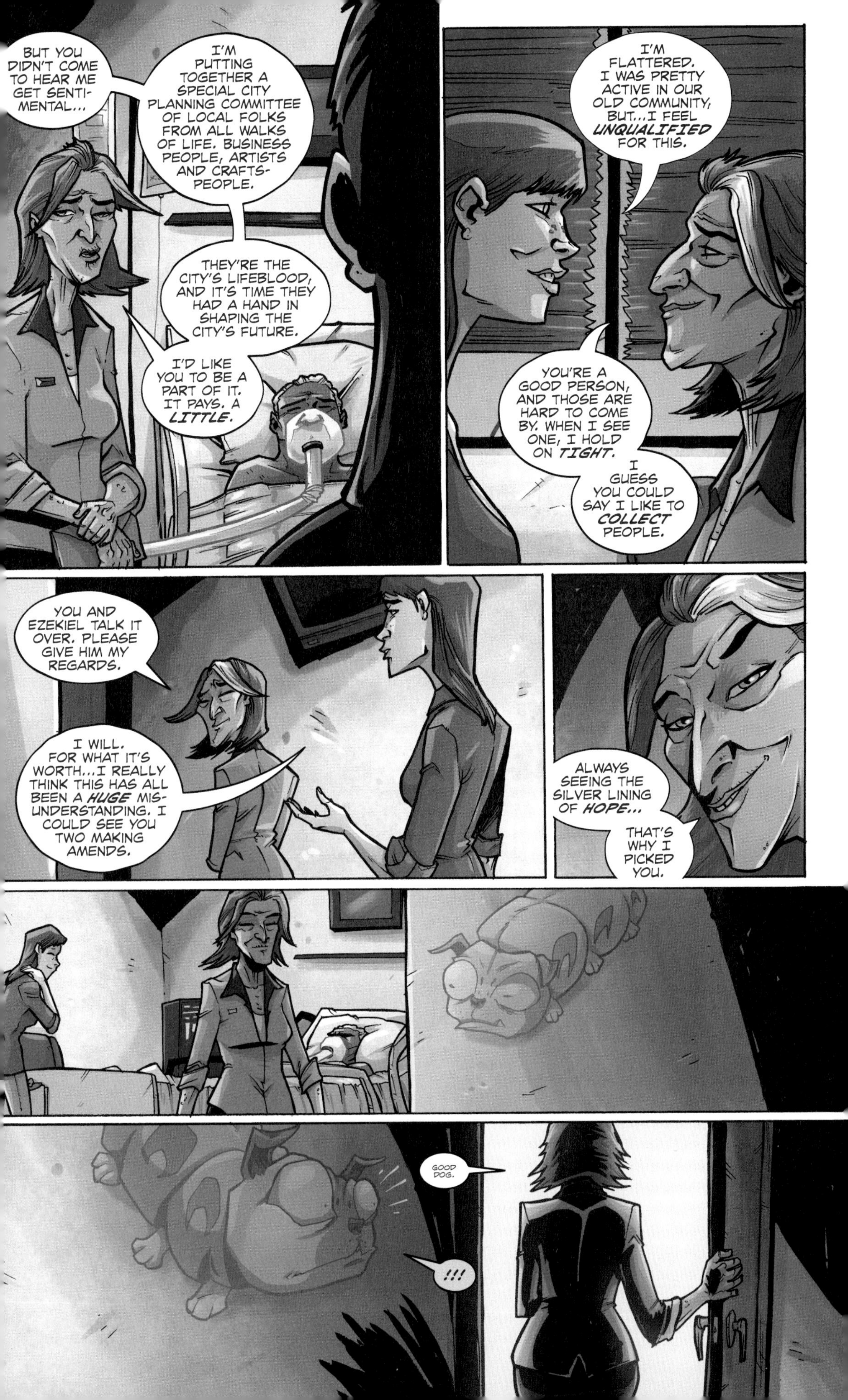
BUT YOU DIDN'T COME TO HEAR ME GET SENTI-MENTAL...
I'M PUTTING TOGETHER A SPECIAL CITY PLANNING COMMITTEE OF LOCAL FOLKS FROM ALL WALKS OF LIFE. BUSINESS PEOPLE, ARTISTS AND CRAFTS-PEOPLE.
THEY'RE THE CITY'S LIFEBLOOD, AND IT'S TIME THEY HAD A HAND IN SHAPING THE CITY'S FUTURE.
I'D LIKE YOU TO BE A PART OF IT. IT PAYS. A LITTLE.
I'M FLATTERED. I WAS PRETTY ACTIVE IN OUR OLD COMMUNITY, BUT...I FEEL UNQUALIFIED FOR THIS.
YOU'RE A GOOD PERSON, AND THOSE ARE HARD TO COME BY. WHEN I SEE ONE, I HOLD ON TIGHT.
I GUESS YOU COULD SAY I LIKE TO COLLECT PEOPLE.
YOU AND EZEKIEL TALK IT OVER. PLEASE GIVE HIM MY REGARDS.
I WILL. FOR WHAT IT'S WORTH...I REALLY THINK THIS HAS ALL BEEN A HUGE MIS-UNDERSTANDING. I COULD SEE YOU TWO MAKING AMENDS.
ALWAYS SEEING THE SILVER LINING OF HOPE...
THAT'S WHY I PICKED YOU.
GOOD DOG.
!!!

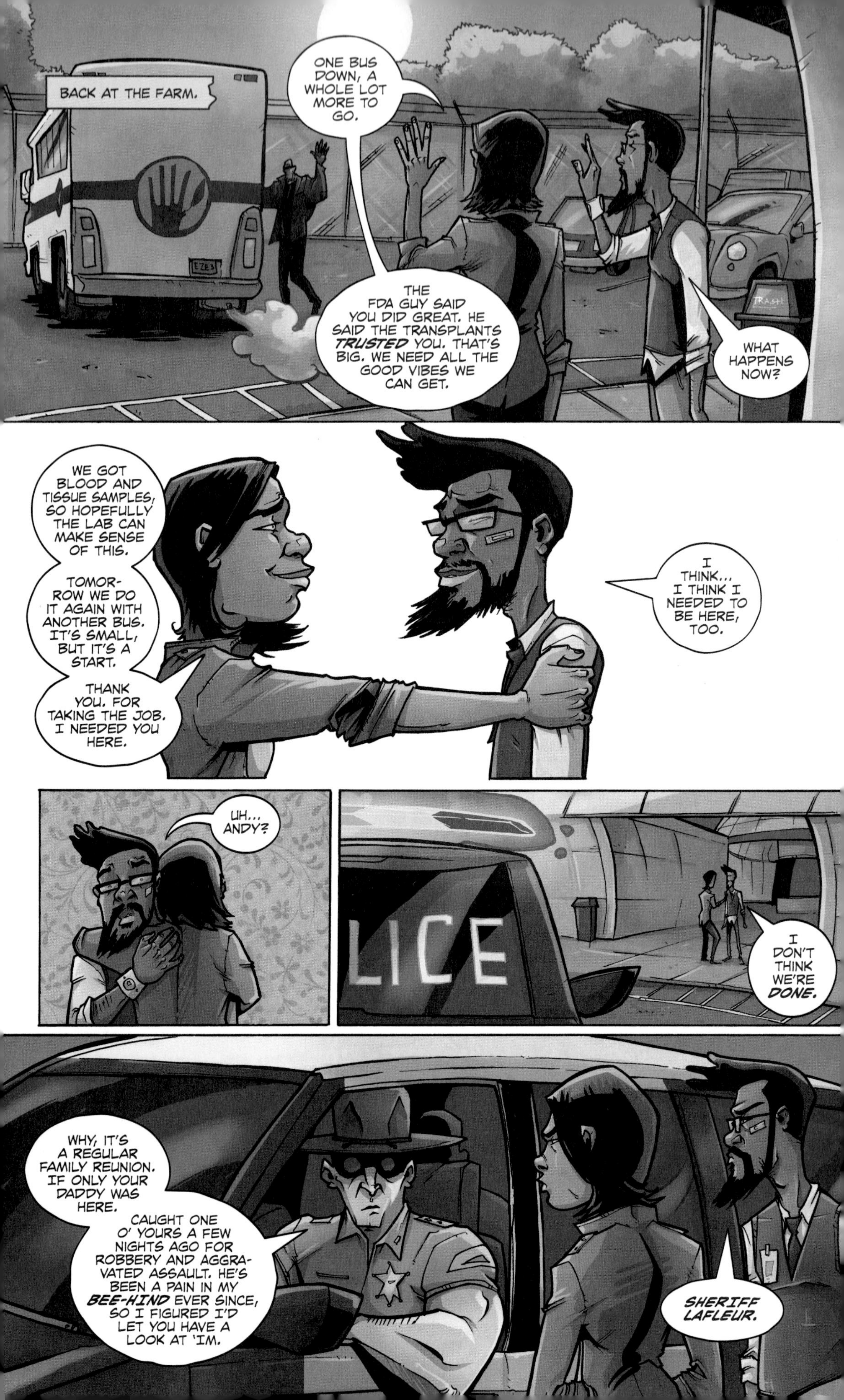
BACK AT THE FARM.
ONE BUS DOWN, A WHOLE LOT MORE TO GO.
THE FDA GUY SAID YOU DID GREAT. HE SAID THE TRANSPLANTS TRUSTED YOU. THAT'S BIG. WE NEED ALL THE GOOD VIBES WE CAN GET.
WHAT HAPPENS NOW?
TRASH
EZE3
WE GOT BLOOD AND TISSUE SAMPLES, SO HOPEFULLY THE LAB CAN MAKE SENSE OF THIS.
TOMOR-ROW WE DO IT AGAIN WITH ANOTHER BUS. IT'S SMALL, BUT IT'S A START.
THANK YOU. FOR TAKING THE JOB. I NEEDED YOU HERE.
I THINK... I THINK I NEEDED TO BE HERE, TOO.
UH... ANDY?
LICE
I DON'T THINK WE'RE DONE.
WHY, IT'S A REGULAR FAMILY REUNION. IF ONLY YOUR DADDY WAS HERE.
CAUGHT ONE O' YOURS A FEW NIGHTS AGO FOR ROBBERY AND AGGRA-VATED ASSAULT. HE'S BEEN A PAIN IN MY BEE-HIND EVER SINCE, SO I FIGURED I'D LET YOU HAVE A LOOK AT 'IM.
SHERIFF LAFLEUR.

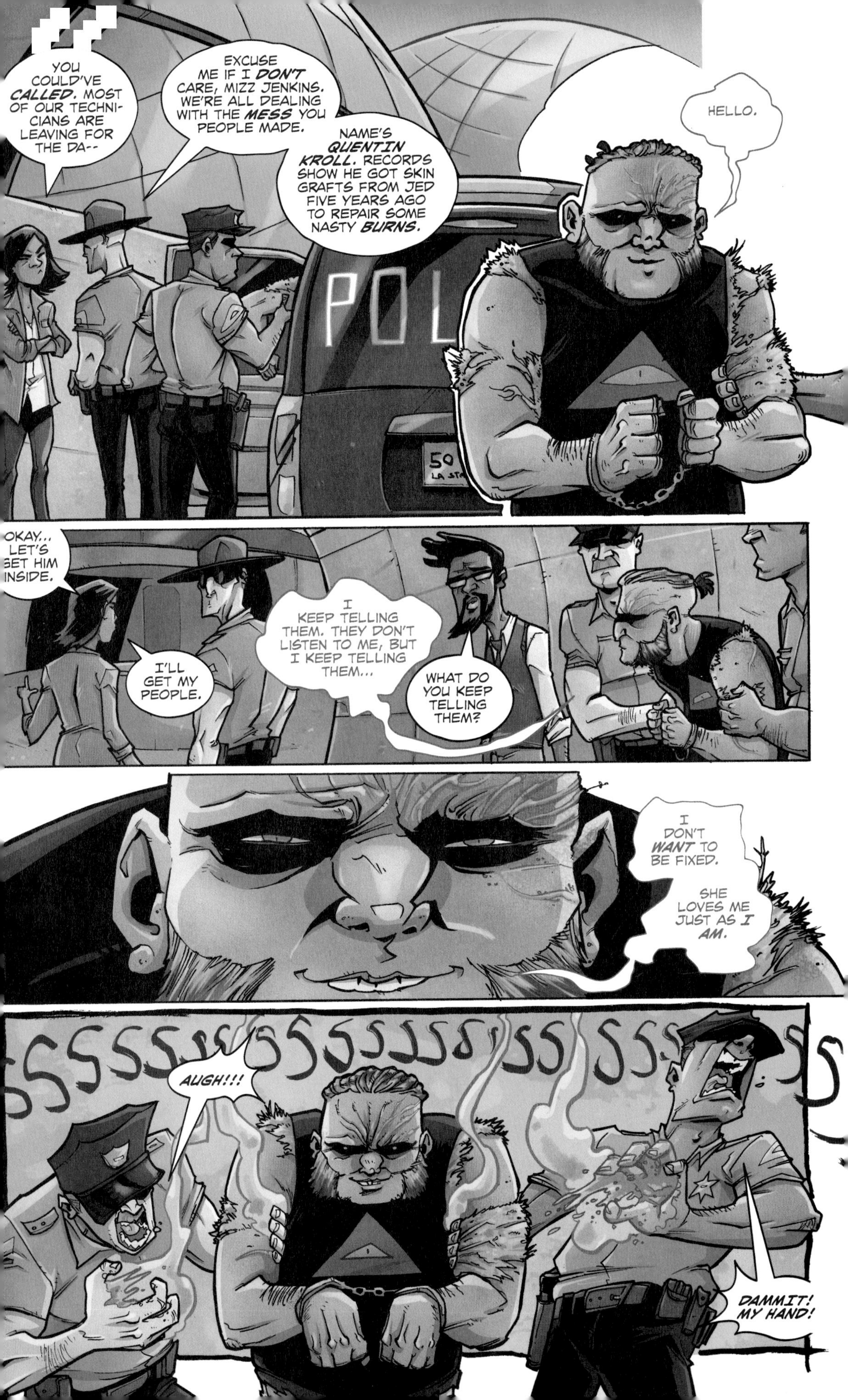
YOU COULD'VE CALLED. MOST OF OUR TECHNICIANS ARE LEAVING FOR THE DA--
EXCUSE ME IF I DON'T CARE, MIZZ JENKINS. WE'RE ALL DEALING WITH THE MESS YOU PEOPLE MADE.
NAME'S QUENTIN KROLL. RECORDS SHOW HE GOT SKIN GRAFTS FROM JED FIVE YEARS AGO TO REPAIR SOME NASTY BURNS.
POL
HELLO.
OKAY... LET'S GET HIM INSIDE.
I'LL GET MY PEOPLE.
I KEEP TELLING THEM. THEY DON'T LISTEN TO ME, BUT I KEEP TELLING THEM...
WHAT DO YOU KEEP TELLING THEM?
I DON'T WANT TO BE FIXED.
SHE LOVES ME JUST AS I AM.
SSSSSSSSSSSSSSSSSSSS
AUGH!!!
DAMMIT! MY HAND!

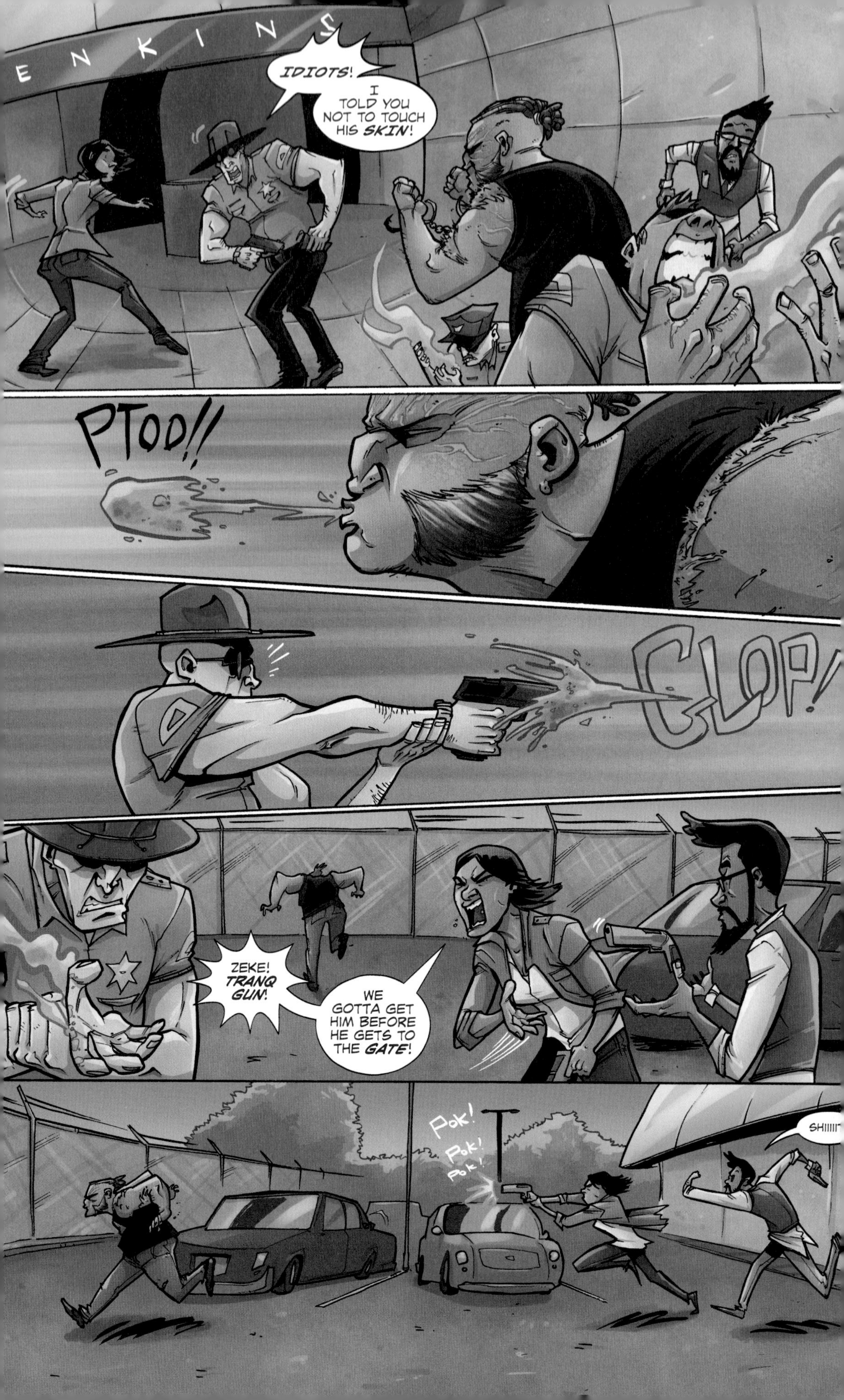

ENKINS
IDIOTS!
I TOLD YOU NOT TO TOUCH HIS SKIN!
PTOO!!
GLOP!
ZEKE! TRANQ GUN!
WE GOTTA GET HIM BEFORE HE GETS TO THE GATE!
POK! POK! POK!
SHIIIII

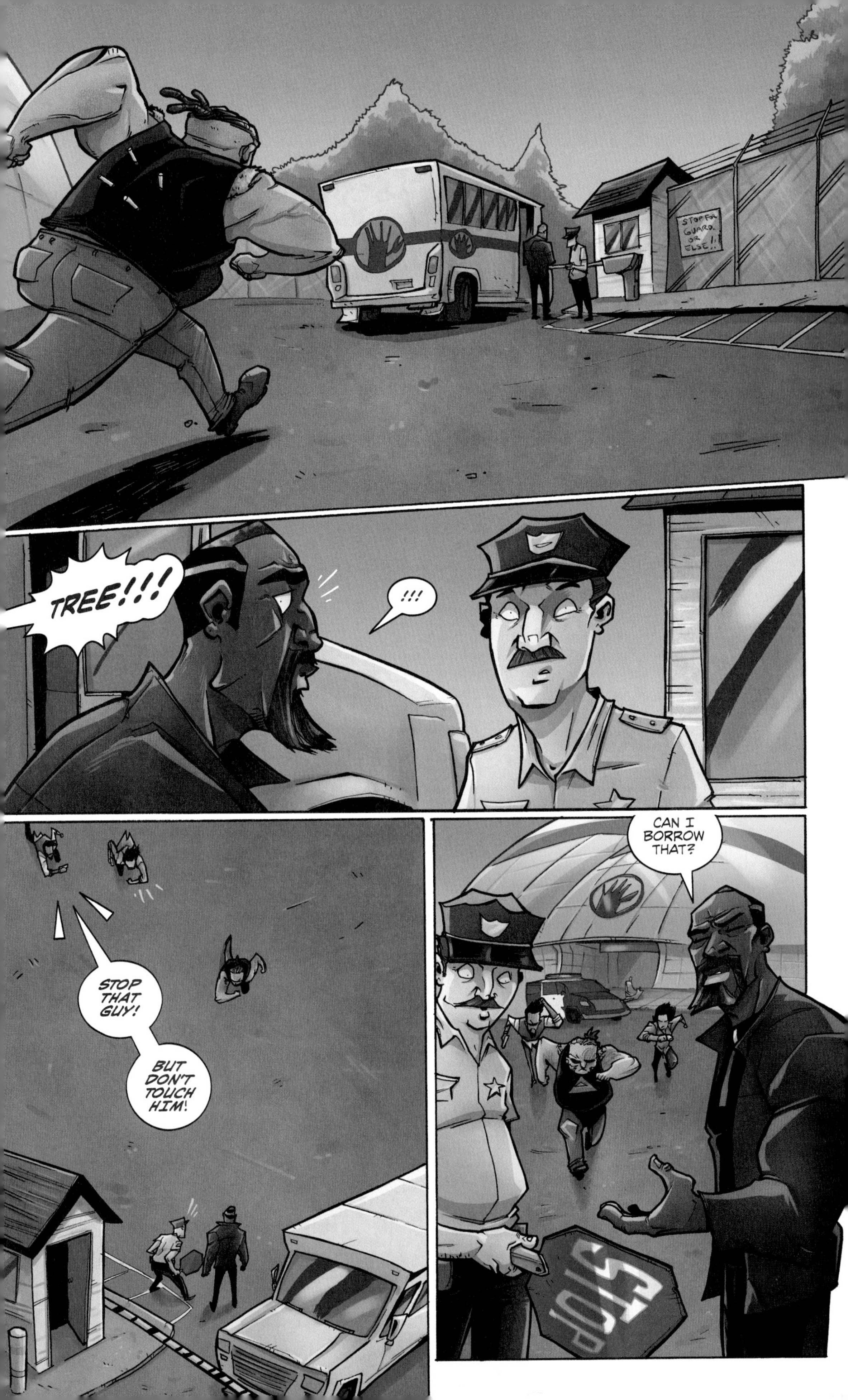
STOP FOR GUARD. OR ELSE!!
TREE!!!
!!!
STOP THAT GUY!
BUT DON'T TOUCH HIM!
CAN I BORROW THAT?
STOP

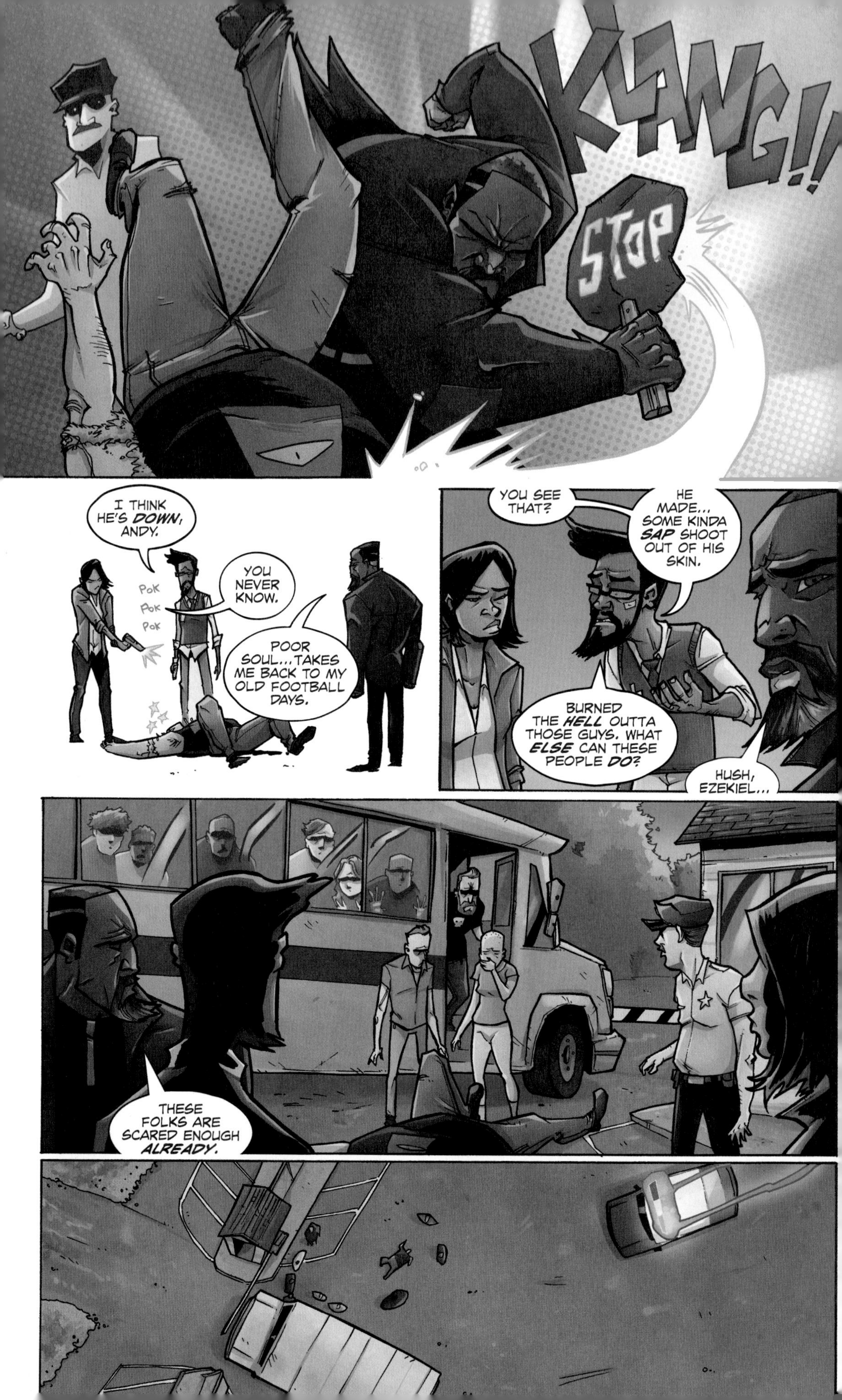
KLANG!!!
STOP
I THINK HE'S DOWN, ANDY.
POK POK POK
YOU NEVER KNOW.
POOR SOUL...TAKES ME BACK TO MY OLD FOOTBALL DAYS.
YOU SEE THAT?
HE MADE... SOME KINDA SAP SHOOT OUT OF HIS SKIN.
BURNED THE HELL OUTTA THOSE GUYS. WHAT ELSE CAN THESE PEOPLE DO?
HUSH, EZEKIEL...
THESE FOLKS ARE SCARED ENOUGH ALREADY.

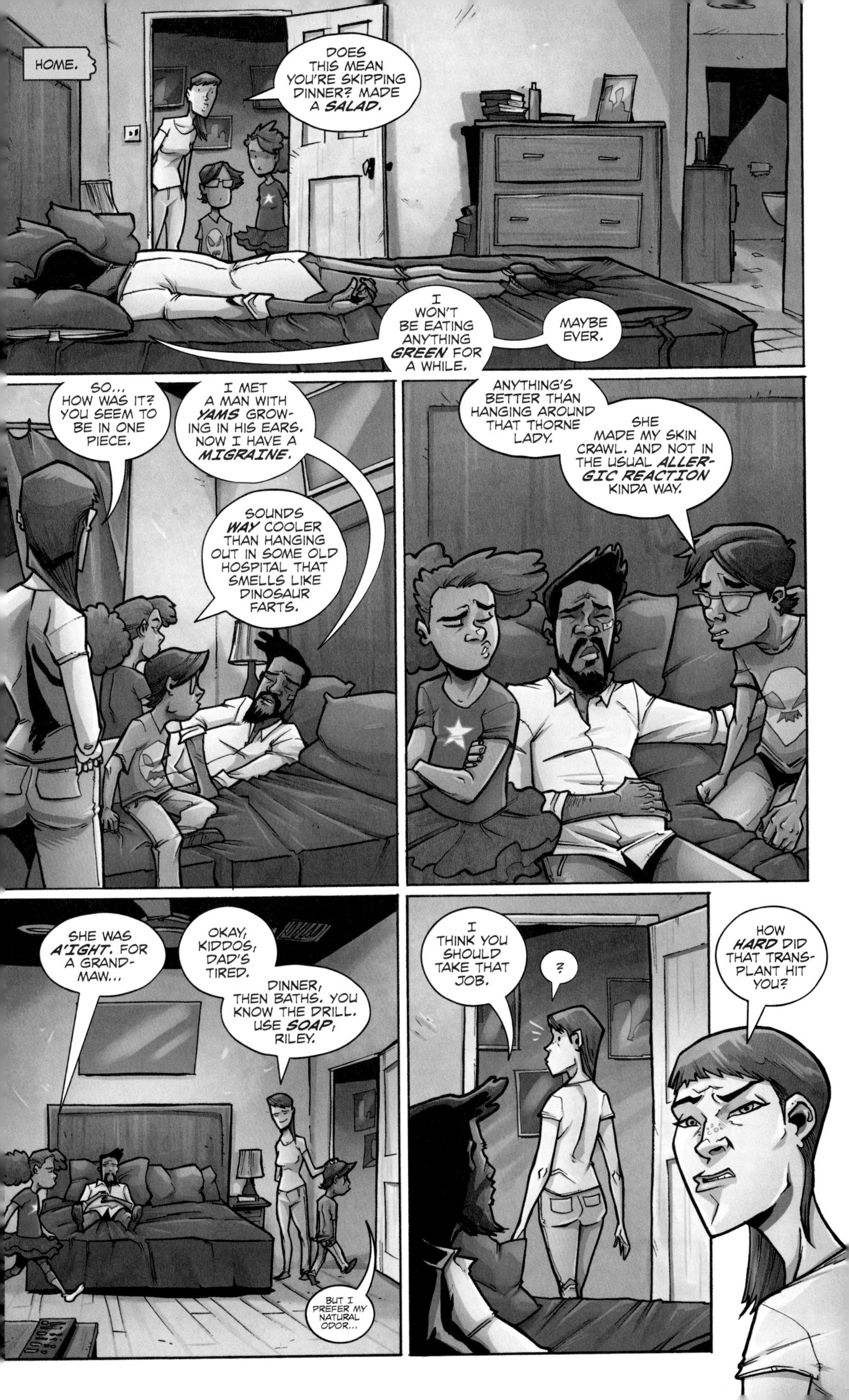
HOME.
DOES THIS MEAN YOU'RE SKIPPING DINNER? MADE A SALAD.
I WON'T BE EATING ANYTHING GREEN FOR A WHILE.
MAYBE EVER.
SO... HOW WAS IT? YOU SEEM TO BE IN ONE PIECE.
I MET A MAN WITH YAMS GROWING IN HIS EARS. NOW I HAVE A MIGRAINE.
SOUNDS WAY COOLER THAN HANGING OUT IN SOME OLD HOSPITAL THAT SMELLS LIKE DINOSAUR FARTS.
ANYTHING'S BETTER THAN HANGING AROUND THAT THORNE LADY.
SHE MADE MY SKIN CRAWL. AND NOT IN THE USUAL ALLERGIC REACTION KINDA WAY.
SHE WAS A'IGHT. FOR A GRANDMAW...
OKAY, KIDDOS, DAD'S TIRED.
DINNER, THEN BATHS. YOU KNOW THE DRILL. USE SOAP, RILEY.
BUT I PREFER MY NATURAL ODOR...
I THINK YOU SHOULD TAKE THAT JOB.
?
HOW HARD DID THAT TRANSPLANT HIT YOU?

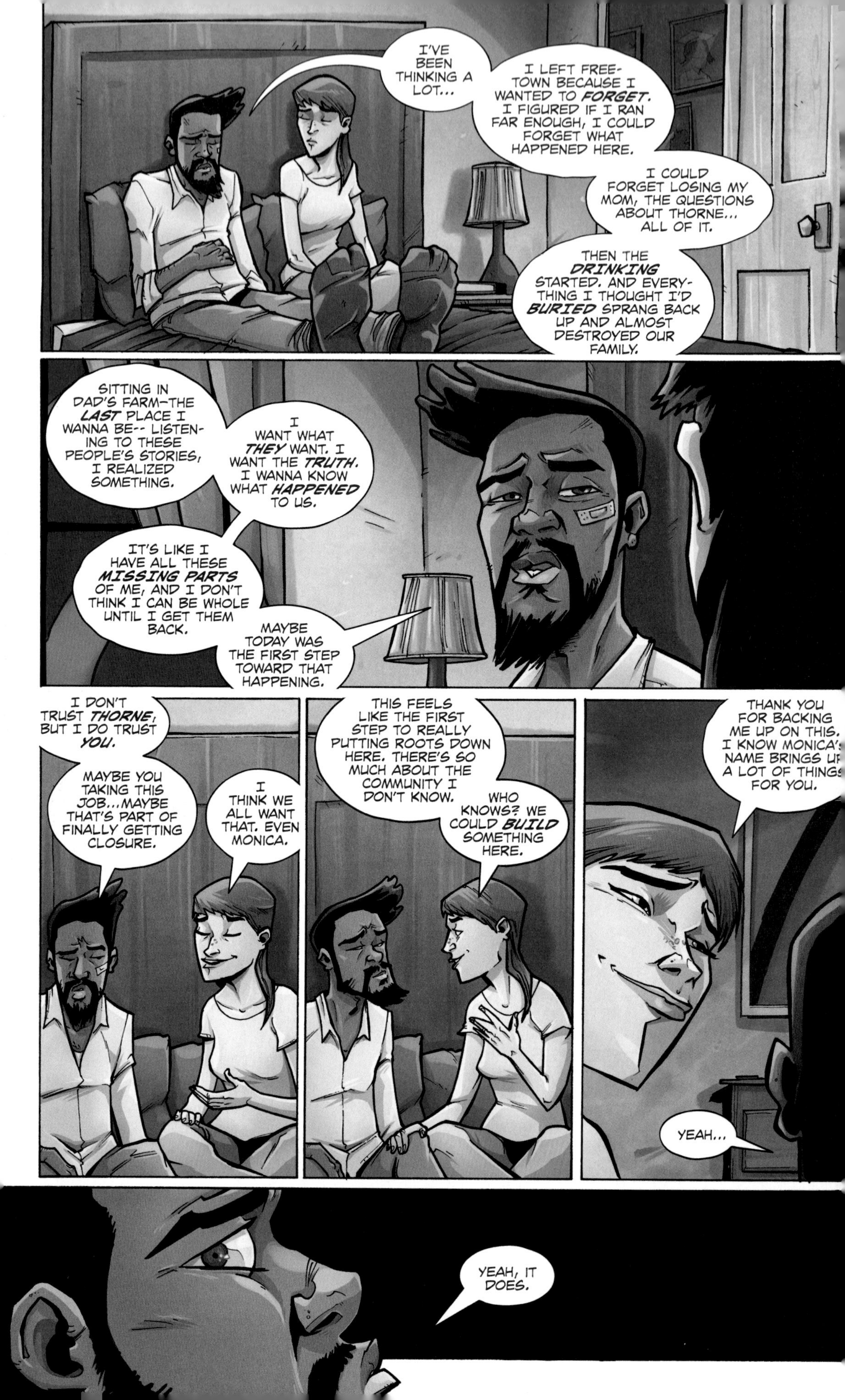
I'VE BEEN THINKING A LOT...
I LEFT FREE-TOWN BECAUSE I WANTED TO *FORGET.* I FIGURED IF I RAN FAR ENOUGH, I COULD FORGET WHAT HAPPENED HERE.
I COULD FORGET LOSING MY MOM, THE QUESTIONS ABOUT THORNE... ALL OF IT.
THEN THE *DRINKING* STARTED. AND EVERY-THING I THOUGHT I'D *BURIED* SPRANG BACK UP AND ALMOST DESTROYED OUR FAMILY.
SITTING IN DAD'S FARM—THE *LAST* PLACE I WANNA BE-- LISTEN-ING TO THESE PEOPLE'S STORIES, I REALIZED SOMETHING.
I WANT WHAT *THEY* WANT. I WANT THE *TRUTH.* I WANNA KNOW WHAT *HAPPENED* TO US.
IT'S LIKE I HAVE ALL THESE *MISSING PARTS* OF ME, AND I DON'T THINK I CAN BE WHOLE UNTIL I GET THEM BACK.
MAYBE TODAY WAS THE FIRST STEP TOWARD THAT HAPPENING.
I DON'T TRUST *THORNE,* BUT I DO TRUST *YOU.*
MAYBE YOU TAKING THIS JOB...MAYBE THAT'S PART OF FINALLY GETTING CLOSURE.
I THINK WE ALL WANT THAT. EVEN MONICA.
THIS FEELS LIKE THE FIRST STEP TO REALLY PUTTING ROOTS DOWN HERE. THERE'S SO MUCH ABOUT THE COMMUNITY I DON'T KNOW.
WHO KNOWS? WE COULD *BUILD* SOMETHING HERE.
THANK YOU FOR BACKING ME UP ON THIS. I KNOW MONICA'S NAME BRINGS UP A LOT OF THINGS FOR YOU.
YEAH...
YEAH, IT DOES.

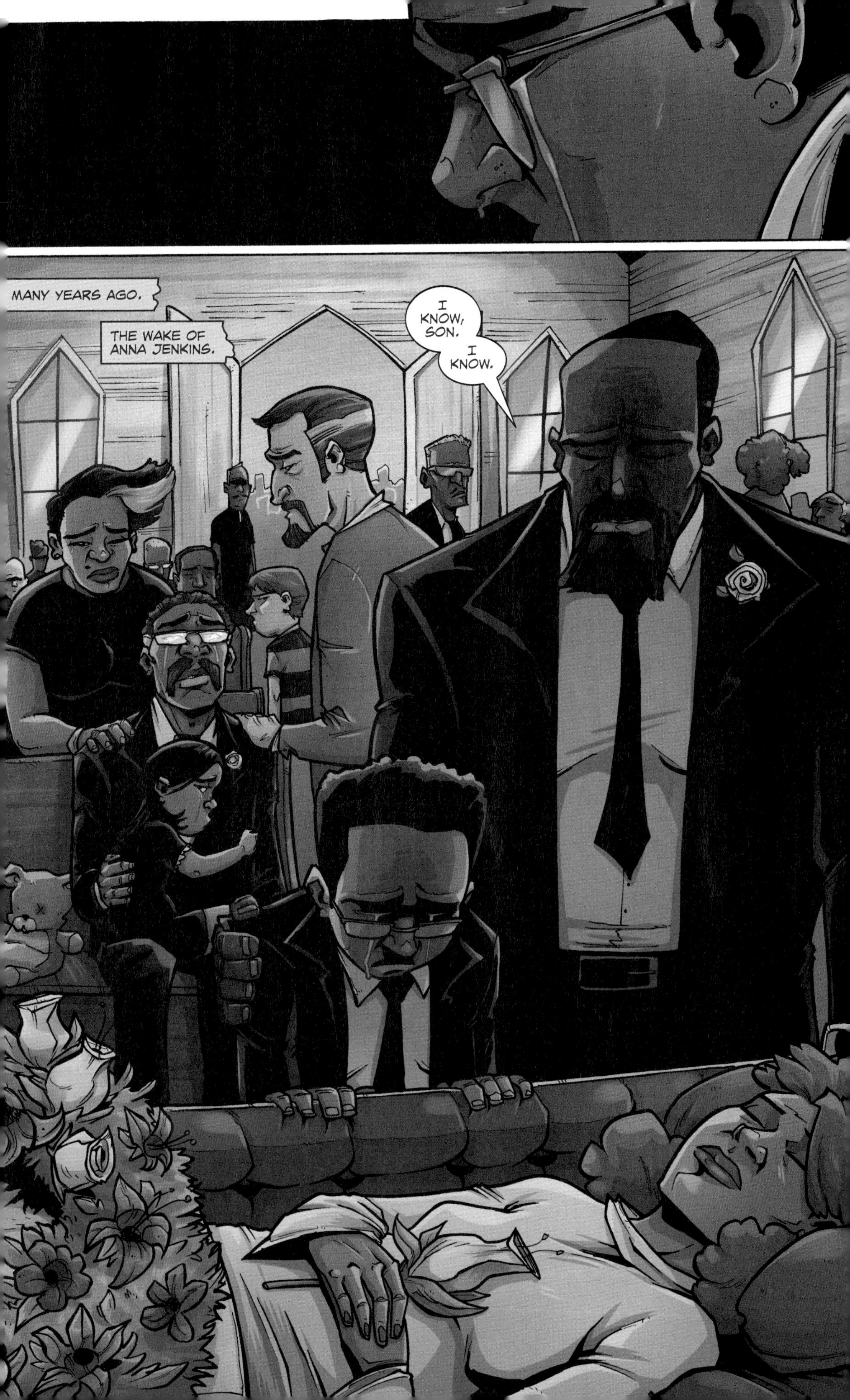
MANY YEARS AGO.
THE WAKE OF ANNA JENKINS.
I KNOW, SON.
I KNOW.

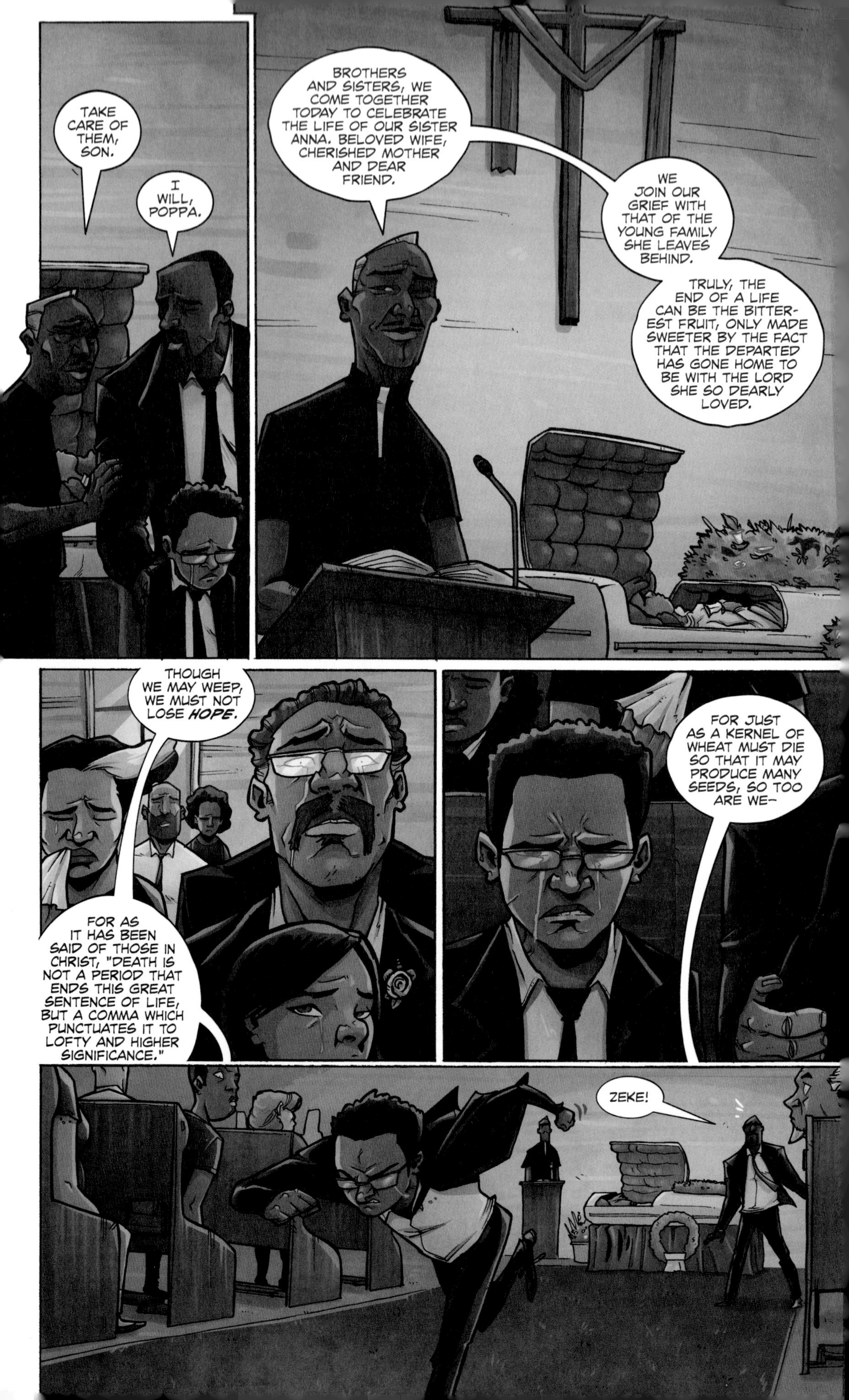
TAKE CARE OF THEM, SON.
I WILL, POPPA.
BROTHERS AND SISTERS, WE COME TOGETHER TODAY TO CELEBRATE THE LIFE OF OUR SISTER ANNA. BELOVED WIFE, CHERISHED MOTHER AND DEAR FRIEND.
WE JOIN OUR GRIEF WITH THAT OF THE YOUNG FAMILY SHE LEAVES BEHIND.
TRULY, THE END OF A LIFE CAN BE THE BITTEREST FRUIT, ONLY MADE SWEETER BY THE FACT THAT THE DEPARTED HAS GONE HOME TO BE WITH THE LORD SHE SO DEARLY LOVED.
THOUGH WE MAY WEEP, WE MUST NOT LOSE *HOPE*.
FOR AS IT HAS BEEN SAID OF THOSE IN CHRIST, "DEATH IS NOT A PERIOD THAT ENDS THIS GREAT SENTENCE OF LIFE, BUT A COMMA WHICH PUNCTUATES IT TO LOFTY AND HIGHER SIGNIFICANCE."
FOR JUST AS A KERNEL OF WHEAT MUST DIE SO THAT IT MAY PRODUCE MANY SEEDS, SO TOO ARE WE—
ZEKE!

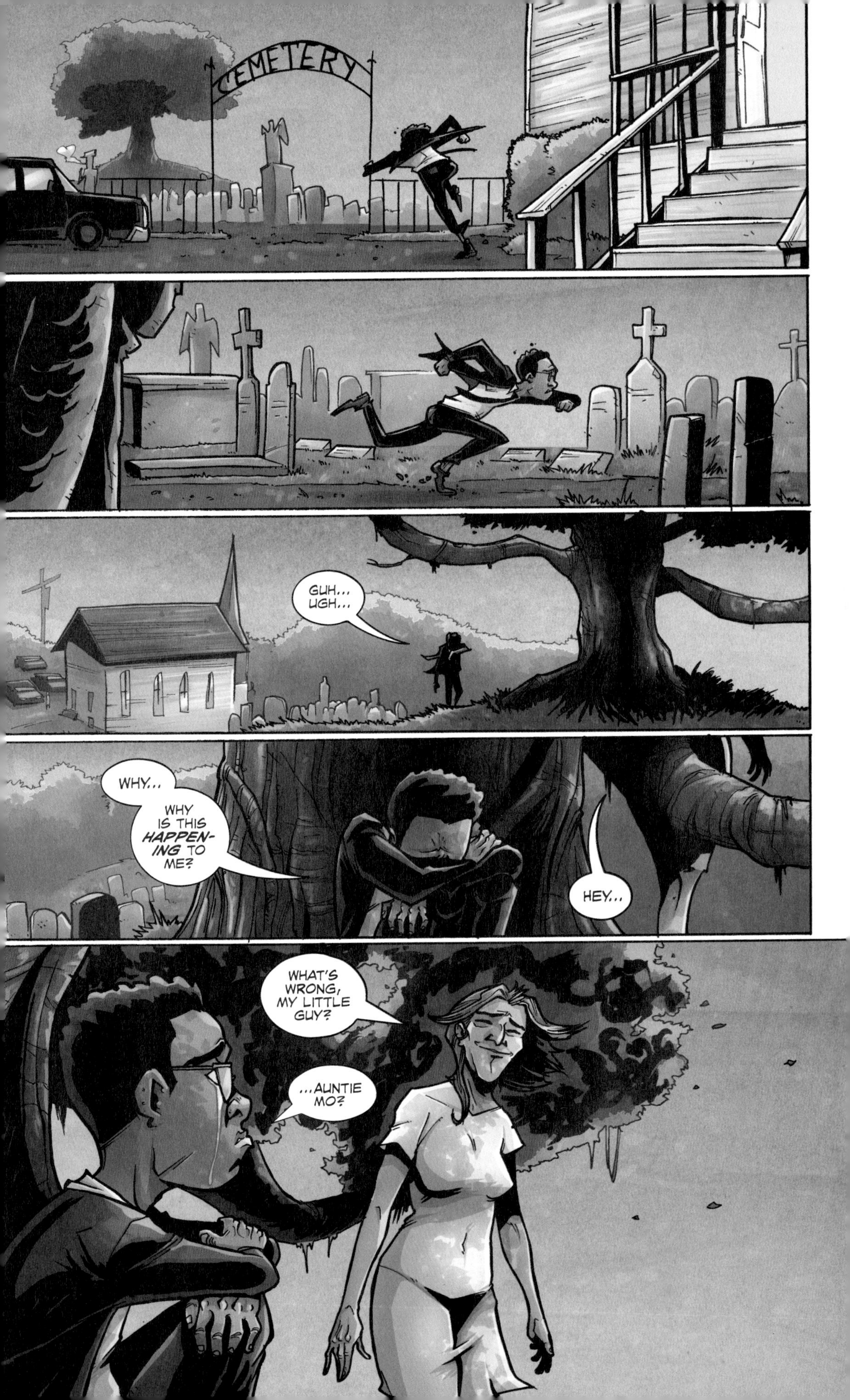
CEMETERY
GUH... UGH...
WHY...
WHY IS THIS HAPPENING TO ME?
HEY...
WHAT'S WRONG, MY LITTLE GUY?
...AUNTIE MO?

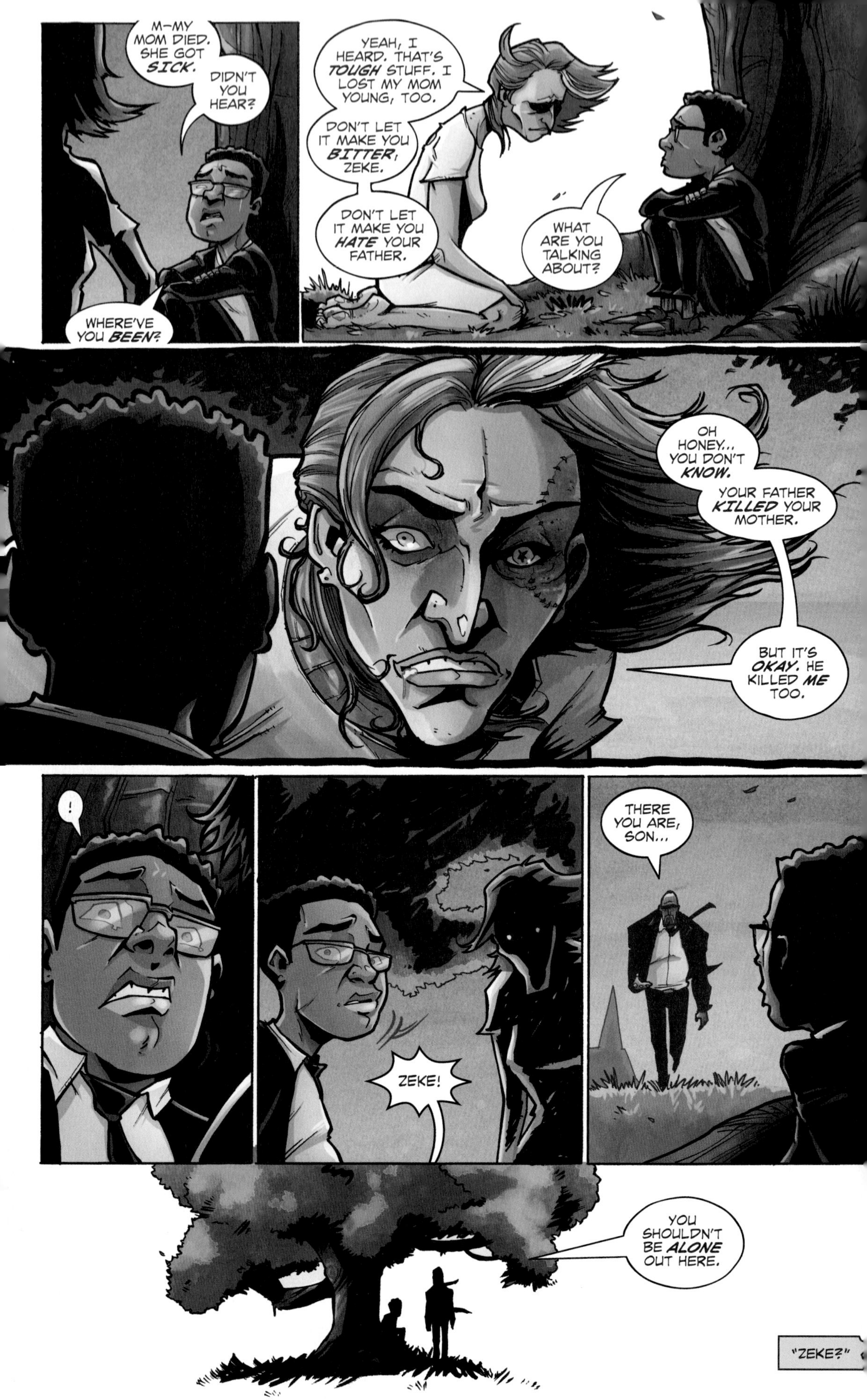
M-MY MOM DIED. SHE GOT SICK.
DIDN'T YOU HEAR?
WHERE'VE YOU BEEN?
YEAH, I HEARD. THAT'S TOUGH STUFF. I LOST MY MOM YOUNG, TOO.
DON'T LET IT MAKE YOU BITTER, ZEKE.
DON'T LET IT MAKE YOU HATE YOUR FATHER.
WHAT ARE YOU TALKING ABOUT?
OH HONEY... YOU DON'T KNOW.
YOUR FATHER KILLED YOUR MOTHER.
BUT IT'S OKAY. HE KILLED ME TOO.
!
ZEKE!
THERE YOU ARE, SON...
YOU SHOULDN'T BE ALONE OUT HERE.
"ZEKE?"

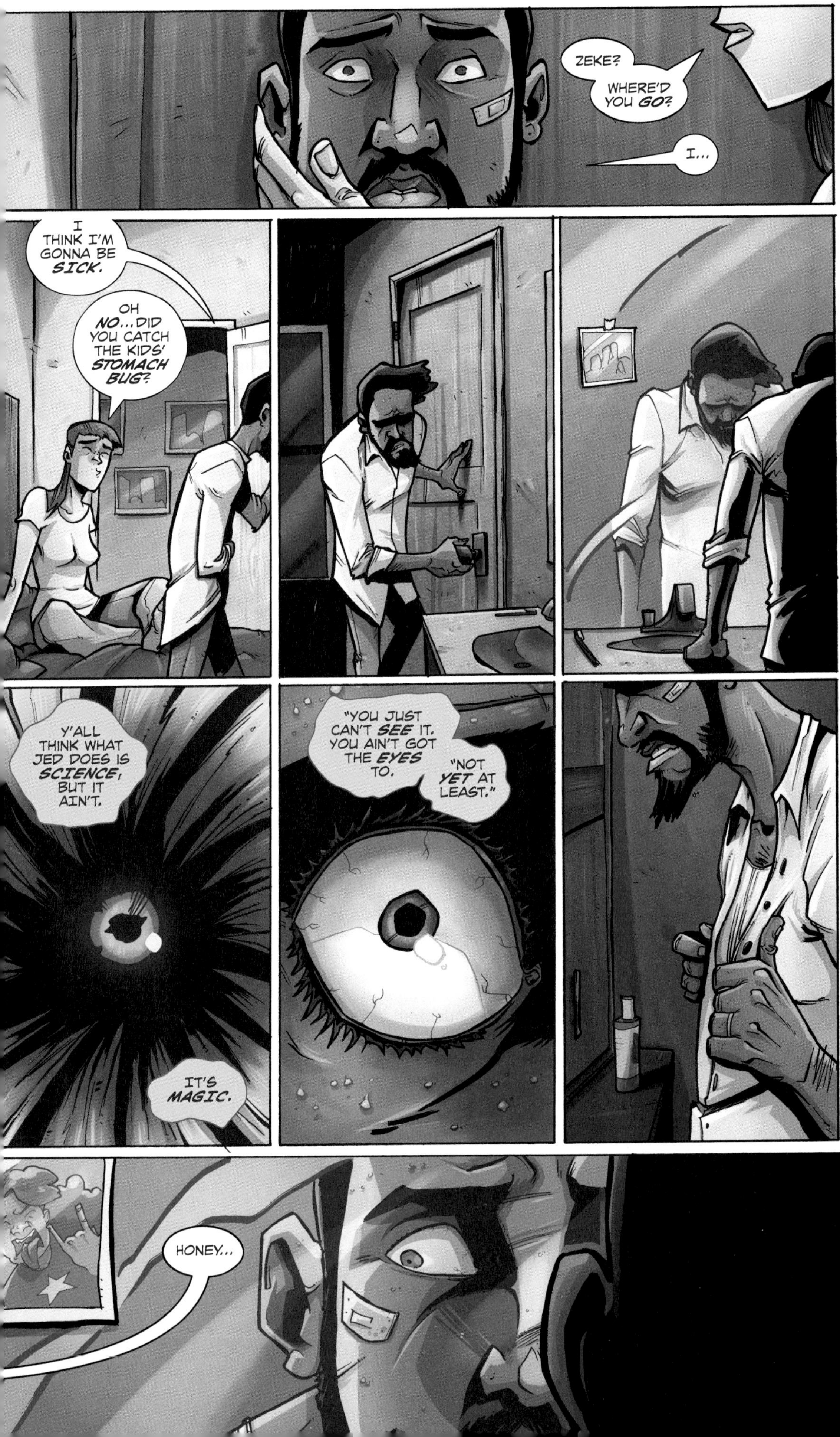
ZEKE?
WHERE'D YOU GO?
I...
I THINK I'M GONNA BE SICK.
OH NO...DID YOU CATCH THE KIDS' STOMACH BUG?
Y'ALL THINK WHAT JED DOES IS SCIENCE, BUT IT AIN'T.
IT'S MAGIC.
"YOU JUST CAN'T SEE IT. YOU AIN'T GOT THE EYES TO.
"NOT YET AT LEAST."
HONEY...

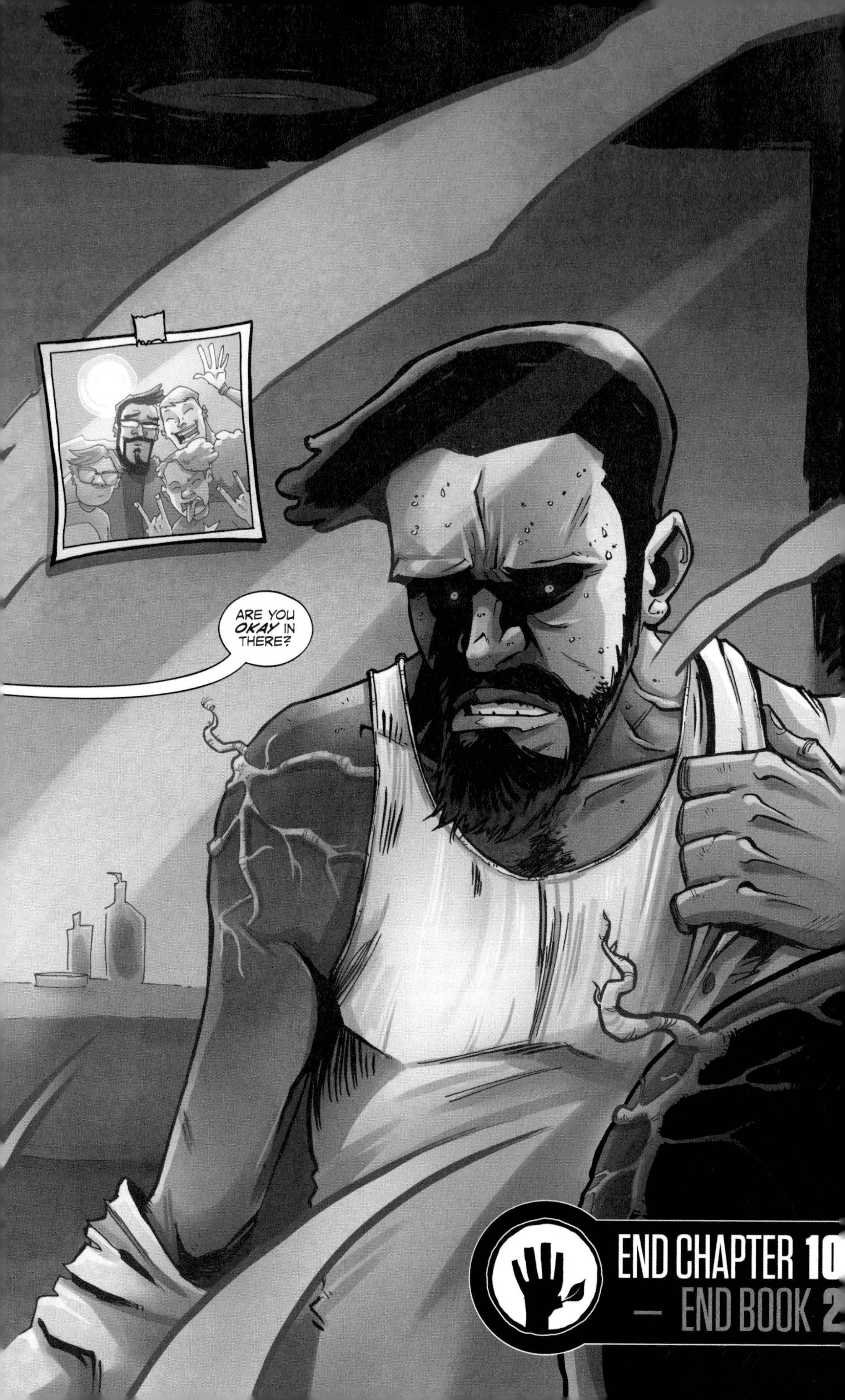
ARE YOU *OKAY* IN THERE?
END CHAPTER 10
— END BOOK 2

Beware of false prophets who come to you in
sheep's clothing but inwardly are savage wolves.
You will know them by their fruit.

Grapes aren't gathered from thorns, or figs from
thistles, are they? In the same way, every good tree
produces good fruit, but a rotten tree produces bad fruit.
A good tree cannot produce bad fruit,
and a rotten tree cannot produce good fruit.
Every tree that doesn't produce good fruit will be
cut down and thrown into a fire.

So by their fruit you will know them.

Matthew 7:15-20 ISV

FARMHAND CONCEPT ART

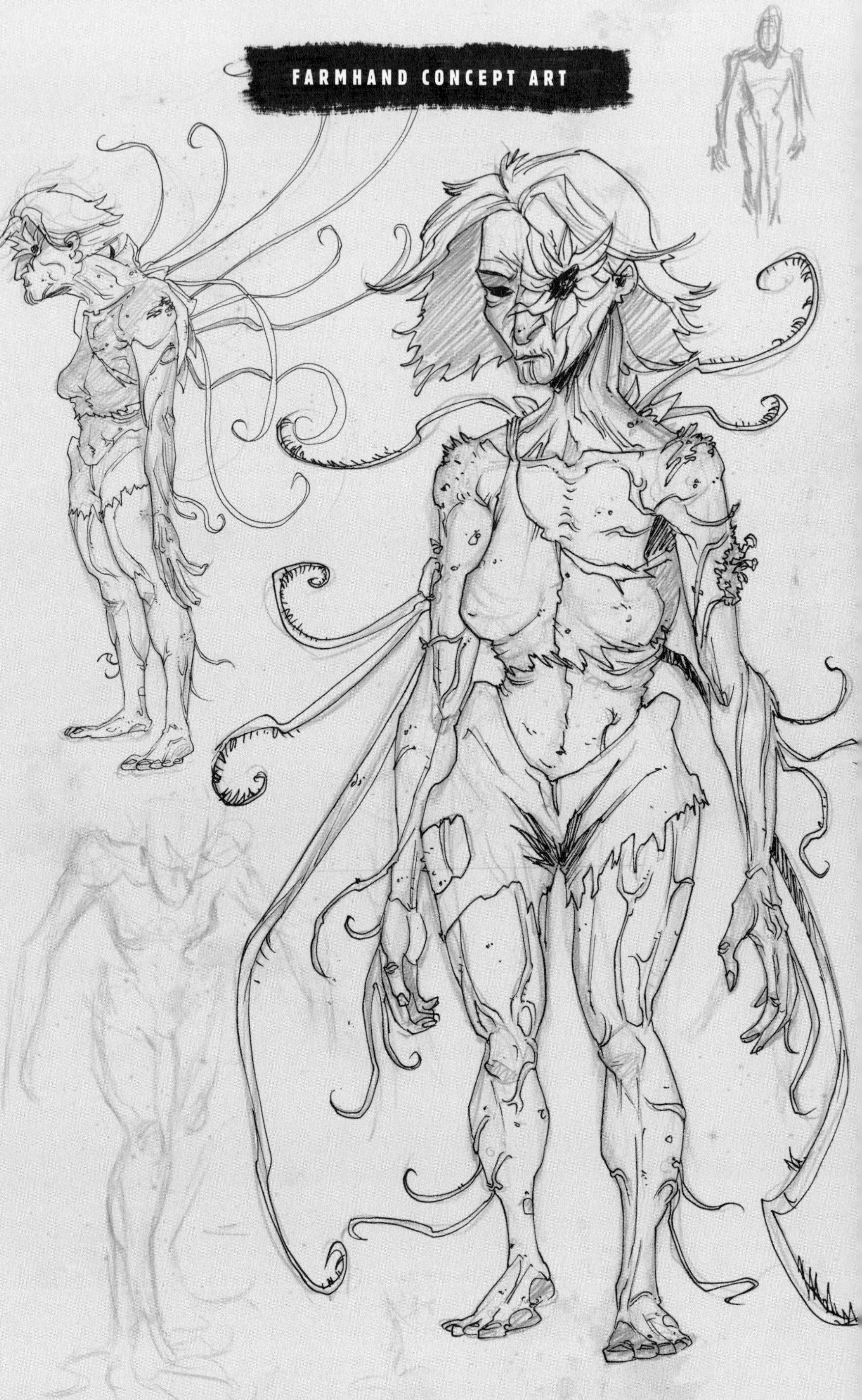

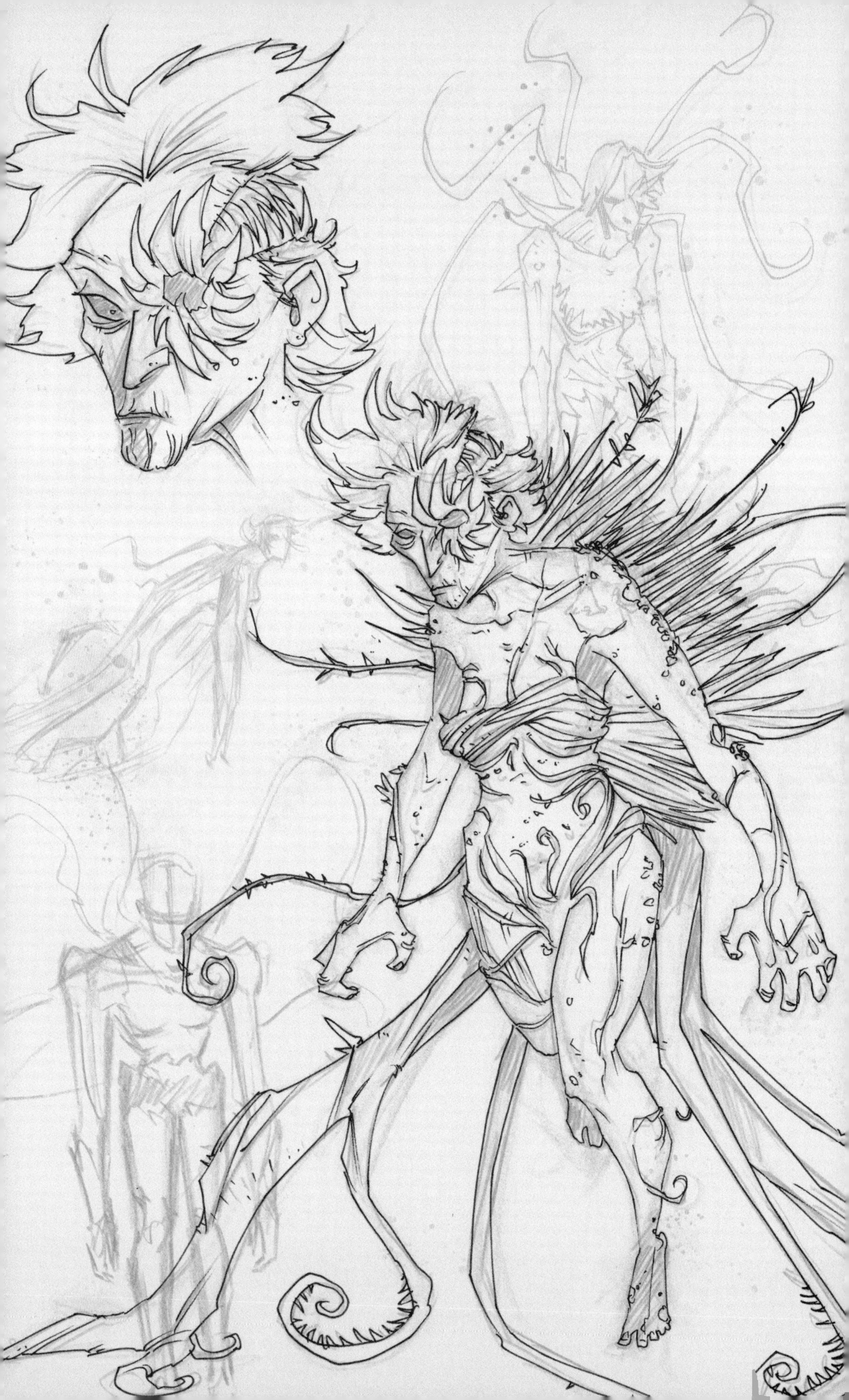

EARLY CHARACTER CONCEPTS

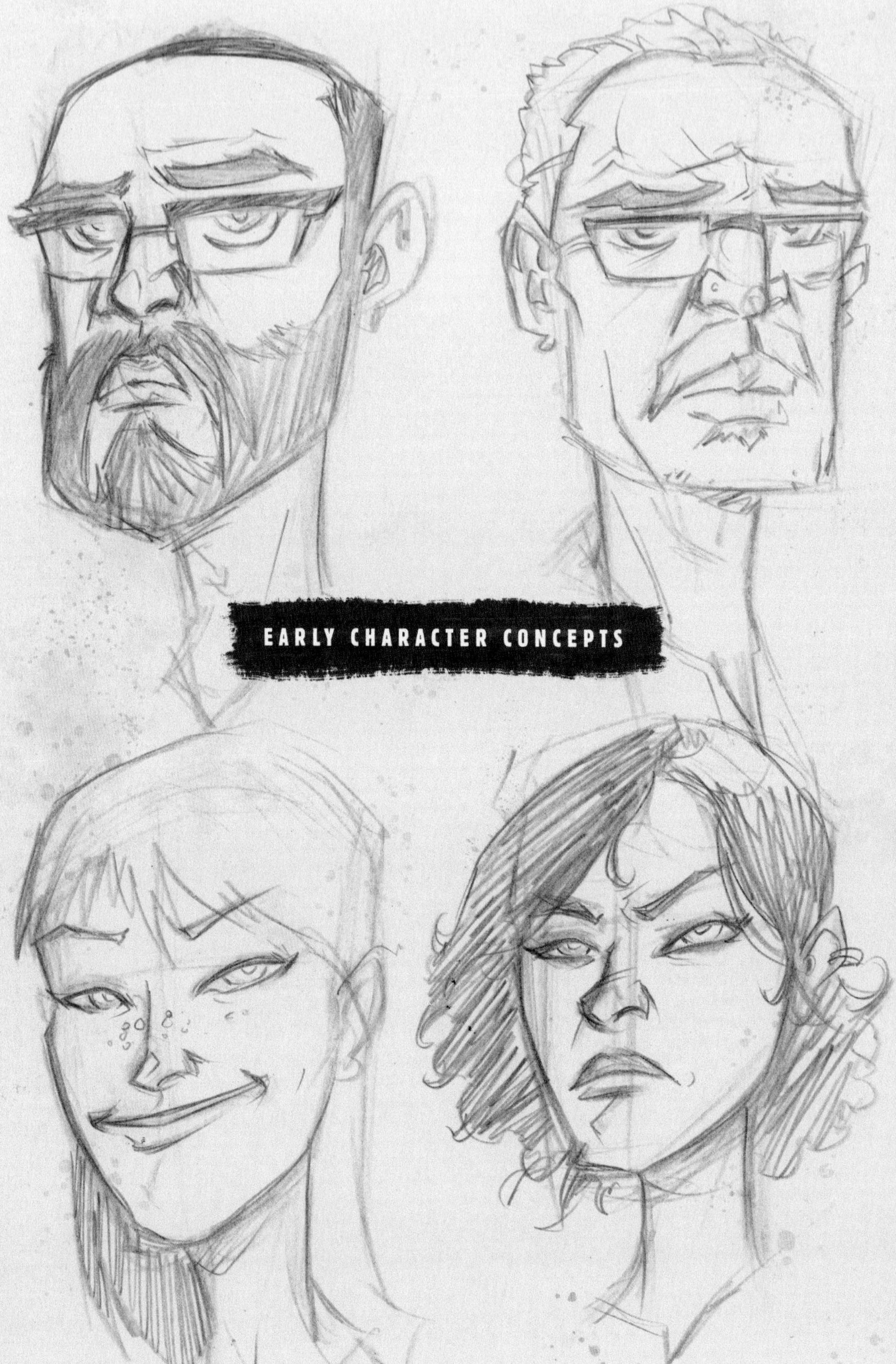

Back when I was a student at the University of Louisiana at Lafayette, I had a five-year tenure as Senior Cartoonist at the school paper, The Vermilion. It was a formative time for me, as I developed my craft, learned to make a deadline and had the pleasure of working with several gifted fellow cartoonists.

Burton Durand was one of those guys. These days, he's an award-winning graphic designer/cartoonist/studio mate of mine. But fifteen years ago, he was the guy whose comic strip *Campus Hijinx* printed right under mine.

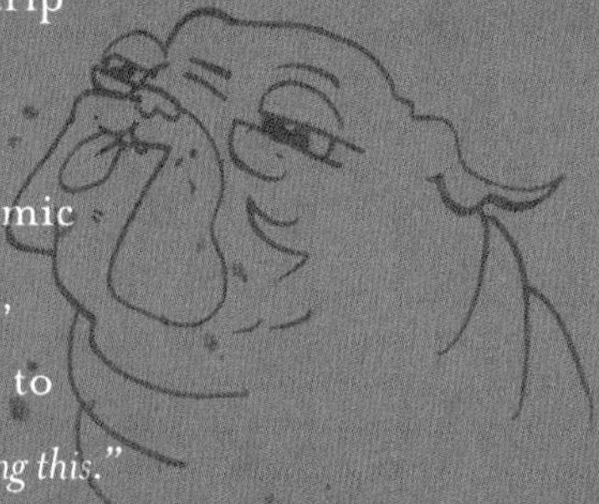

His ever-quirky, sometimes outright bizarre pun-laced comic strips always got a chuckle out of me. Even more than that, Burt's work always betrayed a genuine joy that inspires me to this day. I look at his work and think, *"This guy had FUN making this."* It's a quality I hope comes across in my own work.

Naturally, when Burt agreed to take on FARMHAND's graphic design, it was only a matter of time until I suckered him into doing a comic strip for the book. Just a little something extra, or as the Cajuns call it *"a lil' lagniappe."*

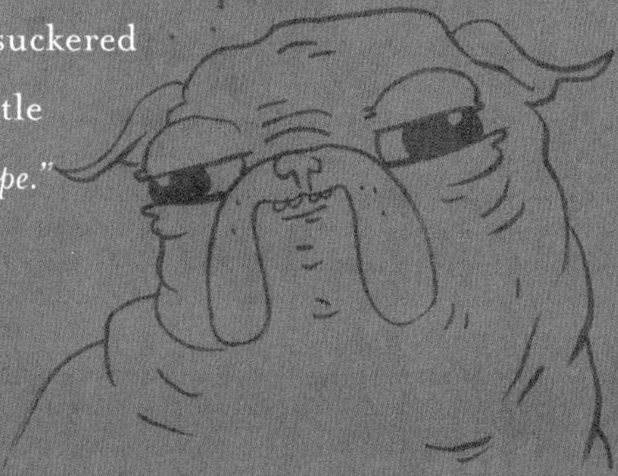

Thus, Freetown Funnies was born. Enjoy.

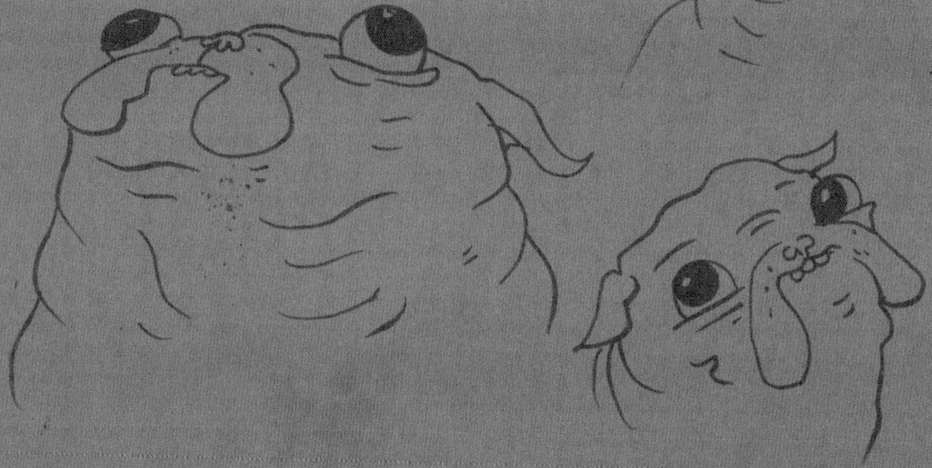

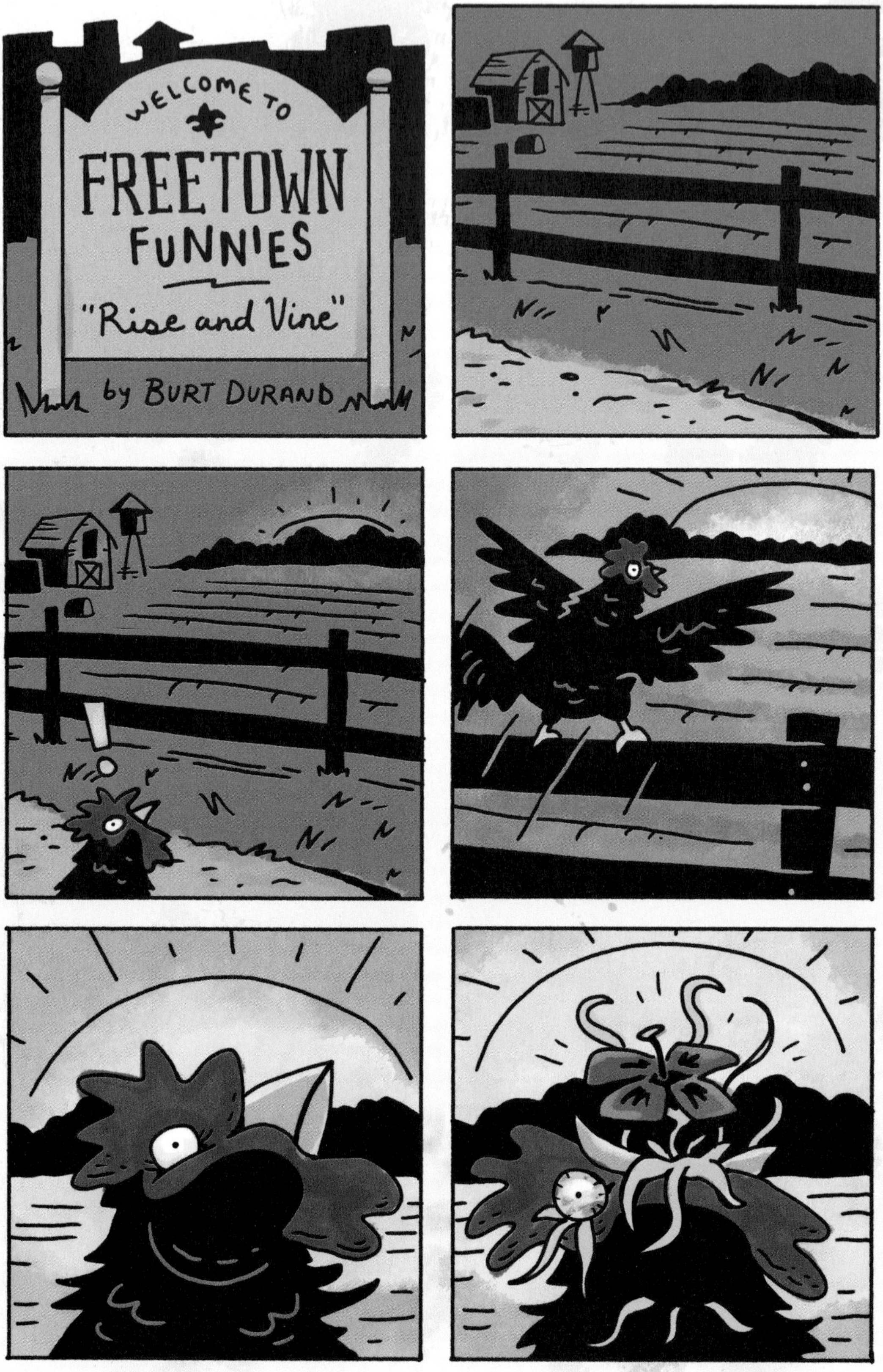
WELCOME TO
FREETOWN
FUNNIES
"Rise and Vine"
by BURT DURAND

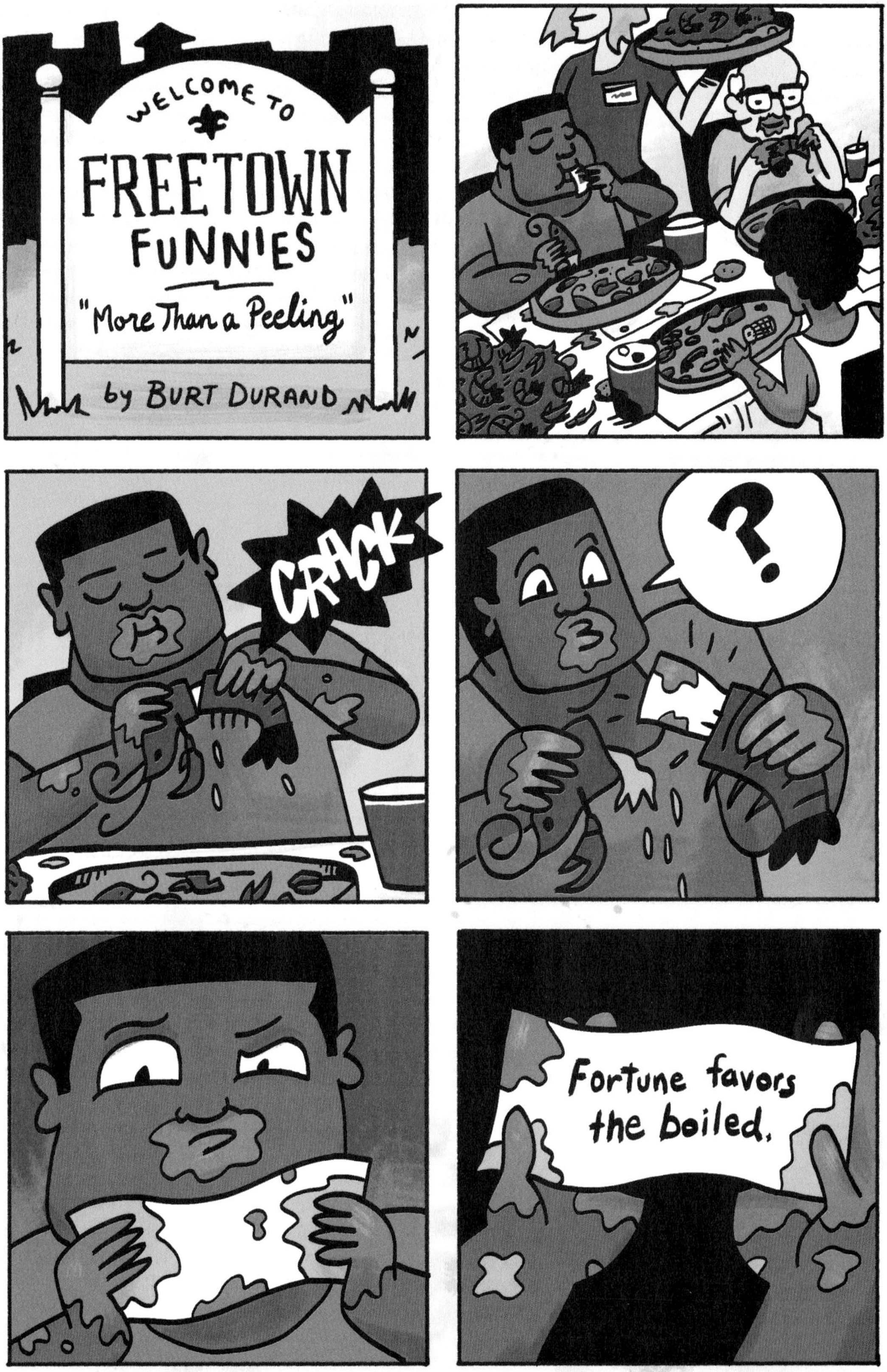
WELCOME TO
FREETOWN
FUNNIES
"More Than a Peeling"
by BURT DURAND
CRACK
?
Fortune favors the boiled.

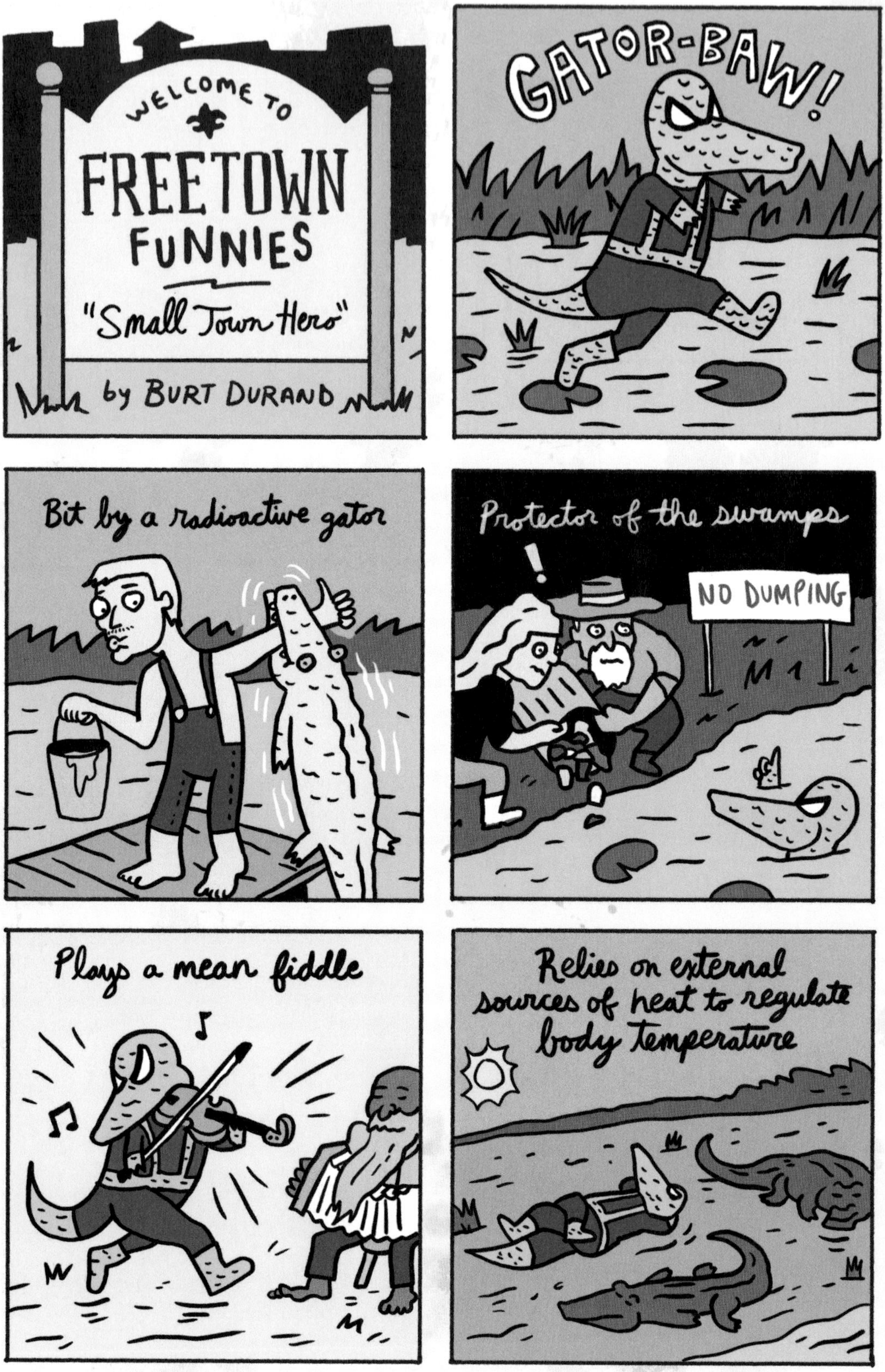

WELCOME TO
FREETOWN
FUNNIES
"Small Town Hero"
by BURT DURAND
GATOR-BAW!
Bit by a radioactive gator
Protector of the swamps
!
NO DUMPING
Plays a mean fiddle
Relies on external sources of heat to regulate body temperature

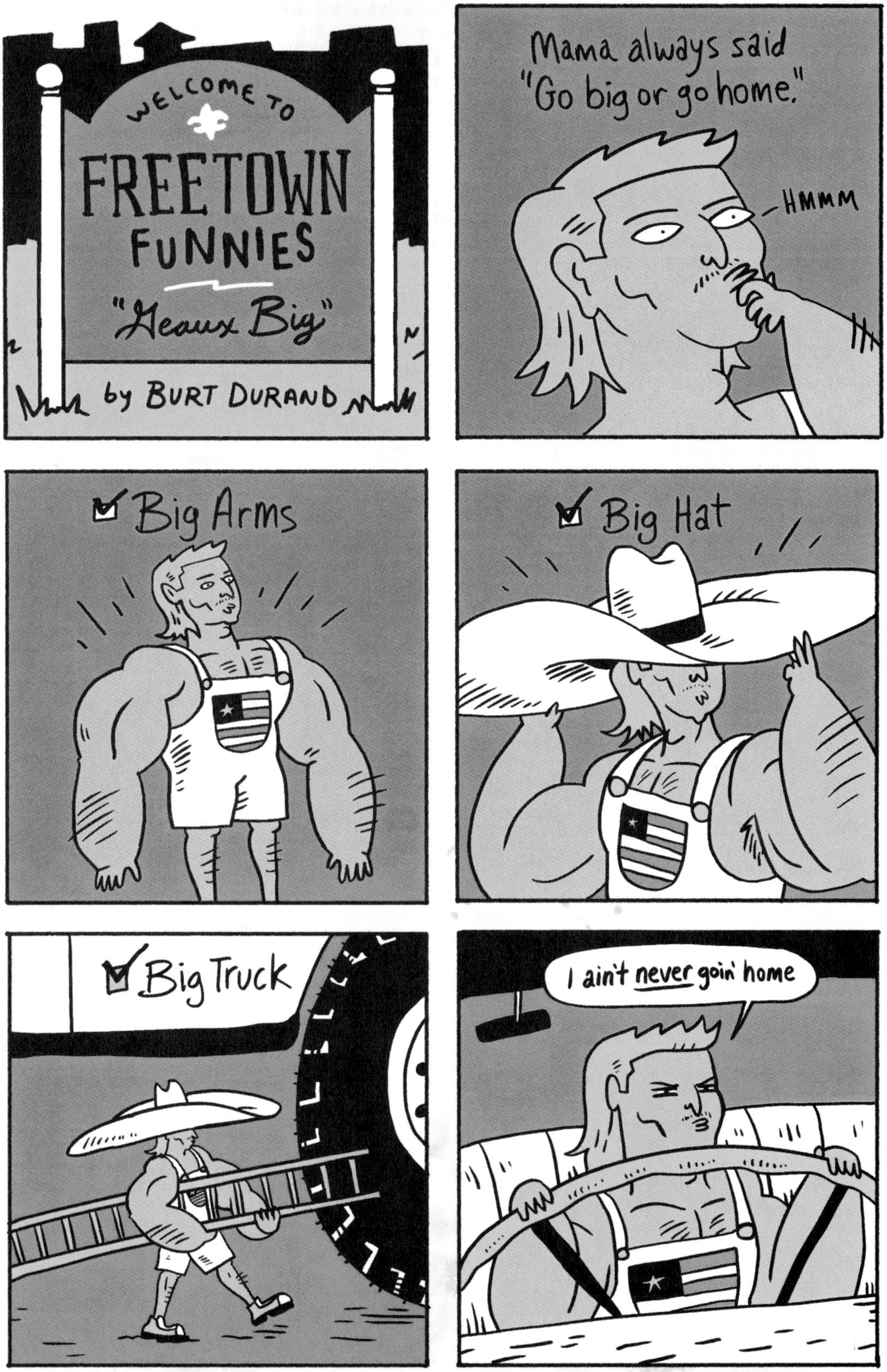
WELCOME TO
FREETOWN
FUNNIES
"Geaux Big"
by BURT DURAND
Mama always said
"Go big or go home."
HMMM
Big Arms
Big Hat
Big Truck
I ain't never goin' home

@BURTDURAND | BURTONDURAND.COM

More books by the author:

CHEW is a 60-issue completed comic book epic by writer John Layman and artist Rob Guillory.

Multiple Eisner Award Winner. New York Times Bestseller. Internationally Acclaimed.

CHEW follows Tony Chu, a detective with a secret. A weird secret. Tony Chu is Cibopathic, which means he gets psychic impressions from whatever he eats. It also means he's a hell of a detective, as long as he doesn't mind nibbling on the corpse of a murder victim to figure out whodunit, and why. He's been brought on by the Special Crimes Division of the FDA, the most powerful law enforcement agency on the planet, to investigate their strangest, sickest, and most bizarre cases.

TRADE PAPERBACKS

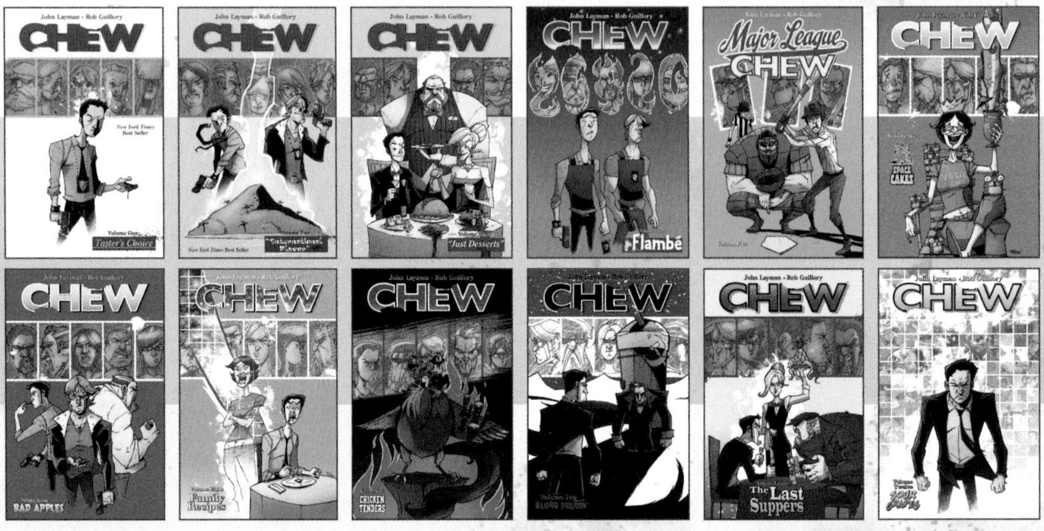
CHEW
Major League CHEW
Flambé
The Last Suppers

OMNIVORE EDITIONS

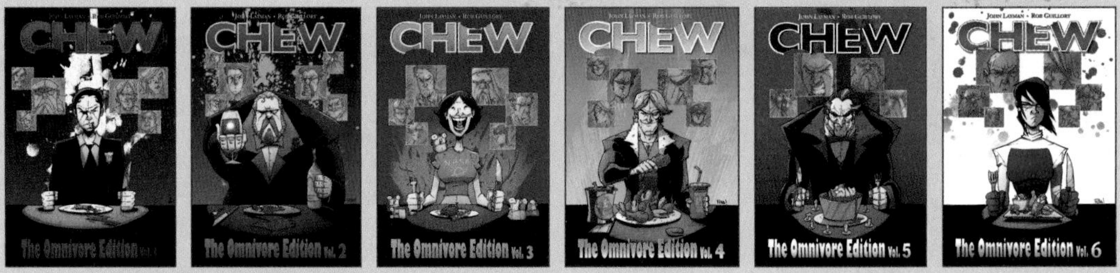
CHEW
The Omnivore Edition Vol. 2
The Omnivore Edition Vol. 3
The Omnivore Edition Vol. 4
The Omnivore Edition Vol. 5
The Omnivore Edition Vol. 6

SMORGASBORD EDITIONS

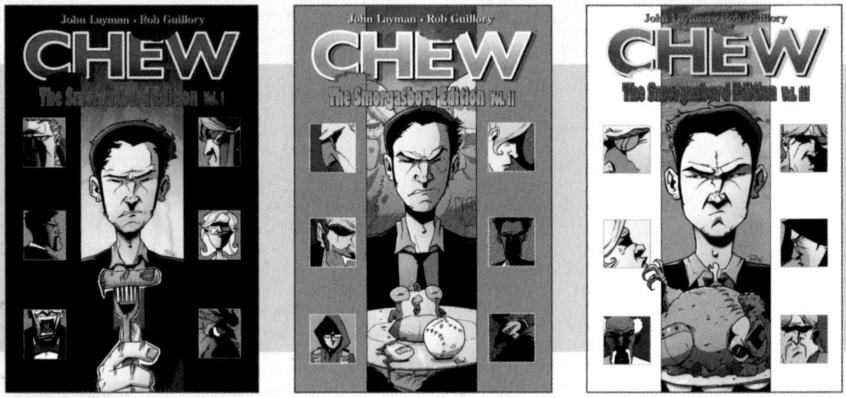
John Layman • Rob Guillory
CHEW
The Smorgasbord Edition Vol. II

Available in Paperback, Hardcover and
20-issue Oversized Slipcase Hardcover Editions where books are sold.

T-shirts available at RobGuillory.com

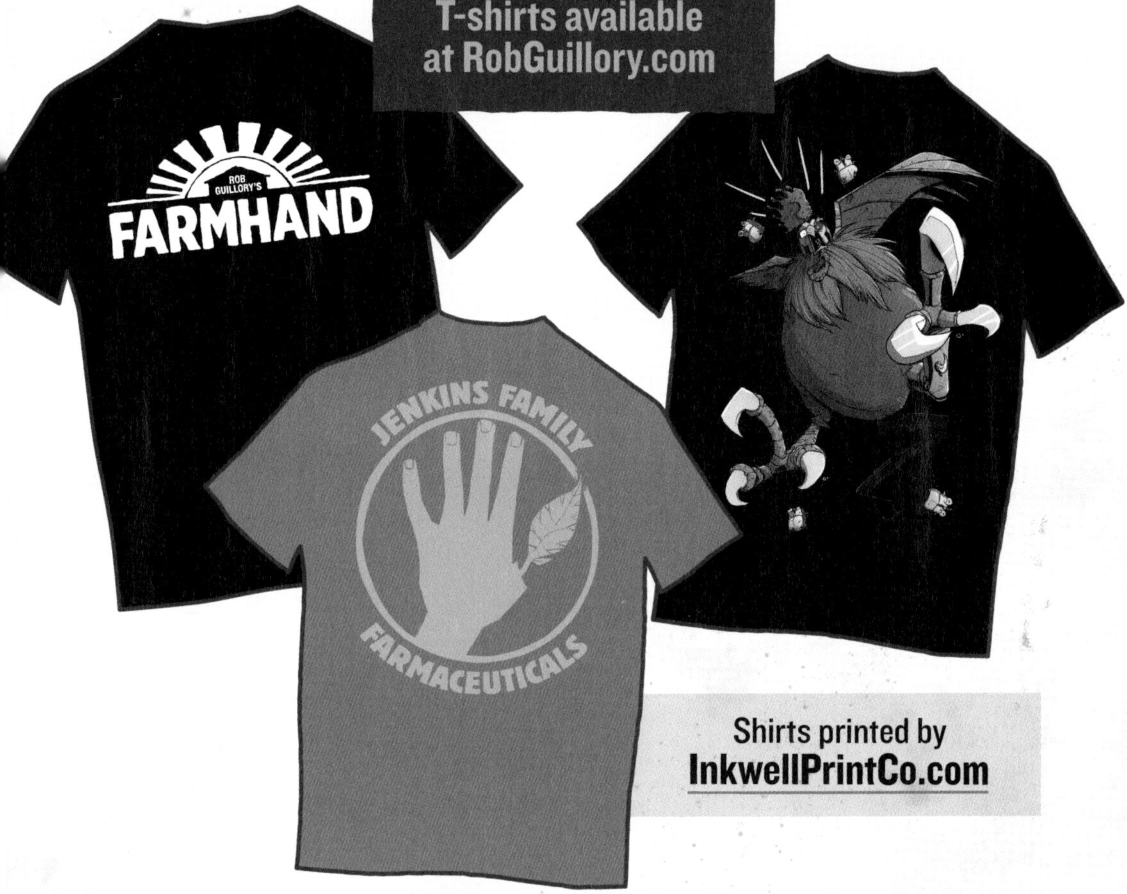
ROB GUILLORY'S
FARMHAND
JENKINS FAMILY
FARMACEUTICALS

Shirts printed by
InkwellPrintCo.com

FARMHAND Original Music Score available NOW.

Fellow Louisiana artist SKIES SPEAK put together an experimental album inspired by the comic FARMHAND.

Moody, atmospheric and absolutely FREE.

Available now at **SkiesSpeak.com**

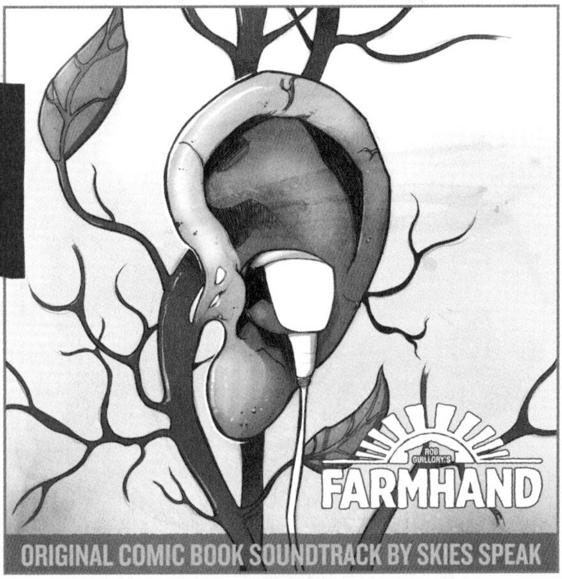
ROB GUILLORY'S
FARMHAND
ORIGINAL COMIC BOOK SOUNDTRACK BY SKIES SPEAK

RobGuillory.com

Original Art + Merch + Signed Books

GRASSROOTS

The Official FARMHAND Letters Column!

Accepting fan mail, gardening tips, haiku poems and random pictures of your dog.

You can email letters to:
FARMHAND@robguillory.com

Or go the snail mail route:
FARMHAND | P.O. Box 304 | Scott, LA 70583